TO VANQUISH DARKNESS

LE SOMBRE

BOOK ONE

CINDY GUNDERSON

WITH GRATITUDE

Editing and Critique
Jordan Truex, Scott Gunderson, A.E. King, Jamie Thornton,
Nicole York, Stacey Prince

Cover Design
Seventhstar Art

Special Thanks
Stacey Prince (assistant)

To Scott. I've loved you in every life.

LE LIVRE DE LA GARDE

Lovely.

Deadly.

Cloaked in shadow,

Bound by light.

Two sides of

The same eternal night.

1

His face haunted her. Branded into her childhood alongside lapping streams and plucked bluebells. Wild and ferocious. His lips smeared with her mother's blood.

As Amalie peered around the stone turret, she dredged up that image from her nightmares to keep from being drawn out of the shadows into the evening twilight prematurely.

Her heart thumped like a war drum.

He is darkness. Evil. Deadly.

She repeated those truths in her mind like a prayer, and still, his beauty—she had no other word to describe it—tugged at her like a cord cinched to her middle. She'd known it would be this way. Not only because of the old myths, the stories of death and seduction, but because even as a terrified child she'd been stunned by him. As an adult, she'd felt that low ache in her gut the day she'd seen Theo Vallon striding down the rain-drenched cobblestones one year prior.

She'd been in the company of handsome men before. Kissed them even. But Theo was a work of art. Tall and powerfully built, his broad shoulders and tapered waist were noticeable even under an overcoat. On the night they'd crossed paths last year in Paris, his jet-black hair had been slicked with rain, but now under the starlight, it was soft and tousled. Amalie wanted to stretch her arm out and thread her fingers through it.

This was why her uncle never let them out after dark, was it not? Amalie clenched her jaw. Her aunt and uncle scoffed at the ancient fables of gods, curses, and creatures of the dark, yet they wouldn't allow the girls out past sunset. Wouldn't give permission for her and Bethany to go beyond the bridge or up the stairs to the abbey.

"Le Sombre reigns in the darkness," Uncle Oren would mutter with a sad shrug of his shoulders, and how could she argue? The world was split into light and shadow. Consciousness and sleep. Pleasure and pain. They were either swayed by Solène or Le Sombre, and there was no middle ground.

You could not serve two masters.

Theo Vallon was proof of that.

Amalie's hands trembled, and she adjusted her grip on the wooden stake. Where was Marcel? She'd been standing here long enough to grow roots, and they didn't know how long this opportunity would last. She listened for his call so intently, she could almost convince herself his voice was floating through the trees.

It wasn't. *Not yet.* She squeezed her eyes shut, praying that Theo's glamour wasn't able to affect her from this distance.

This was dangerous. She'd known it would be. Uncle Oren wasn't wrong for instituting his rules, and she *was* partly grateful. After her mother's death, Oren had kept her and Bethany safe. He'd provided for them both to adulthood. Four years longer than he was required to in her case.

At twenty-two, Amalie should've been married with at

least one babe on her hip. But men didn't jump at the chance to marry a woman with slow blood. And she hadn't been able to keep his rules anyway. Seeing Theo Vallon's face in the torchlight had pushed her down a path she couldn't turn away from.

Yes, Oren was right that the world was torn, but that didn't mean humans had to drop their heads and suffer. It didn't mean they had to live in terror or watch their loved ones be hunted night after night.

Her uncle and the people of France had resigned themselves to their fate, and Amalie refused to join them. So there she was. Standing in the courtyard after sunset. Sweating through her shirt. Waiting for—

The hoot of an owl echoed against the stone, and Amalie tensed. Finally. *Marcel.* It was time.

Amalie wiped her clammy palm on her slacks, then regripped the long, sharpened spike of ash wood before creeping along the wall into the courtyard. She clung to the shadows, cursing their poor luck. All week there had been clouds before midnight, but now the moon hung like a silver dollar above the trees, bathing the courtyard in mellow light.

Don't turn around, she silently pleaded as she flattened her bare feet one after the other over the chilled cobblestones. Was she stupid for insisting she wield the spike? Marcel and Olivie had trained far longer than she had, and both of them had vanquished before, but the idea of setting the flare or blowing the whistles made her nauseous.

Amalie wanted to feel the weapon punch through Theo's flesh. Wanted to see his black blood pour from his chest and stain the worn stone beneath him. She wanted to know without a shadow of a doubt that he was dead and that she'd vanquished him with her own hands.

Just as he had murdered her mother.

This was justice.

Amalie pulled a fabric shade free from her hood, lowering it over her eyes as a white-hot flash burst from the trees. The air crackled, and Theo jumped back with predatory grace, dropping into a crouch and throwing his hands over his sensitive eyes. The shrill squeal of the whistles came next, but they barely penetrated her ear coverings.

Now. This was her chance. She walked faster, and when she reached the corner of the wall, she broke into a sprint toward Theo, who still hunched next to the fountain. His muscles pulled tight, cording his neck and forearms.

He had twice her body mass. At least twice her strength. But she had the element of surprise. She had a spike made of ash wood.

Amalie's heart threatened to burst from her chest as she gasped for breath and closed the distance between them. The rough stone tore at the pads of her feet as blood rushed in her ears.

Theo's ears pricked. His head began to swivel. But Amalie was already leaping, raising both hands high into the inky night sky.

As Theo Vallon shuddered and forced himself up from the ground against the barrage of his senses, Amalie streaked from the darkness and plunged the spike through the fine cloth of his shirt into his flesh. The stake slipped between his ribs and buried itself where she'd intended.

Directly into his heart.

2

1824 BLOIS, FRANCE

Rachel settled onto the verdant spring grass, the sun warming her cheeks. "Amalie!"

Her ten-year-old daughter turned, dark curls brushing her flushed cheeks. She looked so much like her father, it sent shivers down Rachel's arms. Dark eyes set behind thick lashes with a brow always lifted in mischief. "Oui, Maman!"

"The river is full to bursting. No swimming, mon coeur." It was redundant, but she couldn't keep from calling out the warning. Amalie was wise enough to know that when the river reached the fourth stones on the bridge, it was deep and had a current too strong for bathing. Her brother Oren had told both girls the rules at least a hundred times, and yet every summer Rachel worried they'd forget.

There had been fourteen drownings in the Loire River that she knew of, but only one she couldn't get out of her head.

Rachel clenched her teeth and observed the white choppy peaks erupting from the surface of the murky water, listening to the rush of the river through the arches that supported the half of Oren's home where the elements had worn away the foundation.

The girls dipped their toes into the water and giggled, their voices echoing against the tree trunks like bird songs. *They were safe. The bank wasn't steep there.* Rachel drew a deep breath.

She was here for six weeks. Six weeks of planting, pruning, digging, and harvesting. No more dirty streets and smoky air for the girls. No more threading needles and aching fingers for her. And by the time they made their way back to the city, thanks to Oren's generosity, Rachel would have enough to pay off the last of their debt. To leave their flat and move north permanently.

"I thought I'd find you here." Oren strode along the path next to the southern gardens.

Rachel raised an eyebrow. "You can see us from the windows."

He chuckled. "I wasn't coming from the house. I was down at the stables." He sat next to her and watched the girls splashing their feet in the water. "They are happy?"

"Always. Thank you for this." It was their third summer coming to the estate. Rachel had never been one to accept charity, but since Oren allowed her to work and earn her keep, this arrangement was acceptable.

"You look tired."

"My mattress is lumpy."

Oren threw back his head and laughed. "I'll have Patrice take a look."

"You know I'm teasing." Rachel grinned, her heart filling too quickly to keep her eyes from brimming with tears. "Thank you, Oren."

He glanced up, then cleared his throat and stared hard at the river. "This isn't altruistic. You're doing me a favor." Rachel nodded, allowing him to get away with that story for the time being. He straightened his flat cap and pushed himself up from the hillside. "Maurielle wanted me to tell you all that dinner will be served at seven."

"Would she like—"

Oren held up a hand. "Enjoy the afternoon with your girls, Rachel. There will be plenty of work in the morning."

She nodded and turned back to the river as he made his way to the path. She threaded her hands through the soft blades of grass and inhaled the scent of cherry blossoms wafting from the trees as petals danced in the breeze and littered the ground with pink.

Bethany squealed and threw up a hand causing Rachel's spine to straighten. She then relaxed as Amalie pulled her little sister back and kissed her hand. Bethany giggled and resumed her splashing. Tears pricked Rachel's eyes.

For three years she'd been without her husband Romane. Three years, and this was the first moment she'd felt hope.

Rachel wiped her cheeks and was about to lie back and close her eyes when a flash of movement in the shadow of the wood sharpened her senses. Her breath caught as she sat straight and peered into the trees. She glanced back toward the girls, her heart pounding, then scoured the gaps between the tightly clumped trunks.

The light was playing tricks on her mortal eyes as it worked to dispel the darkness.

It was probably nothing.

3

1836 COUNTRYSIDE BEYOND MORDELLES,
FRANCE

Amalie, Marcel, and Olivie let out a collective breath as they passed through the wrought-iron gate in the wall. The stone wasn't impenetrable by any means, but there was a sense of safety that came from leaving the open field.

"That was like a scene from the Grimoire." Olivie clapped her hands on Amalie's shoulders and shook her gently then pulled her close. "You flew through the air, your hair whipping around your face like a goddess."

"It wasn't that dramatic." Amalie squeezed her friend's hand, then stepped back, scanning the moonlit garden. Truthfully, she'd felt as if she was immortal in that moment. Sprinting across the stone. Not giving in to the crushing terror at the sight of Theo crouched in the courtyard. She'd done it. She'd finally avenged her mother's death and prevented the death of who knew how many more innocent people.

It was over.

For now. Until she found the next one.

Amalie exhaled and led her friends through the arbor. "What happens next?"

"Wine." Olivie laughed, and Marcel slung an arm over her shoulder.

"Much deserved. Will you be joining us?" he asked.

Amalie exhaled. "I'll do my best." She wanted to give in to the relief she felt at completing their mission, but her shoulders were still tight. She couldn't wear a loose smile like the ones that hung on her friends' faces. Not yet. She still had one more task for the night.

They'd traveled first by boat directly from the cemetery courtyard where they'd left Theo's body, then stowed Marcel's craft in the brush and taken horses through the wood. After catching a few hours of sleep on the floor of a crumbling stone rectory, they'd continued on at first light and dropped the horses at one of Marcel's contacts in Mordelles, then walked the rest of the way on foot.

Amalie stopped at the steps. This was where she had to continue alone.

"Can I see it?" Marcel, his tunic rumpled and boots coated with mud, held out a hand. Amalie pulled a ring from her pocket. The metal was ice cold and smooth, too dense and heavy for its size. She dropped it into his palm, and he flipped it between his fingers. "D'you think it will be enough?"

Amalie brandished the stake, inspecting the darkened wood where Theo's blood had seeped into the grain. It looked black as death in the moonlight. "It's proof. And if it's not enough on its own, this will seal it."

Olivie blew out a breath, then dragged a hand through her waves. Her hair was cropped shorter on the right than the left, and it made her pointed chin and high cheekbones look almost sinister. "That could be anyone's blood."

"But it's not." Amalie held up the wood to the light filtering through the side window, her heart beating too fast in her chest. *Do you think it will be enough?* She hadn't told Uncle Oren or Aunt Maurielle anything about her association or training with Les Pourfendeurs de Sang. When she tried bringing it up in the past, they'd called Marcel and the rest of the Blood Slayers radicals. Zealots. But there was a reason the Pourfendeurs were growing by the day.

Women were missing. Not only in Paris, but also in the surrounding towns. Amalie had hoped that once the reports had shown up in the papers, Uncle Oren would finally admit that there was more to the reports than political fear-mongering.

He hadn't listened, and she shouldn't have been surprised. Every time she attempted to bring up what she'd seen as a child—who she'd seen clutching her mother's lifeless body with blood dripping from his lips—he insisted her mind was playing tricks on her. That her subconscious was trying to make sense of her grief and lay blame for the pain her mother's death had caused.

But she knew the truth, and now she finally had proof. He would have to believe her. Especially because the symbol on the ring Marcel still gripped in his palm was identical to the one they'd seen carved into the wood in Paris.

Marcel handed the ring back to her and stopped at the corner of the house. He tucked his tunic back into his trousers. "You're sure you want to do this alone?"

Amalie nodded, inspecting the oval etched into the metal, tilted on its axis, half light, half dark. A swirl of gold connecting the two. "Trust me, your face in my uncle's kitchen won't help my case."

Marcel nodded. "We'll see you back in Mordelles, then?"

Olivie reached out and hugged her, and weariness dropped over Amalie like a heavy cloak. "You're one of us now. A vanquisher." Olivie pulled back, clasping her shoulders and running a finger over the barely scabbed line Amalie had carved into her skin as they'd left the courtyard. Amalie ran her eyes over the thin scars ringing Olivie's upper arm. Amalie only had one mark, but she would have more. As soon as she could convince Oren to take Bethany and his daughters out of France.

"I'll be back. Three days at most." Amalie steeled herself. Marcel nodded, and Olivie gave her a tight smile as they retreated back through the gap in the wall.

As soon as they were out of sight and earshot, Amalie wretched in the bushes. The feel of the stake in her hand, the sensation of it pushing through flesh and bone—

She wretched a second time, bracing herself against the wall. It was good. It was right. She had ended the life of a killer.

All the arguments in her head didn't keep her hands from shaking. When her stomach seemed to have settled, she straightened, drawing in a deep breath. She wiped her mouth with the tail of her shirt, still trembling.

She could do this. Olivie and Marcel would be staying in town for the night, and somehow the knowledge that they wouldn't be far gave her comfort. Amalie latched the gate leading to her uncle's house, then drew another slow breath and strode to the front steps.

She lifted the iron knocker and swung it against the plate, hoping her aunt and uncle would at least peer through the window instead of ignoring the sound as they usually did. Bethany would be readying herself for bed, and her cousins, Matilde and Ghislaine, would be tucked beneath their covers at this time of night.

Amalie's heart twinged at the remembrance of routine. She yearned to be the girl who fell asleep with the sound of soft breathing and the croak of frogs drifting through the window panes instead of drunken shouting or the clatter of cart wheels against stone streets.

Mordelles would never feel like home. But neither would this cottage, if she was being honest with herself. She missed the wide-open spaces. The gardens. The trees that scraped the sky. This was countryside, but not at all like Uncle Oren's estate that she'd fallen madly in love with as a child. That was the last place she'd lived with her mother. It was still the only place where she felt like she belonged.

The door creaked open, and Patrice ushered her inside with a puzzled expression. His white hair waved like puffed candy floss and he was dressed in a robe over what looked to be blue-striped pajamas. "Amalie, qu'est que—?"

"Where are they? Uncle Oren and Aunt Maurielle?"

Patrice took in her disheveled appearance, then gaped at the object she held in her hand. "In the study, but—"

Amalie didn't wait for Patrice's carefully curated explanation for why she couldn't interrupt her aunt and uncle. She felt a bit guilty at greeting the man inappropriately, especially since she'd pulled him from his bed, but this couldn't wait.

She charged down the hall, barely glancing at the artwork Aunt Maurielle had hung since the last time she'd visited, and slammed her shoulder into the heavy wooden door.

It flew open, and Uncle Oren jumped from his chair. His hand was halfway to the drawer that held his musket when he recognized her face. "Amalie?"

She straightened her shoulders, then strode to the desk and dropped the ring and the bloody spike onto the polished wood with a hollow thump.

4

1836 COUNTRYSIDE BEYOND MORDELLES,
FRANCE

Amalie worked to catch her breath as Oren stared at the macabre collection of objects in front of him. Aunt Maurielle shoved the book she'd been holding onto the shelf and took a step toward the desk. For a second, she wondered if they'd ignore the weapon completely and start in on her being out after dark.

"What is this?" Her uncle's voice was tight.

"You know what it is." Amalie wasn't going to play his game. Not anymore. There was too much at risk for her to placate him and accept his outdated reasoning.

"I don't—" he started, but Amalie slammed her hand onto the desk, making him flinch.

"This is the proof you said I'd never find. I killed him, Uncle. The man I told you I saw in the city. The vam—"

"Do *not* say that word in this house."

Amalie's nostrils flared. She forced air into her lungs as her hands started to shake. Oren had been the one to teach them from the Grimoire. To tell them the story of Solène and Le Sombre, to explain why their world always teetered between light and darkness, never settling in peace. Yet he would not concede that either god had touched humans with their power. It was madness.

She drew a breath and forced the edge from her tone. "Those dark creatures killed my mother. I saw it with my own two eyes. I've hunted him—the man they call Theo Vallon—for months, and tonight I vanquished darkness." Amalie held up the ring with his insignia. "He is one of them. The brotherhood you refuse to acknowledge. The creatures of the night responsible for—"

"You know nothing of what you speak." Her uncle's voice shook with rage.

Amalie straightened, her palm still stinging. "And you do? You live in a dream, Uncle! Pretending we are not being watched, hunted! Pretending the accounts of corpses drained of blood are not spread to cow us into submission!"

"I told you to stay away from Marcel and the Pourfendeurs. I told you—"

"You told us plenty of things that aren't true, Uncle. You may not approve of Marcel, but he has been willing to do what you haven't." Amalie straightened, stepping back from the desk. "Now there is one less of them prowling the streets."

Oren watched her with barely concealed anger. Amalie waited for him to open his mouth, thrilled and terrified by this break in her uncle's gentle demeanor. He hadn't yelled when she told him she was leaving. When she left with his horse, he hadn't chased after her like she'd half-hoped he would.

"Amalie?" A small voice sounded behind her, and she whipped toward the study door.

"Bethany." The name slipped past her lips as her sister ran forward, wrapping her arms so tightly around her waist, Amalie thought she might heave the meager contents of her stomach. Even though she had nothing left after heaving outside. The adrenaline that had coursed through her for the past half a day seeped out of her at the clean scent of her sister's hair, and she wanted to sink like a stone to the floor.

Leaving Bethany had been the hardest decision of her life, but the ring staring at her from the desk had made it all worth it. *They would be safe.* Amalie would fight until they were safe.

Her sister pulled back, tilting her chin until her deep brown eyes locked onto Amalie's. She didn't have to look far. Bethany had grown a full inch since the last time they were together. She'd had a birthday as well. *Fourteen.* Bethany's jaw tightened. "Why haven't you visited?"

"I—" Amalie paused. How to answer that question? She glanced at her aunt standing next to the desk. "I was working and couldn't get away from the city." She could've visited more if she wanted to. If she'd been willing to lie about what she was doing in Paris. Who she was spending time with. Leaving and defying her uncle's wishes was one thing, but looking him in the eye while sleeping under his roof and partaking of his hard-earned food would've filled her with shame. She'd come back halfway through the year for her blood infusion, and those twenty-four hours had been difficult enough.

"I missed you," Amalie breathed, pulling her sister in again and clutching her head to her chest. That was the truth. Perhaps one of the only truths she could tell her at the moment. "Let's get you up to bed, shall we?" Amalie positioned herself purposefully between Bethany and the desk where the ring and stake were still sitting out in the open.

Bethany nodded, linking her arm with Amalie's and leading her into the hall. They walked together up the stairs and into Bethany's small room. Besides the new clothes thrown over the chair next to her vanity, the room looked the same as it had the day Amalie had left. The same four-poster bed. Same mahogany armoire. Amalie sat on the bed and ran her fingers over the cream Matellase quilt.

Bethany grabbed her brush, then handed it to Amalie as she dropped onto the mattress next to her. Amalie had to reach to pull the brush through her hair from scalp to tip. "You're too tall for this now."

Bethany grinned back at her, her brilliant green eyes sparkling. "Aunt Maurielle passed on some of your old clothes. I wore that blue dress you used to love—the one with the bow?"

Amalie laughed. "That fits you already? I thought I wore that when I was at least sixteen." She hadn't stopped loving that dress. The one with the white swans.

"It's still a bit long in the sleeves." Bethany's eyes dropped.

She understood her sister's impatience. She'd worn everything of her mother's the second it no longer fell off her shoulders, regardless of whether the skirts dragged when she didn't have her boots on. All her mother's frocks, save for one, hung in the bedroom next door. She had no use for petticoats and skirts during her training and only used the one on weekends. Thankfully, there were plenty of women working hard labor in the city. She rarely received strange glances or judgment for her breeches unless she ventured too close to high society.

"You better put it back when you're done," Amalie teased, and Bethany huffed a laugh.

"Are you here to stay?"

Amalie pushed the now gleaming section of her sister's hair to the side and started on the next. "Why would you want your spinster sister to mope around the cottage and accomplish nothing in her life?"

Bethany snorted. "That would only be true if my sister's soul was stolen. The sister I know would find a way to accomplish greatness no matter where she lived."

Amalie swatted her lightly on the hip with the brush. "You have far too much faith in me."

Bethany exhaled, sitting patiently as Amalie finished with the rest of her chestnut locks. Amalie had always been jealous of her sister's stock straight hair. It looked perfect the moment she rolled out of bed, whereas hers looked like a windblown bird's nest.

She could've made conversation about that. She could've teased her about the men who were surely coming around now that she was of age. She could've asked her about her schooling or her plans for the summer, but every time Amalie tried to open her mouth, the lump in her throat bobbed.

So instead, they sat in gentle quiet. The only sound the brush bristles whispering against Bethany's hair. When she finished, Amalie handed the brush back to her sister. Bethany stood and padded back to the vanity, placing the brush next to the jeweled box that used to be their mother's. She wondered if Bethany had hidden any secrets there.

"Why did you come back tonight?" Bethany turned but didn't walk closer.

Amalie drew a deep breath. *How much had her sister heard?* She replayed her conversation with Uncle Oren, regretting instantly how she'd gotten worked up and raised her voice. "I had something I needed to bring to Uncle Oren."

"What was it?"

"Nothing you need to worry about."

Bethany rolled her eyes. "I'm fourteen, Amalie. You hardly need to protect me anymore." She stalked forward and plopped down next to her, making the bed frame creak.

"I'll always protect you, Beth." Another truth. Amalie was grateful for it.

Bethany folded her arms across her chest. "It's about mother, isn't it? About those stories you used to tell?"

Amalie's heart sped in her chest. Uncle Oren had forbidden her from talking about what she'd seen that night. He'd taken the books their mother had found in a closet at the estate. The ones that held the old stories about Le Sombre. About the curse. About unearthly creatures that lured humans into their clutches and drained their victims of blood.

Amalie shivered. "I'm sorry I filled your head with those nightmares."

Bethany shook her head. "You were a child, Ams. We both were."

In her head, Amalie knew it was true, but her heart refused to believe it. She should've known better. *She should've been better.*

"You're not going to tell me what you brought." Bethany lowered her eyes.

"It's not that I don't want to."

"Then what is it?" She looked up, her eyes glassy.

"Beth, I promise I'll tell you the second you turn sixteen." She worried her bottom lip. That was reasonable, wasn't it? This wasn't the same as what Uncle Oren had done to her. Bethany was still a child. "As long as you haven't gone and gotten yourself married by then."

Bethany screwed up her nose. "Married to whom?"

Amalie laughed out loud. "Matthew, for one! Or that boy who always used to wait at the back gate and—"

"Gabriel? Absolutely not!" Bethany playfully shoved her shoulder. "He still chews on the collar of his shirts!"

Amalie pulled a face, and Bethany giggled like she had when they were young. Amalie could still see her there—that wide-eyed girl who had traipsed along behind her on their adventures along the river in the summers. Now her features had sharpened at the edges, and the freckles across her nose had faded. With her long, dark lashes and full lips, she was more beautiful than cute. It made Amalie's heart twinge.

"Alright, time for bed." Amalie pulled her sister into a quick hug and stood from the bed.

Bethany pouted. "You'll be here in the morning?"

Amalie nodded, though truthfully, she didn't know what to expect. Her conversation with Uncle Oren had been cut short. "I'll see you at breakfast." She swept through the door and closed it gently behind her, then strode to her room at the other end of the hall. She hadn't asked if she could stay the night, but given the late hour and the raindrops tapping against the tiles on the roof, she hoped it was a fair assumption.

Amalie slipped through the door and shivered. Her room was on the north side of the house, so the stones didn't absorb much heat from the sun this time of year. She blamed her trembling on muscle fatigue and general exhaustion rather than the lingering sensation of wood punching through flesh. Of blood against her fingertips.

She strode immediately to the edge of her bed and felt along the floorboards for the familiar, uneven edge. When she found it, Amalie pried the edge up with her fingernails, wincing at the pressure, then set it to the side and pushed her hand into the gap.

Amalie breathed a sigh of relief. Still there. She pulled the carved wooden box out of its hiding place and inspected it. Just as she left it.

When she'd run from this house at seventeen, she hadn't known where she'd be living, and the city wasn't a place for flaunting valuables. Though she didn't have the first clue what was inside the box, it had to be something important, didn't it? Else why would her mother have asked her to protect it?

Amalie traced her fingers around the edges, searching for

the thousandth time for a clasp or depression. *Nothing.* She gritted her teeth and kissed the box, then set it on the bed. She wouldn't stay long, and this time, the box was coming with her.

Amalie quickly stripped off her coat and boots, then pulled her shirt over her head. Her skin prickled at the rush of chilled air against her chemise, still damp with sweat. Amalie strode to the armoire to search for clean undergarments, but just as her fingers closed around the knob, a breeze laced with the scent of fresh rain whispered against the back of her arms and neck.

She stilled. Her room had always been cool but never drafty. Her heart jumped to her throat. Perhaps her window had been left open a crack. It had been unseasonably hot the week before in the city, and—

Amalie gasped as a strong arm cinched around her waist and a hand clamped over her mouth. She flailed her arms behind her head, tensing her hands into claws and raking her fingernails over whatever flesh she could find. It availed her nothing.

A man was in her room. Someone strong. How had he gotten in? Her door was still shut and she was on the second story.

She bucked and strained but barely moved inches from the iron chest against her back. The man's grip tightened until her lungs burned, and she was forced to stop struggling or pass out from lack of air.

"Please. Don't make this harder than it needs to be," he whispered, his breath ragged and hot against her ear. He relaxed the fingers over her nose, and she greedily sucked air through her nostrils. A soft scent flooded her senses, and she was immediately transported to the south of France, where they'd traveled with Uncle Oren three summers ago. White jasmine flowers decorating lush green vines. Plump orange fruits hanging like teardrops from thin branches.

Amalie could almost hear the sea crashing against the cliffs. Her wrist twisted, and she slammed back into herself, realizing her cheeks were wet. Her vision blurred as she tried to think past the strange calm coating her like a second skin.

His arms still gripped her. She should be panicking. *Why was she not panicking?* Her body slumped into the stranger, and she nearly growled as she worked to force tension back into her spine.

She had to think, but her mind was cloudy. *What did she know?* He was large, at least a head taller than her, and strong enough that he may have cracked her ribs. *Or had she done that fighting against him?* Either way, she had no chance of overpowering him, though she was struggling to remember why she wanted to in the first place.

As her breathing settled, Amalie became very aware of his forearm against her bare shoulder. The button of his pants pressed into the small of her back. His skin was warm, his breathing deep and heavy. Her eyes darted to the still-firmly closed door of her bedroom. *What did he want with her?* How had he scaled the wall and gotten through her window without her hearing a thing?

He'd been waiting for her. That was the only logical answer. When she'd walked into her bedroom from Bethany's, he'd already been in her room. Plus, he'd brought some aerosolized toxin that was addling her brain.

Amalie held her breath, hoping the effects would clear before her lungs gave out. The man pulled her further from the armoire, away from the desk and the candle that still burned there, and the fog lifted slightly.

His thumb grazed her wrist. "I'm not going to—"

Amalie clawed for every scrap of rage rippling beneath her

consciousness and used the slight distraction of their movement and his words to her advantage. She curled her lips back and bit down hard on the first finger she could draw into her mouth, then slammed her foot against the inside of her attacker's knee. He grunted but never lost hold of her, instead cracking her nose with the heel of his hand as he spun her around to face him. Amalie groaned as he crushed her arms to her sides, and she opened her mouth to scream, but the air caught in her throat.

That face. *His face.* The amber glow of the candle flickered against his dark brow, his angled cheek bones, his coal-black hair again wet with rain like it had been that night on the street.

"It's not possible," Amalie hissed as the room seemed to swirl around her. *She had killed him.* She'd driven a stake made of ash wood into Theo Vallon's heart. Her eyes dropped to his chest, and he noted the movement like a bird of prey. "I watched you die. I—"

"You don't know half of what you think you know." He rubbed his finger, his lips drawn into a sneer.

Amalie's head spun as her eyes shot back to his. The air seemed to thicken, and her heartbeat continued to slow, lulled by his touch and scent. She was breathing. She shouldn't be breathing. Her limbs grew heavy, her thoughts hazy.

His jaw was tense, his brow furrowed as his lips curled past gleaming teeth. "You will remain silent when I release you."

Amalie's eyelids drooped. *Yes.* She wanted to obey him. To please him—*no.* Amalie fought the heat building in her center, searching for the thread of fear and rage quickly slipping through her consciousness. *He is dark. Dangerous. He will kill you, just like he killed your mother.*

The thought of her mother sharpened her senses, and though she nodded her head in acquiescence, the second Theo released her waist, Amalie called on every thread of strength and bolted for the door.

It was stupid. She knew it the second he wrenched her shoulders back. Her face throbbed, pain radiating over her cheekbones as he wrapped around her a second time. Amalie whimpered and tasted iron in the back of her throat as something hot and wet dripped onto her upper lip.

Theo's body went rigid behind her, and the fog in her head lifted instantly. "You shouldn't have done that." His voice was rough, stretched tight like a bowstring.

"Done what?" Amalie coughed, fighting him just as she had the first time, her body no longer numbed by his glamour. *Where was her uncle? Or Bethany?* Surely someone had heard the scuffle of her feet against the floorboards.

"So stubborn." A low growl ripped from his throat as he shifted, forcing her shoulder blades flush against his chest and bending her head at an unnatural angle. Amalie gasped for breath. She begged for strength to stomp against the floor, to scream, but her muscles fell slack as Theo swept her curls from the tender skin of her neck.

Theo's eyes drank in the shadows, glittering onyx in the candlelight. He was feral. He was thirst.

Vampire.

This was how death would come for her. Alone in her room. Her blood drained as she stared at the wooden ceiling beams. Nobody survived a vampire's bite, not in the legends and not in reality. How many corpses had she seen? Lifeless eyes. Sallow, ashen skin.

She wondered if it would hurt. If she'd make a sound.

Amalie imagined her mother's lifeless body draped across Theo's outstretched arms in the woods. She thought of his lips coated crimson. His face twisted into something more animal than human.

This was how she would die then. At the hands of the same creature.

Exactly like *her*.

"Maman," she whimpered as if she still stood on the rocks of the river bed. Hate curled around her bones like smoke as Theo's jaw grazed the shell of her ear. A shudder rolled through his body as he dropped his head and pierced her flesh with needle-sharp fangs.

5

1824 BLOIS, FRANCE

Rachel pressed herself against the garden wall, the stone still warm from the afternoon sun. A sliver of light glowed above the horizon, shimmering like a strand of gold through the gaps in the trees.

The light was not playing tricks on her. *Not this time.* She'd seen the figure of a man move in the shadows between her and the path back to the chateau. She glanced down at her hands clasping the basket of rhubarb stalks. The cut on her finger stung, and there were fresh droplets of blood forming now that she clenched. Why had she been so careless with the knife? Why hadn't she stayed inside the house and let the kitchen staff take care of it?

Because the greenery of the gardens had called to her after staring at stone walls all afternoon. Because this was the countryside. They were supposed to be safe here.

Rachel forced herself to breathe. The girls were inside. They were safe. Oren and Maurielle knew where she was, and if she didn't return soon, they'd come looking for her. Plus, she wasn't the only one in the gardens this time of night. There were men taking care of the animals—the shadow she'd seen had probably been one of the help.

Even as she thought it, she knew it wasn't true. There was something off about the way the man moved and the way her body had reacted to the brief flash of his fair skin.

She should run. Leave the basket and dart for the stables in the opposite direction of the house. Then she wouldn't have to walk back to the front door alone.

Rachel loosened her grip on the basket and was about to set it on the grass and bolt when the brush of boots on grass sounded next to her. She froze as blood rushed to her middle, making her woozy.

"Excuse me, I wondered if you could—"

Rachel's body suddenly remembered how to move. She jumped back, her heart in her throat, brandishing the paring knife and basket of green leaves and raspberry-colored stalks like she knew how to use them. "Don't come any closer."

The man held up his hands and stepped back. "I didn't mean to frighten you."

"Whether you meant to or not, you shouldn't be here."

His mouth quirked. "You're so certain?"

Rachel took a good look at him then, searching for anything out of the ordinary. He was of average height. Strong build. Like he worked with his hands. He wore plain trousers and a linen tunic with sleeves rolled up his forearms. She might've believed he was one of the farm hands, but his skin was too fair. His fingernails too clean. Plus, he wore his chestnut hair loose and long over his shoulders. All the men here had theirs tied back during the workday.

It was different but not strange enough to attract notice. Laborers from different regions were flooding the town, and it was difficult to keep track of who belonged and who didn't.

She didn't feel anything . . . odd. No strange scents either. Her shoulders relaxed a fraction.

"I'm certain." Rachel set her jaw and only then realized she'd dropped her hands. She lifted the knife again, pointing it at his chest, but her heart was no longer in it. He could still be dangerous, but he wasn't one of *them*.

The man took another step back, and that's when she noticed it. The blood on his shirt. "You're hurt."

He glanced down. "Oh. It's not a deep cut, I—"

"Come to the house. I can have one of the servants patch you right up." She took a step toward the break in the wall, but the man didn't budge. His brow furrowed as his eyes lowered to his boots. "What is it?"

"I can't go to the house."

His hands stayed at his side, his posture aloof. He didn't seem threatening in the least, but she shouldn't be with him alone after dark. She should get back to the kitchen, yet something tugged at her. A sense of worry. Pity? Compassion for this man she knew nothing about.

Rachel nodded toward the garden shed on the other side of the pond. "I could do it. If you follow me there."

His eyes lifted, his face full of innocence and surprise. "A kind offer. One I surely don't deserve."

Tending to his wounds seemed like the most important thing in the world. There was something she was supposed to be doing. Something she needed to get back for, but she couldn't remember what it was.

Rachel walked in the opposite direction of the house, her blood humming at the soft pad of his boots on the path behind her. They entered the shed, and Rachel set down the knife and her bowl of rhubarb then lit a candle. She rummaged through dusty shelves, her hands trembling.

"I don't think I asked for your name." The man stood just inside the door, angling himself toward her.

"Rachel." She found an old but clean rag and brushed past him to dampen it with water from the rain barrel outside. When she returned, she found him standing with his shirt pulled up, exposing his left side.

"Florent." He lifted his hand and the paring knife shifted on the wooden shelf.

Rachel swallowed hard. She hadn't been this close to a man alone who wasn't her brother, clothed or unclothed, since Romane's death. It sent a tingle down her spine.

"My name. It's Florent."

Rachel nodded. "I understood." She cleared her throat and stepped closer, focusing hard on the scrape along his shoulder. "How did this happen?" The wound wasn't deep, but the skin was cut, not torn like it would be from a run-in with a natural element. Rachel frowned.

"I'm a carpenter."

Rachel pressed the cloth to the cut, and Florent sucked in a breath. "Are you working on the abby?" Workers had been coming and going for weeks now that the foundation was finished. She'd taken Amalie and Bethany by the construction every afternoon for the past week.

"Yes."

"And you found yourself here? Across the river?"

Florent met her eyes as she reached for a clay pot, retrieving a handful of dried comfrey and yarrow, crushing them into a makeshift poultice and applying it to the wound.

He winced. "I was exploring."

Rachel's fingers hesitated on his skin before she pulled away and tore a strip from a burlap sack then wrapped it around his arm to secure the poultice in place. With a final knot, she stepped back, forcing her eyes from his wholly-masculine form. His chest swelled as he drew breath, and she folded her arms over her chest, turning her head as he tucked in his tunic.

"Thank you, Rachel. For your kindness." Florent straightened and took a step toward the door.

She nodded once and pressed up against the wooden countertop behind her, giving him a wide berth. "Better luck tomorrow."

Florent raised a brow. "With what?"

Rachel's mouth went dry. "Avoiding injury. Finding interesting places to explore."

His expression softened, and Rachel's insides twisted. Florent made her uncomfortable in a strange, exciting way. She wanted him to leave and, in the same instance, wondered what it would feel like to follow him wherever he was heading.

"I think this has been quite interesting. Don't you?"

6

Amalie's eyes rolled back in her head as the sharp sting against her neck stole her breath. *How was she not writing in pain?* Her thoughts scattered. Perhaps there was venom vampires injected that ended life swiftly and prevented suffering. Though the legends she read as a child did not leave much room for compassion.

It was said that vampires and other creatures of the night were created by Le Sombre, a god cursed to dwell in shadows, asleep in the underworld. Le Sombre was awoken by the evil and selfishness of mankind. He prowled the earth in search of men like him—men who were cruel, men who could not be saved—and gifted what he could offer. An eternity dwelling in shadow with him.

No one knew how many vampires and other shadow walkers he'd created, but there was no shortage of their appearances in legend. Demons who feasted on the young and old. Men transformed into creatures by moonlight. Spirits and the walking dead sent to curse men and women, a manifestation of the evil buried in their own hearts.

These shadow walkers sought their own pleasure, terrorized, and murdered, utilizing their eroded divinity with reckless abandon. Though the details of the stories changed with the telling, the result was always the same.

Humans suffered. Having no defense against the damned, they feared and cowered until the god of light took pity on them. They—

She was falling. Her knees struck the floor. Was that it? Was she so weak and pathetic that a few seconds was all it took?

Her lungs burned, her hands clutching at her chest. Amalie whimpered. *Who would protect Bethany?* Who would protect all the other girls and boys growing up believing the Shadow only existed in stories?

She needed to tell Marcel about her mistake. She needed to convince her family to run, to move farther than they had after her mother's death—convince them that there was no safety here. She needed to board a ship and cross the ocean and hope the Shadow didn't follow there. She needed to do so much. *To say so much.*

Amalie would never get that chance.

A wave of nausea threaded itself through her consciousness. *Dying felt much like consumption.* At least it was familiar.

A sound reminiscent of a sigh dragged her up from the depths where she drowned. Just enough that she almost seemed to know her body again. Like if she reached, she could wiggle her toes or flex her fingers.

Another slip of breath and she was pulled as if from the bottom of a lake, her face suddenly breaking the surface. Amalie gasped, her hands gripping tight.

Amalie's eyes flashed open. The sounds she'd heard were from her own lips.

Boots. Why was she staring at boots?

She lifted her head and shoved hard, but her fingers

slipped. Her chest hit the floor with a crack. She scrambled back, her knees weak and her face throbbing as a hand reached for her.

"Don't touch me!" Amalie hissed. Theo loomed above her in a crouch, his chest heaving, a drip of what had to be her blood pooled on his lips. His tongue flicked out and swept it away. "I'm alive." Amalie didn't realize she'd said the words out loud until energy snapped between them.

Theo stood there, his face still trained on hers, contorted in pain or ecstasy she couldn't tell. She flattened her palms against the wood floors and crushed her fingers against the grooves.

She was alive.

She couldn't stop running those words through her head. It was impossible. More than that, she felt like herself. Terrified. Shaking. But her strength was returning faster than it should've been if he'd taken her blood.

What if he hadn't taken her blood? Was there another option?

Amalie paled. "What did you do to me?"

Theo opened his mouth just as heavy steps sounded on the stairs outside her room. Theo tensed for such a brief moment that Amalie wondered if she was hallucinating. Even his slightest movement was graceful and dreamlike, as if he moved on a different plane, obeying different cosmic rules.

Perhaps this was death. Maybe she was lying on the floor, her lifeblood depleted, and she existed only now in memory, in spirit. She was seeing apparitions and—

Another heavy footfall. This time, so close that Amalie felt the vibration through the floor. Theo spun and, without a sound, launched himself through the still-open window and into the night.

Amalie's heart jumped into her throat. *She was alive. She*

was dead? She still couldn't make up her mind, but if she had somehow survived his attack, there was only one explanation.

She lifted a hand to the side of her neck where her skin still burned, then scrambled up from the floor. She braced herself on the vanity and searched for her looking glass with unsteady hands.

Gripping the handle, she leaned toward the flickering candle and positioned it so she could view her flesh. Two tiny marks of deep crimson against her skin.

She inspected the rest of her features to find herself pale, but her cheeks were flushed. Dried blood on her upper lip, her nose swollen where she'd been hit. All of it was proof that her heart still beat deep in her chest.

No. Her thoughts buzzed around the only other possibility like a hornet.

There was a sharp rap of knuckles against wood. "Amalie?" Her uncle's voice called through the door.

Her head was so loud, she couldn't remember how to speak. *What did she know of this curse?*

The histories claimed that vampires could create like Le Sombre. *Create.* She hated that word. "Infect" was more appropriate. In olden times, after their turning, they'd wreaked havoc on humanity, injecting them with venom that turned them to shadow.

They soon learned that their creative powers came at a heavy cost. Their own strength and power were used to form every new vampire they created. They were weakened with each bite.

Nobody knew what powers they could have possessed if they hadn't diluted them by turning others. Vampires had found the curse of Le Sombre in their own desperate search for companionship. Or in their blood lust.

It was just punishment. The gods of legend were selfish,

flawed and imperfect, but it did not please them to witness unfair battles. Though their magic was split at the point of infection, humans still had no recourse.

Amalie choked out a sob. No historian had record of a turned human being in ages. Shame and disgust wracked her body. Perhaps that was why. Once someone was changed, they'd rather fling themselves off the roof than admit they were becoming a creature of the dark.

"Amalie." Another knock.

She ignored it, her mind spinning. If people ran—if they left after being bitten—there could be an entire vampire army growing under their noses. But if the legends were true and his power would be split by turning her, why would Theo Vallon sacrifice any of his power to turn her?

Her brain poked and prodded but couldn't find any explanation.

Amalie began to shake.

Theo's motivation wasn't the most troubling piece of this disaster. The more pressing concern was how this curse would manifest in her. If she stayed, would she keep her own mind? Her own heart? Would she turn into something—some animal or creature—unrecognizable?

Was her family safe? Would she become the threat?

That thought stopped her cold.

Another knock. This time, it made the door rattle.

She wouldn't be able to avoid this. Amalie scrubbed the blood from her upper lip, then snatched the knitted blanket that lay over the end of her bed and wrapped it around her shoulders to stop her shaking.

She couldn't let them in. It was too dangerous. "Yes, Uncle?"

"May I come in?"

"I'm not decent." Amalie swallowed hard, clutching the

blanket and forcing oxygen into her lungs to calm her frantic heart. Her body felt wrong. Like there was something foreign racing under her skin.

Aunt Maurielle murmured something, but she couldn't make out the words.

"We need to talk to you—"

"Through the door is fine." Amalie stared at the open window. Was he waiting in the shadows? Would he come back?

"Amalie, I know you're angry, but this is important." Her uncle's voice was ragged.

She needed to leave. Immediately. If vampire venom was coursing through her veins, she could turn at any moment. What had the history books said about that? There had been conflicting stories. Some said it was a matter of hours before one turned, other accounts listed the process as taking days, possibly a full week. She'd glazed over the details, not thinking them important. Now, she was kicking herself.

"Fine. Through the door." The floorboards creaked as Oren let out a frustrated sigh. "You are right."

Amalie blinked, her mind screeching to a halt. "What?"

Oren's voice was muffled through the wood. "You were always right about the vampires, but we have rules—"

"You told me never to say that word in this house," Amalie hissed, stalking to the door. A hot ache burned down her throat.

"I know."

"You told me what I saw that day in the woods was only my imagination."

"I know."

"You're telling me that you knew they existed?"

Her uncle shuffled his feet, and a slow heat began to crackle. Like dead coals fed with a fresh gust of air.

She clenched her jaw. "You told me I was crazy."

"I never said that."

"You made me *feel* like I was crazy."

"I—"

Amalie's voice built in strength. "You told me we had nothing to fear. You told me that Marcel was spreading hate, that he was deluded by old myths. You told me my mother's death was an accident. You told me that *we were safe*."

"Amalie, Bethany is sleeping." Maurielle's voice was gentle. She was right. Her little sister was sleeping in the room next door, and yet she still wanted to throw herself against the door. To lash out. *Was that the monster inside her talking?*

Amalie paled, stumbling back from the door.

"I know. I'm sorry." Uncle Oren's voice was ragged. "We've always had protections in place. For hundreds of years, our family has been kept safe. I planned to tell you everything on your eighteenth birthday, but you left."

Amalie dropped to her mattress. What? Her aunt and uncle had never mentioned anything about this. She'd come back to visit twice, hadn't she? Why hadn't they told her then? "I don't believe you."

"Amalie—"

"You could've told me any time in the past four-and-a-half years, Uncle. What was keeping you from telling me when I came back at Christmas? Or during my treatments?"

Since she was a child, she'd been warned that her blood didn't clot and heal the way it should. Uncle Oren told stories of her mother refusing to take the needle and then nearly bleeding out from a scrape on her knee. So even though she had run away, she came back for her infusions. Always arriving during the day when she knew Oren was away. Maurielle had given them to her. Why hadn't she said something?

"You know very well what was keeping us." His voice was low.

Amalie clenched her jaw. "You're blaming this on the Pourfendeurs?"

"I couldn't trust you. As long as you were working with them—"

"Couldn't trust me? With what? I already knew the truth. I've been learning the history and training to fight! Who else would be better to hold your secrets?"

Her uncle was silent. There was another murmur from Maurielle. Amalie blinked back tears from her eyes. What good was this now? What could her uncle possibly say that could help now that she was turning into *one of them?*

"Amalie, your mother—"

"What about my mother?" Amalie snapped. Her lungs refused to expand.

"I know you disagree with my methods, but our rules were there for a reason. Your mother went out after dark. She spoke to a man she did not know."

Amalie's stomach twisted. What man? She'd never heard anything about this. She'd never seen her mother with anyone other than her brother and Maurielle, and of course, herself and Bethany. The three of them were always together.

Not after dark. Amalie and Bethany had been in bed after dark.

"She kept him a secret," her uncle continued. "She met with him, she—"

His voice broke, and Amalie's eyes burned. *Theo Vallon.* Her mother had known him. Was it true? She'd met with him, spent time with him, and *then* he had killed her? That low burn flared and threatened to consume her whole.

"That's why we moved north. He was still out there. He and who knows how many others. I left my estate. I left my job.

We took you, and we moved to the opposite side of the region. We changed our name, we did everything we could to keep the two of you safe. I was going to tell you everything when you were old enough—"

"You *lied* to me." Amalie wrapped her arms around herself to keep her guts from spilling out. How would this have been different? Had her aunt and uncle told her the whole story, would she have sought out Marcel? Would she have rebelled against Oren's rules and left if she'd known they were there because of a threat?

It wasn't even a question. Yes. She would have. Because even though her own family had worked to keep the truth from her, she'd known it all along.

But would she have been more cautious?

Would she have had to do it alone?

"There's so much more, Amalie. More I need to show you—to tell you. We were trying to keep you safe—"

"It's not possible. As long as those creatures are out there, nobody is safe, Uncle." Amalie's fingers were numb, and ice seemed to flow through her veins. She hadn't heard Theo—hadn't known he'd even opened the window before he was standing there in her bedroom, his hand over her nose and mouth.

She would be that deadly. And her family was on the other side of the door.

"It's late." Oren cleared his throat. "You're safe. You're home. That's all that matters for now. We can talk more in the morning." Her uncle took a step away from the door. "You'll be here in the morning?"

Amalie's jaw worked. She scanned her body, hunting for any abnormalities. Did her stomach hurt? Did her head ache? Was that an indicator that the venom was working? *She needed to get out of this house.*

Amalie forced her voice to steady. "Of course." She couldn't unclench her back molars.

"You can hate us for now, but don't let it last too long," Maurielle whispered through the door.

As their footsteps retreated, Amalie collapsed onto the bed and gasped for breath, then heaved silent sobs into her rumpled quilt.

7

1836 COUNTRYSIDE TO MORDELLES, FRANCE

When the stairs stopped creaking, Amalie forced herself up. She swiped the tears from her cheeks and clutched the knit blanket as she crept to her window. She ran her hand over the sill, splintering white paint from the frame. A gust, cold and blustery, whipped her hair back, biting against her outstretched arm.

She shivered. The moon hung low in the sky, casting a silver sheen over the garden below. The ground seemed treacherously far below, but she had no choice. She glanced back at the closed door, imagining Bethany tucked into bed across the hall. She had to protect her, even if it meant isolating herself.

Amalie climbed onto the windowsill, the rough wood scraping against her knees. The wind howled around her, tearing at her clothes. Her fingernails embedded in the soft wood as she fought to keep her balance, her heart jerking in her chest. She murmured a prayer, then lowered herself onto the roof. The tiles were slick, and she slid feetfirst until she latched onto a tree branch. Once she caught her breath, she used the branch as leverage to move to the roof of the shed next to the house, then finally dropped to the ground.

The impact jolted through her bones as she landed, her knees buckling. She steadied herself and sucked in a breath of the cold night air. Amalie turned, sure she'd made enough noise to cut through even her uncle's snoring, but there was no movement near the cottage.

She crouched and moved through the garden, a dark, tangled maze of clawing branches. The wind whistled through the trees, putting all her senses on high alert. As soon as she passed through the iron gate and reached the street, she broke into a run.

Amalie flew along the country roads, not at all worried about what might be creeping in the shadows. She'd already met the worst.

Mordelles was eerily silent. Shadows stretched and shifted in the dim light, playing tricks on her mind. Every alley seemed to hide a lurking danger, every corner a potential threat. She would've scolded herself had she not been face-to-face with a nightmare just moments ago.

She was becoming a nightmare.

Tears stung her eyes as she forced herself forward. There was only one option. She needed Marcel and Olivie to take her life before she turned. She'd stabbed Theo in the heart, and he'd still lived. Once she turned, would it be the same for her? Would she live to kill for eternity?

She couldn't let that happen.

The town square loomed ahead, and the house she sought stood at the far end. She searched for light from a lamp or candle in the window and raced toward it, her legs burning with exertion, her lungs aching from the cold.

She stumbled up the steps, her hands fumbling for the

knocker. The cold metal bit into her skin as she grasped it, lifting and letting it fall with a hollow thump. Seconds stretched into an eternity as she waited, her ears aching from the wind. She knocked again, pounding with both fists.

The door finally flew away from her, and Amalie scrambled back, nearly tumbling down the steps.

"Amalie?"

Before she could stop him, Marcel charged past the threshold and gripped her arm.

"No, Marcel, you can't—"

He yanked her inside and slammed the door behind them. "Amalie, what—"

"You have to kill me!" Amalie pressed herself against the door, her palms flat against the polished wood. She couldn't keep her tears at bay, even though it made her look weak. Marcel stared at her, and the physical world around her began to invade her senses. The faint smell of smoke and the flicker of light from the fire burning in the room past the entry.

"Please. Explain why I should kill you?" Marcel raised an eyebrow.

Amalie turned her head, pointing at the marks on her neck. Marcel hissed air through his teeth. There was a creak on the stairs ahead of her. Amalie's eyes snapped up. *Olivie.*

"Amalie? Did your uncle throw you out?" She raced down the steps toward her, but Amalie held out her hands.

"Stay back. Please." She reached for the door handle, but her hands were shaking so hard, she couldn't grasp it. She needed to get back outside. She needed—

"Amalie, stop." Marcel's voice was hard. "Turn around." Amalie obeyed. He pulled her wrists behind her back, and she felt the rough burn of thick rope against her skin. When he'd tied a knot and pulled it tight, securing it to the support beam next to her, he stepped back. "There. That will buy us a few moments if you start lunging for our throats."

Olivie's eyes widened. "What are you talking about?"

Marcel pointed at her neck, and Olivie gasped. "A rope won't stop her, Marcel—"

"Start talking," he growled.

Amalie swallowed the lump still choking her throat. "My uncle didn't need my proof. He's known of vampires all along."

Marcel let out a low chuckle. "'Course he has. They all do. They're too cowardly to admit it."

"I don't give a damn about your uncle, unless he was the cause of this. What happened?" Olivie was singularly focused, her eyes trained on the marks. She'd lost her brother to vampires. Seen him snatched from their doorstep just after dark. Marcel had lost his children. Louisa and Marc were stripped from him as he held their little hands.

"It doesn't matter. I came here because I need you to kill me. Before I turn. Please." Tears stung her eyes. How would they do it? Slit her throat? A bullet to the head? She hoped it would be quick. She hoped—

"Where were you attacked?" Marcel paced in front of her.

"My bedroom, but it doesn't matter! You need to—"

"When?"

Amalie ground her teeth. "Less than an hour ago."

"And you don't feel any different? No added strength or strange thoughts?" Marcel tapped his temple.

"I just asked you to kill me, did I not?" If that wasn't a strange thought, she didn't know what was.

"We need to learn everything we can." Marcel pulled a stake from the pocket of his overcoat hanging on the coat rack. "I can always kill you later."

Her mind, which had been a mass of porridge, suddenly

snapped into focus. "No. You can't." Marcel's expression darkened, and Amalie's mouth went dry. "You can't kill me later. The vampire who attacked me in my room was Theo Vallon."

"That's impossible."

Amalie let out a ragged laugh. "I know! Impossible! Yet I saw him with my own eyes. He gave me these marks, Olivie! He's alive."

Marcel's eyes were predatory. "His blood was on the stones. You took his ring—"

"It was him," she groaned, her wrists aching from the pull of the rope.

"Did you fight him?"

Amalie bobbed her head. It was the answer she wanted to give. She'd tried, hadn't she? Ice slid down her spine as she remembered the feel of his lips against her skin. The rough grasp of his hands on her waist. The fear coursing through her as his fangs broke into her flesh.

Bile rose in her throat at the swirl of clashing emotions. She'd been soothed by him. He'd tricked her. But she hadn't wanted it. *Had she?*

Had that been a survival mechanism? Her body and mind blocking her from the pain and forcing her down from her conscious mind? She couldn't make sense of it. The lack of pain. The calm in her middle. The paralyzing fear of seeing Theo Vallon's face again. The dark desire to search him out again . . .

She was going to be sick.

"You're saying a stake to the heart didn't kill a vampire?" Marcel's jaw worked.

She nodded. "That's what I'm saying."

"Then what will?" Olivie's face was white. "Everything we've done. All the vampires we vanquished . . ." She lifted her hand, running her thumb over her arm where she kept her trophy marks.

"We need answers." Marcel's eyes locked onto hers. "If Vallon was willing to split his power to turn you, there must be a reason."

Amalie shook her head. "He killed my mother—"

"But he didn't kill you. Why?" Marcel took another step toward her.

"I don't know. None of this makes any sense. I—" She flinched as metal flashed, then gasped as her hands dropped free.

"You need to find him." Marcel loomed over her.

Amalie's eyes widened. "No. I can't. I don't have time—"

"You must use the time you have," Marcel snapped.

The silence that followed cooled her skin like mist. Amalie's stomach plummeted to her knees. She'd sat in close to a hundred meetings with Marcel, Olivie, and other members of the Pourfendeurs. They had never preached relocation. They'd never fought for only their towns and villages to be free of the Shadow. They'd fought for total eradication. The Pourfendeurs wanted safety for the region—for the world.

If they couldn't vanquish, the Pourfendeurs were impotent.

But there was nowhere she could go where she wouldn't hurt anyone. Whether tonight or in a few days, she would turn. She would seek out victims and lure them in with the same intoxicating pull she'd felt from Theo in her bedroom. Then she would drain their blood and leave them cold and pale on the ground to rot.

Amalie's heart thumped against her ribs. *You don't know half of what you think you know.* Those had been Theo's words. What if it didn't happen like she thought? What if the venom didn't take over her mind? What if she kept her sensibilities?

"I can't take the risk," she whispered, thinking of Bethany sleeping in her bed. Her cousins in the bedroom next to her.

"What risk?" Olivie pushed off the wall. "Is one more vampire going to make a difference? If we haven't been vanquishing them like we thought, then they're all still out there. We don't have any other ideas at the moment unless you know of some way to stop their hearts."

Marcel scoffed. "They don't have hearts."

Amalie frowned. Hadn't Theo's skin been warm to the touch? Wasn't his heart beating against her back?

Marcel considered, wheels spinning behind his eyes. Amalie wondered if it was already working. If she already had a glamour. If she was manipulating them to preserve her life without knowing it.

But the idea of *not* being stabbed or shot to death against the door had planted itself and taken root. What if this was a blessing, not a curse? What if she could use the time she had? What if this was the key they'd been waiting for all along?

"I can find him," Amalie said with far more confidence than she felt. After they'd attacked him, there was no way Theo Vallon was going to show up along his typical routes. She would have to search like they had months ago and hope a vampire happened to walk past her on a dark street that would lead her to him. A chill slipped down her spine. "I'll go tonight. I'll leave you word in the city. If you don't hear from me by the end of next week, you can assume . . ." She trailed off.

Olivie's face paled, and Amalie read her thoughts. Amalie knew where they met. She knew where both of them lived.

Olivie's features snapped into focus. Her dark waves framed her face, and a splotch of pink bloomed across her cheeks. This was her friend. Marcel was her leader, but Olivie was her confidant. The person she laughed with and complained to. She was almost as close to her as Bethany.

Not anymore. *The risk wasn't small.*

Marcel stepped back and looked at her from under a hooded brow. "Go."

"Marcel—"

"*Go.*"

Amalie choked on a sob as she whirled and pulled on the handle. The door flew open, the wind whipping against her forehead. A drizzle had started while she'd been inside, and the droplets chilled her instantly. She bolted down the path, not looking back. Not because she doubted Marcel or Olivie but because she doubted herself. *What was she doing? Where would she go?*

Amalie's breath came in ragged gasps as she darted through the narrow, cobbled streets of the village, her shoes slipping on the rain-slick stones. This town had once been a place of comfort but now felt like a labyrinth of shadow. The narrow alleys twisted and turned, each one looking the same in the dim light of the torches even though she knew these passages like the back of her hand. The rain soaked through her thin shawl and clung to her skin. Her hair, once neatly pinned, hung in damp tendrils around her face. She needed shelter, and while she knew most everyone in town, she was done putting anyone at risk.

Which meant she had to leave. Survive the night and see what the morning brought her. If she was lucid, she could begin her search for the vampires then. If she wasn't . . .

The rain began to hammer against her skin, and Amalie pulled her shawl tighter around her shoulders, though it did little to ward off the chill. Her trousers clung to her legs, making each step feel like she was slogging through mud. The air around her thickened as she reached the edge of town, leaving the warm glow of windows to fade behind her.

She didn't recognize the road until she passed the gnarled

olive tree on the right, and her internal orientation reset. She was on the north side of town. The Ferrier farmhouse was up the lane on the right, and if she kept on up the path, there would be an old garden shed and—

The back of her neck prickled, and Amalie spun. She pushed her matted hair out of her eyes and blinked into the darkness. It was laughable to think she could see anything in the gray glow of the moon filtering through the clouds overhead, and yet she stood stock-still searching the night. Nothing. Her teeth chattered as she continued on, huddling deeper into herself.

Her thoughts grew darker by the second. Even if she found the shed, she would be soaked through and would likely catch sick overnight. She could freeze to death or succumb to illness before the venom ever took hold.

The idea of lying alone on a cold stone floor without anyone to bring her a hot water bottle or steamed lemon tea made a sob rise in her throat. She'd lost everything. In one night, she'd lost her family and friends, her home, her safety.

Part of her begged for death. But another part clawed desperately for some meaning she could bring to her last fleeting moments. She could find information—she could help the Pourfendeurs and save lives.

Amalie had barely turned off the main road when she felt it again. The hair-raising sensation of eyes boring into the back of her skull. Her breathing quickened as she broke into a brisk walk. She stumbled on an exposed tree root as she pushed further into the trees and fell, her knees screaming in pain as she scrambled back to her feet and started running.

The shed couldn't be much further, but the darkness was all-encompassing as she worked her way up the hill. Amalie spread her arms in front of her, her eyes straining. Just a little further. Just—

A strong hand clasped around her waist, and she was whisked off her feet. Before she could scream, another hand covered her mouth. The air and rain whipping against her skin was her only measure of how fast she was moving. It felt as if she were flying through the air.

She waited for the jolt of her captor's feet slamming against the ground, but none came. They moved seamlessly up the remainder of the hill, and Amalie lost her strength to fight.

Warmth seeped into her from every point of contact, thawing her from the outside in. She gritted her teeth, refusing to feel relief.

It was him. Somehow she'd known it was Theo Vallon before she inhaled the scent of bergamot and jasmine. But why had he come after her? To finish what he'd started? To make sure he was there when she turned?

Amalie wanted to scratch his eyes out. To kick and curse and tear at whatever she could get a hand on. But she needed answers, and she doubted he'd give them to her under those circumstances. She had to be smart. If he was here, she wouldn't have to hunt him down in the morning. Perhaps she could get something out of him that night and go back to Marcel and Olivie before her wits left her.

There was a rush of air, and then Theo slipped his hand from her mouth and righted her, setting her feet on floorboards. The air was black and still. Cool. But no rain fell from above. "Where? How did you—?" Amalie blinked, but couldn't see anything in the pitch-dark of the shed.

Theo left her side, and Amalie curled into herself, tracking the sound of his boots falling across the floor. *So.* He could make noise when he wanted to. She winced at the scratch of a match against wood then blinked as light poured into the room.

Theo walked the flame to an oil lantern hanging on the far

wall. There wasn't much oil in the glass, and what was there looked orange and rancid. As Theo lit the wick, the sour smell that filled the barn confirmed her suspicions.

Amalie stared at him as he returned the lantern to its hook and swiveled to face her. Her gaze traveled over the water dripping from tendrils of his hair. His shirt soaked and molded to his chest.

The same calm she'd felt in her bedroom washed over her, and her chattering jaw went still. "Stop that."

Theo's face was expressionless. "Stop what?"

"Whatever you're doing to make me feel . . . strange."

A twitch of his brow. "I'm not doing anything."

"Liar." Amalie glared at him. So much for catching bees with honey.

"A strong accusation. Why would you want to sully your reputation with such poor company?"

Amalie's jaw worked, just as her stomach swooped out from under her. *Bastard.* The last thing she wanted to admit was that his presence—the mere sight of him—made heat gather at her center. It should've been the opposite after what he'd done to her, but the effect had only grown.

His proximity was intoxicating, and she hated him for it. She hated that every time she looked upon his face, her body twinged, begging for a second dose. It was madness. It was the curse of Le Sombre. It was beyond her mortal understanding, and because of that, she could no longer trust her inclinations. She had to find a way to ignore her emotions, to lean only on her rational mind.

Theo stood unnaturally still, like he was carved of stone. His expression suddenly grew serious. "You know what I am."

Amalie pushed damp hair from her neck, exposing the wounds. "You've made that abundantly clear."

His eyes tracked her movement like a bird of prey, lingering on the marks he'd left. "Let me guess. You're hoping for an apology?"

Amalie scoffed. "If you apologized, I wouldn't believe it."

"You know my thoughts?"

"I know you're not capable of remorse." Her eyes burned.

He chuckled low in his throat. "And how would you know that? You've spoken with so many of my kind?"

Amalie swallowed, clenching her hands to get blood flowing into her numb fingertips. "I know plenty about your kind."

The corner of Theo's mouth twitched. "Of course. From your storybooks."

"History. Fact. Not stories."

"History written by whom?"

Amalie ground her teeth. "I'm not going to stand here and argue with you."

"Then what are you going to stand here and do?" His voice rumbled through her.

Amalie dropped her eyes, busying herself with removing her dripping blanket and scanning the small room. It was sparsely furnished, with rough-hewn stone walls coated with a layer of dirt and dust. The floor was made of cold, uneven flagstones, and a single narrow bed frame without a mattress was pushed against one wall. Shelves lined with grimy jars and gardening tools hung on the opposite side, casting long shadows in the weak light.

Rainwater began to pool at her feet. Her clothes dragged on her frame, heavy and clinging. She needed to get dry. Whatever strange magic Theo was working on her, it wouldn't keep her from freezing to death. "Why did you steal me away from the road?"

"You were seeking shelter here, were you not?"

"That's not what I asked."

Theo's nostrils flared. "I hastened your journey. A bit of gratitude is warranted."

Amalie ignored his jab. "Why?" she hissed. She wanted him to say it. To admit what he'd done and give her some clue as to what she should expect. How her body would betray her. What he wanted with her.

A pit opened through her center as the past hours swam in her head. She couldn't go back. *She could never go back.* Theo was there because he knew what she was becoming. He might've done this before, or at least seen it done. She needed his answers before she lost herself.

Her family wouldn't know what had compelled her to disappear in the middle of the night. What would Bethany think when she woke in the morning and found her gone again? What would she believe when her older sister never came back to visit? Never returned for her treatment?

What was she going to do?

Even after she got her answers—even if she could help Marcel and Olivie—where would that leave her? Amalie shivered, imagining an eternity of hunting as Theo did. Of living alone and never going near her family.

"I pulled you from the road because you're going to help me," Theo snapped.

"And why would I do that?" she spat. She would not allow him to feign altruism when he was the sole reason she'd had to run in the first place.

He shrugged. "I'm not a mind reader. But I assume it's because you'd like my help in return."

Amalie gaped at him, all thoughts of her chilled skin and numb toes disappearing behind white-hot anger flaring through her middle. "Help with what?"

He motioned to the stone walls around them. "Protection.

Food. Shelter. Unless you were planning to run back through Mordelles—"

"You think I'd stay the night with you?"

"Would you rather spend it with your family?" He leveled a stare at her, his eyes cold.

She scoffed. "I'm sure you'd love that. To wait until I transformed into a dark creature like you and killed everyone I love. Is that how this normally works?"

Theo's eyes narrowed. He scanned her face, then glanced again at the wounds on her neck. Darkness flickered across his expression before his lips drew up in an arrogant smile. "Exactly why you need my help."

Amalie's skin heated under his scrutiny. She needed to say something clever, to back him into a corner so he would answer her questions, but she had no leverage. She knew nothing that could benefit him since any plans she'd had with Marcel and Olivie were moot, and her own transformation was a mystery.

Would she have power when she turned? Would she be Theo's equal? Until she figured that out, she was at his mercy. The way Theo stepped forward, slow and catlike, he knew it.

"What will happen to me? How long will this take?"

He ignored her. "You must warm yourself. Rest. Then you'll accompany me to safety and we'll discuss our bargain."

Amalie's heart picked up speed. She didn't want to go anywhere with him. She didn't have time to travel, to wait until her body wasn't her own. And if he took her far, how would she get back to Marcel and Olivie?

A protest worked its way up her throat but couldn't quite break the surface. Theo lifted a hand, and Amalie held her breath, both dreading and wishing for his touch, but instead, he stepped back. "You'll know more soon enough."

Amalie's nostrils flared. Something flickered across Theo's

face, then his expression smoothed over into placid cold. *He was darkness. Evil. Deadly.* Of course he didn't care about her questions. Her fear. Her grief.

Theo exhaled, and the ground seemed to shift beneath her feet as her body grew heavy.

"Stop. That." Amalie's face flushed, and her throat felt singed.

Theo crossed the room with fluid grace and disappeared into the night.

8

Rachel waited near the river, her back pressed against the rough bark of an oak tree. She hadn't thought about how loud the rush of the water would be, otherwise she would've chosen a different spot. She wanted to know when Florent was approaching. Not that she was worried he wouldn't be able to find her—he'd had no trouble the last few times they'd met after dark—but because she hated the feeling of someone watching her.

She hadn't told anyone in the house about Florent, especially not Oren. He'd already pressed her about staying out in the gardens through twilight, at which point she'd decided to avoid him knowing altogether. For the past two weeks, she'd finished her chores early, helped in the kitchens, then enjoyed dinner with her girls and her nieces, Ghislaine and Matilde, and put them all to bed. By then, Oren was locked away in his study or in his room on the third floor with Maurielle. Nobody paid attention to her slipping out through the passageway meant for morning deliveries.

It wasn't wise to be out after dark. She understood Oren's

concern. But her brother would never allow a working man like Florent to come calling at the house, and Rachel couldn't stop thinking about him. Florent was nothing like her husband. He was intriguing. Mysterious. She felt like she knew intimate details about his life and, at the same time, understood nothing about him.

Tonight she would ask what she'd been working up to since their last clandestine conversation in the woods. Rachel had walked past the clawed-up dirt, stone mill, and scaffolding surrounding the abbey. She'd searched for Florent's face in the slew of workers but never saw him. She wanted more than just whispers in the dark. She wanted to see what his life looked like. She wanted to meet his friends and, if she was being honest, hoped he'd want to show her off.

They weren't courting, not by any stretch of the imagination, but the idea of getting closer to him—of being valued by him—sent a shiver through her. Rachel loved her daughters. She was grateful for Oren and all he offered them for the summer, but the idea of true companionship was intoxicating. She missed sleeping next to someone. She missed hands on her waist and lips on her skin.

Florent seemed to look at her with more than simple interest, and she wasn't a child. She wasn't going to get herself in trouble like Oren would probably believe. Florent always acted like a gentleman, which was why she was sure he'd accept her request—

"Good evening."

Rachel spun, her heart jumping into her throat. When she saw Florent smiling at her in the moonlight, her hand flew to her chest. "Do you find it funny to terrify me?"

Florent's grin widened. "Absolutely." He walked closer, and Rachel took him in. He was cleaned up today. While he was always freshly shaven, he didn't always arrive in clean clothes and boots. Tonight his shirt was crisp white, his trousers pressed, and his boots clean.

"What's the occasion?" Rachel asked, her back still up against the tree. She lowered her hand and crossed her arms over her chest.

"Is it a crime to want to impress you?"

Rachel's cheeks burned, and she was grateful for the shadows. "Always so charming," she teased.

Florent strode forward until he was so close Rachel caught the scent of freshly cut wood and the hint of herbs. He hesitated for a moment before brushing past her on his way closer to the river. Rachel's pulse sped at the brief touch.

"What is in your heart tonight?" Florent paused on the bank and crouched, running his hands over the tips of the tall grass.

She loved this question. He asked it of her every time they met after she'd bandaged him up. "Honeysuckle." Florent turned, his eyes alight. She'd thought for hours that afternoon about the answer she'd give, and a thrill passed through her at his obvious delight. "I stood under the vine this afternoon and watched the bumblebees bathe in the flowers. Three different hummingbirds stopped by, and at least four nectar moths."

"You counted?"

"I always count." Rachel walked down to sit in the grass next to him. "The scent was heavenly, and the hum of their wings made me feel like all was right in the world."

"How do humming wings have that enchanting effect?" He sat cross-legged, his knee almost grazing her hip.

"The bees don't worry about what's coming next. They simply get to work. I began to think, perhaps that's my problem. I'm always so worried about the future that I forget to enjoy each day."

Florent watched her, and Rachel turned her eyes to the

river. Her heart was like a treasure chest that she filled to the brim with jewels of his attention. Ones she loved to admire but never knew how to wear.

She pulled her knees to her chest. "And you?"

"Dark eyes," he answered without hesitation. "Flushed cheeks. Hair pulled back tight in a twist that I'd love to let loose." Rachel's throat dried out like the apple slices they'd laid in the sun that afternoon. "And don't say I'm charming. I'm only speaking the truth."

Rachel fixed her gaze on the ripple of moonlight shifting in the water, the ache in her middle so intense, she nearly curled into a ball. She drew a long breath and exhaled, then turned to face him before she lost courage. "I'd like to meet you in the morning. See where you work. I could bring you biscuits or—"

"Women aren't allowed on site." Florent looked amused, and that only hardened her resolve.

"I know. I don't want to complicate things. I could come over lunch if that's better. We could go to the café?"

Florent shifted in the grass. "And what about the girls?"

"I could ask Maurielle to watch them."

"She'd do that?"

Rachel shrugged. "She'd consider it, I'm sure."

"On such late notice?" He pushed forward and settled next to her, his thigh pressed against hers. Slowly, he lifted his hand and reached behind her head, grasping the pin that held her hair in a knot. "May I?"

Rachel's heart fluttered against her rib cage. She nodded, and he pulled, allowing her hair to pool in soft waves over her shoulders. This wasn't wrong. He wasn't asking to pull her trousers off for glory's sake, he only wanted to see her hair let out. She watched his eyes travel over her, tracing the swirls of her hair, then meandering back to her face.

"Beautiful," he whispered.

"Florent—"

"I want to see you at lunch, of course I do, but there's an unspoken tradition there with the other men. I'm barely proving my worth. Would you be willing to give me a couple of weeks more to settle in? Then I don't think they'd bat an eye at me meeting someone."

Rachel's resolve slipped through her fingers. Of course that made sense. Of course that was why he'd been meeting her alone. He was only establishing himself in a new place. She nodded. "That will give me time to talk to my brother. I want you to meet him, and I know it may go poorly at first. He has rigid ideas of who belongs in this family, and I don't agree with him. He's going to have to come around because . . ."

Florent reached out and lifted her hand from her lap, then turned it, placing the hairpin in her palm. "Because what?"

Rachel gazed into his eyes, his hand still cupping hers. Pleasure rippled through her at his touch, sending heat under her skin. She struggled to form words since the only thoughts in her head were far too forward to speak aloud to a man she'd only known for a few weeks.

Florent curled her fingers over the pin, then trailed his hand up the backside of her arm until his fingertips reached the ends of her hair. Rachel couldn't stand it any longer. The heat building at her center exploded into fiery need, and she reached for him, gripping his shirt and pulling him close.

Rachel's lips parted, her silent plea for him to cover her mouth with his. Florent curled his arm around her waist, and when she thought she might split at the seams, he finally acquiesced.

His kiss was hungry, and Rachel reveled in the rough brushes of his tongue, the pressure of his hand against her back. She wanted more. All rational thought fled at the taste of him. He was sweet and warm, and—

Florent pushed back, breaking their mouths apart with a groan. "I must go."

"But—"

"I must go." He stumbled to his feet, and before Rachel could see straight, he disappeared into the trees.

She heaved for breath, her lips raw and buzzing. She pressed her palms against the flattened grass and squeezed her eyes shut. It was only then that she noticed the metallic taste of blood.

9

1836 MORDELLES, FRANCE

The biting chill of the night seeped into Amalie's bones as she lay huddled on the rough stone floor wrapped in a musty potato sack she'd found in the corner. She'd stripped off her damp clothes the second she was sure Theo was gone.

She could only shiver to warm herself. There was the box of matches, but there was nothing to light besides the wood beams of the shed itself. Part of her wanted to shatter the oil lamp and allow the flames to lick across the fuel and shoot up to the thatched roof. To breathe in the smoke until her lungs seized and her heart stopped beating. But if a stake to the heart didn't kill Theo, perhaps all she'd be left with was pain and char for the rest of eternity.

She didn't know how long it had been since Theo disappeared—it could've been five minutes or thirty. Amalie pulled her knees closer to her chest, her breath blooming in front of her. At least her nose no longer ached. She'd always healed quickly, though Uncle Oren forced her to stay home whenever she hurt herself. A cut, a scrape, a bruise, it didn't matter.

"You heal when you rest," Oren always said. *"You must be careful with your blood."*

Truthfully, she'd been glad for the excuse to skip her daily chores. She clung to her thoughts and memories, but they were sluggish, numbed by the cold. Eventually, Amalie drifted in shadows tinged red.

The creak of hinges slashed her consciousness, and her eyelids flickered.

"That doesn't look comfortable." Theo's voice struck like a slap, and Amalie's body tensed until her bones cracked. His shadow stretched across the room, and she squinted to find the source of the light. Another lamp. It sat on the rough-hewn table.

She flinched at a sudden clatter and pressed her forearm against the stone to gain her bearings, then gasped as the potato sack didn't come with her. She scrambled to cover herself, but Theo didn't so much as glance her direction. He was wholly focused on stacking wood in the ancient hearth across the room.

Amalie's fists clenched involuntarily, nails digging into her palms, while her heart tattooed the backside of her ribs. She clutched the rough fabric to her bare skin and shuffled to her knees. He'd come back. He'd brought wood for a fire. Briefly, Amalie wondered at the act of kindness, then quickly crushed her thoughts.

"Is this how it goes? You bite and then play friendly?" Her teeth chattered.

"Do you wish me to be your friend?"

Amalie bit the inside of her cheek. "Gods, no."

"But you do wish to be warm?" He raised an eyebrow, and Amalie shot daggers at him. He was like a wolf offering a rabbit a saucer of cream.

Theo Vallon had created her. He only wanted to keep her

alive until he could use her for his own purposes. That was when fear finally gripped her. She was alone. In the middle of the night with a creature who relished killing her kind. Nobody knew where she was, and her only friends thought her a monster.

Amalie shivered, then gritted her teeth and sat straight. She needed to work faster. Hours. Days. She didn't know how long she had. "I thought vampires had to give up some of their own power to create another like them."

Theo grunted but didn't answer. He stacked the wood and tucked splinters of kindling between the logs, then reached for the matches he'd used earlier and struck one against the bottom of his boot. He tucked it against the kindling and crouched on all fours to blow on the tiny flame.

Amalie's breath caught. The sight of his sleeves rolled up his forearms. The golden glow highlighting the damp waves of his hair. He was beautiful, and she hated it. She'd so rarely had a reaction like this to a man that it felt as if he were stealing more than just her blood.

She hated her fingertips for twitching to trace the line of his jaw. She hated her tongue for losing its ability to speak when he was standing in front of her. It had been over a year since she'd taken a lover, and here her body was betraying her.

Amalie willed her mind into submission. *She didn't want this attraction.* She wanted an experience of flesh and blood, of heart and soul. Not of lust and glamour and darkness. She wanted to be filled, not swallowed whole.

Amalie wrapped her arms around her knees, as if to prove her humanity. At least for a few moments more. Her eyes stung, and as a flame took hold, Amalie forced herself to stay pressed against the frigid stone. She would not take his offering. She'd rather her toes froze off than—

Amalie again flew from the ground and gasped. In a blink,

she was sitting in front of the fire with the sack nowhere to be found. Her whole body seemed to be made of stone. She'd been — How had he—?

How dare he touch her? Amalie curled into herself, her cheeks burning at the lingering sensation of his fingers on her skin, then realized she was sitting in front of him completely nude.

The shame only lasted a moment once she felt it. The warmth from the fire. Heat seeping into her bones.

She nearly wept at the relief and couldn't force herself to search for the sack or scramble back to her damp corner. The crackle of flames consuming the dry wood filled the silence, and Amalie despised her own flesh for being so weak.

The scuff of Theo's boots on stone sounded behind her, but she refused to turn her head. *Let the monster look.* She swiped the tears collecting in the corners of her eyes, pretending the smoke was getting to her. She wouldn't thank him. She wouldn't be a willing participant in his ruse to lure her in and gain her trust.

Unless . . .

Perhaps she should pretend to give it. Pretend she was grateful. If he thought she'd accepted her fate, perhaps he'd bring her into the fold?

The idea made bile rise in her throat. She could pretend, but he wouldn't gain her trust. Not ever. No matter how many fires he built or how many times he swept her off a muddy road or freezing stone. She knew who and what Theo Vallon was.

Amalie's stomach twisted. *And she would soon become exactly like him.* A cold-hearted animal. A killer. She wanted to weep.

Movement caught her eye, and she whipped her head to the left. "Don't touch those."

Theo held her trousers by the waistband. "I was laying them out to dry."

"Don't touch them." Her voice shook.

His face was dispassionate as he set them on the table. "I didn't realize you had an affinity for burlap." He tossed the sack, and it landed next to her on the floor.

Amalie almost screamed, whether from the rage she felt at Theo's comment, the knowledge of what she had to do, or the burning in her toes and fingertips as feeling gradually returned to her nerves, she didn't know. She spun away from him and pressed as many parts of her toward the heat as possible, nearly whimpering at the pain.

Amalie's bones ached against the bare stone. *Breathe.* She swallowed, forcing the venom from her tone. "How are you still alive?"

He had to be arrogant. Self-obsessed. If he wouldn't answer questions about her, she could at least flatter him into talking about himself.

Theo grunted. "After you stabbed me, you mean?"

Amalie sensed his every movement behind her. "Yes." She ignored the fact that most of her upper thighs were exposed as she shifted so the fire could warm the side of her body, like she was slowly roasting on a spit.

"My curse keeps me alive."

Amalie didn't have to feign interest at this. She turned her head to look at him. "Is your curse different than everyone else's?"

He stared back at her, his eyes two shards of midnight. "No."

"So when you became a vampire, you became immortal." That thought filled her with dread so heavy she nearly dropped to her forearms on the stone. How could she live like this? *How could she live like him?* She could not be a killer. She could not—

"Not exactly."

Amalie's eyes snapped to his. "What then?" She worked to keep her breathing even. This was it. If he told her why vampires weren't fully immortal, she could take the information to Marcel and Olivie.

Theo leaned over the table, his shirt barely rumpled from the night's escapades. Amalie shrank into herself, realizing for the first time how she must look. A feral cat hovering for warmth. *When she turned, would she be beautiful?*

"You will learn more once we leave this place." Theo watched the flames curling against the stone.

"I want to know now." Amalie's heart picked up speed.

"Eager to attack me again?"

She nearly flinched. "Of course. As soon as my clothes are dry."

Theo chuckled, and his smile created lines near his eyes that looked almost . . . kind. It was sickening.

Amalie spun back to the fire to keep her head straight. The effect he had on her was lessening, or at least she thought it was. Perhaps a consequence of whatever transformation was happening inside her body. That thought sent ice sliding down her spine. Time was slipping through her fingers, and he was dancing around her questions.

"There are very few ways for us to be released, and they have nothing to do with your stories." Theo's voice was clipped.

At the sound of his steps moving closer, Amalie snatched the sack off the floor and covered herself. "Then what do they have to do with, Theo?"

His eyes snapped to hers. "You know my name."

Amalie scoffed, pulling her knees closer. "You shouldn't be flattered."

"Too late." He pushed off the wooden table and strode

toward the hearth, stopping in front of her. She had to crane her neck to see his face. The flames reflected in his eyes. "An answer for an answer. Why were you hunting me?"

Amalie ground her teeth. She didn't have time for games. "Because you kill my kind." The sack scratched her skin as she shifted her arm away from the fire. Maybe she should've let Theo lay out her clothes to dry, but the idea of him touching her underwear made her insides hollow out.

He waved her off. "All vampires kill your kind. Why me? Specifically?"

Amalie opened her mouth, then closed it. His voice sounded almost eager. She thought of at least ten answers that could work, including the fact that he was the one who'd passed her on the street that night, but settled on the truth. "Because you killed my mother."

It was difficult to rouse the anger she'd felt earlier now that she was thawing out. Grief was strange in that way. Sometimes it filled her to the brim, and sometimes she felt nothing.

A muscle in Theo's jaw twitched. "I didn't kill your mother."

Amalie glared at him. "I saw you. In the woods. You were covered in her blood."

"I didn't kill your mother." Theo spoke slowly, his eyes sharp and focused.

"Then who did?" Amalie couldn't look at him. The outright lie made her blood boil.

"I don't know." Theo's voice was tight.

Was he pretending he knew nothing of her death? Amalie had seen his face, she'd never forgotten it. He'd been covered in her mother's blood. Did Theo even know who her mother was, or did she blend into the thousand other humans he'd fed on over the years?

Panic rose in her chest. She couldn't think about this. She

needed to find her answers, then she could focus on revenge. Amalie drew a breath and tried to center herself. Her turn for a question. "If the truth about death for vampires has nothing to do with the legends, what does it have to do with?"

"I liked the way you asked it better last time."

Amalie shot him a look of disgust. "Just answer me."

"There is only one who knew the location of a relic, an ancient sword, that could release me."

"Who is it?"

Theo stepped back and leaned against the table. "One of your ancestors. That's why I didn't kill you. Why I've brought you here. You're going to help me find it."

10

Amalie blinked. *One of her ancestors?* How could that be possible? She'd never heard of anyone in her family line who was important enough to know of the relics. Though, Uncle Oren had withheld information. *I planned to tell you everything on your eighteenth birthday, but you left.*

What more did he have to tell her? It didn't matter now. Her fate was sealed. She didn't trust a thing coming out of Theo's mouth, but this story she was tempted to believe.

He was a vampire. Vampires wanted power, control. If he had given up his power to turn her, it would have to be for a good reason. Finding a sword that could vanquish vampires would make him the most powerful of his kind.

"If you want my help, tell me what's happening to me." She wouldn't help him. But if there was a sword that could kill creatures of the dark, that was exactly what Marcel and Olivie needed.

Theo tapped his fingers on the table. "That's another question."

Amalie pushed a few inches back from the glowing hearth. "It was a demand."

Theo strode forward and settled into a crouch beside her, the glow from the fire bathing him in warmth. He was so close, his scent mingled with the wood smoke. The marks on Amalie's neck began to throb with the beat of her pulse.

He sat perfectly still, as if posing for her scrutiny. As if he enjoyed knowing her eyes were drawn to him. Any attempts to muster anger fizzled like blazing coals dropped in a lake. *Gods.* If every part of him was meant to lure her in, he was a masterpiece. Even as she reminded herself how this man had killed her mother, how he'd attacked her in her room, how he'd poisoned her blood and stripped everything she loved, her thoughts found no purchase amidst the swirl of longing in her gut.

He finally turned, his silhouette outlined by the nascent glow of the fire, and their eyes locked. Theo's breath quickened, his expression sobering. "You must feel it."

Amalie's skin prickled. "Feel what?" For a moment, she stopped fighting the way her body reacted to him. He was toying with her, and she wanted to punish him for it. *Let him believe she was being lured in.*

The corner of Theo's mouth twitched. He didn't answer her question, and Amalie almost wondered if she'd imagined his words that led her to ask it. *What must she feel?* Was he expecting the change to happen soon?

Was she changing? Besides the strange magic he was weaving, she felt nothing out of the ordinary. Her body still behaved like her own.

Theo's face was again inscrutable. "What do you know about the creation of vampires?"

"I want to know about myself, I didn't request a history

lesson," she snapped, then realized her mistake. He was talking. She needed him to talk.

"Impatient." Theo tsked. "If there's something important I'm keeping you from, please." He motioned toward the door with a self-satisfied smirk.

Amalie's nostrils flared, but she drew a deep breath. Nothing important. Just the loss of her human life.

She slowed her exhale. "I'm sorry. That was rude." Theo regarded her, his face impassive. Amalie continued, "Vampires were cursed by Le Sombre. They wreak havoc on humankind."

She remembered the stories. How the gods took pity on mortals and gifted a defense—humans who had unearthly strength and could see past the Shadow's tricks. For years after her mother's death, she'd searched for them. These golden-haired heroes who would protect her family and push the vampires back.

They'd never come. Her mother was dead, and more humans were going missing every week. That was when she'd sought out Marcel and the Pourfendeurs. When she realized that if she wanted a hero, she'd have to become one herself.

Amalie swallowed. "There were supposed to be guardians. Humans with the strength of the gods who wouldn't be seduced by your kind." *Our kind.*

Theo's eyes were dark. "Are you seduced?"

Amalie's jaw tightened. Regardless of what power he wielded, she didn't want to be, and that was what mattered. "Not for long," she whispered.

Theo leaned closer, and Amalie's breath snagged. She held it as he reached over her and took an iron poker from a hook embedded in the stone. When he rocked back and began prodding the half-burned logs, she let out a shaky exhale.

"I doubt you'll enjoy hearing the true story of our past," he said.

Grief and rage pricked her heart in equal measure. She'd asked about herself, and he'd answered with what was now to become a shared history. A heritage she'd never asked for and couldn't accept. *Why had he done this to her?* Amalie clenched her hands into fists, willing her tears not to fall.

She had to know the truth. She had to take something back to Marcel and Olivie. "Tell me."

Theo laid the poker on the stone in front of him, then sat on the stone beside her. "Ask me nicely."

Amalie shifted so her bare back faced away from him. *What game was he playing?* Amalie had long been acquainted with the oppressive weight of men's expectations. At sixteen, she'd caught the eye of Henri, a wealthy suitor from the south loosely connected to Oren through Maurielle's brother. He courted her with lavish gifts and whispered promises of a comfortable life, then cornered her in the garden, his fingers digging into her wrist as he expressly forbade her to cut her hair shorter than her shoulders.

At seventeen, when she left the countryside, she found work as a seamstress in a high-end fashion house with master tailor Monsieur Dubois. He was a man of impeccable taste and often gave her clothing tailored to her frame that he expected her to wear the next day to work. Then one evening as she worked late, he approached her under the guise of offering guidance, but his hands lingered too long. When she recoiled and told him to stop, he laughed softly and told her all she had to do was *ask nicely*.

Amalie's eyes flashed. "Again. It wasn't a question."

Theo's gaze slowly rose to hers. "Why do you think I made the request?"

"You're a vain bastard, and you wish me to be obedient? That, or you want to hear your name on my lips a second time," she hissed, and regretted it instantly. She was failing.

Theo would never believe she trusted him if she kept biting his head off. But it was like he knew exactly where to push to make her see red.

Theo smirked. "Vain bastard. I've been called plenty of things over the years by women like you, but that's new. I like it." He stood and walked back to her pile of clothes.

Women like her? He knew nothing of women like her. "I told you not to touch those."

"I thought we were both doing and saying whatever we wanted now." Theo picked up her shirt and underclothes. He draped the shirt over the table next to her trousers, then made a point of carefully setting her underclothes on a chair close to the heat.

Amalie clung to the sack as she struggled up from the floor and stood in front of him, refusing to shrink as his eyes dropped to her neck and bare shoulders. "If you want my help, don't treat me like your plaything."

It was a stupid thing to say, and she knew it. Theo had the strength of a god, and she was wrapped in discarded burlap, weak from the cold. *But not forever.* She would gain his power, would she not?

Something inside her stirred, just as it had when Uncle Oren tried to force her to keep his rules. Maybe it was hubris or sheer rebellion, but she wouldn't sit under anyone's thumb. Especially not one like his.

Theo fingered the lace on her bralette, his shadow stretching across the wall behind him. "Fine. Not a plaything." He looked up through his thick lashes, and Amalie's blood burned.

Then in a blink, he stood directly in front of her. She yelped and stumbled back, but he caught her arm. "I will keep you safe. In exchange, you will help me find the relic."

Amalie struggled against his grip, but the sack she held

around her body began to slip. She froze, and Theo dropped her wrist like she was a hot coal. She couldn't accept this bargain. She didn't know the first thing about this sword, and she couldn't go back to her family for answers. But if she didn't accept? She could lose the only opportunity to protect those she loved.

Amalie forced her head to nod and felt invisible knots cinch around her wrists.

Theo took a step back, then pointed at a baguette and hunk of cheese on the table. *How long had that been there?*

Theo unbuttoned his sleeves, allowing the cuffs to hang loose around his wrists. He didn't look like a monster. He never had. That was the problem.

"You've had enough time to rest, and your clothes aren't sopping. Get dressed. We're leaving now."

Amalie reached for her damp clothes. She turned, dropped the sack, and put on her bralette, then pulled her shirt over her head. She tried not to think about whether Theo was watching.

The fabric felt glorious on her skin after being rubbed raw by rough fibers for the past hour. Once she was dressed, she turned and stared at the food, wondering if she could eat it. Did vampires live off of more than just blood? Her heart sped at another thought almost as sinister. Coming from Theo, the food could be poisoned, or worse, drugged. But the ache in her stomach was too strong. She gave in. Her weakness was revolting.

Theo stalked to the door as she tore off some of the bread and ate. When he swung it open, she scrambled to pull on her boots, then swiped the rest of the food from the table and followed. She could go on a hunger strike, but Theo would probably shove the food down her throat just as he'd forced her to sit by the fire, and she didn't want his hands anywhere near her lips.

Amalie stepped onto the mulched path. The night was cool, and a mist rose from the ground like breath, but the rain had ceased. The clouds no longer shrouded the moon, and it bathed the world around them in a soft, silvery light. Their boots squelched in moss and new mud as Theo led them deeper into the woods.

He slowed to a walk only a few paces ahead of her. "Your history books are correct about our curse and the conflict it caused between our kinds in the beginning."

Why was he talking about this now? He'd seemed eager to leave and ignore that conversation, and now he was taking time to explain himself?

Amalie scoffed. "A diplomatic way to put it."

Theo gave her a tired look over his shoulder. "Does guilt eat at you?"

"Over what?"

He pointed at the bread in her hand. "The plants that your kind murder every day, the seeds you steal and grind to dust. The animals you keep captive to harvest their bodily fluids?"

Amalie's expression hardened. "It's not the same, and you know it."

"I can only survive on human blood."

"Then don't survive."

He let out a caustic laugh. "Trust me, I've tried that."

For a split second, Theo looked haunted, and questions exploded like sparks in Amalie's mind. How long had he been alive? Was he being honest that he'd *tried* to starve himself and failed? Theo, just like any vampire, had been human once. How long had it been since he lived a regular life, and who had turned him?

Then, like a bolt of lighting, she understood. Somehow, in his sick mind, he thought he could absolve himself by sharing the past. Or . . . Amalie's thoughts frosted over. *He thought he could absolve her.* She swallowed the lump in her throat.

"Where human history gets it wrong is during the subsequent portion of the story," Theo said gruffly.

What was it that followed? "Defenders. The gifted power to humans by the gods."

Theo nodded and began moving forward again. "Humans were never gifted power, not in the way you understand it. The humans the gods blessed weren't powerful. They weren't warriors. The opposite, actually."

A branch caught on Theo's shoulder, then snapped back and stung her cheek. Amalie winced, holding out her hands to clear her path. "That isn't logical. Humans need protection from creatures cursed by Le Sombre."

Theo had lifted her on the road like she was nothing. When he wanted to, he moved with such grace and speed, he seemed to meld with the air itself. She couldn't see him. She couldn't hear him.

How could humans protect themselves from power like that?

"The gift was in their blood." Theo looked back as if watching for a reaction, and Amalie worked to keep the speeding of her heart a secret. Theo cleared his throat and continued, "The only facts humans care to know about vampires is that we're monsters. They preach about our thirst for blood, never mentioning our admirable qualities."

Amalie laughed out loud. "If you're going to make this a philosophical discussion on morality and ethics, I promise you, you'll lose."

Theo shot her a look. "We're inherently loyal. We cling to our family groups and have a strong instinct to protect those we love."

"Congratulations. Is that before or after you slaughter innocent human beings?"

"Is it possible for you to descend from your pedestal for two seconds?"

Amalie shook her head. "I don't believe it is."

"Fine."

"Fine, what?"

He whirled on her. "You asked for the truth about—"

"Demanded. I never asked." Amalie didn't step back, instead meeting his confrontational stance.

Theo's jaw worked. "The gift from the gods was twofold. Protection for humans, and—"

Amalie waited, but Theo didn't finish the sentence. She had no clue what he hesitated to say. Nothing coming out of Theo's mouth reconciled with the world or history she knew, and despite her desire to believe nothing he said, curiosity ate at her. "And what?"

Theo ran a hand through his hair. "They gave us something . . . we could love."

His words puddled at the surface, then slowly sank in. Amalie frowned. "You're saying the gods weren't only generous to humans. They blessed vampires, as well. Why would they do that?"

"We were cursed. Their pity didn't discriminate."

Cursed. By Le Sombre. *Solène and Le Sombre, once bound as one, now split in shadow and light.* Amalie broke off a piece of cheese and slipped it in her mouth when she was sure he wasn't looking. Solène and Le Sombre clashed like oil and water. One always seeking power over the other. Their world a testament to their battle of light and shadow. Why would Solène or any of the other gods feel pity for the Shadow or any of its creations?

"It doesn't make sense," Amalie murmured. Even if the

gods had been compassionate, Theo said it was a gift of blood, not warriors or protectors. That would be a boon to the vampires, but to humans? Why would they have any need for it when blood ran freely through their veins?

"It was a blood*line*. Humans with blood that could heal. Regenerate. Blood that was—" He paused again, stretching his words. "Highly desirable to us."

Amalie's heart seemed to crystallize in her chest. Bloodline. Lives. Generations. "The gods gave a human bloodline to vampires?"

"In a way, but—"

"They gave you *human beings?* To feed on, to keep as, what? Slaves?"

"It wasn't like that."

"Then please, explain how it was." Amalie quickened her pace, fueled by indignation and disgust. The gods were unpredictable, but this? How could the gods bless humans by forcing them to associate with the cursed? By stripping them of their freedom?

A muscle in Theo's jaw flexed. "It was a bonding between human and vampire. A mutual decision. One that would eliminate the terror and darkness created by Le Sombre, and in exchange, humans of the guardian blood were given safety. Companionship. Pleasure."

That word slipped through her like water, and Amalie's mind snapped back to Theo holding her in his arms. His breath against her skin. The warmth that surged in her veins instead of pain at his bite. "Why are you telling me this?" Her voice was a whisper.

Theo's eyes flicked to hers. He shrugged. "I told you. You *demanded* the truth."

Truth. The idea that she'd hear it from him was laughable.

Wouldn't he tell her anything to suit his purposes? To draw her into his palm and mold her like clay?

Amalie's stomach curdled as a thought slammed into her. "Do you have them? Now? Is that where we're going? If you're expecting me to—"

Theo's face transformed from predatory to devastating. His perfect lips spreading wide over glaringly white teeth, his brow lifting, and his eyes glittering in the hazy moonlight. He threw back his head and laughed.

Amalie was speechless. Somehow, she hadn't considered that his facial muscles could do anything other than glower, brood, or feed, and the result was nothing short of spectacular.

It was like watching a sunrise or holding up a glittering gem to the light. Amalie didn't realize she'd stopped walking until Theo turned back.

"Humans. You're so quick to draw conclusions." He sobered, but a smile still sat on his lips. "And are nearly always wrong."

11

1836 NORTHERN NORMANDY, FRANCE

Amalie stopped where the grass gave way to an endless stretch of sand, her shirt clinging to her sweat-soaked skin. The moon was again obscured by dark clouds, and she was glad to be out of the trees so she could keep track of Theo's shadow in front of her. "How much further?"

"It would be quite a bit less if you'd allow me to—"

"You're *not* carrying me."

Theo had offered more than once, but she couldn't do it. Couldn't willingly be cradled in his arms. She had to keep her wits about her, and that meant distance was necessary.

"Suit yourself, but we have to move faster. The tide will rise before the sun."

Amalie winced as she stepped down onto the packed sand. The edges of her heels burned, rubbing against the damp leather of her boots. She would surely find blisters there when she took them off.

Exhaustion tugged at the edges of her mind, but she gritted her teeth and tromped along behind him, ignoring his annoyed look each time he turned to make sure he wasn't getting too far ahead.

She didn't want to feel tired. She didn't want to feel weak. Any abnormal physical sensation sent streaks of terror over her skin. Was this the moment she would turn? Was that twinge or that stumble proof that her body was groaning under the weight of a curse it could not bear?

To distract herself, Amalie focused all her energy on Theo. She cataloged how his form seemed to blur at the edges when he quickened his pace. How his intoxicating scent became more powerful when he exhibited heightened emotion. How even when she closed her eyes, she could sense him, point to exactly where he stood.

Though not watching him was next to impossible. The fluidity of his movement was just alien enough to create a fixation. She wanted to put him behind glass or creep up on him while he was sleeping so she could inspect him without shame. The thought of observing him without his notice, of touching him or running her fingers over his sharp angles sent a flush across her chest.

No. Attraction wasn't her fault, and she was doing research. Learning everything she could to be of use to the Pourfendeurs.

"Faster," Theo barked.

Amalie slogged through the damp sand, dragging her boots free each time they sank in the muck. "I'm going as fast as I can."

"Do you enjoy swimming?"

Amalie growled and pushed herself into a jog, her feet screaming with each slap against the ground. She caught up to Theo and pushed past him.

"I didn't say you had to run."

Amalie ignored him. He might have power from Le Sombre, but she had an iron force of will. When she was a young girl, her mother had called her "Amalie d'Acier," *Amalie of Steel*, because once she made up her mind, there was no changing it.

Theo might be faster, but he would not beat her.

"Stop!" Theo commanded, and Amalie pushed ten more strides to prove her point. Her throat and lungs burned as she slowed, gasping for breath.

She braced herself with hands on her thighs and looked up. A thread of gold glinted on the horizon, and in front of it—her eyes widened at the sight. A dark silhouette of spires and stone loomed above her. The wind carried the scent of salt and the sharp calls of seabirds.

Theo stalked forward to stand in front of her. He inspected her, his eyes lingering on the hair clinging to her forehead. She swiped it away.

"You are in love with me." His eyes bored into her.

Amalie gaped at him. Yes, the castle blooming out of black granite was impressive, but his glamour was losing its effect on her. If he thought that was all it took for a woman to throw herself at him, he was more vain than she'd accused. "I assure you, I am not."

Theo raised an eyebrow as if he knew exactly how long her eyes had lingered on him while they crossed the flats. "It's a ruse." He turned to the arched wooden doors. "While I'm sure you'd never degrade yourself by sleeping with the damned, in this place, you must pretend to be obsessed."

Amalie wiped at the sweat on her brow, finding her skin gritty. "You said you were taking me to safety."

"Trust me, this is better than the alternative."

Amalie scoffed. "Trust you? If this is some sick game you're playing—"

"It's not optional." Theo turned, his smirk fading. "Everyone past that gate is like me. Equally attuned to the blood coursing through your veins."

Amalie paled. Theo was dropping her into a nest of vampires? Why would he do that? It seemed he wanted her alive since he believed she had some knowledge of this relic he sought, so why put her in danger?

Realization struck. She wouldn't be in danger for long. Once she turned . . . Amalie gazed up at the looming spires. *Was this to be her home?*

Theo stepped closer, his eyes burning like the line of fire creeping over the horizon. The wind tossed dark tendrils of hair over his eyes. "You know nothing of our kind, but we don't often cross another's interests. They will think nothing of you if they believe you singularly smitten."

Amalie's gaze flicked to the massive wooden doors cut into the stone wall, then back to Theo. Her stomach twisted. "They will think nothing because this is a regular occurrence? You whip women into a frenzy and ferry them here to please you?"

Theo leaned closer. "Are you in a frenzy?" he whispered, but before Amalie could slap him, he was ten steps ahead of her. His low chuckle brushed past her ears on the breeze.

Obsessed. Smitten. How could she possibly be believable? If she fell in love with a man, he would be kind. Strong but gentle. He wouldn't tease with cruelty. He wouldn't order her around and expect her tongue to loll at the opportunity to obey him like a dog obeyed her master.

The clock ticked in her head. *She didn't have much time.*

Amalie's heart dropped to her knees as Theo reached for the bronze handle on the door. "Why not tell them I've been turned. Just explain that—"

Theo's expression was impassive as he pulled on the handle, and Amalie answered her own question with the information she had. When she finally turned, Theo would be weak. Maybe he already was. He wouldn't want other vampires to know that. That was what he was trying to tell her. If she wanted to survive, she needed them to believe he was strong. Desirable. *You know nothing of our kind.*

The door creaked, scraping against the drifted sand, and Amalie followed him through the ancient arch. She paused, running her hand over the carvings on the wood. An oval, tilted. Half light, half dark, connected by a smooth swirl in the center. "This was on your ring."

Theo paused. "It's my signet."

"Yours? Do you—are you in charge here?"

Theo turned. "I want my ring back."

Amalie glared at his back as she followed him along the cobbled street. The sky was lightening with the rising sun, but its soft pink and orange rays barely penetrated the high walls. Sand collected in the crevices between stones, and signs for shops and public houses hung from iron bars.

A lead weight seemed to settle in her stomach. This was where they lived. Where they brought their prey—men and women like her, manipulated by their beauty and power. How many others had Theo brought here? How many before her had traipsed up this path unwittingly to their death?

Movement ahead nearly caused her to stumble, and Theo reached out a hand to steady her. When she tried to rip her arm away, Theo gripped tighter and gave her a sidelong glance. Bile rose in her throat. She could run. She could announce the truth and allow her voice to echo off the stone walls as she declared all that had happened since the night before. But the thought of defying Theo's orders while surrounded by vampires felt like slitting her wrists and throwing herself into a pack of wolves.

He was the monster she knew. *But how long would she have to pretend?*

Amalie twisted, wrapping her arm around his and clinging to his bicep. Warmth bled into her through the thin cotton of his shirt. His spiced floral and citrus scent invaded her senses, and she forgot for a few brief seconds that she couldn't allow herself to enjoy it. That calm, that pleasure meant one thing.

Vampires.

As if she'd conjured them with their thoughts, shadows began to shift. They appeared out of thin air from around corners, down stairs built into the hillside, and through the doors and windows of apartments built above the shops. Fluid, like smoke and mist.

Amalie's heart beat hot at her throat. *They could smell her.* She clung tighter to Theo's arm and scoffed internally at the lunacy of it. This creature who had taken everything from her, now a protector?

"Bonsoir, Theo." A voice smooth as silk lifted from a man whose skin looked nearly blue under the moonlight. A sleek black coat hung from his shoulders, moving like liquid as he bowed, his eyes gleaming amber.

"Etienne." Theo nodded. The vampire moved to the side as two women slunk closer and clung to his sides. Even with makeup and brightly colored dresses, they looked small and dull compared to him. *Humans*, Amalie realized, and her stomach clenched.

Another group appeared across from them. Vampires and more humans, men and women this time. She was going to be sick. How many were there? Had they only arrived that night? *Would they last past the morning?*

A vampire wearing nothing but a pair of loose trousers gave a small wave.

Theo waved back. "Paul."

"To what do we owe the pleasure of your company?" A stunning, statuesque vampire with light, silky hair and lips as red as a blood moon assessed Amalie with unveiled curiosity.

She smiled, exposing sharp, white teeth. "Or it seems the pleasure will be all yours."

Theo's arm tensed under Amalie's grip. "Jealousy has never suited you Clémentine." He kept walking as the woman flicked her tongue over her cherry lips. Amalie wanted to run. To escape the narrow chute between the buildings and hold her face to the sun.

She glanced up at Theo. Could he stand in sunlight? The legends said no, but they'd already failed her. She hadn't thought to ask.

"This one must be special." A tall, muscular man with sandy hair that fell to his shoulders sat on the steps next to them. "How long has it been Theo? You never bring your toys home anymore."

"He doesn't like to share." Clémentine pouted.

The man laughed, then sprang from the stone and fell into step next to them. He slung an arm over Theo's shoulders. "We've missed you, love. We wondered . . ."

Theo shrugged him off and stopped, then pulled his arm from Amalie's grip. He ran his hand up her back, then curled his hand around her neck, covering her marks. "Worried I'd moved on without you, Ren?"

This was a game. He didn't want them to see he'd bitten her, and she had to play along. Amalie slid an arm around his waist, doing her best to mimic the other humans she saw and become the naïve, flattered girl while her mind whirred beneath the surface.

By the way they greeted him, it was obvious that Theo landed somewhere at the top of their social structure. His signet was on the doors. Had he found this place and made it his, or had he done something to earn that mark?

"Not worried. Rather. . . interested." Ren stepped in front of

Amalie and crouched to look her in the eye. "She looks terrified, Theo. Your charm may be slipping."

Amalie's heart fluttered in her throat. She wasn't selling it. Keeping her expression even, she flipped through possible responses, roles she could play, but quickly settled on something close to herself. If she *did* love someone, and if they were being taunted by friends—or enemies, she couldn't quite tell —she would want to protect him. She would want to make him appear strong.

She met Ren's stare. His eyes were slate gray, and though his mouth wore a smirk, they seared into her.

Amalie stopped fighting Theo's blanket of calm. She drew a deep breath and let it wash over her. "I'm bored with your friends, Theo. Why are we still standing here instead of finding somewhere we can be alone?" The words came too easily, and the comfort of being close to him too natural. A wave of nausea engulfed her, and she turned her head, pretending to bury it in Theo's shoulder.

His fingertips twitched against her arm as Ren's brow lifted, his lips curling into a wicked grin. "Ah. I see it now. She's got some fight in her. Theo's gotten picky in his old age. Wants a challenge." Ren shoved a hand in his pocket and stepped back, never severing eye contact. "I hope this one sticks around. We could use a bit of fun."

Amalie rolled her eyes, then turned toward Theo, placing a hand on his chest. Her breath caught as she felt his heart beating hard and fast, and she cleared her throat before blinking adoringly up at him.

Theo lifted a finger, tilting her chin up, then lowered his head to an inch above hers. "You've been patient." Amalie quivered, her pulse bucking wildly beneath his fingertips. Theo ran his thumb over her neck and raised an eyebrow. It was wrong how her body couldn't discern between manipulated want and mortal threat. He was a predator. She was prey.

Amalie pulled him closer and slipped her cheek against his. "Don't push your luck," she hissed and felt his exhaled laugh against the shell of her ear.

He pulled back, his eyes glinting as if daring her to stop him, then slowly brushed his lips over hers. The touch was featherlight, and yet it ignited a blaze within her. Her grip on his waist tightened, her ribs cinching around her lungs.

She'd felt this before. There was a flash of dark sheets, Theo's body positioned over hers. In a split second it was over, and she blinked, staring back at him in shock.

"I wouldn't dare." Theo straightened, keeping her collared with his fingers and nudging her forward. "Lovely to see you all."

Clémentine glared at Amalie, then disappeared into the shadows. Etienne and his pets joined three other vampires watching from the far side of the street, but Ren stood with his eyes still fixed on hers. He watched as Theo led her up the cobbled street, and she felt his eyes on her well after they ascended the stairs.

"What was—" she started, but Theo squeezed and shook his head. Amalie clamped her mouth shut and followed, her arm still looped around him. His muscles flexed under her palm each time he took a step.

She peered into the dark, forcing her eyes to trace the intricate carvings on the stone as they spiraled upward into the pinks and oranges of sunrise. What had she seen? Was his glamour strong enough to put images in her head?

She needed to move away from him. Her lips felt seared where he'd kissed her, and his scent still bathed her in calm, willing her to be compliant. With her feet still stinging and her muscles burning, it was becoming more difficult to want to pull away.

Amalie reminded herself this was necessary. She had to play a part. She needed answers, and this was the only way to get them. Then she raced to remind herself why she hated this man. He'd taken her mother. Attacked her in her bedroom.

The only reason he'd taken her in and warmed her by the fire was so he could use her as a tool. That's all humans were to his kind.

She would kill him.

Just as she'd planned to do the first time. Because what she felt and what she chose were two different things.

She would fight his glamour. She would play this game a little longer until she could take information back to her friends, until she discovered her own fate, and until she knew each step it would take to rid the world of Theo Vallon and every last vampire like him.

12

Theo guided her through a gothic archway, its stone protectors glaring down at them with grotesque faces. A gust of wind swept through the stone corridor, toying with the ends of her hair as they finally ascended the steps of the stone, turreted building that sat atop the rocky island like a crown. Amalie looked up, stretching her neck to see where the spires scraped the sky.

They strode through wooden doors similar to the ones at the lower gate, and Amalie blinked to clear her vision in the dim interior. Her eyes widened. Rich tapestries hung on the walls. Carpets covered the stone floors, and vases of fresh-cut flowers sat on tables mirroring each other on either side of the entry. She didn't know what she'd expected. Something like a dungeon, she supposed. Gloomy, dark, and cold. This was the opposite.

"This is where you live?" she asked as Theo walked toward a central stone spiral staircase.

He nodded, maintaining his grip on her as they ascended. She soon saw why. The staircase opened wide at each floor, revealing richly adorned sitting rooms where vampires lounged and fires crackled in the hearth.

"How many of you are there?"

"Only one. I thought you would've recognized that by now," Theo murmured.

Amalie hated that she almost laughed. "You know what I meant. How many vampires?"

"Not all vampires are created equal, so you can imagine my confusion." Theo exited the staircase on the third level, pulling her with him through another common room to a door on the left. They entered a hall that forced them to turn right, then stopped in a large, open room with dark wood paneling on the walls. A sprawling desk and upholstered chairs sat on polished wooden floors.

Amalie's heart sank. "You don't sleep in beds." She longed to curl up on a mattress but now had visions of cold stone floors and potato sacks.

Theo shrugged. "Not always, but they can still be incredibly useful." He dropped his hand, and Amalie's skin immediately cooled. She shuffled away from him, ignoring the hairs on her neck standing at attention. "These are my quarters." Theo strode across the room and motioned to a door at the back. "Everyone will expect—"

"I'm *not* staying with you." She'd done as he asked, and one game was more than enough for her.

He gave her an amused look. "I assumed as much, which was why I was about to say you could have this room if you'd prefer. If you would've let me finish." He pointed to a second door next to the first.

Amalie fingered the hem of her shirt. It had come loose during their trek across the sand flats. She reeked of sweat and dirt from the floor of the shed, and she hadn't eaten more than the bread and cheese Theo had offered her hours prior. All she wanted to do was bolt through that door, strip off her clothes, and take a hot bath. But she didn't know if vampires did that. If there would be a wash basin, or food, or—

"They won't ask questions if that's what you're concerned about. My lifestyle has always been a bit odd. They're used to it."

Amalie swallowed hard. His lifestyle. This place. It felt like she was drinking from a bucket. "You play with your conquests before you kill them?"

"If only all of us could be as morally pure as Amalie Clermont." Theo pushed off of the wall, his expression clouded. "I'll have food brought up to you. If you need anything, you can knock." He pushed her door open. "I don't recommend you leave your room."

Amalie stormed past him, her chest tightening with each breath. *How had he known her name?* 'Amalie' was simple enough, but she hadn't gone by Clermont since she was seven years old. She'd been Amalie Allard since they'd come north.

I didn't kill your mother.

Anger built in her chest like a thunderhead. He'd brought her here, yet since they'd stepped foot on this rock swept by the tide, he'd told her nothing more.

Amalie swore under her breath and glanced around her room. It was much more grand than her room at home, either the one in the city she shared with Olivie or the one at Uncle Oren's. There was already a fire lit in the hearth. Her bed was turned down. A water basin and clean cloth sat on the dressing table.

She dropped to the chaise and stripped off her boots and socks. Just as she suspected, the skin was rubbed raw on her ankles and the edges of her toes. She winced as she ran her fingers over it to check for bleeding. Thankfully, it had already stopped, soaked into her socks.

Her heart started to pound. Did Theo expect her to stay here alone while she waited to change? She'd been so focused on her questions, she still didn't know how or when that would happen. She'd asked in the shed, and he hadn't answered. The least he could do was tell her what to expect.

Amalie flung her door open and stormed into the hall. She pounded her fist on Theo's door. It swung open within seconds, and she stumbled forward.

"Changed your mind?" Theo's shirt was unbuttoned, revealing sun-kissed skin and well-toned muscles. *Nothing like the legends.*

She opened her mouth, then closed it. What had she been wanting to ask? "I thought you couldn't go in the sunlight." Amalie forced her eyes to his face.

"We can't," he answered quickly.

"Then why do you look like that?"

"You'll have to be more specific."

Amalie slid into the room and pressed her palms against the door. It closed with a scrape. "You're not pale or cold like the legends. You don't have bloodshot eyes and fangs showing over your lips."

Theo turned, continuing to undress. He threw his shirt over the post of his bed, and Amalie's mouth felt like it had been swabbed with cotton. Ink-like marks wound over his broad shoulders, connecting along his spine. She caught a glimpse of a sun and moon and a symbol on the underside of his forearm that looked exactly like the signet on the ring she'd stolen.

If Theo saw her gawking, he didn't let on. "We're built to attract those we seek. Our appearance has changed over time. A thousand years ago, humans preferred lighter hair and skin. Now you seem to be preoccupied with . . ." He inspected himself in the mirror along the far wall. "Dark features." He glanced up and caught her eye.

Amalie set her jaw and glared at him. "It's disgusting."

"You set traps for your food. Smear your faces with mud. Dress in colors that mimic the grass or trees. It isn't any different." Theo reached for the button on his pants.

"Can you stop, please? I didn't come here to watch you undress."

Theo smirked. "Then why did you come?"

Amalie bit the inside of her cheek, her heart racing like she'd just climbed the staircase at the abbey. *Vain bastard.* "You said I'd learn more once we arrived."

"And you will." Theo sat on the bed, leaning back on his forearms, his trousers still unbuttoned. Three stripes of black ink dragged over his left hip and disappeared beneath the waistband of his pants.

Amalie blushed in spite of herself. "I've been patient." They were his words she hoped to use against him, but they backfired. All they brought into her head was the memory of his lips on hers.

Theo looked amused. "Hardly."

"You can't keep touching me or—taking things without permission."

"I had permission for that."

Amalie's eyes widened. *He thought she'd wanted his kiss?* "No, I—"

"You agreed to play the part. It kept you safe. I won't apologize."

Amalie wanted to scream. Instead, she drew a deep breath and refocused. She needed to play nice. She needed the answers she came for. "Am I going to succumb to darkness overnight? Will there be pain? Will I burn from the inside out?"

Theo frowned, then cocked his head. "Possibly all of the above."

"Excellent." Amalie's lips pulled into a tight line. She

wished she had another stake in her hands. Even if she couldn't kill him with it, she could at least watch him bleed. Theo's lips curled into a smile, and Amalie couldn't keep her mouth shut. "You find this funny?"

Theo sat straight. "A little. But only because I'd forgotten."

"Forgotten what, exactly?" Amalie seethed, her anger finally killing any desire to rake her eyes down his bare torso. It was a shame that the lithe male form would be ruined for her after this moment.

"The outrageous story you've been telling yourself." Theo pushed up off the mattress. He prowled across the wood floor and stopped in front of her. With him looming over her, her bravado sank, seeping out through her aching feet, leaving only panic.

She'd tried to be strong, but here she was alone with only the man she'd hated her entire life to talk to. Her family, her friends, everything in her life was gone. Pointless. A film of exhaustion and grief settled over her, making her body as heavy as lead.

"Why would you do this to me?" she breathed.

Something flickered in Theo's eyes, and his jaw tightened. "Besides saving you from frostbite, feeding you supper, and providing you safety for the night, I've done nothing else." He turned from her and stalked to the table at the edge of the room, pouring himself a glass of amber liquid.

Amalie's eyes burned. "How dare you pretend—"

"You want to know what to expect? Why you're still living after a bite from a vampire?" Theo turned, his lips wet, the glass in his hand.

Amalie swallowed hard. Why had he used those words? Why would he talk to her about living? She wanted to know what to expect when she turned. It was no life to be proud of.

Could he be attempting to distract her? The old stories

poured through her mind. *Le Sombre cursed to quell his loneliness, but it was insatiable. Vampires, in their lust for companionship, turned others with their bite only to discover their power was split, shared with their victims. They became weak, drawn further into shadow, forced to accept their isolation or shrivel in darkness without the power they'd been given . . .*

Theo took three slow steps toward her, his eyes fixed on hers. "You believe I turned you. You think I gave up the power of Le Sombre to curse you like the rest of us."

The name of the Shadow pulled her above her racing blood. *Le Sombre.* His power. Was Theo asking if she believed he'd transferred that power by turning her into a vampire like him? Was he amused because she was naïve enough to believe the legends or foolish enough to believe he'd act in such a way?

Amalie swallowed the shame working its way up her throat. His venom was the reason she was standing there, wasn't it?

Theo took another step. "If I turned you, I wouldn't be standing here."

"Why not?" Amalie felt like she was standing on the edge of a cliff. She held her breath, desperate for the answer about to slip through his lips.

"Because I'd be a weakened sop."

Amalie's hands started to shake. It was true, then. When vampires were created, they sacrificed. Which meant—

"And you decidedly wouldn't be," he finished.

Amalie's breath hissed between her teeth. *She wouldn't be?* There she stood like a drowned cat, her bones frosting over, in front of a creature that only half a day prior she'd stabbed in the heart with a stake. She was sick of him dancing around her questions, batting at her like a mouse hanging on a string.

"Humans don't survive vampire bites," she snapped. "Your

kind feed like gluttonous dogs. I should be dead on the floor of my bedroom."

Theo shook his head, the light flickering from lamps hung on the walls warming the right side of his face. "Almost always wrong."

He thought her stupid. So be it, but she at least needed to force a straight answer out of him. Amalie was shivering again, and just as she was about to insist he stop talking nonsense, Theo opened his mouth. "I thought you'd know something. That you'd—" He caught himself, his hands balling into fists. "You have no idea who you are, do you?"

The walls seemed to close in on her, and Amalie put a hand on the armoire next to her. She wanted to shout back at him. To fight and kick like she had when his arms were around her, but his words held her in a choke hold as his eyes traveled over her, the smirk fading from his lips.

That question should've felt like the others he'd asked, a half-truth, a slap, but it didn't. His words struck her like a mallet, ringing her from the inside out.

It wasn't only this night she couldn't make sense of.

She'd seen with her own eyes that her mother had been killed by Vallon, but her family had tried to bury the truth. They'd never let her see her mother's body. Her uncle had never talked about it since that day.

Then her uncle's refusal to admit the truth followed by their conversation outside her bedroom door. What else would he have told her? Missing pieces that she'd stored carefully in her memory over the years splayed out in her head. Their hushed relocation. The change of their names. Uncle Oren's rules.

There was something there. Something she wasn't seeing. *What did Theo know that she didn't?*

His eyes were sharp as he gave a small smile that seemed

disarmingly sincere. "It's true that humans die when they are bitten, but you misunderstand the reason why. You call us 'gluttonous dogs,' and I won't refute that point, but humans would die regardless of how much or how little we drank. Their blood reacts to our saliva. It coagulates within minutes. So, yes. We drink fast and fully. Waste not, want not."

Their blood, not hers. *You have no idea who you are, do you?* Amalie pressed harder against the smooth wood. He spoke about death as if he were recounting a trip to the market. "You drank my blood."

"I did not."

Amalie's frown deepened. "I have the marks to prove it."

"A bite does not equal feeding."

Amalie's throat was thick. No wonder it had felt like seconds. "I don't understand." If he hadn't fed, then that solidified her assumptions. He'd injected his venom. Why else would he bite?

Her breath came quickly then as a tiny spark of hope flickered to life within her. Was he saying she wasn't turning into a monster? That there was some other explanation for why she still stood there, herself, after his bite?

Theo took another drink from his glass, and Amalie's mind reeled. He could drink something other than blood? He swirled the last inch of gold in his glass. "I told you a story of a bloodline."

"Of your slaves, yes, I remember." Amalie twisted her hair around her finger.

Theo's eyes hardened. He walked forward, stopping close enough that Amalie expected to smell the sour odor of his drink on his breath, but there was nothing. "I hoped you'd think beyond your judgment, but since you seem incapable and my body needs rest, I'll state it simply. You would survive any vampire bite because your blood was made to be taken. You are born of the guardian bloodline I spoke of."

Amalie blinked, his words so far beyond the realm of possibility, she couldn't make sense of them. Made to be taken? What had he said of the bloodline? That they'd been a gift from the gods. That the gods had dealt mercy to humans and vampires alike.

But she, a member of that bloodline? "No!" The word sprung like vomit to her throat. Amalie stumbled back, moving as far from Theo as she could. *No. This had to be another one of his games.*

Theo had bitten her. She'd survived because he'd turned her into a vampire like him. It had nothing to do with a gift of the gods or magic in her blood.

Humans would never have accepted that agreement. To live as offerings to vampires, to allow them to freely drink of their blood. Vampires were powerful—deadly. What would stop them from harming them? Slaughtering them if they desired? Theo's words resonated through her. *Companionship. Pleasure.* "I don't believe you."

Theo shrugged, but his eyes were still sharp. "You don't have to believe me, but like you said. You standing there still human is all the proof you need."

"That isn't proof of your story. It's a fact. Somehow I lived, but I have no evidence that your explanation is the right one." She took a step toward the door, but Theo shifted like smoke to block it. "You say you didn't drink. If my blood was so desirable, such a gift, how could you stop yourself?"

"Perhaps I don't always take without permission."

That time Amalie did laugh out loud. "You kill humans! You feed and take their lives!" She turned her back on him, running her hands through her hair. There had to be some other explanation, but as Amalie searched her memories for something to prove Theo a liar, pieces of her life story began to create more questions than answers. The strict rules of their childhood. The medical condition she'd been born with and the management it took.

She whirled back to face him. "I have a blood condition. I receive treatments every few months to make sure I don't bleed out from a simple scratch." Amalie's hand flew to her neck. Without her treatments, there was a good chance Theo's bite could've killed her. Or maybe that's how she survived? Because her blood didn't clot as quickly?

"Is that why you chose me? Because you knew my blood was slow? Is it thickening inside me now, and you're just waiting for me to drop dead?" Every cell in her body held its breath. She didn't want to accept any of this, but at the same time, she'd always felt that there was something off. Last night proved that her instincts were good. Uncle Oren *had* been keeping things from her. He'd been planning to tell her everything.

She'd left. She'd ignored his rules and run off trying to save the world. Had it cost her the truth about her family? Her mother's death? The blood that ran through her veins?

Theo's eyes were dark and glassy. "What proof do you want? Would you like me to take you into the square and prick your finger? Leave you to be hunted and possessed? You live in a world where death is the worst horror, but I promise, there are worse fates."

Amalie thrust a finger against his chest. "I live in a world where the worst horror is *you.*"

Truth resonated through her at that declaration. She wouldn't be able to find her answers there because Theo would never give them. He would use her. Manipulate her. She could never be sure whether her beliefs were her own or a manifestation of his power to twist her mind at his bidding.

She jutted out her chin. "If this story is true, then I could leave. Go back. I won't be a danger to my family."

"You can't go back."

Amalie's blood began to simmer. "Don't tell me what I can and can't do." Despite how many times he'd proven that he could force her to comply, she wouldn't give in. Let him force her. Let him take away her will. She would never give it freely.

Theo shoved his hands into his pockets. "You'll put your family and friends in danger."

"How? You're the only one who knows about me, so are you admitting you'll come for us? Are you threatening me?"

Theo shook his head. "If you think I'm the only one who saw you and your friends in the courtyard that night, you're more naïve than I thought."

"You didn't see us in the courtyard. We saw you. We hunted you—"

"I knew you were there."

Amalie laughed out loud. "You knew? And yet still allowed me to stab a stake through your heart?"

Theo stood to his full height. "I welcomed it."

That shut her up. It seemed each conversation with him took a turn she wasn't expecting. She folded her arms over her chest. He was manipulating her again. "You don't feel pain, then?"

"I feel it."

Amalie thought back to Theo sitting at the table when she suggested he starve himself to death. *Trust me, I've tried.* Her eyes narrowed. "How long have you lived?"

"Two thousand and twenty six years. Are your feet cold?" he asked. Amalie ground her teeth realizing she'd placed one of her feet on top of the other. "An answer for an answer."

"Yes."

He glanced up from the floor. "Why didn't you wear your boots?"

Amalie didn't answer, only pressed both swollen feet to the wood. "Are you sick of it?"

"Your stubborn attitude? Absolutely."

Amalie shot him a look. "Living."

He didn't blink. "More than you could possibly know."

Amalie moved further along the shelf, and her cheeks heated when Theo's gaze stayed fixed on her. She understood, then. Theo hadn't brought her to the castle to answer her questions.

She cleared her throat. "That's it, then? After living so long, you've found another member of guardian blood, so you want me to stay? To bond with you and live out my days with you feeding on my blood? Blood that was a gift from the gods. That belongs to your kind. That gives you . . . pleasure?"

Theo was silent. When he finally spoke, his voice was so low it hummed. "If I thought that would make life worth living, I might consider it." He took a step closer, and Amalie froze. "You're too fresh to understand, but pleasure is fleeting. Pain seems to leave a more lasting impression."

Amalie felt like a caged rabbit with him standing so close. That low burn, that deceptive calm threatened to wash over her, but she fought it. "What then? Why force me here?"

"Because we both want the same thing." Theo reached out to straighten her collar, but she slapped his hand away.

"You don't know half of what I want."

His mouth curved at the edges. "You won't be hunted here. Guardian blood is strong. We can sense it above anything else. But the scent of yours is disguised."

Amalie scoffed, then thought of Uncle Oren's questions. *Did you hurt yourself?* His eyes always darting over her and Bethany. Checking them carefully.

If this was true—if Theo's story about blood and bonds had merit—then her whole family was at risk. Bethany had treatments just like she did, but did Uncle Oren? Did his daughters? Blood was passed from parent to child, but did this heritage come from her mother or father or both? Had her mother received the injections? It was so long ago, she couldn't remember.

Amalie glared at Theo. "You lied to me in Mordelles."

"I never lied."

"I thought I was turning into a vampire, and you let me believe it." Fingers of ice spread over her spine. Why would he have done such a thing? "Did you think that would make me more malleable? More willing to follow along?"

It had worked. She hadn't taken much convincing when she believed herself a threat to her family and friends. He'd dangled the relic in front of her, and she'd trotted along, salivating at the chance to discover his secrets. But if Theo's story was true and she was of guardian blood . . .

She clenched her hands into fists. "You brought me here. Into a den of vampires. You offered me protection for my help in finding the sword—"

"But that wasn't ever what you were interested in, was it?" Theo raised an eyebrow. He walked back to the desk and set his glass on the table. "You attacked me with those revolutionaries. What do they call themselves, the Pourfendeurs? The Slayers?"

Amalie swallowed hard. "Yes."

"And you went to them. After you left your room."

The blood drained from her face. "You were watching me?" Amalie replayed her run through Mordelles. Her begging Marcel and Olivie to stay back, to take her life before she turned and took theirs.

"It seems I wasn't the only one withholding information."

Amalie steeled herself. "At least mine wouldn't lead to your imminent enslavement" She thought of the streets below. Of the vampires she'd been only a few paces from.

Theo scoffed. "No. Just my death."

Amalie opened her mouth and closed it. She'd wanted him to believe she was pliant. Innocent. But she'd been fooling herself. The night had started with her stabbing him in the chest. She was a fool to think—

"I'm glad we're at least on the same page." Theo stepped closer, his trousers riding dangerously low on his hips.

"What are you talking about?" Amalie's eyelids flickered, his scent suddenly swirling around her.

"I want the relic for the same reason you do."

Amalie barked a laugh. "Doubtful."

Theo was suddenly right in front of her. He lowered his chin to meet her eyes. "You can vanquish me yourself. And then I don't care what you do with it. Kill them all if you want."

Amalie's heart skipped a beat. She'd assumed Theo wanted the relic to hold more power, to control his coven or threaten other vampire groups. But find the relic to take his own life? It didn't make any sense.

Theo fixed his eyes on her. "The injections from your uncle mask the scent of your blood unless it's fresh. I only caught the scent when you broke your skin. The others won't sense you if you're careful. Stay in your room—"

"How am I supposed to find a sword while locked in my room in the middle of the sea?"

Theo's hand twitched, and he shoved it in his pocket. "I've collected books. Histories, not the ones you're used to. I'll have them sent to your room."

"So what, I read? Look for something that could lead us to a vampire murdering relic? What am I going to find that you haven't?"

Theo was silent for a moment, his eyes scanning her face. "You seem motivated." He stepped back. "I must leave tomorrow in a few hours. I'll send for you when I return."

"Theo—"

"Leave me. I need rest. And you need to bathe."

Amalie clenched her jaw. "How do you expect me to take care of that with only a wash basin?"

He looked at her, a strange expression on his face. "Did you not open the other door?"

13

1824 BLOIS, FRANCE

Rachel sat upright in bed at the metallic click of a latch. She pulled her sheets to her chest, her breath coming in quick bursts as her window swung open, sending chilled night air sweeping across her skin.

She threw her covers off and leaped from the bed, then worked to untangle her nightdress as she bolted for the door. "Or—" Her brother's name disappeared under a warm palm clapped over her mouth.

"Shhh, Rachel. It's me."

Rachel stilled, her fingernails still digging into the man's skin. Florent? But how had he gotten to the second story? The house spanned the river and the walls were sheer. She worked to draw air into her lungs as he dropped his hand and settled it on her shoulder.

"I'm sorry. I didn't mean to frighten you," he whispered, brushing a kiss across her temple.

Rachel spun to face him. "You came in through my window in the middle of the night."

Florent grinned. His hair was loose as it always was. His

skin looked almost velvet in the moonlight spilling in from the window. "I had to see you."

Rachel's heart fluttered, but she pushed him back toward the wall. "You can't be here." For so many reasons, Florent couldn't be there. Amalie and Bethany were sleeping in the next room over, for one. Oren would kill him, for another. And Florent still hadn't answered her questions, for the last. "I told you I wouldn't meet you again—"

"That's why I'm here." Florent grasped her wrists and held them in front of her. "I knew you wouldn't meet me in the gardens, and I owe you an explanation."

Rachel searched his eyes, her pulse quickening. "You're going to tell me why nobody knew your name when I stopped by the abbey? Why you will only see me after dark?"

Florent held her gaze and nodded. "I thought—well, I'd rather show you." He pulled her closer to the window.

Rachel stopped in front of the open shutter and shivered. The thin fabric of her dressing gown did nothing to fight off the damp breeze. She stared into the shadows, broken only by reflected moonlight on the river. "What is there to see?" Florent slung a leg over the window sill, and Rachel gasped. "Don't, you'll fall—"

"I won't fall." Florent tugged on her hand, pulling her against his side. He wrapped her arms around his chest then gripped her waist. "Hold on. I promise I won't let you go."

14

Amalie scanned her room a second time, searching the back wall. There. The door was hardly obvious, hidden in the paneling.

She strode across the room, the idea of a bath so enticing, her breathing quickened. Her skin was covered in a fine layer of silt, and she didn't want to know what her feet smelled like.

You need a bath. Theo was rude. Not exactly cruel, but definitely not kind. He seemed to both despise her and . . .

Amalie's cheeks flushed as she remembered how he seemed to undress her with his eyes. It was because of what he was. What she was. He desired her blood, nothing more.

And yet he hadn't taken it.

Amalie frowned as she reached for the handle and pulled the door open.

Her eyes widened as she took in the scene before her. The room was bright, a long window on the far wall letting in streams of golden sunlight. It was morning, Amalie realized. They'd reached the island when the sun was barely rising. No wonder she was exhausted.

A woman in a cap and apron stood by a large copper tub, her brow furrowed in concentration as she stoked the fire beneath. Her eyes widened as she noticed Amalie. "Oh! Mademoiselle, I didn't hear you come in." The servant girl stood frozen, her hands trembling slightly as she clutched the iron poker. She was young, perhaps no older than Amalie, with wide brown eyes and a smattering of freckles across her nose. Her dark hair was pulled back in a loose knot at the nape of her neck, wisps escaping to frame her face.

She was human. Amalie's pulse sped. Did this woman know she was working in a vampire's lair?

"The water's warm enough. Master Vallon insisted you'd want it steaming. If you wait a few moments, it will get there." The servant stood, wiping her hands on her apron, leaving a streak of ash on the fabric.

"Thank you." Amalie's eyes darted around the room. The scent of eucalyptus and lavender hung heavy in the air, her favorite herbs for a bath. *Strange.*

She walked to the edge of the tub and dipped her hand in the water. She couldn't keep from sighing. A bowl of rose petals floated on the surface of the water, their delicate pink hue contrasting with the copper of the tub. Amalie's lips parted in wonder. She'd never been treated to such luxuries. Aunt Maurielle was a practical woman. She believed in oregano soap and a stiff brush.

Amalie turned and took in the array of jars and bottles lining the shelves. Each was meticulously labeled in elegant script, boasting names like lavande, romarin, and chamomile. She stepped closer, her fingers brushing over the glass, feeling the cool, smooth surface beneath her skin.

"For your feet." The servant handed her a jar of salve, then paused. She glanced between the shelves and Amalie, her mouth opening and closing.

"What is it?" Amalie asked.

The servant's cheeks flushed. "Master Vallon said it wouldn't be necessary to provide monthly cloths. You may n-not . . . I only meant that your visit may be short, but—"

"It's not necessary." Blood rushed in Amalie's ears. The servant girl bobbed her head and exited through the door to Amalie's room. She hadn't been there before, had she? She must have come in while she was talking with Theo, which meant . . .

Amalie looked down at the ointment in her hands. Had Theo planned this? Had he known she'd come to his room, or had he planned to provide a bath well after they arrived? Had he noticed her feet before they'd arrived at the castle?

Why had he told his servant not to provide monthly cloths? Surely he couldn't know . . . Amalie tensed. Could vampires sense a woman's menstruation? The thought made her stomach roil.

It didn't matter for her. She set the jar on the counter. She'd never bled, and neither had her sister. It was part of their blood condition, and she'd never quite understood it. If they didn't bleed, they couldn't become pregnant. Yet her mother had birthed two healthy girls—

Blood rushed in Amalie's ears as another piece slid into place. It wasn't a blood condition. Was it possible she didn't bleed because she was a guardian?

Amalie felt suddenly woozy, and her gaze shifted to a tray set on a small wooden table. Fresh bread, a wedge of cheese, and a cluster of grapes. Her stomach growled, and she realized with a start how hungry she was. She'd been so consumed with her mission, she'd scarcely thought about food.

Amalie reached for a grape, the skin taut and glistening. She popped it into her mouth, savoring the burst of sweetness on her tongue. There was a knife on the tray, and she used it to slice off some cheese, briefly wondering if she should hold onto the blade. Keep it hidden in her trousers.

But what would be the point? If Theo or a vampire in his coven decided to attack her, there was nothing she would be able to do to save herself. She set the knife down and tore off a piece of bread.

After her stomach was moderately full, she reached for the buttons of her shirt. She undressed quickly, her movements efficient. She didn't want to linger on the fact that she was standing naked in Theo's home, that she was about to immerse herself in a bath he'd arranged for her.

Why had he done this? It wasn't to be considerate, that she was sure of. He'd been happy for her to huddle on a stone floor wrapped in a potato sack hours earlier. Maybe this was how he treated all his human guests. Pampered them before he drank their blood. Maybe the servants here didn't know how to offer anything different.

She stepped into the tub, hissing as the hot water lapped at her skin and stung the raw skin on her toes. She lowered herself slowly, the heat seeping into her muscles, melting away the tension that had coiled there. It was heavenly.

She closed her eyes, letting out a sigh of relief as she sank up to her neck. She could enjoy this couldn't she? It didn't make her any less dedicated to killing Theo Vallon if she savored a few moments of pleasure in the midst of her most disturbing nightmare.

Then Amalie remembered how easily the servant had entered her room. She was surrounded by vampires. There wasn't time to relax. She needed to start searching for answers so she could find the relic, kill Theo, and take it back to Marcel and Olivie.

A lump formed in her throat as she thought about returning to Mordelles. *She could go back.* She wasn't going to turn into a monster. Tears welled in her eyelids at the realization that she didn't have to lose her life or her family and friends.

That was the moment she chose to believe Theo's story. If he was wrong, at least she would turn into a vampire with hope blooming in her chest instead of cowering in fear.

But how much did she believe?

Amalie reached for a bar of soap, inhaling the scent of lavender as she lathered it between her hands. She worked the suds into her hair, scrubbing at her scalp until it tingled. She rinsed, then repeated the process with a cloth, working the soap over her skin, scrubbing away the dirt and sweat.

Some of his story was simple to grasp, but she still couldn't wrap her head around her mother's death. She'd always assumed Theo had killed her out of thirst, but now . . . Theo recognized her blood. He hadn't taken hers when he had the chance. Wouldn't he have known her mother was a guardian? Wouldn't he have kept her alive like he'd done with her since her mother could have helped him find the sword just as well as she could?

But if another vampire killed her mother, they also would've recognized guardian blood. Theo had said they could sense it above anything else. Wouldn't they have come after her? Or Bethany? Her entire family?

Her head felt like it had been stuffed full of stinging nettle.

Amalie scrubbed until she was raw, and after rinsing, was tempted to lie back and soak. Instead, she forced herself from the tub. She stepped onto a clean cloth on the floor, the water cascading from her skin as she reached for a towel. She wrapped it around herself, feeling the soft cotton against her skin.

Amalie dried herself quickly, then noticed a set of clean underwear, a blouse, and trousers folded on the counter. She frowned. It wasn't common for women to forego a corset or wear trousers, and yet that was exactly what the servant had left for her. She pulled the blouse over her head. The fit was perfect. *Very strange.*

She finished dressing, applied the salve, then ran a comb through her hair and braided it quickly, tying it off with a ribbon. She took another bite of bread and cheese, pulled a few grapes from the vine, and was about to exit when the servant walked back into the room.

"Dressed already?" The woman looked surprised.

Amalie nodded. "I have work to do. What is your name?"

The woman smiled and bobbed a curtsy. "Henriette."

"Thank you, Henriette. This was lovely."

Her smile widened. "I've never run a bath in this room, but 'ave always wanted to."

"Never? Not for . . . Master Vallon's other guests?"

She crossed the room, using the poker to smother the flames beneath the tub. "Master Vallon does not have other guests. Not since I've been 'ere."

Something flipped in her chest. He didn't bring other guests? What had Theo said, that the others were used to his odd lifestyle? Amalie thought of her uncle. How he'd described her mother slipping out at night, meeting with a vampire after dark. Theo had snuck in her window, hadn't he? Maybe he preferred to do his killing away from home.

"How long have you been here?" Amalie asked, moving toward the door.

"Three years." Henriette set the poker in a cast iron rack.

"And you only work for Master Vallon?"

Henriette shook her head. "I work for the north wing. There are three other servants, one of them my sister."

"And all of you are . . . safe?"

Henriette's lip twitched. "Of course. Why wouldn't we be?"

Amalie's heart thudded in her chest. "Right." Her eyes flicked to a chain around the woman's neck. For a moment, she was back in the house on the river. Her mother tucking her in at night. A locket hanging off a chain, so close to her face, she thought she could kiss it.

"Don't worry, this key will go straight back to Master Vallon when he returns," Henriette lifted the chain, showing her the key that hung there. "It's the only one for this room, so you don't have to worry about anyone else interrupting you."

Amalie nodded, her words sinking in. Only one key. Henriette would give it back to Theo when he returned. "Do you know where he's off to?"

Henriette shook her head. "Master Vallon is extremely busy. He rarely sleeps here two days in a row. I was surprised to 'ear that he planned on returning in the morning."

Amalie put a hand on the door. "Thank you again, Henriette."

The woman bobbed her head. "I'll finish up here, then I'll pop back through your room. You won't even know I'm there."

Amalie nodded and pushed the door open. Her room looked exactly as she'd left it, besides the three stacks of books that now sat on the writing desk. She yawned and covered her mouth with her hand.

Time to get to work.

15

Amalie woke with a start, nearly ripping a page from the book she'd been reading. She peeled the paper from her cheek and straightened. Her brain moved slow like molasses as she stretched her arms over her head. She turned and scanned the room. Light poured through the windows stretching toward the domed ceiling. It had to be mid-to-late afternoon.

Though her eyes felt like they'd been scrubbed with sand, her mind raced. She couldn't afford any more sleep. She turned, and her gaze settled on another tray. Henriette had been there. Amalie walked to the nightstand. There was a ham and cheese sandwich with a ripe apricot.

She picked the fruit up, feeling the velvet skin against her palm, and held it to her nose. The scent was sweet. Amalie sat on the bed and devoured it. It couldn't have been long since her breakfast in the washroom, but she was starving.

When she finished with her meal, she swung her legs over the edge of the bed and padded back to the table, her fingers brushing the spines of the books stacked in neat piles. She pulled out a few leather-bound volumes, flipping through the pages and scanning the titles. *Le Savoir des Vampires*, Vampiric Lore. *Les Gardiens de la Lumière*, The Guardians of the Light. *La Fracture et le Sombre*, The Shattering and the Shadow.

She flipped through the pages of the first book that claimed to hold the legends of the guardians, skimming passages. She found nothing different than what she'd been taught as a child. The guardians were stronger, faster, and more resilient than ordinary humans. Heroes.

Amalie scoffed and flipped to the middle. *It is believed their blood has regenerative properties.* That, at least, seemed closer to the truth. But the book didn't talk about their blood being used to satiate a vampire's thirst. The guardians in the books didn't bow to vampires, they held them back. They were a military wall protecting humans from shadow. Exactly what she'd always hoped for.

She closed the book and picked up another. *Methods of killing vampires.* Much more her speed, though she now knew all of it was nonsense. Well, not all of it. She only had proof that a stake hadn't killed Theo, though that was enough to breed doubt in everything else she'd been taught.

It was a strange feeling. Watching the foundational truths she'd built her life around crumble. It was even stranger to construct a new reality based on the words of her enemy. She wanted to strip her life bare and start with a blank slate. But how could she fill it? There was nobody left whom she trusted to guide her. She wasn't even sure she trusted herself.

Amalie spent hours poring over the texts, her fingers flipping through pages and her eyes scanning the words. She jotted down notes in the margins, her pen scratching against the parchment. The light outside the window shifted as the sun dipped lower in the sky.

Amalie shifted in her seat, her muscles stiff from sitting for so long. She rolled her shoulders, her joints popping. There were hundreds of references to relics, and even narrowing her search to swords didn't help much. There were still too many references to count.

With a groan, she strode to the bed and flopped onto the mattress, then pulled her knees to her chest and ran her fingers over her blistered feet. They were inflamed and sore, possibly worse that morning than they had been the night before.

Amalie thought back to the moments preceding her bath. Had it only been hours before that her entire life had flipped on its head?

When Theo was there in front of her, the story he told made sense. But now, staring at the cherubs and clouds swirled in paint on the ceiling, nothing did. How had she allowed herself to be fooled and lured here? She should have demanded answers in Mordelles. She could have gone home— she could have stayed with Olivie and Marcel.

Even as she thought it, that assumption fell flat. Staying wouldn't have brought her any closer to helping the Pourfendeurs, and besides, she hadn't been in a position to demand anything. Not when she thought she was being acted on by forces beyond her mortal control. Theo had allowed her to believe that, and maybe he was only spinning another story now.

Amalie buried her face in the down pillows. If Theo was to be believed, not only had her family lied about vampires, they'd lied about their own heritage from the gods. Oren had lied about the injections he gave, but why? If the gods had granted this gift for humans and vampires alike, why were they in hiding? Why did they allow other humans to die when their blood could bridge the gap?

Amalie rolled, staring again at the vignettes above her. She didn't know if Theo was drawing her into his web, but she had proof he'd been honest about two things. The stake to his heart hadn't killed him. His bite hadn't killed her. Whether his explanations for both were honest, she had yet to judge.

Amalie sat up and pulled out her disheveled plait, then ran her fingers through her hair. When it was smooth, she wove it back into a tight braid. *If only she had pins to hold back the curls around her ears.*

Her eyes landed on a set of carved boxes on the polished dresser. All the furniture in the room was delicate. Thin legs that curved into patterns of inlaid wood. She wondered who had lived here before Theo and his coven.

His coven. That's what he'd called it. Had he only meant that he belonged to it? From the way his friends reacted to him, she doubted it. Theo was important to them, but she had yet to figure out why.

Amalie lifted the top off the first box and found an array of hairpins. Perfect. She put two in place then repositioned the lid and lifted the top to the second box. She sucked in a breath as ice slid down her spine.

There was a strip of azure fabric curled at the bottom, marked with intricate white shapes. Swans. She'd only ever seen that pattern once before in her life.

On her mother's favorite dress.

Amalie ran to the door and burst into the hall, gasping for breath with the strip of fabric curled in her fingers. She stumbled to Theo's door and raised a hand to knock, then hesitated. What would she say to him? That this was fabric her mother used to wear? That she'd found it in *his* castle?

Theo was gone. She sucked in a breath and stepped back from the door. He was gone, and even if he were there, she had no proof that it belonged to her mother. There had to be hundreds of women who owned pieces of clothing in that print, and Theo would likely tell her as much.

Amalie whirled, retracing her steps and stopping in front of her door. What did it matter even if it was her mother's? She already believed he'd killed her, so what more did this tie prove? That he'd brought her here? That he'd done to her exactly what he was doing to her now?

She needed more information, and she needed to find it herself. Not from Theo's silver tongue or her uncle's guarded one. She couldn't believe what either of them said because, for reasons she didn't understand, even Oren was hiding things.

Amalie needed to find proof, and she needed to see it with her own eyes. She turned to face the empty hall. The vampires would most likely be sleeping. *What Theo didn't know wouldn't hurt him.*

She crept forward and tied the swan fabric around her neck. Theo had led her by the neck to cover proof of his bite. Though the marks were fading, she'd be stupid to walk around with it showing now.

Theo had also said her blood was masked. As long as she didn't cut herself, there would be no reason for any vampire to be suspicious of her, especially not when Theo had made it clear that she was his. Amalie shivered at that, disgusted that she'd gone along with his suggestion.

Colors splashed across the floor from the oval stained glass that faced the sun on the other end of the hall. Though she'd walked here with Theo, she'd been distracted and didn't remember which direction they'd come from the front steps.

Left. She didn't question it and turned right instead. The castle was eerily silent, and Amalie wished for gusts of wind against the walls to hide the brush of her sore feet against the stone floors. At least one piece of the legends seemed to be true.

She came to what looked like an open common room and paused in an alcove, craning her neck to see if it was empty.

She waited and listened. When she was sure she heard nothing, she peeled herself off the stone and padded forward, keeping to the wall as she entered the room.

The room was so large, it made the furniture seem sparse. Tapestries hung on the wall, freshly cut firewood sat stacked next to the hearth, and an array of canapes and chaises were available for seating. It was informal but cozy.

Her eyes snagged on a bookshelf along the back wall. She strode forward, feeling more exposed than a deer in the middle of a clearing. Her pulse quickened as she began to read the titles. *Le Comte de Monte-Cristo. Madame Bovary. La Chartreuse de Parme.* They seemed to be fiction, mostly, along with maps and encyclopedias. She crouched to look at the next row, when a gasp sounded behind her.

Amalie whipped around, then released a breath when she saw Henriette staring at her.

"Oh, Miss Amalie. I thought—I'm so sorry, I didn't mean to disturb you." Henriette bobbed and walked with purpose toward the fireplace. "Just 'ere to warm the room."

Amalie clasped her hands in front of her, still working to settle her heart. "Do you do this in every room?" As soon as she asked the question, she remembered what Henriette had told her as she drew her bath. "But only in this wing?"

Henriette smiled. "Yes. I have seven fires I start in common areas and six more in the bedrooms. I'll start yours in just a few moments."

Amalie blinked. There were that many rooms in one wing of the castle? "Thank you."

Henriette stacked another log and looked up. "I don't mean to be rude, but Master Vallon told me you shouldn't leave your room . . ."

"I know. I was just—I needed to stretch my legs." Amalie gave a small smile.

Henriette's eyes flicked to the books she'd been inspecting. "Do you need more? I can find more titles if you tell me what you're interested in reading."

Amalie laughed. "No, I haven't even gotten through the ones in my room."

Henriette nodded. "Then I would listen to Master Vallon. He knows the house best." Her eyes dropped, and she resumed her task.

The house or the creatures in it?

"Right." Amalie pursed her lips. "But if I wanted to take a quick peek at the library?"

Henriette frowned. "It's too far, miss. In the east wing."

East. Her room was in the north. "So this hall, I'd have to follow it from here to the right?"

"Yes, at first. Then down the steps and back to the left." Henriette looked up. Her eyes wide. "But don't tell Master Vallon I told you that."

Amalie smiled. "Of course not. I was just curious. I'm sure he would've told me had I thought to ask."

"When you're ready, make a list and I'll gather more books." Henriette nodded as if convincing herself that Amalie was going to be perfectly obedient.

"I will. Thank you." She turned and strode back to the hall, her face flushed. She'd hoped to walk more than twenty paces before being caught by the woman drawing her baths, but at least now she had direction.

Light still poured through the window. *She had time, didn't she?*

Amalie hurried down the hall, pausing at every archway before hustling on. She passed four closed doors, and each of them bore Theo's signet. *A bit heavy handed.*

A small stairwell leading to a higher floor, a parlor, a small passage leading to a terrace, and two hallways before she finally made it to the wide stone steps that swirled downward. She put her hand on the center stone column and began to wind her way down.

Down the steps and back to the left. It wasn't that far from her room, though the idea of making her way back made her stomach flip.

She'd be quick. She only wanted to see—

Amalie saw stars as she slammed into something solid. Her heel slipped on the step and she fell back, landing hard on her bottom. She flattened her palms on the stone to make sure she was steady before glancing up.

A man. *Not a man.* A vampire stood in front of her. His hair was thick and fell in waves across his forehead. His eyes a startling green. Amalie's breath caught in her throat at the sight of them. They were so close to the color of Bethany's eyes, it was eerie.

His glamour trickled through her. Cold. Like mist. Though the same calm washed over her, there wasn't any warmth. The knowledge that she already knew Theo by feel filtered through her in layers.

Amalie blinked. "I'm sorry, I wasn't watching." She lifted her hands, searching for any sign that she'd broken the skin. *Stupid.* She'd been careless to leave her room, to risk herself like this.

"Well, neither was I." He reached out a hand, but Amalie didn't take it. He observed her as she rose from the stone. "I'm Marx. Your master wouldn't approve of you touching another?"

Amalie pursed her lips. She hadn't seen this man in the street when they'd arrived, but he had to be a part of the coven. Why was he awake and walking the halls when everyone else seemed to sleep? "I have no master."

She regretted it the instant the words came out of her

mouth. She stood mere feet in front of a vampire. Less than a day ago, that would have filled her with fear so thick she would've run. Or thrown up. Or possibly both. Now her desperation to gain some semblance of control was dangerous. After hearing Theo's explanation of her bloodline, shouldn't she have felt more trepidation, not less?

Marx's smile widened. "A guest. You arrived with Theo?"

Amalie worked to keep her expression blank. "A bold assumption."

"But a correct one." Marx shoved a hand in his pocket. "It's exactly like him to force others to keep his rules."

Enemy then. Though Amalie wasn't sure if that made him her accomplice or if her list of threats had just grown longer. "Well. It was nice to meet you." Amalie took a step back on the staircase and turned, but before she could climb, he was there in front of her. She jolted, and he caught onto her arm to keep her from tumbling down the stairs.

Marx assessed her. "I *am* curious."

Amalie tried to pull her arm free, but he held firm. "About what?"

"Why you aren't warming his bed." Marx's lips curled, and Amalie's breath caught. There was something there—something familiar. She'd never seen this vampire before in her life, and yet the way his eyes crinkled when he smiled—

She blinked. *It was his damn glamour.* She needed to keep her wits.

Amalie planted her hands on her hips, her temper flaring. No one had ever been so bold to discuss what happened or didn't happen in her bedroom. Then, as she stared at Marx, Amalie almost laughed out loud. Of all the events of that night, that was what offended her sensibilities? "We had a long journey. He needed rest."

She didn't want to tell him Theo was away from the castle. In case that gave him ... permission.

"Ah." Marx chuckled, his eyes traveling down her torso, lingering too long on her hips. "Theo does like his rest. It is rare, though. For his pets to be wandering alone through these halls."

"Is it not rare for one of his coven to be awake before sunset?" Amalie didn't understand the game she was playing. What did Marx want with her? Why wouldn't he let her leave?

Marx shrugged, finally releasing his grip. "Perhaps I also have no master. Certainly not Theo."

Amalie nodded, sliding along the step and pressing against the other side of the stairwell, then hurried back up the stairs.

When she reached the top, she pressed her back against the wall and sucked in a ragged breath. She needed to get back to her room. She'd been lucky, but she wasn't going to push it.

Amalie d'Acier. She could do this.

Amalie forced air into her lungs, then started back down the long hall. She passed the path to the terrace, the stairwell, and two of the empty halls, but when she paused at the archway to a common room, she heard voices. Female voices. Laughter. It was coming from the parlor.

"The apricot cake was divine. You may get to try it tonight. I had it the first night I was here, and Ramon promised a repeat."

"Three nights?" A second voice sighed. "This has already been the best day of my life."

Amalie chanced a look. There, sitting on embroidered armchairs in a room with windows overlooking the sea at high tide, were two of the women she'd seen clinging to the vampire Theo had called Etienne in the courtyard. They were giggling, their heads thrown back as they whispered to each other. *They were alive.*

They were also facing the hall. There was no way she could cross without being spotted.

A third woman stepped into the frame, her hair a riot of red curls, her skin so pale it was almost translucent. She was draped in a gown that looked like it belonged in a painting from the Renaissance. The fabric clung to her curves, the neckline plunging dangerously low.

Amalie's stomach churned. Had she been the one talking? Had she already lived here three nights?

Perhaps if she moved quickly, purposefully, they wouldn't be able to stop her.

She was about to straighten and skitter across the open archway when two men crossed behind the chairs. One with his hair shaved close to his scalp. He wore a tunic and breeches that accentuated the well-formed muscles in his arms and legs. The other had fair hair, almost white. He was taller, his frame lean. *Who did they all belong to?*

"Excuse me, but who are you and why are you spying on us from the hall?"

16

Amalie froze. The women were staring directly at her. She pulled back, then realizing she couldn't pretend she hadn't been noticed, stepped out into the archway. "I was only passing by."

The first woman motioned for her to come closer, and Amalie glanced down the hall. "I need to—"

"You're the woman we saw arriving last night. With Theo?"

Amalie nodded. She needed to get out of there. But the idea of being rude to humans who were most likely going to be dead by morning made her queasy. Though, they'd survived this long, hadn't they?

"Theo is so mysterious." The first woman raised an eyebrow. "I'm Marie, this is Sarah and Penelope. Have you gotten to know him yet?"

Amalie tapped her foot on the stone. "No. I've been resting. In fact—"

"It's exhausting isn't it?" The woman with red curls, Penelope, gave her a knowing smile. "The journey alone. Then settling in to someone else's room. Did you know Ramon has a closet filled with costumes? Suits and frills for every occasion. After our time together last night, I suggested we throw a masquerade. Just so I can see him wear something other than a tunic and slacks."

Marie winked. "I'm surprised you're up and about after the first night. I still don't leave Etienne's bed by choice."

"Especially since I've joined you." Sarah laughed, and Amalie thought she might be sick. When would he kill them? Would he do it one at a time or make the other watch?

The man with the close-cropped hair turned from a painting he was admiring. "Has anyone seen Clémentine recently?"

"Or Everly?" the second man asked.

Amalie clenched her jaw, nearly biting her tongue. *Careful.* But she was so angry, her hands were trembling. Knowing vampires lured humans into their beds and seeing the reality of it playing out in front of her were two very different things.

They were entranced. Obsessed. *And it wasn't their fault.*

"You spent the night here." Marie leaned in conspiratorially. "So tell us. How was he?"

Amalie wanted to scream. To shake them. To tell them to run. To get as far away from this place as possible. But she couldn't. Not unless she wanted to announce that she was different, that she knew exactly what she was walking into. It seemed like the worst possible choice since she wasn't supposed to be out of her room in the first place.

"Excellent. He was an attentive lover." Her voice was tight, her cheeks on fire. "Anyway, it was nice to meet—"

"I'll make sure to give him that glowing report."

Amalie spun to find Ren, Paul, and Etienne behind her in the hall. She scurried back, closer to the other humans as they entered the room.

Their glamours rippled through the space, and Marie,

Sarah, and Penelope reacted as if they'd just been plunged into the copper tub she'd used the night before. Their eyes rolled back in their heads, their breath slipping between their lips in a soft hiss.

"I missed you." Marie rose from her chair, but Etienne motioned for her to sit. She did so instantly.

Amalie exhaled, forcing her mind to focus. Four vampires. She'd left her room once and run into *four vampires.* If one of them didn't kill her, Theo surely would. Stay calm. She only had to pretend she was socializing, there was nothing wrong with that.

Amalie drew a deep breath. Each of their influences felt different. Paul was smooth like melted chocolate. Etienne more vibrant, like a sour cherry or crisp apple. And Ren . . . she couldn't sense him well. Or perhaps he was more purposeful in how he used the gifts of his curse.

Regardless, it only took seconds for her to push back the fog. Was she getting better at it, or did Theo affect her more than others? The idea sent a shiver through her.

"I've always wondered how Theo's lovers would describe him. I can't say I've ever had the pleasure of speaking to one of them in person." Ren sauntered closer. "How did he come upon you? He's been traveling so much, I was surprised he'd found a willing companion. Especially one so lovely."

Amalie stepped back, pressing her palms against the stone wall. "I was walking one evening."

"Where?"

"Rennes," she lied. "He was sitting on a bench in the court-yard. We struck up a conversation."

Paul chuckled. "A conversation with Theo? Must have been short-lived."

"Yes, please. Tell us what you spoke about." Ren's voice was smooth as melted butter, but there was an edge to it. It made

Amalie's skin prickle. Could he have been the one to kill her mother? Could it have been Paul or Etienne? Why would they have left the rest of her family alone?

Amalie swallowed, her throat dry. She scrambled for inspiration to answer Ren's question and landed on her last conversation with Olivie. "We spoke of politics."

Ren's eyes widened, and a moment later he burst into laughter along with Paul and Etienne. "Politics?"

It was a reach, but she couldn't very well tell them the truth. That she'd been hunting him. That she knew who and what they were, and that she despised them.

She forced a smile, playing the part of the enamored damsel. "His ideas are revolutionary." Amalie moved toward the open archway, noting how low the sun was in the sky outside the window. She'd thought it was only midafternoon, but she'd calculated wrong. It was nearly twilight. She needed to leave. To get back to the safety of her room.

Ren sighed, leaning against the armchair and playing with Marie's hair. She nuzzled into him like a cat.

Paul yawned, and as he lifted his hand to cover his mouth, Amalie's eyes narrowed. He wore a ring. One she'd seen before —one she'd taken off of Theo's hand as he lay dead on the stone. Did they all wear one?

Amalie couldn't get a good look without drawing too much attention to herself.

"And what happened after that? Did he ask you back here to continue your discussion?" Paul asked, dropping his arm.

Etienne laughed. "Whatever he said must've worked. Didn't you hear her? He was an attentive lover."

"Who is an attentive lover?" Theo's voice sent a shock shooting down Amalie's spine. Her head snapped to her right.

Theo stood in the archway. He wore clean black trousers, a

crisp white shirt, and a vest that fit him like a glove. And he was glowering at her.

Ren walked toward him, clapping a hand on his shoulder. "Amalie was just regaling us with tales of your love making." Marie and Sarah, still seated in front of her, leaned toward Theo as if hoping for the briefest scent of him.

"No, I—" Amalie's mouth snapped shut as Theo raised an eyebrow. She spun to face the window, searching for anything to burn that expression from her mind's eye. *Thank the gods he was at least fully dressed.*

Theo cleared his throat. "I thought I'd find you in your room."

Ren tsked. "Leaving Master Vallon waiting after his long journey. What a naughty girl."

Marie and Sarah giggled, and Penelope sighed. "I'd never keep Ramon waiting."

Amalie wanted to smack her.

"Did you enjoy the books?" Theo asked, and Amalie drew a deep breath before allowing herself to turn back.

She met his eyes. "I did. Thank you." Before she'd fallen asleep, she'd studied without breaking. She'd consumed the deep myth of Le Sombre and his relegation to live interminably in darkness after refusing a marriage to Leviathan. The eldest daughter of the sun god. She'd turned page after page detailing Le Sombre's curse and the plague of vampires on humanity. It all held more weight than it had when she'd heard the stories as a child, but it hadn't gotten her any closer to finding the sword.

Ren gave a lazy smile. "We've heard you're interested in politics, Theo. Please, tell us what you shared with this lovely young woman that was so intriguing she followed you here."

Theo's lips twitched, then he leaned against the wall and scratched the stubble on his chin. The action was so human,

Amalie almost forgot the truth of what he was. Then the soothing blanket of his glamour enveloped her, and she stiffened.

It almost hurt to look at him. The sharp angles of his face, the gloss of his hair.

Theo exhaled. "I believe our monarchy has become lax. We've all agreed to the rules given, and yet many refuse to follow them. Even when they serve as a protection to our citizens." His words were sharp. Pointed.

Amalie's eyes widened. He was going to play this game, was he? "An interesting statement, considering it's only the wealthy who get to have their say."

Theo took a step closer. "Do we not all benefit from the laws?"

"So they tell us." Amalie stood her ground.

"You're not convinced? Tell me, what would a king have to do to convince his subjects that he was only concerned with their safety?"

Amalie glared it him. "He could probably start with keeping their family alive. And telling them the truth in the first place."

Theo's jaw tightened. He was close enough now, his scent washed over her. She fought against it, but her body was suddenly liquid. Amalie put a hand on the wall to steady herself. He definitely affected her differently.

"Paul, would you lead our wonderful guests to the dining room for cocktails?" Ren gave a winning smile.

Amalie's eyes flared as the other humans were herded from the room and she was left alone with Ren, Etienne, and Theo.

"As riveting as it is to watch the two of you posture, I believe you've broken one of your own rules, Master Vallon." Ren crossed his arms over his chest, all hints of amusement gone.

Theo glanced at him. "Which one?"

Ren shrugged. "You've instructed us never to bring someone into the castle who understands our true natures." He looked straight at Amalie. "Tell me, why do you flinch when I appear? Why do your hands clench into fists? Humans are always more relaxed in our presence, more docile, but you seem to be the opposite."

Amalie's throat worked. She could pretend she didn't know what he was talking about, but he'd already called her out. How could she explain herself?

"Amalie is a historian." Theo turned to face Ren. "She's been studying our history, and since she's only been reading human accounts, her research is hardly fact."

Etienne groaned. "Theo, this again? Why does it matter?"

"It matters that humans know the truth." Theo turned back to Amalie.

Ren's gaze flicked to her, then back to Theo. "A historian. And you brought her back here? Pretending she was your lover?"

Theo's lips twitched. "You heard her. I didn't pretend anything. I only thought it would be . . . educational."

A flush climbed up Amalie's neck.

"She doesn't seem too fond of you." Etienne looked between the two of them, shoving a hand in his pocket.

Ren's eyes narrowed. "It's always fun to have a challenge." He strolled forward, his eyes locked on Amalie's. "Quite the turn of events. A historian who pays attention to something other than human folly. What have you learned, then? Besides how tender Theo is in his lovemaking." He winked at Theo. "None of us were surprised to hear it, by the way."

Theo's already thunderous expression somehow darkened.

Amalie wet her lips. "I've learned that the histories I've read are incomplete."

Etienne dropped onto the chair next to her. "Because nobody has bothered to write our history."

"Why haven't you?" Amalie looked between the three of them. That was an honest question. With all the books she'd read, all the research she'd done, she'd never come across one reference to a story told from a vampire's perspective.

Etienne laughed. "Humans would never believe it."

Theo ran a hand lazily through his jet-black hair, smoothing it into place. "Human histories are necessary because your lifespans are short. Those stories must be recorded more permanently."

"And your stories aren't worth recording?" How much time would it save them both if vampires or guardians had written anything down about the sword?

A thought struck her. Was it possible her family did have a record? She thought of the books her mother had once kept in her study. Where had they gone?

"We remember everything perfectly," Ren said.

Amalie's eyes narrowed. Everything? Did that mean he had been there at the beginning? Had all of them?

"I personally think the human histories are pure comedy." Etienne stretched his arms over the back of the chair. "The way they think they can kill us with pieces of silver or stakes of ash."

Amalie stiffened, and Ren locked onto the movement.

"Oh, don't tell me you believed that was true?" He purred, dropping his eyes to the pockets of her trousers. "Theo, did you tell her she could bring a stake to protect herself?"

Theo shrugged. "I didn't check her pockets."

Ren's eyes gleamed. "And yet you still let him have his way with you? Or was that for research as well?"

"Ren. Enough," Theo growled.

Ren laughed. "I'm sorry, you'll have to forgive me. After

living for centuries, I latch on too quickly to shiny objects. But I have to say, this conundrum you've brought to our attention is sparkling indeed." He planted his hands on his hips and looked between Theo and Etienne. "What do you say we have a bit of fun in the courtyard tonight?"

"What are you proposing?" Etienne kicked a leg over the arm of the chair.

A slow grin spread over Ren's face. "It won't do for Amalie to perpetuate antiquated and dangerous beliefs. Let's give her some hands-on research."

17

Rachel grasped the stone wall in front of her, so dizzy she thought she might hurl her dinner into the glittering night sky.

"Breathe." Florent rubbed a hand over her back.

She did as he said, forcing air into her lungs and squeezing her eyes shut. "You can fly," she gasped,

"No." Florent's chuckle was low. "I can move quickly. There's a difference."

Rachel opened her eyes, still pressing the pads of her fingers into the rock. "I've never been up this high."

"Only because your brother keeps you so busy, you have no time to explore."

Rachel scanned the treetops and rolling countryside. "Where is Oren's estate?"

Florent pointed to the south. "There. After the bend in the Loire."

Rachel nodded. There were candles burning behind many of the windows. "What is this place?" She turned and scanned the roof beyond the turret she stood on, and her eyes widened with realization, the red tiles. Black shutters. "This is Place Deaumont."

Florent nodded. "It's my home."

"But it's abandoned. Monsier Deaumont refuses to sell—"

"Monsier Deaumont has lived beyond our borders for two years past. He will not miss it."

Rachel frowned, her heart beginning to skip in her chest. How was this possible? How had he taken her safely to the ground and covered this much distance in the blink of an eye?

As panic built in her chest, another sensation crept over her like morning mist. Peace. Calm. He'd never harmed her. He'd never done anything untoward. She should give him an opportunity to explain, shouldn't she? "Florent—"

"You have questions. I will answer them. But first, let me bring you inside so you don't catch a chill."

Rachel nodded, giving the home where Amalie and Bethany were still fast asleep in their beds one last look before following him into the dark stairwell.

18

1836 NORTHERN NORMANDY, FRANCE

Amalie stood at the edge of the courtyard, gaping at the pastel sky mixed with dark thunderheads beyond the castle spires. It was better to look there than at the pile of weapons at her feet.

Days prior she'd catalogued the same items in Mordelles with Olivie in preparation for their attack on Theo. Now there were no torches, whistles, or bells. There was no need when the vampires were willing participants.

Theo stood ahead of her, his chest splayed and arms bound behind him with braided leather cord. Ren had laughed as he'd tied them himself and pulled the knots tight. Theo wore no shirt, only trousers, and Amalie felt sick seeing his broad chest rise and fall. The fact that guilt crept into her heart only fueled her anger.

"What the hell were you doing outside of your room?" Moments before, Theo had prowled in front of her once they were behind closed doors. His hair was mussed, his eyes wild.

Amalie had argued. *"You told me my blood was masked—"*

"I told you to stay in your room!"

She wasn't proud of how she'd reacted. She'd just been accosted by one of Theo's vampires in the stairwell, then forced to converse with other humans who were delighted to be fattened up for slaughter.

She'd taunted him. Needled. It wasn't as though he didn't deserve it, but there hadn't been a point. Being there at the castle had made one thing clear. Amalie didn't only hate Theo. She hated the world she lived in.

Theo glanced up at her, and the rest of their argument replayed in her head.

"You've made it clear you own me. Isn't that enough?"

"That won't matter." Theo raked his hands through his hair, then drew a deep breath and dropped his hands.

"So this is my life. I stay locked away in my room hiding from your vampire coven who wish to kill me until I can bring you the sword?"

Theo shook his head. "They wouldn't kill you."

"More stories? To keep me clinging to you in the streets? Safe in my room where only you can access me? Does it make you feel powerful to force humans to do your bidding?"

Amalie gasped as Theo shot through the air like smoke, stopping with his chest pressed against hers. His eyes burned. "This is protection. If my coven caught the scent of your blood, they would rip themselves apart to possess you, and they're not even close to the real monsters you need to worry about."

"You should start, séductrise. The sun is nearly set." Etienne's voice snapped her back to the rooftop. He rubbed his hands with anticipation, and Amalie noticed the ring he wore on his finger. The same as the one Paul had been wearing in the parlor.

The courtyard teemed with members of Theo's coven, and they all had silver glinting on their fingers. Was a simple ring what bound them? Or did they have marks on their skin like

Theo? What commitments had they made to be there? What did Theo offer them? By the gleeful looks on their faces, she wouldn't call them his friends.

She turned to Theo, bound and shirtless. His pants hung low on his hips exposing the tight V of his abdomen, and the inky marks on his skin seemed darker now than they had in his bedroom.

She should have felt nothing.

But "nothing" was the opposite of what Theo brought out in her.

"I am not a seductress," she muttered.

"You caught his attention, did you not?" Ren raised an eyebrow, then turned to Theo. "That's difficult to do. If I didn't know better, Theo, I'd think you'd lost hope."

Theo clasped and unclasped his hands, the blood already struggling to force its way past the cord around his wrists. "Don't mistake my interest for affection, Ren." His eyes were cold as he looked up at her.

Amalie scoffed. *Of course, not.* Theo wouldn't care about anyone. But what was Ren referring to? What would give a vampire hope?

She cleared her throat. "Can someone else take the lead so I can observe? I'm much more comfortable collecting evidence." Even though the vampires now knew she wasn't Theo's besotted lover, she didn't want any of them to think she was a threat.

Was that the only reason she didn't want to wield the weapons?

Amalie's stomach flipped. Compassion or empathy should never have entered her head, and yet she couldn't push it away. Life wasn't something to toy with. Suffering shouldn't be entertainmnent, regardless of how terribly a creature deserved it.

But this hadn't been her idea, and Theo Vallon, along with the rest of his coven, were monsters. Who knew how many times they'd murdered without remorse. *I can't survive without blood. Do you feel guilt?*

No. She would not allow his words to prey on her mind. The Grimoire didn't give an explanation for why Le Sombre chose to curse those he did. Perhaps they'd earned it. By the actions she'd observed, they'd certainly done their best to keep their place with the Shadow ever since.

This wasn't survival. This wouldn't make the cities and villages of France safer. This was entertainment.

"A woman with arms like this does not sit inside at a desk." Ren's hands were suddenly on her, and Amalie's entire body went rigid.

"Ren," Theo growled.

Ren dropped his hands and grinned. "Sorry, sorry. I didn't mean to overstep." He turned to Amalie. "Did Theo tell you that bringing you here meant he'd staked a claim? I assume you understand all about our hierarchies."

Amalie nodded, though Theo had barely alluded to this the night before.

"Once a human steps foot on this island, they belong to the vampire who brought them." Ren ran a hand through his hair. "Forever."

Amalie flinched. She thought of the humans in the study. "Do you ever let them go? If they're . . . not a good fit?" She wanted to believe that was possible. That Marie, Sarah, and Penelope could one day walk down the steps and back onto the sand flats at low tide.

A female vampire sitting on the wall behind Ren sighed. "Oh, they always become a good fit. In the end."

Amalie nodded once, trying not to let the hatred in her soul bleed out through her expression.

"But I didn't answer your question, did I?" Ren looked down at the pile of weapons. "I think it would be best if you did the killing. Just so you know we didn't use any tricks. Plus, I've never seen what happens to a human when they're violent up close."

Amalie had mentally prepared for this. She'd decided to start with the easiest, least violent option. Exposing Theo to sunlight.

She stalked forward. "Can we move him over there." *Be docile. Uncertain.* She pointed to the swath of sunlight warming the stones to their left.

Theo nodded once and stepped forward, then hesitated as his boots neared the light. Amalie put a hand on his shoulder and pushed him forward, not giving herself time to consider it. The sooner this was finished, the better.

But as Theo's face hit the light, nothing happened. He drew a deep breath, closing his eyes a moment, then turned to face her.

"I don't understand."

Ren clapped his hands together. "Ah, I should've stopped you sooner, but I wanted to see if you'd actually do it." He stepped forward, standing close enough the cloth of his shirt brushed hers. "None of us understand. The sun would roast any of us alive—burn our flesh—but Theo has never had that problem. Well, not *never*. Only after Helena—"

"Would you like me to tell your life story? We could start with the vial." Theo snapped. Something dark flashed through Ren's eyes.

Helena. Had Amalie seen that name before? Yes. She was sure of it. But where? And what had the book said?

Theo turned to Amalie with a smile. "Did you hear that? I'm one of a kind."

Ren forced the smug look back onto his face, then stepped

back. "Here. I believe this was what you were after." Before Amalie could process the movement, Ren grabbed Etienne by the collar and hauled him into the sunshine.

She stumbled back, knocking Theo to the side. She was not prepared for the smell. Or the sounds that tore from Etienne's throat. Her entire body went rigid as the muscles of his back grew taught under Ren's hand, still fisted in his shirt.

She coughed at the acrid smell of charred meat laced with the distinct smell of sulfur as Etienne's skin began to blister and crack. It wasn't only the flesh on his hands and arms. Since his entire torso faced the setting sun, every inch of him above the waist sizzled and split, revealing raw muscle and sinew underneath.

Amalie's breath came in wheezing gasps as she whirled around, covering her ears to keep the guttural screams from piercing her to the core. When she could endure it no longer, she lunged forward and grabbed Etienne by the arm, yanking him back into shadow and out of Ren's grip.

He stumbled and fell, landing on the stone and staring up at the sky from a face stripped of flesh. His chest gaped, revealing bones and organs burnt beyond recognition. Like she'd pulled him directly from the coals in her hearth.

He was dead. He had to be. Half his body was eaten away, and the other half lay lifeless. There was no breath in his lungs, no thump of his heart.

"Some friend you are." Amalie wiped at the tears streaking down her cheeks, only then noticing that she was on her knees next to Etienne's body, her chest cinched so tight, she thought it might crack. Killing in one shot to the heart was one thing, but making someone suffer—even a vampire—left bile sloshing in her throat.

Etienne's cries still echoed in her ears as celebratory hoots and laughs sounding all around her, and Amalie's head snapped up. Paul, wearing a shirt today, was doubled over, his shoulders shaking. Clémentine was gaping, a broad smile stretched across her perfect face. And Ren, he was the worst of them all. Howling at the thin crescent slice of the nearly transparent moon like a fool. And Theo. He stood there, his hands still bound, watching her.

Why had he been able to withstand the sunlight? *Since when?*

"What is wrong with you?" Amalie pushed up from the ground. Had they no shame? While she wasn't going to cry over one less vampire in the world, Theo had said vampires were loyal. Now here they were dancing over their friend's grave.

Ren sighed, clutching his stomach. "It probably seems cruel to your human eyes."

"Yes. It does." Amalie glared at him.

The smile faded from Ren's lips. "Strange to find a human with compassion for our kind. Don't you think, Theo?"

"I told you. She's a historian."

Ren shrugged. "When you've lived for thousands of years, even pain is better than boredom. I wouldn't expect you to understand." He looked at her like a father would look at a sniveling child. "But this little experiment hardly gives unequivocal proof. Why don't you try this instead."

Ren pulled a long, sturdy stick from the stone floor and held it out for Clémentine to tie what looked like an old dirty rag to the end of it. Then he shoved the cloth into a bucket and pulled it out, sopping.

Amalie shivered. Two thousand years. They'd lived through wars and revolutions. Watched humans suffer through reigns of terror, pestilence, and plague. No wonder they were cruel. Humans must seem the equivalent of ants crawling under their boots.

Ren held the stick out to Paul who fished a flint and steel from his pocket. He struck for sparks, and in seconds, the rags were aflame.

"Care to do the honors?" Ren held it out, and Amalie took it from him.

She turned, taking in Theo's rigid posture, then turned back. "Who is this for?"

Ren's eyes sharpened. "Theo, of course. Unless I sense . . . affection?"

Amalie turned back, blood rushing in her ears. What part did Theo want her to play now? There was no affection, and yet he'd asked her to pretend in the beginning. If she'd done a more believable job, they wouldn't be in this mess in the first place.

Why couldn't she have drowned in their glamours and flushed when they appeared in the doorway? Oh, yes. Because she'd spent her entire life hating their kind and working to overcome their seductions.

But could she do this? Could she purposefully light Theo on fire? Amalie thought back to the night in the courtyard. How she'd run and stabbed Theo through the heart. She'd been sick. Disturbed. But she'd done it.

Now she had to do it again. Not only would it prove that she was an obedient little mouse, but she'd have more than Theo's word that the other strategies for vanquishing vampires were obsolete.

Yes. She could do this. She *had* to do this. Marcel, Olivie, and the Pourfendeurs were counting on her.

Before she could second guess herself, she lunged, thrusting the flaming torch against Theo's chest.

He didn't move. Didn't try to stop her. As the flames licked up his shirt, he simply closed his eyes as his lips curled, baring his teeth.

Again, the scent of burning flesh. The growls ripping from his throat. Amalie turned, unable to watch as acrid smoke filled the air. She flinched as Theo's body hit the ground behind her, his cries interrupted only by scuffling against stone. She squeezed her eyes shut, clenching her jaw until the sounds died out.

Ren's eyes were alight. "Beautiful work. Truly."

Amalie gasped for breath. Was it done? She couldn't bring herself to turn around and see the wreckage.

"You have to pay up." Paul wiped the tears from his eyes and put out a hand. Clémentine scoffed and handed him a thin metal object. He slipped it into his pocket with a cheeky grin.

"What was that?" Amalie snapped.

Paul sauntered over the stone. "Clémentine didn't believe you'd do it. She thought you were only trying to impress him, but that you'd end up licking his shoes before you ever caused him harm." Amalie's eyes flicked to Clémentine. The woman winked at her. "I have to admit," Paul continued, "this is the most fun any of us have had in ages."

"Perhaps not Etienne." Ren grinned. He walked past her and nudged Etienne's lifeless form with his boot.

Without thinking, Amalie shoved him. Hard. Ren didn't even wobble. He caught himself, spinning and moving close enough that she could hear his intake of breath. "Feisty. I can see why Theo likes you."

"*Liked*," Amalie corrected.

Ren's face split into a grin. He nodded toward Etienne's body, and Amalie followed his gaze. She held her breath, readying herself to view grotesque, mutilated flesh, then froze. Her brow furrowed as she stepped back and dropped to the stone.

What was happening? Moments before, Etienne had been lifeless. Burnt to a crisp, and now . . .

Her head shot up, and she scrambled across the ground, landing next to Theo. He looked worse. His skin and muscles were ash, his bones charred. Bits of hair melted against the few pieces of flesh that hadn't been consumed by the flames.

She clapped a hand over her mouth, about to be sick. But then she saw it. Fresh. Pink. Amalie ran her fingers over the new, perfect skin forming over his shoulders, his arms, and—

She yanked her hand back as Theo's heart started beating in his chest. The fibers of muscle flushed red, then squeezed and released once, twice, before flesh and muscle corded over his ribs and in a flash, sealed shut.

Ren sighed above her. "Impressive, I know."

Amalie yelped and scrambled back as Theo pushed up from the ground. "You—I saw you. You were dead."

"I'm beginning to doubt your observational skills." Theo shot her a look, then curled over, as if taking stock of his limbs. A sheen of sweat coated his skin, and his face held a ghoulish tint as dark shadows bloomed under his eyes.

"You can regenerate," she hissed.

"So it seems." Theo grunted and hauled himself to his feet.

Amalie forced herself to stand next to him, only then noticing that Etienne was on his feet next to the others. The whole world seemed to spin. "How is this possible?"

Ren leaned against the wall. "Le Sombre was thorough in his cursing."

Thorough. They couldn't escape it.

Amalie's mind reeled as they crossed the roof toward the rest of Theo's coven. That was why they'd been laughing. They hadn't been concerned for either of them in the least. Did all vampires know this? Had they all experienced death at some point without giving up the ghost?

"What's next on the list?" Ren rubbed his hands together.

"Garlic first. I love how that makes your mouth burn, and then …" He reached down and lifted the stake from the pile.

"No." Amalie shook her head. "I'm sure about that one."

Etienne gave her a strange look, and she realized her mistake.

"You've seen a vampire stabbed?" He twisted the sharpened ash wood in his hands.

Amalie swallowed hard. "Once."

"The Pourfendeurs in the city. They've grown more brazen. Trying to show off their skills in public." Theo stopped next to her, and his glamour hit her with full force. Her emotions were compromised, and she didn't have her normal walls up. Amalie swayed on her feet, pulled like a moon to orbit a planet of greater mass.

Theo turned his head, and though a smile was on his lips, something pooled behind his eyes. Pain. Sadness. How had she never noticed it before?

She shoved her hands into her pockets to keep them from trembling. *I feel it.* She'd set him aflame, heard his groans of agony. Was she going to continue with this?

Was it truly possible that Theo was above death like he'd said? That all of them were? That there was no mortal weapon strong enough to take their lives?

The rest of Theo's story began to carry more weight. If this was the best entertainment they had to look forward to, why wouldn't they want to be released?

There it was. Another pang of compassion.

Amalie gritted her teeth and turned away from Theo. Her eyes settled on the smooth arc of a blade protruding from the weapons pile. *Maybe it couldn't be a mortal weapon.* Theo had said this sword he hunted had supernatural power. Maybe there were other blades with similar qualities. Especially one blessed of the gods.

"Is that authentic?" Amalie pointed, and Ren's eyes glittered.

He reached into the pile and pulled out the sword, its sharpened edge gleaming in the waning light. Platinum. A naturally weak metal fortified by the gods to exceed even steel in its strength. It was mined and traded, forged and fought for throughout history.

Ren passed her the handle, and Amalie coiled her fingers around the carved wood. The sword was weighty. Top-heavy.

Ren's smile was wicked. "This is capable of more than stopping his heart." His eyes landed on Theo's neck, and Amalie swallowed hard. Her own wounds, the marks he'd given her, throbbed under the strip of fabric around her neck.

Theo leveled his eyes on hers. "Where would you like me to be?" His tone was low and soft, and Amalie's center dropped out of her. Why was she agreeing to this? Why was he allowing her to torture him at Ren's command if he knew he'd continue living?

He scrubbed his hand over his jaw, and Amalie's heart picked up speed. This was unfair. It was wrong. Vampires prowled in the shadows hunting humankind and then here she stood feeling sorry for one?

Anger solidified within her like shaken cream. Her father wasn't given a second chance when his head was split by a rock and water flooded his lungs. Her mother wasn't given mercy when Theo set his sights on her blood.

I didn't kill your mother.

Her breath came quick. He had to have been the one to kill her. She'd seen no one else.

Amalie pointed to a stone lifted up from the rest of the courtyard. She had to know. If this blade wouldn't kill him, how could she be sure the relic he hunted would?

Theo's eyes flickered, but he nodded, clasped his hands

behind his back, and crossed the space toward it. The edges of his form blurred in the quickening twilight as he dropped to his knees.

Amalie took shallow breaths, hoping to clear her mind of his scent. She shook the memory of his smoky eyes peering out from under long lashes and hair falling over his forehead as she clenched the handle of the sword and strode forward. This would be quick. It wouldn't cause him pain if she struck clean.

She lifted the sword higher as Theo bowed before her, laying his cheek on the stone. His collar gaped, baring the tanned skin of his neck. Blood rushed in Amalie's ears.

He couldn't survive this. Even if he could regenerate muscle and flesh, he couldn't heal a severed head.

He was evil. Darkness.

She could feel nothing. She could earn her mark.

Amalie gritted her teeth and planted her feet, raising the weapon over her head with both hands. Years of grief and fear swelled like a symphony, and a ragged cry burst from her lips as she threw all her strength into her shoulders.

This was for not having her mother there to teach her how to plait her hair. For not having her there to teach her how to wash the stains from her clothes. For not having a mother to teach her how to raise her little sister, for the years she'd spent questioning her memory and yet still shivering under her blankets every time the sun dropped below the horizon.

Amalie's strangled cry echoed through the courtyard as she swung the sword in a smooth arc toward the stone below.

19

Rachel curled her legs closer to her chest, watching the dancing flames. Florent sat straight in the chair next to her. His eyes were on her, but she wasn't ready to meet them. She was sitting in Place Deaumont. *With a vampire.*

"This isn't possible," she whispered against her knees. The words were empty husks. She felt numb. Like she was hovering just outside of herself.

"Have you never heard the stories?" Florent's voice was gentle, and it only tightened the knot in her chest.

"Of course I've heard them." Her parents had used myths from the Grimoire to keep them from sneaking out after dark. To remind them to light their incense and recite their prayers. She'd been steeped in tradition since she could walk and talk, and while she knew the stories were true, she never thought she'd encounter them. *She'd been careful.*

She'd done everything her parents had told her to, had never questioned. She may not have kept Oren's rules perfectly, but close enough. And now there she was. Raising two girls alone without two francs to rub together.

She finally turned her head. Florent sat on the floor with his back against the wall, one leg stretched long and the other pulled in, his arm slung across his knee. "I know it's a lot. It's why I waited to tell you."

"Why did you tell me?" Rachel's heart began to pound. She couldn't explain how Florent had swept her from her window and brought her here in mere minutes. She couldn't explain how he appeared in shadow without making a sound or how he always knew where to find her. But this . . .

"Because I love you."

Rachel's heart beat faster, warmth spreading under her skin like she'd lowered herself into a bath. "You don't love me. You barely know me."

"I know enough."

Rachel shook her head. This was impossible. "Vampires can't love. If you are what you say you are, then—"

"I'm a monster?"

Fear gripped her heart. What was she doing? She was sitting here, far from her two girls asleep in their beds, conversing with a man who had admitted to being a creature of the dark. Who fed on human blood. Who killed each time he satisfied his thirst. Was that why he'd brought her here? Did he always seduce his victims? Toy with them before taking their life?

"I told you the truth."

Rachel nodded, unable to think of a response. Could it be possible? Florent spoke of vampires living in peace with humans. Of a time when they didn't kill to survive. But how could that have turned into the world they lived in?

Rachel pushed herself up from the floor and stumbled back until her palms pressed against the wall. She could make it to the window, but Florent was between her and the door.

"I won't stop you. If you wish to go." Florent stood and moved closer to the hearth.

Rachel watched him warily. "Florent—"

"I won't harm you. I can't, actually."

Rachel frowned. "What do you mean, you can't?"

Florent took a step closer. "It wasn't our fault, Rachel. So many of us were fooled, victims of vampires who believed they were above the agreements with those of guardian blood."

"Were you a victim?" Rachel asked.

Florent's expression hardened. "Yes. A vampire, Helena, who I thought was a friend, gave me up for a chance at power."

"What do you mean, 'gave you up'?" Rachel groaned and leaned against the wall. "I'm trying to understand, Florent, but you speak of this world as if it's part of my own. My family is supposedly of this guardian blood, and yet I know nothing of these stories. I only know that vampires are our enemies. That they abused their power and we had to flee."

"Shh, Rachel." Florent closed the final space between them and placed his hands on her waist. "Your ancestors were victims, yes. But we were not your enemy."

20

Amalie's hands shook as she heaved again over the wall. Her stomach was empty, but she couldn't settle it. A hand rubbed in slow circles over her back, and another held her hair away from her face.

"You've never seen that, then, have you?" A male voice chuckled. Ren.

No. She had not seen that, but it wasn't the visual of the sword slicing through Theo's flesh. It wasn't even the feel of it. The blade hitting bone, then giving until it hit the stone beneath. The crunch of his spine, the ting of the metal.

It was the flash of an image through her head. Theo wrapping his hands over hers. Showing her how to hold a broad sword, how to position her feet to keep her balance.

The scene was so real, she could smell him. Feel his stubble on her cheek. Hear the smile in his voice.

Amalie heaved again, her stomach clenching so hard, she clutched her middle to keep from bruising a rib. *It wasn't real.* Theo's clothes had been strange and they were in a clearing she'd never set eyes on. Her mind was playing tricks on her.

"Ah, shhh." Ren moved his hand to her shoulders, and his fingers grazed the tie around her neck. "It's not as bad as all that. He's already half repaired if you want to—"

"I'm not looking." Amalie swiped the tears from her cheeks as she flinched away from his touch. She didn't like that he was close. That he'd been the one to swoop to her side the second she'd dropped the sword and bolted for the wall.

Ren considered her, then pulled a handkerchief from his pocket. He held it out between them, and Amalie finally took it. She wiped her nose and lips and focused on the branches of the tree in front of her to keep the images of pooling blood and raw bone at bay. She could barely remember why she'd done it in the first place.

Amalie looked over the wall at the encroaching sea. She felt the cloth between her fingertips. She was here with Theo's coven. She'd come to find a way to vanquish vampires, to kill Theo Vallon and avenge her mother's death. To take that knowledge back to the Pourfendeurs so they could finally protect their villages.

Her breathing finally slowed, and she turned to face the wreckage. *It hadn't worked.* She'd severed his head from his body, and Theo was still alive. She wanted to weep.

Ren sighed, leaning back against the sun-bleached stone. "I have to say, Etienne was right. I spent the last two weeks in Paris, and this was far more entertaining." Despite her best efforts to keep it, Ren took the soiled handkerchief and shoved it in his pocket. "I'm not afraid of a little bodily fluid." He grinned, and Amalie clenched her jaw, willing her stomach to stop roiling.

She had to get off this island. Peering over Ren's shoulder, she inspected the ground below. Water still lapped at the rocks, but it was lower than it had been when they'd come out onto the roof.

"It will be low tide in an hour or so. If you wish to run," Ren taunted. "I'd like to see that, actually. Theo having to chase after someone for once."

Panic surged through her as the depth of her situation settled like a thick blanket. What could a sword do that a platinum blade couldn't? *And how was she going to find it in the first place?*

"Are you satisfied?"

Amalie's head snapped back at the sound of Theo's voice. He stood next to Ren, his ashen skin marked with a new deep purple line around his neck.

Tears pricked her eyes a second time. Theo had held her with such tenderness. He'd helped her, he'd—

No. That imagination wasn't real. A Theo like that had never existed.

Amalie turned to Ren. "I've seen enough."

Theo nodded once, then stalked across the stone courtyard to the door leading to the staircase they'd climbed earlier. "Clean this up," he barked to the onloookers, motioning to the pile of weapons and his own blood that still stained the stone.

The members of his coven no longer laughed.

"If you're going to run, I'd do it now. Seems he's in a poor mood. Bit distracted." Ren grinned, then turned and crossed the rooftop toward Clémentine.

Amalie had to run to catch up to Theo. She barely saw him disappear through the door and bolted after him, taking the stairs down to his quarters as fast as she could without slipping on the narrow steps. She was breathless when she put out a hand to stop his bedroom door from slamming shut in her face.

"Why did you do it?" She slipped in, and the door closed behind her. She kept her hand on the knob. After Theo had allowed her to do her worst, she doubted he'd turn on her now, but she was still wary.

"You wanted proof of my integrity. Now you have it."

Pain. He felt it. Amalie's hand rose to her neck. Her cheek. She'd burned him alive, then sliced through his flesh and bone. He'd felt all of it, and it was as if the ghost of his wounds hovered over her own skin.

Ren's goading had worked. Not in the way he'd hoped, no doubt. But despite her commitment to not believe a word out of Theo's mouth, her resistance was weakening. She was alive after being bitten, and Theo had proven definitively that he couldn't die.

Her questioning mind had gone silent.

Theo stalked to the washbasin and plunged a cloth into the water, then wrung out the excess water and began washing his own blood off his skin.

"Do you not have a tub?" Amalie asked.

Theo glanced up, his eyes hooded as he shook his head.

Amalie frowned. "You're the master of the house, and my room is better outfitted than yours?"

Theo rinsed his blood from the cloth. "This isn't my normal room."

Amalie's heart stuttered. She couldn't ask the question that sat on her tongue because hearing the answer would only confuse her further. Monsters didn't give up their rooms for humans. Even if they wanted their help.

Theo dragged the cloth over his side. Over the marks on his hip that she'd never seen the end of.

He didn't look like a monster.

He never had.

That was the problem.

"Tell me more about the sword." Amalie's heart began to

pound, and she lowered her eyes. She didn't want to see more of him. Not when his glamour still drew her in like a moth to a flame.

"All it took was a severed head and you believe me?"

Amalie's stomach churned. Standing near him felt more difficult than it had before. Heavier. Everything she'd done on the roof had leached her anger, and she couldn't even cling to fear. Theo wasn't going to hurt her. It didn't make sense, but she knew it with a surety.

He'd allowed her to set him aflame. To slice through flesh and bone.

Amalie's hands moved to her middle as she curled into herself. It was only then that she became aware of a strange pulse through her center. *Had that been there before?* It felt like a hum, a warmth. Sitting directly over her spine.

"There's something wrong with me." Amalie stumbled forward, bracing herself on the edge of his bed. In her peripheral vision, Theo set down the blood-soaked cloth and dried his hands and chest with a towel.

"What do you feel?"

Amalie froze. The words he'd used. Not, "Do you feel faint?" or "Would a cool compress help?" but *"What do you feel?"*

Theo watched as if waiting for something, and her skin pricked.

She hunched over her knees, forcing a deep breath. "Just start talking. I need a distraction." What was happening to her? Was she breaking down like she had after stabbing Theo the first time? As much as she'd trained with the Pourfendeurs, she didn't seem to enjoy the realities of violence.

Theo turned and stalked toward his armoire. "It's said that in the fifteenth century, a female warrior discovered the sword within the depths of an old church. The walls were crumbling, ivy curling between stonework, overtaking what had once been holy ground. There was no light inside save for the slivers pushing through stained glass windows high above." Theo paused and glanced up through his lashes, studying her face. "She brought it back to their castle, discovering almost by accident that it was capable of vanquishing creatures of the dark."

"Creatures like you," Amalie murmured. She had never heard this story, and the detail in which he told it was unnerving. The Grimoire spoke of ancients, but nothing in the last century.

Theo nodded and took a step, pausing at the end of the counter. "That weapon was misplaced."

"The warrior lost it?"

"It was taken from them."

Them. Amalie's heart picked up speed. Talking with Theo was like treading water and then suddenly being yanked below the surface.

Had he lived during that time? Had he known the warrior who found and lost the sword?

Amalie wracked her brain. What did she know about that period of human history? Not much besides turmoil and suffering. Witch hunts. A war with the King of England.

A knot tightened behind her ribs. "I know nothing of any sword, Theo." She straightened, her stomach beginning to settle. "Do you believe someone in my family line stole it? I assure you, if my ancestors held onto such a powerful relic, they've kept their secret well."

Theo shook his head, pulling a shirt from a wooden hanger. "No, I don't believe your family has it. I believe . . . You may have a connection to it."

Amalie stilled. "To the relic?" Theo nodded. "How would that be possible? I've never seen anything like that in my life."

He took another step toward her, a muscle in his jaw ticking. "I've spent centuries looking for a way to end my curse. You—" He cleared his throat. "Your lineage leads back to those who first discovered its power. I've traced your bloodline through generations of guardians."

Her hands began to tingle. He'd been tracing her bloodline? He was still keeping her in the dark. The realization was like straight oxygen over coals. "What else do you know, Theo?"

He regarded her a moment, then a door seemed to close behind his eyes as he strode to his writing desk. "The gods created guardians because they couldn't reverse the curse of Le Sombre. Not without risking another rift between light and shadow."

Another history lesson, it seemed. Amalie focused intently on the carved wood of Theo's bed, ignoring the thrum in her core at the sight of him shirtless.

The Grimoire spoke of Solène and Le Sombre. How they were once bound as one god, then ripped in two when they sought to create beyond their natural order. Their rift threw the world into an eternal spiral, spinning between light and dark.

She ran a finger over a knot in the wood of Theo's bedpost. It was split with a dark crack. "And you think this sword is like that? A work-around. A way to release you from a curse you're supposed to be tethered to for eternity."

Theo nodded.

Would he become what he was before or would losing the power of Le Sombre be enough to finally allow him to pass from the world?

It was silent a moment, and just as she was about to brave a glance to the side, Theo appeared in front of her, still holding the shirt in his hands. A slim cord of leather wrapped around his neck, a key dangling from it. *The key to her room.*

He seemed oblivious of his indecency. "That's what I want."

Theo pulled the tunic over his head, and she swallowed, forcing her eyes away from his flexing abdomen as he pulled the sleeves over his arms. Her mouth kept moving even though she willed it to be still.

She could draw her own conclusions after experiencing the rooftop, and yet she couldn't keep the words from spilling past her lips. "It seems you have everything you want. A richly adorned home. The freedom to go wherever you wish, the ability to seduce humans to satiate your . . ." Amalie pursed her lips.

"My what?" Theo faced her, his hair disheveled and almost boyish.

Amalie's throat grew thick. She thought of their entrance through the gates. The other vampires praising him for his lasciviousness. Inspecting her like a prized hog. *Ants beneath their boots.*

But Theo didn't look at her that way. He scoffed and teased, but when his eyes met hers, it was as if they were trying to send a message he couldn't speak with his lips. He didn't look amused. He looked tortured.

She cleared her throat. "You know what I meant."

Theo straightened his shirt. "I'm not sure I do. I have plenty of needs, and I assure you, not all of them are sated."

Amalie's cheeks flushed. Heat flashed across her thighs, and she took a step back. "I only wondered why you wouldn't want this life."

"Because vampires are monsters. Your words." Theo blew a breath through his nose. "Or perhaps, like Ren, I'm sick of it."

Amalie watched, waiting for him to continue, but he didn't. He simply shrugged, then turned and plucked his discarded shirt from the bed post, then placed it in a basket next to the window. Amalie's fingernails dug into the soft underside of her arms.

Was he still playing a game? Pretending to be civilized so she'd let her guard down? She couldn't tell anymore. But suddenly she felt so tired, she wanted to collapse to the floor and close her eyes. She would have done it if she had any hope she'd wake from this nightmare. She'd already slept once and it hadn't changed a thing.

Theo poured himself a drink. "Some secrets are so dangerous, they're hidden even from ourselves."

His words swirled around her head like warmed fat on a skillet. Secrets? He had the audacity to bring up secrets? "If you didn't kill her, why were you there?" Amalie snapped.

The pit inside her grew wider. Every second she felt torn between her desire to help her friends, to protect those she loved, and her hunger for the truth about her mother's death. With everything Theo told her, both objectives seemed to knit into one.

Whoever killed her mother knew of the guardians. Finding the sword would allow her to take revenge and protect her family, but only if she knew who it was.

If she could find them. If she could discover the sword. If the sword worked as Theo expected.

It was too many 'ifs.'

Theo didn't ask her to clarify. "I told you, I don't know."

"Was it someone here?" She rounded the bed, scrutinizing his face.

"No. I don't believe so. I—"

"You knew her last name, *my* last name. You admitted you've been following my line. How could you not know?"

"Amalie—"

"Why did you choose me instead of her? Why couldn't my mother have found the relic for you? Or—" A thought struck her like a battering ram. "Did she try? Did you ask her to do this for you, and—" Amalie clapped a hand to her mouth. Had her mother been hunting for the sword and someone had killed her for it?

"Stop. I didn't ask her."

She glared at Theo through the tears welling in her eyes. "Why not? Her ancestors are the same as mine."

Theo growled in frustration. "I understand you want answers, but there are forces beyond my control—"

Amalie dropped her hand. "What forces!" She charged forward. "If you want my help, I need to know what I'm working against. Besides knowing the briefest history of this relic, you've given me nothing to go off of."

Theo crossed the room giving her a wide berth. "There's a reason for that."

She threw out her hands. "Please! I'm all ears."

"Go back to your room, Amalie." Theo turned to the window.

"I will not."

His form was black against the twilight beyond the glass as if drinking in the shadows from every corner of the room. Amalie felt like she was going to rip at the seams. She wished she was back on the rooftop because she would have no problem swinging the blade a second time.

She grabbed the glass from the table and hurled it at his head. He spun, snatching it out of the air. "You've decided to throw a tantrum?"

"You're treating me like a child. May as well act like one."

Theo's grip on the glass was so tight, she thought it might shatter. "Fine. It seems I'll have to throw you out."

Amalie held her ground. "Don't touch me."

"Then leave." His eyes were black, his lip curled.

And suddenly, Amalie wasn't standing next to Theo's

writing desk. She was in a dark room made of stone. A torch hanging on the wall. She wore a white cloth that was wrapped around her torso and draping over her sandaled feet.

Theo stood in front of her wearing a leather breast plate with a cloak over his shoulders. "Life would be easier for you if you followed the rules."

"I don't like Alain's rules."

Theo laughed, sweeping his cloak over his arm. "Well, unfortunately for you, I've been tasked with enforcing them."

The vision fractured, and Amalie stumbled back, knocking into Theo's writing desk and sending his glass bottles crashing to the floor. "I—you were there. I saw you in a different time—a different place."

A muscle in Theo's jaw flinched. "You need rest." He put out a hand and grasped her elbow.

Amalie yanked her arm away, but instead of ripping her arm free, she lost her balance and snapped against Theo like a cracked whip. His scent filled her nostrils. Jasmine. Citrus. And suddenly she remembered it. Not from the courtyard. Not even from her bedroom. From a place so deep in her soul, she couldn't sense the bottom.

"I know you." Speaking the words sent an ache thrumming through her, gripping her throat and searing her insides.

"You're mistaken."

Amalie's eyes snapped open and she reached up, catching his face in her hand and forcing him to look at her. "I'm not. Don't lie to me, Theo. Not about this." Theo's cold expression softened for a split second before he tried to pull back, but Amalie held tighter. "Why didn't you ask my mother to help you? Or my uncle, my aunt, someone else in my family line?"

He opened his mouth, then shut it again.

"Answer me!" Her voice was hoarse, her breath coming so fast, she was becoming faint.

"Because the ancestor I needed was *you*," he rasped. The room seemed to swirl around her. The tips of her fingers turned white. "You're a guardian, Amalie. Guardians are reborn."

The word pounded against her skull. *Reborn*. She couldn't make sense of it. What she was hearing, what she'd seen. She knew him. She'd been with him, somewhere. Hundreds, possibly thousands of years ago.

Theo didn't bend to comfort her, didn't wrap an arm around her shoulders. He stood there, stiff and cold, even as she dropped a hand to his chest. Felt the beating of his heart. Amalie squeezed her eyes shut as her world fractured into a million pieces. "You believe I was the one who took the sword." *Stolen*. That was the word he'd used.

Theo shook his head. "I don't believe anything. I saw it firsthand. You found it, Amalie. You were drawn to it."

"That's impossible."

"It's not."

Her eyes flew open. "I'm not a warrior."

Theo scoffed. "The stake to my heart begs to differ."

Amalie's eyes narrowed. "That was self preservation."

"Do you know how few humans and guardians alike are willing to fight to protect themselves? Since you seem to have forgotten every last scrap of the last two thousand years, let me give you the answer. Not many." He finally pulled away from her, and Amalie curled into herself.

Two thousand years. The numbers stamped themselves across her consciousness. Reborn. Warrior. She strode toward the door, a sob building in her throat.

"I tried to wait. To make this gentle for you."

"Don't say another word." Amalie hissed. He'd lied to her, they all had. Was this what Uncle Oren had planned to tell her on her birthday? That she'd lived before? That there were creatures who walked the earth who'd known her as . . . as what? A warrior?

Theo had known her. He'd seen it with his own eyes.

She grasped the handle and pulled, but the door didn't budge. Amalie yanked again, and that time she saw Theo's palm pressed against the wood.

"You need to listen—"

"I'm done listening for the moment," she whispered. "Let me out."

"Amalie—"

"You knew who I was. You'd been watching me since when? Since my birth? Plotting this moment? Wondering how old I'd need to be before you could use me?"

Theo shook his head. "No. I made a promise. I watched your family, made sure they were safe—"

"A promise to who?"

Theo's eyes darkened. "Amalie—"

"STOP SAYING MY NAME."

Theo pulled back as if she'd slapped him. He stared at her, unblinking. "Hate me. You can hate me. But don't doubt that what I'm telling you is the truth." He snatched his hand away from the door. "I didn't know it was you. Not at first. Not until I smelled your blood."

Amalie scoffed. "It was that recognizable?"

"Yes." Theo answered without hesitation. "I'd know it anywhere."

Her throat grew so thick, she thought she might asphyxiate. Amalie turned the door handle. "I'm leaving. Tonight."

"Do what you need to."

"You won't try and stop me?"

Theo's eyes were cold. "No. But I can't promise the other members of my coven won't."

Amalie's eyes shot to the window. Dark. The sun had set after they'd left the rooftop.

Everything she'd seen, everything she'd learned since Theo appeared in her bedroom seemed to ignite and turn to ash. Amalie threw the door open and fled from Theo's room with rage so hot and choking, she forgot all about the thread of light that grew inside her.

21

1824 BLOIS, FRANCE

Rachel pulled Florent closer, dragging the quilt higher to keep out the chill. It had been unseasonably cold the past few days, and her fingers and toes still ached from tilling the rows for tomato planting. But Florent always had a fire burning in Place Deaumont when he came to draw her from her room.

"Will it hurt?" she whispered.

Florent smiled against her cheek, dragging his lips along her skin as he traveled past her jaw. "I don't know what you should expect, but I don't believe so."

"But you've fed before." Rachel hated the word. Even though she'd accepted what Florent was, she didn't enjoy ruminating on what it meant. That Florent had killed. That the stories she'd heard about creatures dragging women and children into the shadows painted him as the monster.

"Of course, I have." His breath tickled her skin. "But never with someone like you." Rachel's pulse jumped in her throat, and Florent let out a low groan. "You smell like heaven."

"I thought you couldn't sense my blood?" she ran a finger down his throat and traced his collarbone, threading her bare leg with his.

"When I'm this close, I swear I can." Florent's voice hummed against her skin, and Rachel drew a breath.

She swallowed hard, and despite her willingness, her palms grew clammy. "You're positive this won't harm me?" She'd already asked the question, but she had to be sure. Florent had told her the stories about her bloodline. About the guardians who were created to complete the curse. Solène's answer to Le Sombre's dark plague on humanity.

That, of course, hadn't been enough to convince her. Amalie and Bethany depended on her—she was their only living parent. But then she'd asked Oren about her father's things and they'd finally opened the crates Oren had taken from their old house and stored in the attic for the past ten years. Oren had supported their parents in their old age, just as he was supporting her then. She'd never considered that there could be something of worth in their inherited belongings.

It was when she'd opened the book that Oren told her the truth.

Florent brushed a tendril of hair from her cheek. "It won't harm you. Your blood was made for my kind. But it might sting."

Rachel nodded. She didn't mind if it hurt. She wanted to do this, to give him every piece of her. Florent had already given her so much—new clothing for the girls, money to add to her savings each week as the summer drew to a close, and companionship and pleasure every night when the lamps were snuffed out. Since Romane had left her, she'd never been so blissfully happy. Though she didn't have much, she knew how much Florent desired this, and she would give it.

She pressed her fingers against the back of his head, urging him forward. Florent ran his tongue over her skin, and she shivered, then gasped at the flash of pain.

22

Somehow, Amalie slept. She dreamed of her mother. Of the two of them finding each other in different lives. Sometimes they were friends, sometimes family, and once she held her mother in her own arms as a baby. She woke in the darkness coated in sweat wearing the same clothes from the rooftop.

It took a moment for the events in Theo's room to connect themselves in her head. When they did, warmth spread through her chest. Her mother wasn't gone. Not forever. She couldn't have her now, but the thought that she existed somewhere was a salve on her broken heart.

The warmth was driven out as cold dread settled in her stomach.

Theo knew her.

He'd been with her in another life, possibly more than one if the flashes of memory in her head were to be believed. Had he been her captor in each? If Theo had seen her find the sword, why hadn't he used it then? He said it had been stolen, but wouldn't he have had time? Couldn't he have ended his life?

The questions flowed in a constant stream, and she had answers to none of them. Amalie hugged her knees to her chest. She'd left Uncle Oren's to avenge her mother's death, yes, but it wasn't only justice. She wanted to protect her family and all families like hers. Innocent people attacked every day in their cities and villages.

It had been simple. Train. Fight. Vanquish.

Amalie ran her thumb over the puckered flesh on her forearm. Nothing was simple anymore.

The door to her room opened, and Henriette entered carrying a tray and a candle. "Oh! You're awake. I was going to leave this for you—"

"I need more books." Amalie dropped her legs to the bed. "Specifically on France in the fifteenth century. Anything on a female warrior, a sword, or—"

"On Joan of Arc, then?"

Amalie frowned, then shook her head. "No, this woman wouldn't have been that impressive."

Henriette bobbed her head. "Of course. I'll find what I can." She left the tray on the nightstand, lit the candles hanging in their holders on the wall with her flame, and exited the room.

Amalie ate in silence, and by the time she finished, Henriette was already back carrying a stack of books.

She grunted as she set them down on the writing desk next to the others. "Some of these may not be relevant, but I thought it best to be thorough."

Amalie scooted off the bed. "Thank you, Henriette." She could hardly wait to crack open the first cover. Henriette quietly cleaned and removed her tray behind her. Amalie barely heard the click of the door as she left.

She scanned the sections of the first book, Vies des Saints et des Martyrs. It seemed to be a religious text recounting the lives of saints and martyrs, an inspirational work. She flipped to halfway through the book and paused. Joan of Arc. Martyred in 1431 and later canonized.

Amalie set the book down and grabbed the next. Le Traité de la Guerre et la Paix, a treaty on war and peace. While she was interested in the philosophies surrounding chivalry and governance during times of war, it wasn't likely that this tome held what she was after.

She opened book after book. The Annals of the House of Valois. The Fall of the Plantagenet Empire. All of them spoke of the war that raged through France for over a hundred years. All of them spoke of Joan.

There was nothing on another female warrior. Nothing on a woman named Helena or a sword. Amalie exhaled and closed the books, then stood and stretched her arms over her head. She stalked to the window and released the shutters, swinging them open so she could peer out into the lightening sky. There wasn't much of a drop to the roof below, and it wasn't angled. If she couldn't leave her room and wander the castle, perhaps she could at least get some fresh air.

The latches bit into her fingertips, but she eventually convinced the casements to release. The frame swung outward, ushering in a whoosh of sea air. Amalie closed her eyes as it brushed across her cheeks.

She pulled herself up onto the sill and carefully lowered her feet to the tiles, then stepped away from window and sat, taking in the scene below her. The tide was out, the sun barely burned on the horizon. The wet sand glistened in the orange light.

"You nearly have a library in there."

Amalie jolted, slamming her palms into the tile beneath her, and whipped her head in the direction of the voice.

Marx. He stood below her on a terrace. Even in the low light, she could make out the green in his eyes and instantly thought of her sister.

Amalie pushed up from the tile and turned to escape back into the safety of her room. Would it keep him out? Theo had proven a vampire could easily enter an upper floor window.

"I'm not going to hurt you, I promise." Marx chuckled. "What did Theo tell you to keep you so frightened?"

She shouldn't talk to him. But she hadn't seen him on the rooftop. She hadn't seen him anywhere with the other vampires. "Who are you?"

"I told you already."

Amalie crossed her arms over her chest, the wind picking up around her. "I know your name, but why are you never with the others?"

Marx grinned up at her. "You've noticed my absence?"

Amalie pursed her lips. Why had she noticed? Shouldn't she have been as afraid of Paul, Etienne, or Ren as she was of Marx? Yet there was something different about him. Something she couldn't place.

"Theo would not be pleased to know I'm speaking with you, if that's what you're wondering." Marx leaned on the stone wall in front of him. "Are you going to rat me out?"

"That depends."

Marx's eyes flicked back to the open window and the glow of candlelight. "What are you studying?"

Amalie's stomach tightened. "Botany." She wouldn't admit to him what she was after. Amalie found herself wishing Theo was there. Not so she could cling to him, but so she could gauge this man's place. Would he defer to Theo as Etienne had? Or tease him like Ren? Something told her Marx would do neither, and her skin prickled.

"You love plants."

"Of course. What woman doesn't?" she answered blandly.

Marx turned his attention back to her, and Amalie gripped the window sill.

"Don't you have your own humans to bother?" she asked.

Marx grinned. "Plenty. But when Theo brings one to his castle, I tend to put my plans on hold."

"Why do you care?"

Marx shrugged. "Call it a personal hobby." He pointed at the scarf still tied around her neck. "Do you always wear that to bed?"

"It's sentimental."

"Uncomfortable to sleep in though, wouldn't it be?"

Amalie shook her head. "It reminds me of my mother."

He blew a breath out of his nose. "Sweet. I'm not quite sure I believe it, though."

Amalie's hand tightened on the wood. "It doesn't make much difference to me what you believe."

Marx straightened, trailing his hand over the stone railing. "Has he fed yet?"

"I don't know what—"

"Don't play dumb with me. I heard about your escapades on the roof. You know what we are. So has Theo fed since he brought you back?"

Amalie's cheeks flushed. "Not on me. Obviously."

Marx's grin widened. "Obviously." He ran a hand through his hair even though the wind threw it back around his face within seconds. "Nearly three days. He must be aching with thirst."

Amalie's stomach turned. Had he killed while she'd been

there? Was that where he went during the day? Did he leave to hunt and then come back to the castle?

Marx turned and walked a few paces before turning back. "Those books aren't on plants. If you struggle to read, I can help." He held her gaze for one last moment, then disappeared into the shadows.

23

Amalie closed the windows and the shutters with shaking hands. How had he found her a second time? Had he been watching or did she have terrible luck?

She slumped against the wall and pressed a hand to her chest when a knock sounded at the door. Henriette knew she was awake. She probably wanted to give her privacy. "Yes, come in."

A woman's tinkling laugh lifted in the hall. "I'd love to, but Theo keeps the door locked."

Amalie bristled. Who would be coming to her door at this hour? "Who is it?"

"Are you trapped in there like a scared little mouse?"

Amalie pushed off the wall. Theo was next door, wasn't he? If someone tried to attack her in such close proximity, he'd hear her screams. Hopefully before she bled out. Regardless, her curiosity got the better of her.

She strode to the door and flung it open to find Clémentine on the other side.

"Not a scared little mouse." Clémentine smoothed the fabric clinging to her hips. She wore a black gown with straps like string over her shoulders and a deep "V" revealing the swell of her breasts. Her skin was creamy white and so smooth it looked like velvet. "Breakfast in the hall. Interested?"

This was what vampires wore to breakfast? Amalie's stomach grumbled despite eating what Henriette brought for her, then twisted as she parsed out Clémentine's meaning. Why would a vampire be inviting her to a meal?

Has he fed yet?

Amalie shivered. "I'm exhausted."

"I can see that." Clémentine put out a hand and her manicured nails scraped her skin as they tipped Amalie's chin up. "Low blood sugar. Iron deficient. Your skin is sallow."

Amalie flinched and pulled away. "I'm fine." The assessment felt oddly personal, even though she was sure it was automatic. It was the same as her inspecting an apple.

Clémentine gave her a look, then pointed down the hall. "Lie to me and yourself if you want. I know better than you what your body needs." She turned and took a few steps, then looked back over her shoulder. "I've never seen any human challenge our males like you did on the roof. I don't think I've ever been so aroused."

Amalie's mouth fell open, making Clémentine grin wider. She quickly recovered. "Shouldn't you be sleeping? I didn't think your kind was interested in daylight."

Clémentine stretched her arms like a cat. "Last night was raucous. I'm barely winding down."

A party? Was that why Marx was out on the rooftop?

Clémentine spun and strode past Amalie, lifting her hand and rapping on Theo's door. "Theo, darling, if you think this charade will absolve you, you're fooling yourself!" She sighed, tossing her sleek hair over her shoulder. "It happens to all of us. We get this idea in our head that we *could* change things. Be something we're not. It's a *stage*. His is just lasting longer than most."

What charade? Theo hadn't wanted to participate in Ren's challenge any more than she had. Looking in Clémentine's eyes, Amalie realized that wasn't the show she was referring to. Amalie was still there in the castle. Alive.

A chill swept down Amalie's spine. "Will the other humans be at breakfast?"

Clémentine shrugged, then stalked closer and leaned in. "Can you give him a message for me? Tell Theo that if you're only interested in pain, I can provide plenty of pleasure." She brushed her lips over Amalie's cheek, then hissed a breath through her teeth. "I've always been excellent at sharing."

Amalie's lungs burned as Clémentine turned and swayed down the hall.

The vampire lifted a slender arm into the air. "Don't worry, doll. He'll be thirsty soon enough! Then you'll get plenty of attention."

She needed air. Not the window. Where could she go without risking discovery? Without risking her life?

The castle walls seemed to draw closer, squeezing the air from the hallway. Amalie vaguely realized that her mind wasn't functioning properly as she retraced her steps to the staircase and climbed to the roof. She knew it wasn't safe, but in that moment, she simply didn't care.

Let them discover her blood. Let them consume her, possess her. At least then she wouldn't have to keep fighting *everything*.

As soon as the cool night air hit her face, she gulped it in and dropped to sit on the cool stone. She stared up at the last twinkling stars and the sliver of pale moon, buried in thoughts that layered through her mind like laminated dough. She couldn't pull one from the next without making a mess of the whole of it.

Vampires were evil. They were darkness. She pulled the words out and stretched them like toffee. What she'd seen since leaving Marcel and Olivie blurred the edges of her belief. Just as she'd slammed the stake down on Uncle Oren's desk, Theo had opened her eyes to a cold reality she wished she could forget like everything else in her history.

Vampires were prisoners. They were bound to their fate. Her blood had been created to meet their curse, to prevent human suffering.

And where had her people gone? Where were they now?

Those questions tilted her world on its axis, and the ground was still shifting beneath her.

Vampires were evil, and yet it was her bloodline who'd disappeared and allowed them to begin feeding on humans again. It was her own family that hid the truth of their past, who'd opted to live in shadow. *Why?*

A breeze whispered over her cheeks, making her skin prickle as the door to the stairs pushed outward. Amalie pushed to her feet, ready to bolt, but it was Theo who stepped onto the roof. He walked out into the sunlight, his eyes locking onto hers.

"Save your breath. I know. It's not safe for me to be wandering alone." Amalie had meant it to be a dig, but she was too tired to put any force behind her words.

"I thought it would take you longer." Theo's voice was soft. He lowered his head and crossed the roof to stand along the wall, far enough from her she still couldn't make out his face.

"For what?"

"To lose hope."

Amalie tensed. "I haven't lost hope."

"And yet you sit up here as a willing sacrifice."

She ground her teeth. "I only needed air."

Theo huffed a laugh and scrubbed his hand over his jaw. "I didn't plan it this way."

"What was your plan, then? How did you intend to lightly break it to me that my entire life has been a lie?"

Theo's face was a mask. "I didn't want it to hurt. I doubt there's much I can say to convince you of my intentions."

"Considering you stabbed your fangs into my neck, that's true enough." Amalie turned to rest her arms on the wall, allowing the morning sun to kiss her cheeks.

Theo stepped up next to her, and Amalie's nerves stood at attention. His scent was intoxicating in the sunlight. A swirl of toasted bread and lemon jam.

"I'd like to try."

Amalie blinked. It took her a minute to remember what they'd been talking about. When she did, she nearly laughed out loud, then bit the inside of her cheek. None of this was remotely funny, but the fact that Theo was working to change his image was almost ridiculous enough to be a joke.

Theo ran his hand over the stone, and the sound made her shiver. "I told you vampires hunt your blood. It's been like that since the beginning. Guardian blood is most desirable, and since your kind went underground, vampires have longed for it. When I had proof it existed, I needed to keep it safe. I knew what would happen if your secret got out."

When I knew it existed. Amalie's chest tightened. *It.* That's all she was to them. A resource they wanted to deplete. It shouldn't have hurt, but it did.

The flashes she'd seen in her mind's eye showed that she'd been a captive before. Was that why guardians left? Were they sick of being kept like birds in cages?

Amalie wanted to dig into *how* exactly Theo knew she existed. He said he'd scented her blood, but he'd been watching before then. Waiting. Had the death of her mother been the cost of that discovery?

It was then that a thought hit her like the gong of a church bell.

"She couldn't die." Amalie spun to Theo, wincing at the rising sun. "If you bit her and fed, she wouldn't have died because she has guardian blood." But she'd seen her mother's lifeless body. She'd pressed her fingers to her colorless cheeks.

"She couldn't have died by feeding alone."

"Then how?"

Theo's face hardened as he watched the sea. "I don't have the answers you seek."

He was there. He'd been there as her mother died. He had to know something. "Why are you doing this? Why when I ask questions do you close off? Have I not shown that I'm working to find this relic? Have I not proven—"

"There's nothing to prove." Theo pushed back from the wall and motioned to the door leading to the stairs.

Amalie glared at him, her whole body beginning to shake. She'd seen him there—memorized the planes of his face. How could he say that this was the end of it? "I saw you there when she died. Did you know her? Did you meet with her at night? My uncle said she was breaking the rules, and I need to know—"

"I made sure you were safe. I made a promise, and I fulfilled it to the best of my ability."

"She wasn't safe!" Amalie growled in frustration, turning away from him and blinking back tears. She'd lost her mother when she was barely old enough to remember her. Theo had watched her. Had seen her going about her daily life while Amalie had been distracted by childhood.

Her death was a tragedy. Her mother had been happy. She'd laughed and played with them in the stream that summer. She'd worked in the gardens and sat with them at the dinner table. She'd saved enough money for them to start fresh in the city after harvest, and . . .

She was in love.

Rachel had plucked flowers from the garden one evening after Amalie and Bethany helped pick blackberries. Amalie's arms stung where thorns scratched her skin as she'd reached between the canes for the berries, but she hadn't wanted to interrupt her mother's humming. That night, as Amalie and Bethany were tucked into bed, her mother whispered, *"There's someone I want you two to meet. This Sunday. At sunset by the water. Something to look forward to."* Then she'd kissed them on the cheek.

Her mother died that Sunday afternoon.

At the edge of the woods.

Uncle Oren's words came back to her. *She didn't keep the rules. She went out after dark and spoke to a man she did not know.*

A lump formed in Amalie's throat. She needed to be crystal clear. "The man my mother spoke to after dark. Was it you?" Something pinched deep in her gut.

"No." Theo's voice was close. She turned, and found him there in front of her. His fingers brushed her elbow, then disappeared as quickly as they'd come. "I wasn't there watching. I couldn't be."

"Why not?"

Theo's eyes turned cold again, hardening like stone. "The more I pay attention to things, the more other vampires pay attention to things."

"Is that true of all vampires? Or only you?" she asked. Theo didn't answer. "Why do they pay attention to you?"

Again, he remained silent. Amalie pressed a finger into his chest. "The only reason I can think of for you to clam up when I ask these questions is that there's something you're hiding. I just can't figure out what."

"You'll have to inform me when you come to it."

Anger flared in her chest. "Perhaps you didn't kill my mother like you say, but I saw her blood on your hands. Maybe you're only opportunistic."

Theo's jaw twitched. "I was there because I smelled her blood. Because my throat burned and I was driven mad, is that what you want to hear?"

Amalie's mouth grew dry. "If it's the truth."

"You've already decided what the truth is. So *you* tell me why I was there. You tell me why I can't go anywhere without someone watching. Please, Amalie, tell me why I waited forty years to have the pleasure of arguing with you at sunrise. It will be much faster and easier that way."

"Only forty? That's like a split second for you," she snapped, but her mind was spinning. *Theo had waited for her?* She suddenly recalled the first flash she'd seen of him. His hands had been on her waist. His lips—

Amalie straightened even though her body still felt like it was being dragged down by anchors. "I'm so sick of arguing with you, I could scream."

Theo turned his head. "Then do it."

"I'm too tired."

He huffed a breath. "Hungry, too?"

Amalie pursed her lips. "I'll survive."

"I believe you were invited to breakfast."

She planted a smile on her face. "Everything I've ever dreamed of. Cracking into an egg in a sea of vampires telling me 'don't worry, doll. He'll be thirsty soon enough.'"

Theo laughed out loud. "Is that what she said?"

"Word for word."

He shook his head and ran a hand through his hair.

Amalie hadn't meant to gawk, but she didn't catch herself in time. Even leaning over, he was a head taller than she was. It gave her a perfect view of his mouth.

Theo blew out a breath. "Breakfast would most likely be vegetarian."

Amalie blinked. "You're joking."

His laugh was rich and low. "We can't eat like humans, but Etienne enjoys cooking like them. Especially when there's company."

Despite the sun on her cheeks, Amalie felt cold. Were the others still alive? She drew a breath and steadied herself with a hand on the wall. She needed to lie down. Needed to sleep.

Theo gripped her shoulders, and Amalie felt a jolt of energy run from her head to her toes. He spun her toward the door.

She tried to pull away, her muscles didn't obey. His hands were gentle as he led her to the stairs. At least he wasn't picking her up again. It was a small win, and she was going to take it.

By the time they reached their quarters, Amalie was barely able to walk on her own. "I still hate you." Amalie stifled a yawn as Theo stopped in front of her door.

"I know."

"The fact that you allowed me to kill you doesn't change that."

"Very aware." Theo dropped his arm, and Amalie reached for the knob. She turned it, then noticed that Theo was heading in the opposite direction of his room, his hands shoved deep in his pockets.

"You're not sleeping?"

He slowed, then stopped, turning back. In less garish lighting, the circles under his eyes were more obvious. He looked exhausted. He—

Amalie froze. *Has he fed yet?* "Where are you going, Theo?"

Theo scrubbed a hand over his jaw. "I'll come for you when—"

"Theo, stop." Her pulse quickened. "Wherever you're going. Don't." She didn't know how often vampires had to feed, but he'd been there at the castle for at least twenty-four hours, and she'd seen his blood on the stone. His body had been through enough to hasten the process.

She hated where her head was going, but she couldn't stop it. The idea of her allowing any other human to be attacked—to die. It was unthinkable.

"Drink from me," she said in a rush, and Theo stilled. "If you drink from anyone else—"

Theo blurred and appeared in front of her, his finger on her lips. He shook his head slowly, then glanced down the hall and pulled her into his room.

24

"I'm sorry," she whispered as Theo stepped back to lock the handle. "I wasn't thinking."

Theo pinched the bridge of his nose. "You don't seem to grasp—"

"I do. I grasp it. The danger you've talked about."

"And yet I found you in the parlor. I found you alone on the roof."

Amalie swallowed hard. She didn't need to mention the meeting with Marx outside her window. "I said I was sorry."

Her hands were shaking. In the hall she'd blurted out those words, but now that Theo was there in front of her, she wasn't sure she'd been thinking clearly.

Her blood hummed under her skin. She knew what it felt like when his fangs pierced her skin. When his body was pressed up against her.

It was his glamour. What she'd offered was purely rational. Theo needed to feed. They'd already established that he could drink her blood without harming her, so how could she allow him to prey on another person? How could she allow another human to die when it would cost her nothing? It didn't matter how much she hated him. She could endure anything to save a life, couldn't she?

Theo met her eyes, his hands resting on his hips. His eyes flicked to her throat, and Amalie's skin tingled. She was instantly back in her bedroom, frozen as his fingers moved her hair from her cheek, as his lips brushed her skin, and all justifications dissolved behind a flare of carnal curiosity.

I didn't drink. What would it feel like if he did? She clenched her jaw at the slow ache of longing. The sudden pang of desire.

An image of him hunting in the shadows, of choosing his prey, flashed through her head, and Amalie felt something primal rear its head. The idea of his mouth on someone else's neck sent a flash of ice down her spine.

Shame swirled in her gut. This was practical. A kindness. *She didn't want this.*

"I can't be gentle. You need to be sure." Theo's eyes locked onto hers. *Had her thoughts been written all over her face?* There was hunger in his eyes. Desperation.

She could turn back. Retract her offer. Instead, Amalie nodded toward the door to the hall. "Is it safe here?"

"Follow me." He strode across the room and opened a narrow door.

Blood rushed to her middle as Amalie slipped inside. Once she'd snuck into the back room of the abbey with Oliver Bland when they were supposed to be polishing the columns of the chapel. He'd shoved his hands up her shirt, and she finally worked up the courage to slip her tongue into his mouth. When he flipped her skirt over her hips, she thought she'd die from the ache between her thighs.

That had been nothing.

Her thoughts scattered like seeds in the wind as darkness enveloped her. Amalie threw up her hands as her head knocked against the wooden hangers hooked to a solid beam stretching from one side of the closet to the other.

Theo pushed them to the side and moved in next to her, closing the door behind him. They were plunged into complete darkness, and Amalie stilled as Theo's arm grazed her shoulder. She worked to steady her breath.

This was smart. Practical.

"We're behind two heavy doors. I don't think it would be possible for anyone to catch the scent of you unless we made a mess of it," Theo whispered.

Her eyes nearly rolled back in her head from his voice as it rumbled through her skin, her muscles, and bones. "Mmhmm." It came out more like a whimper than a response. Theo reached out a hand, and his fingers brushed her forearm, then moved up to wrap over her shoulder.

Amalie cleared her throat. "Just do it. You don't have to ease me into this."

Theo's hand froze. "No woman has ever uttered those words."

Jealousy flared within her. He'd been alive for two thousand years. *Why did it matter?* Why did she care if he was thinking of the endless throng of women he'd used in the past? "You had no problem before," she snapped.

Theo grunted. "This won't only be a bite."

His hand shifted, sending a pulse of energy down her arm. The rest of her body might as well have faded from existence. She couldn't feel anything besides his fingers wrapping over her shoulder. "You said you couldn't be gentle. Have you changed your mind?"

"Stop talking, please." Theo's lips grazed her temple, and Amalie had no trouble shutting her mouth. She was on fire. Her heart pounded in her chest, loud enough she was sure Theo could hear it.

Hate him. She needed to—

His fingers traced a feather-light path down her neck. "Leaving a mark here will be too conspicuous. Other vampires will notice," he murmured, his breath hot against her skin.

"They didn't notice earlier."

"You're nearly healed, and this time there may be bruising. Do you prefer wearing a scarf for another week?" Theo brushed her hair back from her cheek. Since the moment they'd stepped into the closet, his hands hadn't left her skin.

He was doing research. Hunting for a strong pulse. It wasn't that he wanted to touch her.

Still, Amalie couldn't control her quick breaths or flushed cheeks. She'd checked the mark on her neck earlier. It was healing well. She'd always recovered quickly. Now she understood why.

"What are you suggesting?" Her voice was hoarse.

Theo's breath stuttered, his hand still resting over her collarbone. He swallowed hard. "There are other options for strong blood flow." His fingers slid under the edge of her blouse, pulling it over her shoulder. He slid two fingers under her arm. "Here. Still visible depending on the situation, or . . ." He cleared his throat. "The inner thigh. Much less noticeable."

Amalie's skin tingled. *This was practical, nothing more.* It was wise to hide the marks, especially in a place filled with vampires who would notice if she was still walking around the castle after Theo fed.

Her arm would suffice. But the thought of lowering her trousers. Of watching him drop to his knees. Of feeling his hands on her knees as her leg butterflied away from her. Of feeling his hot breath against her sensitive skin.

She *was* curious. *About so many things.*

"Arm," she rasped. "I've never had a dressing maid and I

don't plan on stripping down in front of your friends. Nobody will see it."

Theo's fingers trembled as Amalie pulled up the fabric of her shirt, exposing the bare skin of her stomach and her bralette. *Maybe she should've been willing to wear a corset.* It was dark enough, even as her eyes adjusted, she couldn't even make out a vague silhouette of Theo's head.

That meant he couldn't see anything either. A slight pang of disappointment hit her gut.

She pulled one arm out of its sleeve, offering it to him. Amalie held her breath as he ran slow fingers over the tender flesh of her underarm.

Then his other hand was on her hip, pressing her back against the closet wall. "This may help. To steady yourself."

She leaned her head back, her pulse fluttering wildly at her throat. "If I fall—"

"You won't fall." Theo's hand still clasped her hip, and his chest pressed up against her as he lifted her arm over her head. She forced her lungs to expand, willing her heart to settle.

Could he feel this?

Theo's hand settled on the crook of her elbow as he dropped his head. Of course he could. Her face grew hot. She closed her eyes as her pulse grew frantic.

"It's been so long," Theo whispered against her skin, so soft she wasn't sure she'd heard the words.

Then his grip tightened, his whole body tensed, and something flared within her. A sharp burst that flashed behind her eyes. She sucked air through her teeth and grasped his upper arm with her opposite hand as Theo's fangs broke her flesh.

25

She drew a shuddering breath as she clung to him, the sting quickly fading into a flood of warmth. The world seemed to flip on its head as raw heat rolled through her like honey.

Theo was everywhere. Pressed against every inch of her body, caging her in as he drank. Amalie's eyes fluttered closed, a soft moan escaping her lips as Theo pulled blood from her veins. This wasn't pain. It wasn't gentle, but it *wasn't pain*. It was a heady rush that buried all rational thought.

She was color and light. Warmth and ache.

Theo pressed her harder into the wall, his fangs piercing deeper. She wanted to cry out, but clamped her mouth shut.

Amalie teetered on the brink of madness as images flickered to life. Memories? Fantasy? She couldn't tell the difference. She saw her eyes on a different face. Theo's eyes, so close she found flecks of gold hidden in their depths.

There it was again.

That buzz of warmth. The shimmering thread of light tied to her spine. It seemed to grow taught and stretch out into the world. And then shadow moved through her like ink spilled on a manuscript. She forced herself to breathe as her knees went weak, and Theo tightened his grip on her waist. Her head tilted back as she lost all sense of grounding. Pictures formed with more intensity, more focus—

"Amalie!" The sharpness of her mother's voice broke through the haze, and Amalie froze against the heavy wooden door. It was a small sanctuary tucked within the north turret, its tall windows framed by ivy and overlooking the sprawling gardens below. Amalie hadn't dared sneak in before, though she was regularly drawn there. That day, she'd battled her curiosity and lost.

Inside, the air felt different. Dust motes danced in shafts of sunlight. Books were piled on shelves, their leather spines cracked and faded. A heavy oak table dominated the center, cluttered with odd trinkets.

There, her mother hunched over an ancient tome, her expression stern. "What have I told you about following me up those stairs?"

Amalie's cheeks heated. "I can climb them now."

Her mother raised an eyebrow. "I can see that."

"Can I read with you?" Amalie asked, taking a step inside, heart racing.

Her mother sighed, then beckoned for her to sit on the stool next to her. Amalie ran forward, nearly knocking into the corner of the table. Her mother grabbed her waist, lifting her, and Amalie immediately began to scan the pages in front of them.

"What is that?" She pointed at a man with long, pointed teeth.

"Silly stories. Isn't he strange looking?"

Amalie giggled. "Yes." She wanted to impress her mother with her maturity, though the picture made her pulse quicken. "A little scary," she admitted.

Her mother nodded, pulling a jewelry box toward her and

allowing her to peek inside. "That's why I study here. Some things aren't meant for your eyes and ears."

Amalie played with a locket on the end of a chain, trying to figure out how to open it. "What if the silly stories are real?"

Her mother tsked. "We mustn't let fear take root." She leaned over the table, pointing at the necklace. "That will be yours some-day." Amalie's eyes lit up. "It was my mother's once . . ."

The room shifted and she was standing in a wood. Ancient trees stretched around her as she crouched, readying herself.

"You're not protecting yourself," a man growled, and she landed hard in the dirt. Her feet swept out from under her.

Amalie scrambled back up, assuming a defensive position. "You can't use your advantage," she hissed.

With a flash of smoke, the man appeared in front of her. "Do you think you'll be fighting humans?" Theo's eyes drilled into her. "If you'd start taking my advice, you'd be able to see it coming."

"It's impossible."

Theo rolled his eyes. "Go again."

The memory blurred at the sensation of a sharp sting, and Amalie dropped back into herself. She drew a ragged breath.

Theo's mouth was no longer touching her arm. Instead, there was pressure. His hand still circled her waist, but he wasn't so close, and she felt the loss of him. Euphoria danced in her chest, igniting every nerve ending like wildfire. She was both alive, electric, and seconds away from collapse.

"How do you feel?" Theo's voice hummed against her temple.

Amalie swallowed. She wanted to tilt her chin. Press her lips to his jaw . . . *She wasn't in her right mind.* "A little weak."

Theo was still. "To be expected."

"What is it like for you?" The words spilled from her lips before she could filter them.

"Feeding?"

She nodded, still clinging to him. Theo dropped his hand from her waist and stepped back, still pressing something against her arm.

"Much like how it feels for you to eat a meal, I expect."

Amalie's heart dropped. A moment later, lamp light streamed in through the open closet door. Amalie winced, blinking until her eyes adjusted.

Theo checked the cloth he held to her arm. Was it one of his shirts? Amalie couldn't tell. When he was satisfied, he retreated into the room.

Cool air rushed against her, and she shivered. Her shirt was still pooled against her neck, and she quickly pulled it down, returning her arm to its sleeve. She felt strange. Different. That ball of light and warmth she'd felt before swelled.

Theo didn't look at her as she exited the closet. When he finally turned, his eyes slid away from hers. "I'll take you back."

The words stung more than his bite. "Is it safe?"

He nodded once and stalked to the door. She followed, then stopped as Theo reached for the door handle.

Amalie pursed her lips. "You could say thank you."

He pulled and the door swung open. "You offered."

Her eyes flashed, shame burning hot in her throat. "That doesn't mean you can't show gratitude."

His jaw worked. "Thank you."

The light inside her dulled, and her cheeks stained pink. "You're so very welcome."

Amalie swept out into the hall, walking straight to her

room. She shouldn't have allowed herself to be vulnerable, even inside her own head. Theo Vallon was a vain, selfish bastard, and no amount of compassion on her part was going to change his nature.

She stormed into her room, breathless, and closed the door behind her. Leaning against the cool wood, she pressed her palms to her temples. Images of her mother still danced in her head. The image of Theo in the woods. The feel of him against her . . .

She wanted to scream.

She wanted to weep.

"Fool," she muttered under her breath, heart racing as she pulled off her shirt, lifted her arm, and stared at the two new perfect marks on her skin.

26

Rachel curled into Florent's chest, her fingers tracing circles over the palm of his hand as they sat in the hollow of their tree by the river. "Do you have friends?"

"Of course, I have friends."

She grinned. "Vampire friends."

"Yes." He kissed the top of her forehead.

"Will I get to meet them?"

Florent blew a breath out of his nose. Rachel knew what that meant. He was always so cautious, so worried about how other people would react to him. But she knew of vampires. Her parents had been relentless in their teaching, and recently she'd learned the reason why.

Even after Oren had told her the truth, they'd still decided to protect their own children from it while they were young. There was no need to terrify them, especially when they were never far from their parents.

Now that she'd met Florent, she wondered about that decision. Had they been wrong? Rachel still had so many questions, none of which she'd get the answers to now that their parents were gone. Where were the other guardians? Why had they decided to go underground?

Her relationship with Florent was proof that guardians and vampires could live side by side. Their blood had the power to save humankind—to keep vampires from feeding. It seemed selfish to keep masking it.

"I'm going to talk to Oren."

Florent stiffened under her. "I don't think that's a good idea."

Rachel pushed up to look at him, her hair falling like curtains around her face. "I can't live the rest of my life sneaking around in the shadows, Florent. I want to be part- ners. Equals."

"Your family won't accept me."

She exhaled, dropping back to his chest. "I don't under- stand. You won't allow me to introduce you as human, but I'm not allowed to be honest either?"

"Your brother would figure it out."

"I didn't!"

"You weren't looking for it."

That was probably true. She'd been so enamored of him, she hadn't thought to question much. She was lucky it had turned out as well as it had, considering.

"My girls are only going to get older. They're going to stay up later. They'll notice if I'm always slipping in and out without a good explanation."

Florent brushed his hand up and down the side of her arm. "Then let's find a good explanation."

27

Amalie's fingers trembled as the cool water hit her face. After tossing and turning for most of the day, she finally opened the shutters. The afternoon light filtering through her window had been a welcome reprieve. She'd taken a cold bath, not calling for Henriette, and pulled a coarse linen towel from the shelf, pressing it to her cheeks.

She glared at the far wall, the knot in her stomach tightening. How dare he discard her like a used handkerchief? Amalie dropped the towel. It wasn't anything new, though, was it? Men were always interested until they got what they wanted. That was why she tried to steer clear of them as of late.

Her stomach growled as she ran her fingers through her hair, pulling it back into a tight braid. She'd given him her blood, and now her body was starved. She would have to wait for Henriette since traipsing around the castle wasn't an option. She doubted Clémentine would be waiting outside her door with another offer. She hoped she wouldn't be.

What had Clémentine meant about offering pleasure? Did vampires . . . couple? She'd always assumed they were only interested in humans, but Theo had only touched her out of necessity.

The other humans assumed she'd slept with him. The thought of them doing such things with their minds addled made her want to vomit.

Amalie stared at her face in the mirror. She looked well. Normal. Pink cheeks and an even complexion. Not like a vampire had feasted on her the night before. *Hopefully.*

Heat pooled below her belly button thinking of his breath against her cheek in the dark, and she gritted her teeth. The memories were so visceral. She groaned and turned from the mirror.

She hated Theo Vallon. She needed to discover how to vanquish him and his kind, which meant she could not give in to this sick curiosity for one second longer.

But would it hurt anything? It wasn't as if she *would* develop feelings for him. She was only experimenting. Gathering information. As long as she wasn't wasting time . . .

No. Exploring anything with Theo was a terrible idea. She would only allow him to feed when it was necessary. To protect the people unlucky enough to live beyond the castle walls.

With a deep breath, Amalie gathered her long, dark hair back from her face and tied it up with the swan fabric tie since she no longer needed it for her neck. She needed food, something substantial, to regain her strength, and she was *not* going to go begging Theo to help her.

If she stood in her doorway, she could hopefully catch Henriette as she passed, and it would be easy enough to close the door if she needed to. Amalie crossed the room and turned the knob. She hadn't even pulled when the door swung open, and Amalie yelped, jumping back.

Theo lay sprawled out on the floor, his head now inside her room. He bolted up, his eyes blinking and his hair tousled.

For a moment, Amalie stood frozen, trying to make sense of it. Why was Theo sleeping against her door? Was he guarding her? Trying to force her into compliance? She clenched her jaw at the surge of annoyance in her chest, the echo of his snide farewell the night before still lingered in her ears.

"Afternoon." He cleared his throat.

"What are you doing here?"

He blinked, and his dark lashes splayed over his cheek. "I could ask you the same thing."

"I was looking for Henriette."

He assessed her. "Why?"

Her grip tightened on the door knob. "To find food."

"I can help you with that." Theo ran a hand over his face, and as he turned, Amalie's breath caught. He was practically glowing in the morning light filtering through the glass at the end of the hall. He looked vibrant. Fresh.

Because of her blood.

"I don't need your help. I can wait for Henriette."

"Henriette isn't here today."

Amalie's stomach plummeted. "Theo, if she—"

"She's with her family. It's her day off."

Amalie swallowed, wetting her lips. "Oh. Good."

Theo motioned for her to walk with him down the hall. She closed the door and followed. At the end of the hall she turned left, and Theo snagged her elbow.

"Wrong way."

She yanked her arm back. "Don't touch me."

"Don't turn the wrong way."

She glared at him, only realizing then that they'd both stopped. "Please. Lead me, oh great one."

The corner of his mouth turned up. "That's more like it. Someone told me recently that gratitude was a virtue—"

Amalie growled in exasperation. "You're a bastard."

"*Vain* bastard. Don't forget the qualifier." He led them down another hall, then through a door that opened to a descending spiral staircase.

Amalie kept her mouth shut. She had nothing else to say to him. She would get her food, then escape to her room and figure out what in the world she was going to do next. *Theo still wouldn't let her in on something.*

That knowledge made her insides squirm. It had to be something terrible. Something that would change her mind, and since he already knew she hated him, she couldn't imagine how anything he told her could make things worse.

But the whispers wouldn't stop. It was the feeling of hairs lifting on the back of her neck. Like the buzz in the air before a storm.

Something was there. She'd been collecting slivers of information the best she could. Flashes of memories. The threads she felt ebbing and waning within her. By the way he soured whenever it was brought up, his secrets had something to do with his promise.

"This way." Theo led her past the parlor and down the steps. The rounded walls of the stairwell encircled them, and she tried to focus on anything other than Theo's proximity. She counted the number of stones under her feet, analyzed the fading tapestries as they passed.

When they reached the bottom, Amalie glanced back and caught a glimpse of the library she'd been searching for the other day.

The castle halls glowed golden as they walked, rays of sunlight filtering through the high arched windows. Theo led her through an arched door and down a second, smaller spiral staircase. As they entered the kitchen below the main floor, she gaped at the high vaulted ceilings. There were dried herbs hanging with copper pots and pans. A gorgeous brick oven and iron stove.

Theo walked straight to the pantry. He pulled open the cover to reveal loaves of baguette that were fresh, no doubt. Delivered discreetly for their human guests. Amalie nearly scoffed at the word. Humans here were like fatling calves. Given their last supper before heading to the chopping block.

There were cheeses wrapped in cloth, fruits preserved in jars, and a hanging rack holding cured meats that swayed lightly at his touch.

Amalie pursed her lips. "How many humans do you and your friends plan to kill this week?"

"Depends on how perturbing they are."

Amalie rolled her eyes and picked up an apple, inspecting its glossy red surface for blemishes. She remembered Clémentine's assessing gaze. Theo prodding her for a pulse.

Amalie's mouth went dry. "It's a well-stocked pantry. For creatures who don't eat."

"Occasionally we do entertain humans." Theo said. "And not always for feeding."

"Comforting." Amalie squeezed the closest baguette, then tore off a piece. The bread's interior was pillowy and soft against her calloused fingertips. She selected a jar of confiture, its lid adorned with faded cloth, and pried it open to reveal the deep purple preserves nestled within. Lastly, she grabbed a hunk of cheese. She set her makeshift feast on the butcher block, and set to work.

She sliced into the creamy cheese with a knife, spreading it over the torn end of the baguette before adding a dollop of tart preserve. She didn't waste time admiring her work. Amalie took a bite and closed her eyes as flavors danced across her tongue.

It took her a few seconds to remember she wasn't alone. She glanced up at Theo who was leaning against the counter, watching her. "What?"

He crossed his arms over his chest. "Nothing."

His attention made the hairs stand up on her arms. Choosing to ignore him, she spread the jam on the bread with a spoon she found in the drawer next to her, then stacked the cheese and took a bite. She sighed as the tart sweetness melded with the earthy flavors of Camembert.

"Good?" Theo asked.

Amalie sighed in response. She hadn't realized how hungry she was, and while she didn't want to look like an absolute hog, she was already deciding to go back for seconds even before she finished the first chunk of baguette.

Her eyes flicked up. Theo's expression was unreadable. "Do you miss it?" she asked, swallowing. Before he could answer, she shook her head. "You probably don't remember."

"No, actually. That I do think about."

Amalie tore off another bite-sized piece of bread. "Can you still try it? Even if it won't . . . I don't know, digest?"

Theo shrugged. "I could. If I enjoyed chewing ash."

She spread the jam. "You can't taste anything?"

Theo's lips twitched. "I can taste plenty of things. Just not food."

Amalie's cheeks heated. He hadn't said words that should make her blush, but the way he said it . . .

"You drink. In your room."

His tongue flicked over his lips. "Absinthe. It has no flavor, but it stings."

"And you like that?"

"Sometimes." His voice was steady, casual, but there was a

physical shift in the energy in the room. He watched her, his hands going still.

She wet her lips. "What are you looking at?"

He exhaled. "You've always done that."

"Done what?"

He motioned to her eyes. "That squint. Where your right eye gets a little smaller than the left. You do it when you're ready to go to battle."

Amalie dropped her eyes to the baguette. *You've always done that.* She wanted to ask since when? But the words died on her tongue. He wouldn't answer her, and that would hurt more than pretending not to care.

The air in the kitchen felt thicker than the preserves in front of her. Amalie struggled to expand her lungs. *He knew things about her.*

"Theo!" The kitchen door swung open, and Amalie froze.

Ren wore dark pants with leather boots that laced up his calves. He swept his hair back from his forehead before setting eyes on the two of them. "Well, well. Hope we're not interrupting." His lips curled. "Amalie, what a pleasure. With Theo looking so well-fed today, I wasn't expecting you'd still be with us. I'd love to hear *all* about your evening."

Amalie clenched her hands into fists and stepped back from the counter. "Good morning, Ren." She needed to stay calm. "Theo and I have an agreement."

Clémentine stepped in behind Ren, her movements predatory despite the flowing skirts of her dress. Her curls tumbled over her shoulders, and she placed one long white finger to her lips, smiling when her amber gaze landed on Amalie. "Please tell. I love games. Especially Theo's."

Amalie swallowed against the fear and felt resolve build in her chest. She wasn't frightened. Not anymore.

They wouldn't kill her. Try to possess her, yes. Consume

her, absolutely. But they would have no reason to take her life if they knew who she truly was. With that knowledge, she no longer imagined escape. Instead, she found herself fantasizing about holding that sword in her hand. Plunging it into their chests.

She glanced down at her hands. She could nearly feel the weight of it.

"Amalie is under my protection while she's here." Theo rounded the counter. "Including from myself."

Clémentine's expression hardened. "You put too much trust in his restraint."

Theo stopped next to Amalie, his hip brushing hers. "You should know better than most about my self-control."

"I didn't see you leave the castle to feed," Clémentine snapped. "Do we have other guests I'm not aware of?"

"My evening didn't progress as smoothly as I would've liked," Theo said coolly. "Would you like me to knock when I leave next time? Wear a sign stating how many hours it's been since my last meal?"

Clémentine's laugh tinkled through the air, and she moved like water across the stone floor. "No need. I can smell it on you." She stopped short of the counter, inhaling deeply before closing her eyes and letting out a satisfied sigh.

Amalie's heart sped. Could Clémentine smell her blood? Could she sense that Theo had fed on a guardian, not a human?

"It seems Theo's made his choice. He prefers pain over pleasure. Or maybe it's possible for them to be the same thing," Amalie snapped, glaring at Clémentine as Theo tensed next to her.

The vampire's grin faded. "For now."

Amalie cocked her head to the side. "Is that how it is? You bide your time, waiting to strike instead of being loyal to your friends?" She'd been thinking of it since the rooftop. When Ren threw his friend into the sunlight. How they'd remained a coven was beyond her. They should have torn each other apart.

Clémentine's lip curled. "Our loyalty runs deeper than you know."

"Clearly. A new body in bed every night—"

Clémentine lunged over the counter, but Ren clamped his arms around her chest, dragging her back just as Theo bore his teeth, shoving Amalie behind him.

"Shh, darling. She's an ignorant human," Ren purred, his eyes locked with Amalie's as he nuzzled Clémentine's cheek.

"Get off me, Ren." Clémentine shoved at his arms, but he didn't let go until she stopped struggling. Clémentine shifted to the end of the counter, glaring at the three of them.

Ren sighed. "While I've always enjoyed a bit of female on female action, I don't think it wise to push her further, Amalie."

"It wouldn't be wise for Clémentine to approach my—" Theo caught himself, and Amalie's breath hitched. *My what?* She was suddenly desperate to hear what words he'd wanted to end that sentence with.

Ren chuckled. "Researcher? Historian? Quite fond of her after only a day, aren't we, brother?" His gaze was assessing, and Theo immediately relaxed, moving out from in front of her.

"If you're going to keep her as a pet, you should at least teach her manners." Clémentine glared at her, but Amalie didn't look away.

Ren leaned against the counter. "It was rather offensive. Considering."

Amalie glanced at Theo. "Considering what?"

Theo wet his lips. "It's part of our curse." He turned his

head. "Our souls crave eternal connection, but our immortal forms are destined to destroy it."

Amalie pondered this. "Because you feed."

"Because we have to kill. And even those we save and love *die*," Clémentine growled. "Perhaps if your lifespan was more than that of a moth you'd understand."

Amalie swallowed hard. "But you don't—you can't love each other?" Her eyes flicked to Theo.

Ren barked a laugh. "We love each other plenty. But we aren't built to attract other vampires. We aren't built to bond with them."

Bond. Amalie hadn't heard that term before. "But you can bond with humans?"

Ren's eyes flicked to Theo's. "Something like that."

The kitchen door swung open and Etienne strolled in. When he saw the food on the counter, his face lit up. "What are we making this morning?" He looked genuinely curious, oblivious to the tension in the room. "I've always been interested in how humans prepare their snacks."

"A bit pandering, even for you," Theo muttered.

"What? It's interesting." Etienne strolled over and glanced down at the bread and cheese on the cutting board. He nodded appreciatively. "Good choice."

Ren took another step forward, crossing his arms over his chest. "Perfect timing, Eti. We were just discussing where Theo found his meal last night—"

"Stop." A low rumble started deep in Theo's chest. He shot a glance at Clémentine who was stretching her hands over her head, showing the flat of her stomach. "Both of you."

Etienne stepped forward, rolling the sleeves of his white linen shirt to his elbows. "Mind if I help?" He glanced up at Amalie through dark lashes, then winked at Theo. Grinning, he picked up a sprig of thyme, stripping the tiny leaves from its stem with practiced fingers. His silver signet ring glinted in the light from the window. "I've heard herbs add a brightness to flavors—"

"Is this what we're doing? Playing chef?" Theo glowered at Etienne as Amalie pulled her hand away to pinch the small spears between her fingers.

"Not playing. I've always been fascinated by the evolution of human cuisine." Etienne set down the herbs he'd gathered and picked up another leaf, this time tearing off small pieces and placing them neatly in a row along one side of the board before reaching for more. "The flavors, the textures . . . so different from when I lived."

"When was that?" Amalie asked, her interest piqued.

"Second century."

She blinked, then turned to Theo. "You're older?" Theo nodded. "How did you meet?"

Etienne cocked his head. "You haven't told her?"

"Told me what?"

Theo crossed his arms over his chest. "We met at a party."

Etienne laughed out loud. "Oh. It was definitely that." He waited for Amalie to spread more cheese, then sprinkled the herbs. "Tell me, what is your favorite dish to prepare?"

Despite herself, Amalie found her lips curling into a smile. If he was attempting to put her at ease, he'd failed miserably, but there was something undeniably charming about Etienne's curiosity. And the way he got under Theo's skin.

She glanced down at the fresh ingredients spread across the counter. "I suppose it depends on the season. In the summer, I love making ratatouille with vegetables from my garden. And in winter, there's nothing better than boeuf bourguignon."

Etienne's eyes lit up. "You're from the south?"

Ren's eyes narrowed just as Theo's hand wrapped around

her elbow. "Enough." His voice was low when he spoke. "Unlike the others, she isn't here for entertainment."

"No?" Clémentine purred, twirling a lock of hair around her finger. "Seems like you're quite amused."

Amalie bristled, dropping the preserves over the herbs Etienne had prepared, then allowing Theo to draw her toward the door. Her curiosity ate at her like acid. *What about this party? And if vampires didn't bond with each other, why did Clémentine act like Theo was hers to claim?*

He paused, his eyes dark. "I don't question your escapades."

"We're all glad you've found good company. We know the last few years have been . . . difficult." Ren stepped in front of Clémentine. "I think—"

The door slammed open, and Amalie jumped as Theo threw her again behind his back.

A vampire Amalie didn't recognize appeared in the doorway, breathless. His coat billowed behind him as he strode into the kitchen, eyes wide with urgency. "We've found another."

Clémentine straightened, her amber eyes flashing. "Where?"

"Mordelles." The man sucked in a haggard breath. "A Guardian. He's been changed."

28

1836 NORTHERN NORMANDY, FRANCE

Amalie jogged to keep up with Theo as he stormed up the stairs and down the hall. "A guardian? They've been turned?" She looked back and lowered her voice. "How does your coven know about them?"

"Everyone knows about guardians, Amalie." His expression was hard as he started up the second staircase. "What they don't know is where they are."

They. Because Theo did know where they were. Where her family was. Her stomach dropped. Now his whole coven knew about someone else.

She panted as they climbed. "Well. Seems like the secret's out." The words hissed through her lips like venom.

"It's only one."

Amalie scoffed. "Only one? How many of us are there?"

Theo stopped when they reached the top. "I'm trying to protect them," he growled. "To protect *you*. Do you have any idea what would happen if every vampire knew of the guardians walking among us? I've seen it. I know—" He shook his head, fury flashing across his features. "But that's exactly what's happening now. This will spread. All vampires will hear of this soon enough, and there's no telling what chaos will ensue." He whirled on her. "You need to stay here. I can't risk your safety outside these walls."

Theo started down the hall to their rooms. *Stay?* Her fingers curled into fists at her sides. The idea that she could sit idly by while Theo figured out who had changed one of her blood. . .

"Who is it?" she snapped.

"I don't know."

"You don't know." She scoffed. "Right. You never—"

Amalie's breath caught as she noticed a figure ahead of them. A woman. Bathed in red.

Amalie rushed forward, dropping to her knees. "Penelope?" It was the third woman she'd seen in the parlor. "Who did this to you?"

Her dress was torn. It hung off her in ribbons, barely covering her bare skin underneath. She wore no corset or underclothes. The skin on her throat was bruised and mottled, and a long cut on her left shoulder dripped blood down her arm.

Theo knelt beside her, his body rigid. "Who is your host?"

Amalie swallowed the bile rising in her throat. *Host.* He said it like she'd been invited to a party and had an unfortunate accident. She grabbed at the shredded fabric with numb fingers, trying to piece it back together. "We have to help her. She's bleeding, she—"

Amalie froze. Penelope was bleeding. In a castle where vampires roamed. Had the others left the kitchen? Would they walk down this hall?

Penelope looked up, her eyes red and swollen. "I tried," she whispered. "I did everything he asked."

"Who?" Theo demanded, his voice like steel.

Penelope's eyes filled with tears, and Amalie's heart shattered. "He said I wasn't good enough," Penelope choked out. "That I w-was a disappointment."

"His name started with an 'R,'" Amalie murmured. "She mentioned him in the parlor, but I hadn't met him."

"Ramon," Theo growled.

Amalie didn't know what she expected from Theo in that moment, but it wasn't what she saw. The air around them went cold as Theo's entire being threaded with shadow. He moved with it. Became it.

There was a click of a door opening. Then another. Amalie's head snapped up as two figures emerged from the rooms lining the hall. Shadows with eyes that gleamed like polished steel. Only two of them. Theo could outrun them, couldn't he? Henriette could help them patch her up.

"To my room," she hissed, the glamours already swirling around her like she'd been soaked in perfume.

Theo shook his head, his body tense as he watched the vampires approach. Amalie turned. There were no longer only two.

She swore under her breath. Why would a vampire do this? Why would he bring a human here only to hurt her and set her free?

Penelope clung to Amalie, hyperventilating. This was why. Ramon wanted to create a feeding frenzy. He wanted Penelope to be terrified in her last moments. To beg for life.

Amalie gripped Penelope's hands, dragging them off her and rose. She didn't have a weapon, but if she could find—

"Stay with her." Theo stepped in front of her. "Don't move."

Amalie's breath caught. Theo was cloaked in black mist, his eyes dark as coal. He flexed his hands and faced the vampires that still edged closer.

Theo's voice was like a whip crack. "Go back to your rooms."

The vampires snarled, their eyes glittering. These were the same men who'd been on the rooftop. How human they'd looked then. Now they were feral. Driven by blood lust.

"To your rooms." Theo's growl sent a shudder through her. His glamour, normally warm and peaceful, had turned to January wind.

One of the vampires took a step forward, and Amalie's heart leapt into her throat. He was tall, with a lean, athletic build and hair as dark as Theo's. His eyes were wild, and his lips curled back to reveal fangs that gleamed in the dim light.

Theo's hand shot out, and the vampire stumbled back, hissing. "I won't say it again."

The vampires looked between Theo and Penelope, their nostrils flaring. They were like wolves, circling a wounded deer.

The vampires pounced, swift and predatory. Theo moved like smoke. He ducked under a swipe of claws, then spun, delivering a kick to the vampire's chest. The creature flew back, crashing into the wall with a sickening thud.

Another vampire lunged, fangs bared, but Theo grabbed the vampire's wrist and twisted, the bones snapping with a sickening crack. The vampire howled in pain, and Theo's fist connected with its jaw, sending it sprawling.

They couldn't die, but they could feel pain.

Theo delivered it. He caught a vampire by the throat and squeezed, then slammed his head into the floor. He broke skin. He shattered bones.

When they were down, Theo turned, his gaze locking on Amalie. For a moment, she couldn't breathe. Theo Vallon was deadly. A Darkness.

He was beautiful.

Theo stepped forward, his movements slow and deliberate. He reached down and scooped Penelope into his arms. Amalie winced at the blood smeared on his skin and the torn fabric of his shirt.

He rose. "Are you coming?"

Amalie nodded, and Theo shifted Penelope so he could reach out and hold on to Amalie's waist. He lifted her like she was nothing, and then the hall seemed to bend around them.

When the stones stopped blurring, they stood in front of another door, but Amalie didn't recognize her surroundings. It had to be a different wing of the castle.

Theo didn't knock. He set Amalie down and kicked the door open with his boot. A man skittered back, raising his hands as his eyes widened in horror.

Ramon. He was short. Thin. With pale eyes and hair that fell to his shoulders. "Theo, I didn't—"

"Shut your damn mouth." Theo walked in and lay Penelope on the bed. He turned, his voice a low growl. "You will put her back together."

Ramon's eyes glinted. He took a step back. "She's a human. I did as I wished."

In an instant, Theo knocked him against the wall. He caught Ramon's left wrist as he tried to rise from the floor and raised the vampire's hand in front of his face. Without a second's hesitation, Theo pulled a knife from his boot and sliced off Ramon's first two fingers.

The vampire howled in agony. "I will do this every day, slowly, for the rest of your life if I don't return and find this woman cared for. Do you understand?"

Ramon fought to get up, but his right hand slipped on the stone, already slick with his blood. Theo held the knife to his thumb, and Ramon gasped.

"I understand! I understand."

Theo cut it off anyway. The man howled as Theo dropped his arm and wiped the blade on Ramon's shoulder before putting it back in his boot.

He didn't say another word as he walked back toward Amalie. He didn't ask before wrapping his arm around her waist and lifting her into his arms.

She buried her face against his chest as he carried her back to her room, breathing him in. He walked quickly, but he didn't run, and by the time they stood in front of her door, his scent had warmed and the shadows had almost fully receded.

He set her down, but her arms lingered around his neck. He reached around her and opened her door. "Clean up. I'll be back."

She nodded, swallowing hard. She'd forgotten all about the kitchen, about their argument as they'd ascended the stairs.

"Theo? Are you ready?" Etienne appeared at the end of the hall, seemingly oblivious to what had just occurred.

Amalie pulled her arms off of him. She didn't argue as she slipped into her room and closed the door.

29

Amalie's legs felt barely capable of holding her up. A cold sweat broke out on her skin as she dropped onto the bed.

It shouldn't have been shocking. None of it. What she'd seen in Ramon had been the vampires of legend. The cruelty. The evil.

But then there had been Theo.

Breathe. Amalie curled over her knees. She'd been so sure he was the enemy. But now? He'd defended a human. He'd harmed his own kind to keep Penelope safe.

She felt the last of her resolve crumbling, and the walls she'd built around the stories Theo told her turned to dust.

She believed him. All of it. And that was almost more terrifying than holding onto hope that there was an alternative explanation.

Amalie forced herself off the mattress and walked to the washroom.

Theo hadn't killed her mother.

Theo protected guardians.

Theo wanted the sword.

Theo wanted to die.

That last truth slapped against her consciousness. Her fingers shook as she knelt to inspect the coals that were still warm beneath the tub. Even though Henriette had the day off, she'd already filled the tub, and the water was tepid.

Amalie grabbed a handful of kindling, her fingers still trembling, and forced them to hold steady as she fed the fire. She used the poker to stir the coals until embers glowed red, then dropped to her knees and blew, the coals sparking, then catching, flames curling around the logs and sending light flickering across the stone and copper.

She stripped off her clothes, inspecting the dark stains where Penelope's blood had soaked into the cloth, then noticed the fresh clothing already sitting on the counter for her.

Amalie wanted to weep. Here she'd been complaining that she was stuck in her room, enjoying hot baths and trays of food whilst studying her books, and Penelope—

She pressed the heels of her hands over her eyes. Did Penelope have it worse or had it been worse for the others? Marie and Sarah? Had death come quickly, or had Etienne and Paul toyed with them like Ramon?

When the water was warm, Amalie dropped into the tub. She scrubbed Penelope's blood from her skin, then dunked her head under the water. She held her breath until her lungs screamed, until her body forced her back to the surface, gasping for air.

She held onto the edges of the tub, staring at the pink-tinged water. When she couldn't bear it any longer, she stepped out and grabbed the towel, her skin prickling as she dried herself off.

Amalie finished drying herself, then plucked the comb

from the shelf and worked it through her hair. She needed to find something else in those books. They needed a way to stop vampires like Ramon, to vanquish them permanently.

But Theo?

Amalie's thoughts snagged. She set down the comb and lifted her arms to braid her hair. When she was finished, she dressed in the clean shirt and slacks, then re-entered her bedroom. No sooner had she crossed the room to her writing desk than a knock came at the door.

"I want to come with you." Amalie gripped her mother's coat.

Her mother turned and crouched in the hall. "There is something I have to take care of, mon chou. I'll be back soon, and I need you to protect your sister."

Amalie looked back at their bedroom door. "But I'm scared."

"Go in and lock the door. I'll do our special knock when I return ..."

Theo didn't have a special knock. And even if he did, he couldn't possibly be back so soon.

"Don't worry, I'm not going to come in." Ren's voice slid through the crack like butter, sending shivers across her skin. "I couldn't even if I wanted to."

She tiptoed to the door and checked that the lock was turned. He didn't have the key, but with one kick, Theo had leveled Ramon's door. What was keeping Ren from doing the same?

"Why couldn't you?" Amalie asked.

Ren was quiet a moment. "This room is warded. It's the only room in the castle with enchantments. It's why Theo claimed it."

Amalie stared at the back of the door. "It's warded?"

"Nobody can get in without the key."

"Not even through the windows?"

"Not unless you opened them."

Amalie blanched. "Right." She glanced back at the shutters. They were drawn. She vaguely wondered if she'd see the pinks and oranges of sunset if she pushed them open.

"You're on guard duty, then?" It wasn't really a question. Theo would never leave her with another vampire. Not even one from his own coven. But he did have reasonable doubt that she'd stick to her room. Perhaps he thought if a vampire was in the hall, she'd be more likely to follow the rules.

"There was a complication earlier. Theo felt it necessary that I stay back. To make sure his objectives were prioritized." Ren's shadow moved across the thin gap at the bottom of her door. "I'm glad for the task, actually. The last thing I want to do right now is traipse around Mordelle. The town is a dung heap."

Amalie pursed her lips and didn't speak. Theo hadn't liked when Etienne noticed her southern traditions in the kitchen. She wouldn't give any more details that could link her to her family.

Ren sighed. "Not much of a talker, are you?"

She waited a moment. When he didn't continue, she said, "I'm not going to leave my room. You can go."

He chuckled. "So you do know Theo. You'll understand, then, if I stay. The last thing I want to do is upset him. Didn't go well for the last vampire who crossed him."

Amalie's stomach soured, remembering Ramon's fingers landing on the stone with a sickening thump. "You don't say," she murmured.

Wonderful. She was going to have to study with Ren sitting

there. He'd hear her moving around the room. Possibly keep wanting to talk.

Amalie took a step back and paused. If he wanted to talk . . .

"Why do you listen to him?"

Ren scoffed. "Theo? Why do you?"

Amalie pursed her lips. "Don't all humans get drawn in if you desire?"

"Fair enough." There was a long pause. "Theo is stronger than most. I suppose I listen for the same reasons you do."

Did she sense a hint of bitterness in his tone?

"So. Tell me, Amalie. What is in your heart tonight?"

Amalie frowned. An odd question. "Why do you care?"

His laugh drifted through the door again. "Because I've lived for years without anything beautiful or interesting to look at, and now I have both standing right behind that door."

Amalie shivered thinking of Marx in the stairwell and on the roof. Was this how covens worked? As soon as Theo was gone, others swooped in for the kill?

"I'll start with an easier question. Where are you from?" he asked.

"Here. Normandy," she lied, hoping Ren hadn't paid much attention to her food choices earlier.

"Mmm. And what does your family think of you living so close to us monsters?"

Amalie scoffed. "They don't know about the monsters. Or at least they pretend not to."

"But you're different than your parents?"

"My parents are dead." Amalie snapped her mouth shut. Why had she said that?

Ren chuckled. "Ah. A perfect target. Does nobody miss you, then?"

Amalie sat on the bed. "I have a family. Seems you do, too.

Your coven?" She needed to turn this around. She needed to be asking the questions.

"They are my family. And just like brothers and sisters, we don't always see eye to eye."

"You disagree with Theo?"

Ren sighed. "I don't think he should have locked you up. You would've been safe with him, and then you could've seen more for your research."

Safe. That was the last word she would've used to describe how she felt with Theo up until an hour ago. Confused? Agitated? Intrigued? Still all of the above. Heat flushed her cheeks.

Ren exhaled. "You know, you remind me of someone. A woman I knew years ago."

Amalie's thoughts snapped to attention. "Well, whoever she was, I'm sorry to disappoint you."

"Lucky for you, I find disappointment intoxicating. It's boring to constantly get everything you want. Like Clémentine, I love games. Secrets are even more delicious."

Amalie's heart hammered in her chest. His questions and comments no longer seemed random. He was leading her along, dangling a treat in front of her face. "I'm all out of those, I'm afraid."

"I'm not. What would you like to know?"

She stood and crossed to her writing desk, holding onto the back of the chair. She shouldn't engage with him. It was dangerous. But the idea of finding out more about Theo . . .

"When were you changed?" she asked.

"Before Theo. I remember the day he arrived."

Amalie moved back to sit on the floor next to the door. "Arrived where?"

"Back then there weren't divisions in the land like there are now. The Roman Empire stretched to our borders."

Romans. That empire spanned too much time to narrow it down. "Were you conquered?" Amalie picked up one of her books, flipping through the pages.

"No. We lived on our own. We didn't meddle in the world of humans."

Amalie scoffed. "Except to kill them?"

Ren sat and leaned against the door, his body fully blocking the strip of light at the bottom. "We didn't harm humans then."

Amalie's pulse thrummed in her throat. "How did you survive?"

"You heard what was said in the kitchen?"

"Yes."

"Have you heard of the guardians?"

"No." *Had she answered too quickly?* She swallowed hard, her fingers pinched around the cover of the book.

"Well, it's more than you need to understand. But we lived in harmony once. Their blood sated us without the need for death."

Amalie ran her fingers over the tender skin of her underarm. "Sounds idyllic."

"It would've been. Had they not gone into hiding."

Amalie's pulse quickened. "Why would they do that? If your relationships were so perfect, why would they leave?"

Ren tapped his fingers on the stone. "That's probably a better question for Theo."

It felt like bait, and yet she couldn't help herself. She took it. "Why?"

"He was one of the vampires who enslaved them."

A pit opened up in her stomach. Enslaved? That couldn't be true. Theo said he protected guardians. He'd rushed from the castle to find one who was in danger.

Amalie drew a deep breath. "But you didn't?"

"Of course not. That's savagery. It's no surprise Theo left the second he got word. He's been obsessed with finding the guardians ever since."

Obsessed. Amalie set down the book.

Was it possible? She considered all her points of data from this alternative explanation. He wanted power. He wanted control.

Amalie bit the inside of her cheek. No. It didn't make any sense. If Theo wanted guardians, he knew where her entire family was. He could've taken them at any time. "They said a Guardian was changed. But how? I thought when vampires choose to use their venom, they lose power—"

"They don't always choose." Ren's voice was sharp, and Amalie sucked in a breath. "But yes. They lose strength. Power."

Amalie waited, not sure what to say next. She'd obviously hit a nerve. It wasn't surprising that vampires took losing their abilities seriously.

"I think I will sleep after all." Ren's shadow lifted from the underside of the door. "Theo shouldn't be too long. Unless he gets held up with the man's family."

"Family?" She'd asked Theo if he knew who the guardian was. He said no. "You know who was changed?"

Ren paused outside her door. "He lives outside of the city. Has a farm. Allard is the surname, I believe?"

30

Amalie scrambled back, clutching the edge of the windowsill to keep from crumpling into a pile on the floor. *Allard?* No. It couldn't be possible. He'd heard wrong, repeated an incorrect name. The world seemed to shrink and expand in a never-ending cycle, and she squeezed her eyes closed against the spinning walls.

People said that time slowed and your life flashed before your eyes in the moments preceding death, but she didn't expect it to happen by proxy. Images flashed through her mind. Her uncle's laughter as he tossed her in the air when she was young. His strong arms catching her again and again. Sitting by the fire while he told stories of battles fought long ago. Of heroes in France who risked everything for those they loved.

She couldn't imagine it. Him. Transformed into one of these monsters. Somehow she'd believed that it wouldn't be possible to turn a guardian, but that belief was based on nothing. Theo had never said as much. She'd assumed, and it seemed her assumption was proven false.

What kind of power would a guardian have if they were cursed? Her blood and body healed and replenished. She could withstand glamours. But vampires could do all of that, too. What kind of gift was guardian blood if it didn't give her anything to fight with?

Amalie pressed her lips together, staying silent. She couldn't admit she knew the name. If what Ren said was true, Theo had known her family was in danger and had kept information from her. Again.

It didn't make sense.

Ren's explanation didn't make any sense, but she couldn't think of a better one.

Unless.

Theo still held his secrets. Had he brought her here because he knew something more about her family? Had he plucked her out because he needed her and believed they were in danger?

Her heartbeat felt like thunder before a storm.

She should stay here behind the wards. She should listen to Theo and wait until he returned.

She should stay in after dark. She should stay away from Marcel and the Pourfendeurs. *Should, should, should.*

She should've done so many things. But she hadn't.

That night would be no different.

———

Amalie sat on the edge of her bed with a small satchel in her arms, her toes tapping on the floor. Voices echoed along the castle walls, the sun had already dropped over the horizon. This was not her moment. But she was taking it anyway.

Quietly, she rose from the bed and tiptoed to the window, praying that no vampires would be on the lower terrace. The salty sea air greeted her as she opened it, sending a shiver down her spine. She peered out, her eyes scanning the roof outside her window. It was a precarious route, but it was her only option. She couldn't afford running into any member of Theo's coven inside, especially since Ren was on high alert.

Amalie took a deep breath, her senses skittish. With one last look around her room, she climbed up onto the window ledge. The rough stone dug into her palms as she steadied herself. Her heart raced, but she forced herself to stay calm. She had to move now, or she'd lose her nerve.

At least she'd already had practice with sneaking out a window once in the past week. It was becoming an unfortunate new habit.

She swung her leg over the ledge and carefully lowered herself onto the roof. She hadn't counted on the mist. The tiles hadn't felt precarious when she'd stepped out the other day, but now they were cold and slick under her boots. She took a moment to steady herself, then hissed as her sole slipped.

For a heart-stopping moment, she teetered on the edge, her arms pinwheeling for balance. Her heart skipped a beat and she bit back a gasp as the tile cracked and a piece of it skittered off the edge of the roof. She dropped into a crouch, waiting for any sign of life on the terrace. After she caught her breath, and nothing moved in the shadows, she stayed low, moving quickly but silently.

The rest of the castle loomed above her as she took calculated steps, keeping to the wall. She couldn't afford to make another sound. Vampires had heightened senses, but with the number of gulls nesting on the roof, she hoped her scuffs wouldn't attract attention.

Sweat beaded on her brow as she reached the edge of the roof and peered over. On one end of the terrace, a set of stone stairs led down to the cobbled street. She steeled herself, then swung over the edge, lowering herself down. Her feet hit the ground softly, and she let go.

Amalie dropped to her stomach, rolling away from the windows, then crawled toward the stairs. When she finally arrived, she lowered into a crouch, then began to descend.

She kept low until she reached the street, then darted between the buildings. She stepped lightly, her footsteps silent on the cobblestone. Traveling in solitude made her skin itch. It was only days since she'd run through Mordelles and found Theo on the path to the shed.

They could be out there. Any of them. She wouldn't even hear them coming.

Amalie pressed on. She tried to remember the path they'd taken when Theo had brought her through these streets. Hard to grasp, considering the situation. Her mind flashed back to his firm grip on her arm as he guided her up the winding alleys. They had passed a graveyard and a small chapel with a crumbling facade and stained glass, of that she was certain. Amalie turned left and followed the street down, hoping it would lead her to the front gates.

The wind whispered through the narrow passages, rustling the leaves of ivy that clung to the stone buildings. With adrenaline coursing through her veins, she picked up on everything. The distant crash of waves against the shore, the creak of a wooden sign swinging above a shop. Every sound made her shoulders tense.

Her family wasn't safe. Amalie quickened her pace, tears pricking the corners of her eyes. What a mess. How had she gotten here? She wanted to retrace her steps and figure out which one she'd gotten wrong, but even when she stretched to her childhood, each pinpoint in time seemed to tumble into the next.

Her father's death. Her mother's loneliness. Her uncle's

deceptions. Amalie's desperation. If she'd been different as a child, would her mother have been a target? If she'd stayed until her eighteenth birthday, would Uncle Oren have told her everything?

Had she known then what she did now, she would've acted differently, wouldn't she? She would've gone to Oren if he'd been honest with her, they could've had warning—they could've fled.

But Oren was a guardian, too. He only knew as much as his lifetime allowed. As much as their history and stories told him.

Theo had seen her. He'd known her. He hadn't died and forgotten.

She swiped the tears from her cheeks as she passed under an archway, spotting the church ahead. As she neared the edge of the abandoned village, anxiety clawed at her throat. Soon, she'd pass through the doors and stand exposed on the flats.

She'd checked the tide. She should have an hour at least before the water rushed back in. Amalie paused at the last building, pressing her back against the cool stone. She allowed herself two breaths, then scanned the area ahead, looking for any signs of movement, any hint of danger.

Nothing.

The wind whispered against her cheeks as she pushed through the door. There was no one there guarding the entrance, because why would they have to? Anyone who wandered in here would be a welcome guest.

Her foot sank as she stepped onto the sand flats. There was nowhere to hide, no way to make this less conspicuous. She gripped the strap of her bag on her back and made a run for it. Thanks to her training with the Pourfendeurs, her lungs and heart were strong. If she kept a steady pace, she'd be able to make it to the trees without stopping to rest.

The soft sand shifted under her boots, but she maintained

her balance. As her breathing quickened, she searched for something to distract herself.

Her mother. Bethany. Uncle Oren. Not helpful to think of them, but she couldn't keep their faces out of her head. They were tied by blood. *Oren had secrets.* She'd lived before, she'd been a warrior. *Theo had secrets.* There was a sword, but the books—

A flash of a memory surfaced—her mother and Uncle Oren in hushed conversation. She focused harder, but it was like grasping at smoke. The words were just out of reach, slipping away before she could piece them together.

They were always talking. Every day when her mother came in from the gardens. They laughed together, argued about whether it was best to butter the bread before or after baking, and played games of stones in the garden at sunset.

That was how Amalie had learned to be a sister. She wanted a friendship like that with Bethany, and she'd earned it. *She had to get to her before another vampire did.*

Amalie pushed harder, and when she finally entered the cover of trees, her breath came in short bursts. She dropped to the ground, resting her back against the trunk of an oak.

And like a crack of lightning, the words from her memory surfaced.

Amalie was a child crouching at the top of the staircase, peering through the gap in the stairs. Her mother's voice floated up to her . . .

"That wasn't my goal, Oren." Her mother paced, her long skirt *brushing against the stone floor.*

"Then what is it? Please, Rachel. I'm all ears."

Her mother dropped a book with a frayed black cover and gold lettering on the table. "We've broken our bonds. It says so right here!"

Oren placed his spectacles on his nose. He stood near the window, his hands clasped behind his back. "I don't need to read it."

"Oren—"

"They kept that record from us for a reason! It's dangerous."

"Or they were afraid." She planted a hand on her hip.

Oren shook his head. "Maybe we should be afraid."

It had been almost twenty years since that night. How had she never thought of it? She replayed the dialogue, searching for anything she'd missed. It was like hunting for coins scattered across the damn flats.

Her mother's books. Where had they gone?

Amalie forced herself up. She needed more than half-remembered conversations and cryptic phrases. She needed concrete information—something tangible she could use to find this relic Theo had spoken of. If Uncle Oren was turned, he wouldn't help her, would he?

Her fingers brushed something cool and sticky as she stood. Sap. It was all over the arm of her shirt. And in her hair. She groaned, opening her satchel. At least she'd thought to bring an extra pair of clothes.

She stripped off her shirt and pulled the new one from her sack.

"I'll give it to you Amalie, had I not been watching, I wouldn't have heard a thing."

Amalie whirled at the voice, her heart leaping into her throat.

Ren stepped out from behind a tree, his eyes gleaming. He tsked. "Where are you headed, little bird?"

31

1824 BLOIS, FRANCE

Rachel laughed, the sound bubbling up from her chest. "Do you ever take a break? Let loose?" Her breath clouded the stars overhead.

Florent reached for her hand. "Only when I'm with you." She rolled her eyes, but warmth spread through her at his words. "How are Amalie and Bethany?"

Rachel's heart swelled at the mention of her daughters. "Amalie is more stubborn by the day."

"Shocking."

Rachel elbowed his ribs. "Bethany refuses to leave the kitchen. Our poor cook."

"She wants to help?"

Rachel laughed. "She wants to take charge, and don't say it." Florent grinned down at her, moonlight bringing out his high cheekbones.

Florent sighed. "I caught a cat in the bedroom last week. It seemed to think it owned the place."

Rachel burst out laughing. "Another squatter at Place

Deaumont. You should've brought him home! The girls would've died with delight."

"Animals won't come within ten meters of me. He hasn't been back."

Rachel's eyes widened. "So you've never made a cat purr?" Florent shook his head. "Well. That's tragic."

He laughed. "At least I don't have to worry about fleas."

They walked on in silence, listening to the babble of the river.

"It's hard to believe summer's almost over," Rachel murmured.

A shadow passed over Florent's face, but he quickly masked it. "Paris, then."

"Paris." She didn't know what she wanted Florent to say then, but she held her breath. *Something.* She hoped he wanted something more than just these last few weeks.

When they reached their hollow in the trees, Florent pulled Rachel into his arms. "I've always loved Paris."

"Have you?"

He grinned, brushing the hair from her face and dropping his lips to hers. Rachel's stomach flipped. She loved his kisses. Soft and gentle in some moments and desperate in others.

Rachel sighed against his mouth, reaching up to thread her fingers through his hair. Florent pulled her backward, dropping to a soft patch of grass near the water's edge and pulling her over him.

Florent's hands roamed over her back, tracing patterns that sent shivers down her spine. She arched into him, pressing closer. It had been over a week since they'd last been able to get away, and her body was impatient.

His lips moved to her neck, and she gasped, heat pooling low in her belly. Rachel nipped at Florent's earlobe, delighting in the way he groaned against her skin. His hand slipped under the fabric of her blouse, and heat shot down her thighs.

She wanted him—all of him. To feel him completely, to understand what he'd been hiding from her all these months. With trembling fingers, she began to unbutton his shirt, exposing the smooth planes of his chest.

Her breath hitched when she saw the rune etched into his skin, glowing faintly in the moonlight. "Florent," she whispered, brushing her thumb over the intricate design. "What is this?"

Florent's muscles tensed beneath her touch. "It's nothing."

Rachel frowned, brushing her thumb over the design again. "It doesn't look like nothing."

His chest rose and fell against her ribs. "Runes tell our story."

"You had someone place this here?"

He shook his head. "They appear throughout our life." He pushed up on his elbows, and Rachel rolled to the grass at his side. "This is a symbol of Le Sombre. Of our origins." He paused, seeming to weigh his next words carefully. "It represents my past—who I was before this life."

"It looks like the sea."

"I worked on a fishing boat."

Rachel followed the curves of the dark lines. She wanted to comfort him, but how did you make this better? How did you glorify a curse? "I'm sorry," she whispered, pressing her palm flat against his chest. "I didn't mean to pry."

Florent shook his head. "No, you have every right to be curious. It's just difficult to talk about sometimes." He dropped his hand from her back, and Rachel shivered.

"That's why you're strong. Why you know how to fix things."

Florent gave a mirthless laugh. "Strong. If only."

Rachel frowned. "What do you mean?"

He sat, draping his arms over his knees. "I used to have strength you couldn't imagine."

She swallowed, pushing up and settling next to him. "Do all vampires start out strong and then lose their abilities over time?"

Florent's eyes flicked to hers. He watched her a moment, then sighed. "I'm not sure where to begin." Rachel bit her lip, not wanting to say anything that would stop him from sharing more. "When humans are changed, they are gifted a portion of the vampire's power who changed them."

Rachel frowned. "They aren't given the power of Le Sombre?"

"All power comes from the Shadow. But it flows through us."

She nodded. "So if you change someone, your power is given? Shared?"

He huffed a breath. "Taken is more accurate."

She watched him, the moon reflecting in his eyes. "You didn't know this? When you changed someone?" He shook his head, and Rachel didn't know whether to cry or clutch her stomach. The idea of Florent's mouth on someone else's flesh made her want to vomit.

"Can you ever get that power back?"

He turned to her, his eyes liquid. "I believe there is a way."

She put a hand on his arm. "What is it?"

He shook his head turning back to the river. "It's not an option."

"Why not?"

"Because it's not something I can do myself. It's something another has to do for me."

Rachel put out a hand and turned his face to hers. "All you have to do is ask."

32

Amalie's palms grew clammy as she struggled to pull the shirt over her head.

"What is that?" Ren snatched her wrist, and Amalie's heart jumped into her throat. No. The marks. She hadn't checked to see if the cuts left by Theo's fangs had healed.

Stupid. Ren was going to see that she'd been bitten—that they'd tried to hide it. The fabric obscured her vision. She tried to yank her hand from his grip.

"Did you hurt yourself?" he asked, his voice low and calm.

"Yes, I—" Amalie froze as her head popped free and the shirt pooled around her shoulders. She looked down. Ren wasn't staring at the place where Theo had fed. He pointed to a small, gray—nearly midnight blue—faded blotch on the underside of her arm. Higher than her wrist, but not quite to her elbow.

"A strange looking bruise."

Amalie blinked. "I spilled ink," she murmured. "It stained

my skin." Ren let go of her arm, and she shoved her arms into the sleeves of the shirt.

How had she not noticed a mark like that? She had used ink, but she hadn't spilled any. Ren seemed convinced by her story, but Amalie's skin prickled.

"Theo would be quite displeased to know you've wandered off." Ren took a small step back, but was still too close for comfort. He was powerful in the coven. When Theo wasn't present, it seemed the other vampires deferred to him. But he wouldn't cross Theo's claim, would he?

She acknowledged him coolly, suppressing the tremor in her voice. "Theo understands I have my own priorities."

He smiled, his teeth glaringly white. "I'm curious, were you lying to me when you said you didn't plan on leaving, or did something I said change your mind?"

Amalie scrambled for an excuse, but her mind scattered. If Ren discovered she knew the name he'd given, she'd be as good as dead—or worse.

Ren circled her like a predator, his gray eyes flashing with amusement.

Amalie found her part. Angry. Sick of being controlled. "He left me there. After a few hours of twiddling my thumbs, I decided I had plenty of personal research. I've moved on to other projects."

"Don't lie to me. I've sensed your affection, Amalie."

"You can hardly expect me to withstand his glamour," she snapped. "With him gone, I found more clarity of mind."

Ren regarded her. "These lands are dangerous for a delicate thing like yourself."

"They shouldn't be." Amalie glanced back at the flats. "You said you were going to be sleeping."

"Then I guess we both told little white lies." Ren took a

step closer and leaned in. "Theo may be more compelling in person, but he's not the only one who can offer protection."

"Protection is the last thing I want from Theo. I've had enough of his games."

Ren raised an eyebrow. "Is that so? Your agreement seemed rather . . . binding."

Amalie thought back to their conversation in the kitchen.

We aren't meant to bond with them.

But you can bond with humans?

"Theo said I could leave when I wanted."

"Kind of him. But now you don't have his protection."

Amalie clenched her jaw. "Are you telling me I need it? I know what to look for."

Ren chuckled. "Knowing is only half the battle. Like you mentioned, fighting the glamour isn't always possible."

Amalie's eyes narrowed. Odd that she'd never felt anything when Ren was close. She'd felt more pull from Etienne in the kitchen than from him now alone in the woods. "Have you never used yours on me?"

Ren's expression hardened. "I haven't felt the need." He clenched his hands into fists, and Amalie's eyes snagged on his fingers. There was nothing there. All the members of Theo's coven wore their signet ring. Had he taken his off? Or had she never noticed that he didn't have one?

"Lucky me." Amalie started off through the trees.

"I think I've proven you can't outrun me."

Amalie threw up her hands. "Don't care. Follow me if you want, Ren."

"Where are you going?"

She shrugged. "I guess you'll have to watch and find out." Panic surged through her. Where was she going? She couldn't head to Uncle Oren's farm, not with Ren on her heels. She would have to convince him. Prove that she was doing as she said, getting away from Theo.

Amalie took a sharp turn north into the trees, heading in the opposite direction of Mordelles.

"Interesting." Ren's footsteps sounded behind her.

"Please stop talking."

"I understand you're upset, but I have my orders. I can't leave you unprotected."

"Oh, please. Like you're so loyal." Amalie wheeled on him. "A moment ago, you were threatening me. Seems like you pick and choose the orders you follow."

Ren studied her. "You don't know me as well as you'd like to think. You'd be surprised what lengths I'd go to to get what I want." He stepped closer. The air around him seemed to hum with energy. "You're lucky Theo found you first."

Amalie drew a breath. "Go ahead and rat me out to Theo. Tell him to come for me. I'd love to tell him all about our little conversation."

She didn't look back to see if Ren was following until she reached the market square of Valenciennes. Despite the late hour, there were still a few people milling about, finishing their supper. There was a group of men laughing loudly near the fountain. She angled past them, then ducked into a narrow alleyway. If Ren insisted on following her, she wouldn't make it easy for him.

The cobblestone streets glistened with recent rain, the air cool against Amalie's cheeks. Her footsteps echoed off the stone buildings lining each side of the street, casting long shadows in the moonlight. She glanced over her shoulder, her heart leaping into her throat as Ren turned the corner.

Amalie wound through streets and alleys, weaving back and forth until even she wasn't sure which direction they were headed. Finally, she burst out onto a street lined with shops and cafés.

This was ridiculous. She needed to go home. She was hours in the wrong direction with no hope of losing her tail. Had Theo found her uncle? Was he trying to keep her family safe like he'd said? The idea of staying there in town for the night not knowing felt like drinking straight poison.

Why hadn't Theo told her? Why hadn't he let her come?

Anger welled within her, but she tamped it down. Now wasn't the time. She needed to stay focused.

Amalie spun in the dimly lit alley, heart pounding as she weighed her options. She wouldn't be able to travel tonight. Ren was right about one thing, the roads between towns were dangerous. Each route carried its own risks, plus, traveling at night could lead Ren or other vampires straight to her family. She couldn't let that happen.

She would find a bed for the night. Leave in the morning.

Just as Amalie made it to the street, a voice called out from behind her. "Amalie?"

She spun, then blinked at the figure striding toward her. "Marcel?" He was dressed well. Black trousers, an ivory cotton shirt, and a waistcoat. *What was he doing there?* The Pourfendeurs rarely left their radius, and this was too far north.

He pulled her close to the wall and glanced behind him. "There's someone following you." Amalie eyes locked onto his hand on her arm. He quickly pulled it away.

She swallowed and stepped back. "I'm aware."

Marcel studied her. "What are you doing here?"

"I could ask you the same thing."

He scanned the street. "There was another attack."

"I know." She spoke too soon, realizing they probably

weren't talking about the same thing if he was there. Ren had said the attack was in Mordelles. A lump formed in her throat. "Have you—do you know if my sister Bethany is alright?"

Marcel shrugged. "I haven't been to the country since the last time . . ." His eyes dropped.

The last time. When they'd walked past her uncle's gate together. "Marcel—"

"You didn't come for us. You're still . . . you?"

Amalie drew a breath. "I am." She felt guilty, even though it was the truth. She *was* human. She was herself. But she also very much wasn't. How was she supposed to explain it?

Marcel studied her a moment. "I don't believe you." He nodded curtly and turned toward town.

"Marcel." Amalie rushed after him, and though heads turned her way, she didn't slow. "Marcel, I can prove it to you," she hissed. "In the morning. I'll step out into the sunlight—"

Marcel frowned. "That would hardly be definitive proof."

Amalie pursed her lips. "Vampires can't go in sunlight. How would that not be enough?" She kept her own rebuttal to herself. Theo had been capable of standing in full sunlight without turning to ash. She'd seen it with her own two eyes.

Marcel crossed his arms, his expression cold. "I need to find Olivie."

He stalked away from her, and Amalie stood in the street, defeated. She needed to talk to him. To tell him what she knew. But if he wasn't going to listen, fine.

She clenched her fists, not even glancing back to spot Ren, and rounded a corner, her gaze catching on a wooden sign swinging in the breeze. The image of a horse and rider was painted on the weathered surface, and warm light spilled out from the windows below. An inn.

Amalie slowed, her senses on high alert as she approached the door. He was watching. Ren would know that she'd come here for the night, and there wouldn't be wards or enchantments around these rooms. But she had no choice. She needed a place to rest until morning.

As she reached for the door handle, a flicker of movement caught her eye, and she turned, her heart leaping into her throat. But it was only a cat, its eyes glowing in the lamplight as it darted across the street.

She stepped into the inn, the warmth and light enveloping her like a cozy blanket. The interior was as expected. Wooden furniture, a roaring fireplace, and candles casting a soft, golden glow through the quaint room.

A middle-aged man stood with a ledger book open in front of him. His hair was graying at the temples. "Bonsoir."

Amalie nodded. "I'd like a room for the night if you have one." Her voice was steady despite the fatigue tugging at her limbs.

The innkeeper nodded, sliding the ledger toward her. "Sign here, mademoiselle. Payment is required upfront."

Amalie froze. Money. How had she forgotten money? "I—" Her mind spun, searching for any possible solution. She couldn't sleep in the streets, but she had nothing of value on her person.

"I didn't realize you'd already gone in." Ren strode through the door of the inn, raising an eyebrow as he approached the counter. "Here you are." He reached into his pocket and pulled out a small pouch, placing it on the counter. The innkeeper's eyes widened, and he quickly counted out the appropriate number of coins before sliding the ledger back toward Amalie.

It felt as if the air going in and out of her lungs traveled through a pinhole as she scrawled her name on the line. He was there. He was watching. She hated that she was desperate enough to take his money.

"Glad I could help." Ren's voice was like velvet as he turned and strode out of the inn.

Amalie snatched the key from the innkeeper's outstretched hand, her stomach churning. She rushed out of the room and ascended the staircase, the wooden steps groaning under her weight. The dim lighting from wall-mounted sconces cast long, flickering shadows along the walls. She reached a narrow hallway, and the flames sputtered as she passed.

Her room was at the end of the corridor, the number eleven etched into the wood of the door. She frowned, realizing she'd been looking for Theo's signet.

She slid the iron key into the lock and twisted, the mechanism clicking in protest before the door swung open. The room was simple. A wooden bed with a thick quilt on top, a washbasin with a pitcher of water beside it, and a small open-air window with heavy shutters.

Amalie locked the door behind her, then crossed the room to check the latch on the window. Satisfied it was secure, she poured water into the basin and splashed her face. The cold shocked her senses, bringing her mind back into focus.

How she wished for Henriette. For a warm bath and clean clothes.

Amalie couldn't bring herself to undress. If Ren came in during the night, she wanted to be ready.

She slid under the quilt and lay on her back, staring at the wooden beams above her. It was a relief to lie down, but she didn't see how she could sleep. Not knowing she was being watched.

Although, Theo had been guarding her at the castle, and she didn't mind that as much as she thought she would. There she'd been a priority. Here, she was nobody.

She turned on her side, trying not to think about Ren

finding a way through her window. He would wait. Theo had asked him to watch and wait.

As she pulled the quilt higher over her shoulders, Amalie stilled. Had he asked? It was what Ren had told her, but since she'd been taken to the abbey, Theo had never once asked for Ren's help. Or any of his coven's help for that matter. He'd been careful to keep her away from the other vampires. If he truly thought she would leave, wouldn't he have sent Henriette? Or one of the other serving girls?

A shiver passed through her. If Theo hadn't asked Ren . . . then why had he been at the door of her room?

33

Somehow Amalie slept. It was fitful, but it was something. When she noticed thin strips of morning light forcing their way through the shutters, she threw off the quilt and strode to the washbasin.

Her hair was still sticky where she'd sat against the tree, but there was nothing to do about that. She couldn't waste another second of daylight, especially if it meant Ren couldn't follow her as easily. Her mind wandered back to the quandary of which route to take.

First, she thought about the main road leading directly to Mordelles and the countryside. It was the fastest way, but also the most obvious. Ren would anticipate that route, and she couldn't afford to be predictable. Too risky.

Next, she considered cutting through the forest. The dense trees would provide cover, but it was always dangerous. Even during daylight hours. The forest was known for its treacherous paths and wild animals. Though she'd never believed the attacks spoken of were committed by anyone other than vampires. And now she was sure there was one tracking her.

A shiver ran down her spine as she remembered Theo's words. *There are some fates worse than death.*

Her mind raced, considering the narrow, winding streets of Valenciennes. She could weave through the alleys and side ways, hoping to lose Ren in the labyrinthine layout. It was a longer, more complicated route out of the city, but it might be her best chance.

Could she ever be sure she'd lost him? She still didn't understand how powerful he was. Theo had been able to track her, but once she thought he was dead, she hadn't been careful.

It wasn't an option not to go to her family.

She'd have to do everything she could to mitigate the risk.

Amalie took her key to the innkeeper, thanked him, and asked if she could leave through the servant's door. He gave her a strange look but acquiesced.

She pushed through the steamy, bustling kitchen and exited into the back alley, filled with food scraps and a striped tabby cat, most likely the same one that had given her a start the night before.

Amalie made her way to the street. She looked both ways, scanning for Ren amidst the vendors and townsfolk visiting the boulangerie for their morning baguette. When she was sure he wasn't there, she lowered her head and started walking.

She should've found a disguise. Something to cover her hair, at least. It was too recognizable. Her attention snagged on a rack of scarves on display on the other side of the street. She crossed, her heart picking up speed.

Amalie wasn't a thief, but she didn't have any money and her family was in danger. She ran the soft fabric of a midnight blue scarf through her fingers and memorized the location of the shop. She could come back and pay them later.

When she was about to pull the scarf into her shirt, the hairs on her neck prickled. Amalie's eyes snapped up, and there he was. Ren was strolling leisurely past the shops, his hands tucked into his pockets. He caught her eye and smiled.

A bead of sweat trickled down her temple as she let go of the scarf and jogged down one of the side streets. She swiped it away, clenching her jaw. Ren was like a cat. Toying with her until he pulled her back into his clutches.

She was more convinced by the second that he wasn't on Theo's errand. But why was he there? Did he suspect that she was a guardian? Is that why he'd told her the name of the man who had been attacked?

As Amalie turned onto a side street, she paused, catching her breath. She wouldn't be able to outrun him. It had been stupidity to think she could escape the town unnoticed.

Pressure built behind her eyes as her breathing quickened, panic gripping her chest. She pulled at the neck of her shirt. Her clothes were too tight.

She looked up, expecting to see Ren's gray eyes peering at her, but instead she froze. Marcel and Olivie strode up the street toward her. Marcel wore the same clothes he'd been in the night before. Olivie, on the other hand, looked more like a stable boy than a woman. Her hair was pulled up under a cap, and she wore a plain white shirt, her mustard colored trousers cinched at the waist with a brown belt.

Amalie straightened, forcing air into her lungs.

"Amalie." Olivie moved as if she wanted to rush toward her, and the thought of her friend wrapping her in a hug made her lip tremble. "Good to see you're still alive."

Amalie coughed a laugh. "See, Marcel? Olivie knows how to be polite."

Her comment pulled a hint of a smile from him. "You're still here."

Amalie pursed her lips. "You found Olivie." She looked to her right, then stepped out into the street, allowing the morning sun to wash over her. Olivie's eyes widened, and Amalie could barely speak around the lump in her throat. "This is all I have to offer. I can't think of any other way to prove myself, but if you have ideas—"

"Follow me." Marcel turned and walked back the way they'd come. Olivie matched his stride, glancing over her shoulder as Amalie tagged along like a baby duckling.

She refused to scan the streets for Ren. She didn't want to see him there leaning against the wall, smirking.

It felt as if a lead weight sat on her chest, and her stomach grumbled as they reached the edge of town and paused in front of a café tucked along the river walk. Marcel asked for a table, and when the two of them sat, Amalie took the chair across from them in the shade.

The other tables were full. Men and women sat with their coffees, reading the morning paper. Two older men smoked while they puzzled over a chessboard. Such normalcy. It made her heart ache.

Marcel and Olivie ordered coffee and croissants. Amalie abstained. She didn't have any money, and even if she did, her hands were already shaking.

Marcel grunted. "Why didn't you send us information?"

Amalie exhaled. Did this mean he believed her? Or was he playing a game of his own? "I didn't have everything I needed yet."

"You do now?"

She held her breath, wondering what the right answer was. Did she have what she needed to help the Pourfendeurs? Yes. And no. She shook her head.

Marcel watched her. "What have you found so far?"

"Will you believe me if I tell you?"

He shrugged. "Depends."

Olivie leaned over the table and lowered her voice. "Amalie, we're your friends." Her fingers twitched, but she didn't move. Neither of them had touched her or come close enough that she could touch them.

Amalie wanted to be angry, but she couldn't. If it were Olivie in her position, if she'd never come to Normandy and learned the truth about guardians, she wouldn't have believed it either.

That understanding clarified what information she could share, even if they were friends. "Nothing the Pourfendeurs do will vanquish a vampire, Marcel. They feel pain, but they regenerate."

Marcel's eyes narrowed. "Amalie, we've killed hundreds—"

"No." She shook her head. "It doesn't work. Not permanently. I saw it with my own eyes." Amalie watched them both, but couldn't discern their thoughts. "I have no motivation to lie to you."

He scoffed. "No motivation? A vampire telling the Slayers that they should stop slaying?"

Amalie swallowed hard. "An excellent point." She dropped her eyes, searching for some other explanation, but found every argument besides the truth wanting. And she couldn't tell them that. "There's a relic."

"What kind of relic?" Marcel asked.

Amalie looked up. She took the olive branch. "A sword."

"And you know where it is?"

Amalie pursed her lips. "No, but—" She paused and glanced up, scanning the passersby for stormy eyes and sandy, shoulder length hair. He was there somewhere. "I'm going to find it."

The server brought their coffee in delicate porcelain cups set on saucers with a small spoon for sugar and cream. He set the croissants in the center of the table, and bits of buttered pastry flaked onto the embroidered tablecloth.

"How?" Marcel picked up his cup and held it in front of his nose, breathing it in.

Amalie's shoulders tensed. "I need to get back to my family first. Then . . . I have some ideas."

"Why are you up north?" Olivie broke off one end of her croissant and dipped it in her coffee.

"Someone has an interest in her." Marcel flicked a glance at Amalie before taking a sip from his cup.

Amalie realized two things at once. Olivie was nearly her same height and she was wearing a cap, and they'd passed a storage closet when they'd entered the café. "Olivie, I need your help. If you'd be willing to give it."

34

1824 BLOIS, FRANCE

Rachel's footsteps echoed against the cobblestones, her breath coming in quick bursts as she wove through the narrow streets. The city around her buzzed with life despite the gloomy weather—merchants calling out their wares, the clatter of horse-drawn carriages, the scent of burgundy stew wafting from homes nearby. She scanned the faces of the people passing by the abbey, searching for any sign of Florent.

She hadn't seen him for six days. Each day she'd woken, reaching for him, only to find the bed cold and empty. That wasn't unusual. He often left early or arrived late, but the fact that he hadn't come at all niggled at her. Making her desperate enough to trek into town after harvesting green beans since dawn.

Her mind wandered back to the girls at home, and her chest tightened. She'd noticed Maurielle's side-long glances whenever she disappeared into her room at odd hours. She'd noticed the way her sister-in-law held back when she spoke.

Things had been tense for weeks now, but she didn't know how to rewind.

Rachel's heart twisted as she thought back to the night before. She'd been reading a book in the parlor when Bethany had burst in, tears streaming down her cheeks. "I had a bad dream," she said. "There was a monster. It was—" She'd paused when she saw Rachel's face, and her eyes had widened.

Rachel had pulled her into her lap, stroking her hair and whispering that it was nothing but a nightmare. That she was safe. But Bethany had wriggled from her grasp, calling out for Maurielle.

The next instant, Maurielle had appeared, her eyes tired but soft. Rachel had looked away as her husband's wife carried Bethany upstairs and tucked her back into bed, humming the same lullaby their own mother had sung to them when they were children.

Rachel's face burned with shame. She'd been so consumed with her own search for answers that she'd neglected the girls. She'd ignored her brother and his family.

Rachel quickened her pace, her eyes darting from side to side. She had to find Florent. She had to know what he was hiding from her. She needed to be at peace.

Ignoring the questioning glances from a few passersby, Rachel turned down a side street and found herself in a quieter part of the city. The buildings here were older, their stone facades weathered and crumbling. She passed a small chapel with its heavy wooden door ajar, the sound of chanting drifting from within.

Rachel's heart skipped a beat as she caught sight of a familiar figure in the distance. Sandy hair. A distinctive gait. She'd know it anywhere. Her breath caught, and a rush of adrenaline washed over her like a wave. It was him. It had to be.

She quickened her pace, her eyes locked on Florent as he wove through the crowd. The noise of the city faded into the background until it was nothing but a dull hum in her ears. She had to get closer. She had to see his face.

Rachel's pulse quickened as she rounded the corner, her eyes scanning the street ahead. She caught sight of him again, but his head was turned away from her. For a moment, her heart jumped. She thought he might look back. That his heart might tell him she was there in the street behind him.

He didn't turn. Instead, he slipped into a narrow alley, disappearing from view.

Rachel hesitated, her heart pounding against her ribs. *Was he meeting someone?* She drew a shaky breath, her mind racing. She couldn't back down now. She had to know. If there was someone else . . .

Her throat constricted. She couldn't handle that, could she? Ignoring the voice in her head warning her to be cautious, Rachel hurried forward and pressed herself against the wall at the mouth of the alley. She peered around the corner, her breath catching in her throat.

Florent stood with his back to her, his shoulders tense. He was speaking to someone, but Rachel couldn't see who. She strained to hear, her pulse thrumming in her ears.

"—don't understand the risks." Florent's voice was low and angry, the words barely audible.

A man's voice responded, sharp and biting. "I'm not the one who's careless."

Rachel's stomach clenched. She wanted to step forward, to demand answers, but she stayed where she was, her fingers gripping the rough stone of the building. *What was he talking about? What risks?*

Florent's voice rose, his words echoing off the walls of the alley. "I have a chance, Paul. I'm going to take it."

Rachel's chest tightened as the man's response was lost in the wind. She bit her lip, her mind racing. What were they planning? And why did Florent seem so desperate? Was he planning to leave without her?

Her legs trembled with the urge to move, to confront him, but she forced herself to stay put. She knew he would be angry. She couldn't risk him pushing her away again.

She gasped as a man stormed around the corner, pulling his hat onto his head. Rachel pressed her back against the brick and held her breath until he was at least ten paces away. After drawing a few breaths, she clenched her fists and strode into the shadowed alley.

That time, Florent turned.

Rachel stepped forward, her heart pounding in her chest. "Florent?"

His eyes narrowed as he took her in. When he recognized her, his jaw tightened, his eyes burning like coals.

"Rachel, what in the hell are you doing here?" His voice was laced with irritation. "Do you think this is a game? Showing up unannounced and sticking your nose where it doesn't belong?"

Rachel flinched, her eyes widening. He'd asked her not to bother him in the city. She looked down at her feet, the weight of his words pressing on her shoulders. "I—I'm sorry, I just—" Her voice cracked, and she bit her lip, trying to hold back the flood of emotions threatening to spill over.

Florent's eyes bored into her, his nostrils flaring. He didn't move, and Rachel's pulse quickened. She couldn't bear to see him like this, so distant and angry. It was tearing her apart.

She had to do something. *Tell him the truth.*

Rachel swallowed hard, the taste of fear and regret bitter on her tongue. "I couldn't stand it any longer." Her voice was barely above a whisper. *Was this a good idea? He could laugh in her face and tell her to leave.* She held her breath, praying she'd made the right decision. She couldn't stop herself. She stepped forward, her legs shaking as she locked her eyes on Florent's. "Why have you been so distant, Florent?"

She reached out, touching his arm, but he jerked away, his eyes wild. Rachel's heart twisted in her chest, the pain like a knife. "I can't live like this." Her voice cracked, and she felt tears well in her eyes. "It's tearing me apart. Every morning I wake and remember that you were absent the night before. I know nothing of what you're doing when I'm not there, and the girls and I are leaving in less than a week. I don't—"

She wrapped her arms around herself, trying to keep her heart from spilling out like a cracked egg. Florent's jaw tightened. Rachel forced her eyes to his. "I know you're hurting, and I want to help you, Florent. Whatever it takes. Please, let me help you. Let me help *us*."

Florent's expression twisted, his eyes flicking over her face. He didn't move, but Rachel could see the conflict in his eyes. He was angry, but there was something else there too. A softness, a flicker of the man she'd fallen in love with. She held her breath, praying it wasn't just her imagination.

Florent's eyes softened, and Rachel's heart skipped a beat. *There.* She hadn't imagined it. She took a step forward, her fingers trembling as she reached for his hand.

Florent's eyes locked onto hers, and Rachel's pulse quickened. He didn't pull away this time. He didn't reach for her, but it was a small victory, and she was clinging to it.

Florent's pupils dilated, and he took a step forward, his chest brushing against hers. "You're sure?" His voice was rough, and a shiver ran down Rachel's spine. She nodded, her throat too tight to speak.

Florent's fingers tightened around her wrists, and Rachel's breath caught in her throat. She couldn't look away, couldn't breathe. She was suspended in that moment, the world fading away.

She pressed her palms against his chest, her heart pounding so hard she was sure he could feel it. Florent's arms wrapped around her, pulling her close, and Rachel's eyes fluttered shut. She leaned into him, her cheek pressed against his shoulder, the scent of his skin filling her lungs.

This was air. This was life. The way his body felt against hers, the way his breath tickled her ear. Her fingers dug into the fabric of his shirt, and she let out a shuddering breath. She didn't want to ruin the moment, but she had to know. "Why, Florent?" She drew a deep breath, her body trembling. "Why have you been distant? I'm trying to be patient, but this has been—" Her voice cracked, and she pressed her lips together. "I've been tearing myself apart."

Florent gripped her tighter. "It's not as simple as all that."

"Then explain it to me."

"You wouldn't understand—I don't want you to understand."

Rachel pulled back, and she opened her mouth to respond, but Florent cut her off. "You have no idea what you're asking for. What you're offering." He stepped closer, his breath hot on her face. "This isn't a game, Rachel. This is life and death."

Rachel's heart pounded in her chest, and she forced herself to meet his gaze. "I know that." Her voice was steady, despite the fear coursing through her veins. "I'm not a child, Florent. I understand magic holds risks. But I also know what I want. I know what I need."

Florent's eyes darkened, and he shook his head. "You don't know what you're saying." His voice was a low growl, and Rachel's breath hitched.

"I do." She stepped closer, her fingers brushing his cheek. "I know what I want." She leaned in, her lips grazing his ear. "I want you."

Florent's jaw clenched, and Rachel's heart raced. He was going to push her away. He was going to tell her to leave, to forget about him, to—

"What do you feel? When you close your eyes and send your thoughts deep within you."

Rachel frowned. The question was so strange, she wasn't sure how to answer. "I feel many things."

He wrapped his arms around her waist. "Close your eyes, Rachel. Sink into yourself. What do you feel?"

Rachel did as he asked, but how to put it into words? Her thoughts raced, making it difficult to focus.

"Breathe." Florent ran his hand over her back.

Rachel inhaled and imagined herself dropping into the river, her body sinking into the soft mud and river rock. "I feel warm. I feel . . . tight. Like there's something lodged against my spine. I don't know how to describe it."

"Is it cool? Dark?"

Rachel's brow knit together. "I don't know. It's just there. A knot I should unravel, but don't know how."

Florent smoothed her brow with his thumb. "Good. Well done."

Rachel's eyes fluttered open. What had she done to deserve such praise?

He pursed his lips. "There is a way."

Rachel's heart skipped a beat, and she pulled back, her eyes wide. "What?"

Florent's eyes were dark, his expression pained. "There is a way to solidify what we have. To make it permanent. To give me back my power." Florent's jaw tightened, and he looked away.

Rachel brushed her fingers over his arm. "Tell me."

Florent's eyes met hers, and Rachel's breath caught in her throat. There was something in his gaze—something dark and dangerous. But there was also something else. Something that made her heart ache.

Florent's voice was low when he spoke. "There's a ceremony."

Rachel nodded. She wanted Florent. Not just as a secret. "Show me what to do."

35

Amalie hesitated. There was a chance she'd be putting Olivie in grave danger if she followed through with this. But Ren hadn't attacked her yet, and if he was after her blood, Olivie would be nothing to him.

She grabbed Olivie's hand and yanked her toward the storage closet after mumbling something about an asp sting to the server. Dust motes danced in the stream of light pouring through the small round window above the door, and the room smelled faintly of dust and old wood. Without a word, Amalie began stripping off her clothes.

Olivie stood frozen for a moment, her eyes wide as she watched Amalie toss her blouse and trousers into a pile on the floor. Then, as if realizing they didn't have all morning, she fumbled with the buttons on her blouse, struggling to undo them with shaking hands.

"Here." Amalie stepped forward and yanked the fabric down over her shoulders.

Olivie let out a small gasp but didn't protest as Amalie pulled the shirt free and tossed it aside. She shivered, goosebumps rising on her arms, and undid her belt. She darted a glance around the room as she stepped out of her trousers like she expected someone to burst in at any moment. To be fair, it was a real possibility.

Amalie ignored her nervousness, focusing on getting dressed as quickly as possible. She slipped into Olivie's trousers, ignoring the way the coarse fabric scratched against her skin. Before pulling on the blouse, she handed her own clothes to Olivie.

"Thank you."

Olivie shoved her arms through the arms of her shirt. "Don't thank me yet. Do you think it will work?"

"I hope so."

"And I won't be in danger?"

Amalie shook her head, guilt blooming in her gut. "As soon as he realizes you aren't me, there will be no reason for him to bother you." She was almost certain that was true. Even if Ren knew the Pourfendeurs, he seemed motivated enough to keep his eyes on her. But the fact that she didn't know why niggled at her.

"We both need to stay hidden," Amalie muttered, more to herself than to Olivie. She reached for Olivie's cap, tucking her dark hair beneath the edges until only her face showed. Satisfied with her disguise, she turned to Olivie.

Her friend had managed to get dressed, though the trousers were tight around her hips, and the blouse hung a bit loose on her frame.

Amalie stepped back and surveyed their work. They wouldn't fool anyone up close, but from a distance, she was positive it would work. She led Olivie back toward the door, her hands shaking.

"Amalie . . ." Olivie grabbed her arm.

Amalie froze and glanced down. She was touching her.

Olivie pulled her hand back. "Take this. Please." She handed her a small satchel that Amalie hadn't noticed her carrying. Coins clinked as she took it. "Be careful."

Amalie clutched the satchel to her chest. "Tell Marcel it was good to see both of you, and I'll be in touch." There was so much she wanted to say. So much she wanted to explain. It would have to be later.

Amalie left the closet and exited the café. She walked leisurely, blood rushing in her ears as she paused, pretending to be interested in a shop or two as she made her way down the street. More people were out, and that worked in her favor.

She could hide. Better yet, she could hopefully find someone willing to take her on as a passenger.

Amalie quickened her steps, and when she reached the main thoroughfare, she hailed a passing cart, shouting in French. "I need a ride to Mordelles. I'll pay." She held out the satchel.

The driver, an older man with a scraggly beard, eyed her warily before slowing his horse and nodding. "Get in."

Amalie climbed up and handed him the coins, then settled onto the wooden bench beside him. The cart jolted forward, and she gripped the edge to keep herself steady. With each turn of the wheel, they moved farther from the center of town, the buildings thinning out until they were surrounded by fields and orchards. The smell of growing things barely drowned out the scent of sun-warmed horse hair.

She couldn't force her shoulders to relax even though everything had gone her way that morning. Something still didn't feel right. It was too easy.

Amalie shook her head and scanned the horizon, taking in the rolling hills and neatly manicured fields. *Why couldn't it go her way for once?*

The cart creaked beneath her as they rumbled over century

old roman stone, then jolted onto a dirt path lined with wild-flowers. She gripped the bench tighter, her knuckles white against the rough surface.

A flash of movement caught her eye, and she turned to see a young girl riding a velocipede along the side of the road. Her hair streamed behind her like a banner, and Amalie's heart clenched at the sight.

Oren had taught her how to ride when she was no older than that girl. He'd held the back of the seat steady while she wobbled and swayed, his laughter filling the air as she'd finally found her balance and pedaled down the lane on her own. She could still feel the wind in her face, hear the sound of their joy echoing through the trees. It had been one of those rare moments when everything felt right, when the world seemed full of endless possibilities.

The cart rounded a bend, and her gaze landed on a small farmhouse nestled among blooming flowers. The colors were so vibrant they almost hurt her eyes, and another memory surfaced unbidden.

She and Oren had spent hours planting tulips and daffodils in the garden outside his study. He'd shown her how to dig the holes just right, how to space them evenly so they'd have room to grow. Their hands had been covered in dirt by the time they finished, and they'd laughed when they looked up to see each other's smudged faces.

Amalie blinked back tears, the ache in her chest growing stronger with each passing second. Those simple, happy times were gone forever. She couldn't bring them back, no matter how desperately she wished otherwise.

She let out a shuddering breath, the memories clinging to her like burrs. Oren's warm smile, the way he'd tugged on his beard when he was deep in thought, the sound of his voice reading poetry aloud in the candlelight.

Would she find him there? Would she be able to get to her sister or cousins, to Maurielle? Amalie's throat constricted, and she forced herself to take a deep breath.

Another jolt nearly threw her from the bench, and she squeezed her eyes shut, willing her mind to still. Instead, a vivid image of Theo laughing filled her vision. His midnight hair tumbled over his forehead, his mouth open wide in delight.

Amalie's eyes flew open. *That was not real.* She shook her head, willing the intruding image to disappear. But it stayed there, taunting her with its familiarity.

Had she seen that moment and forgotten? Had she experienced it firsthand, or was her brain making things up? Meshing bits and pieces together until they formed a cohesive whole?

It didn't make sense. And yet, the more she tried to unravel it, the more tangled her thoughts became. Something was happening to her. It was like she was being cleaved apart, separated from the woman she thought she was and forced to meld with a woman she knew nothing about.

Tears pricked at the corners of her eyes again, and this time she didn't fight them. They spilled over, tracing hot paths down her cheeks. Amalie buried her face in her hands and sobbed, her shoulders shaking with the force of it.

"Ah, mademoiselle, peut-être voulez-vous en parler?"

She shook her head. *No.* She didn't want to talk about it.

How could she do this alone? How could she save her uncle when she didn't even know where to begin? She knew nothing of guardians, nothing of relics or ancient rituals. Every scrap of information she had came from Theo, and now she wasn't sure what was true and what was fabricated.

Would finding Oren even help? Would he want her to go after him if he knew what she was seeking?

She didn't have the answers to those questions. *Because he'd never talked to her about the truth.*

———

Nearly four hours later, the cart entered a narrow lane flanked by tall hedges. Amalie's pulse quickened, and she leaned forward, recognizing it immediately.

She stared at the shed she and Theo had sought refuge in. It felt like a lifetime ago. Her shivering next to the fire. Theo laying out her clothes to dry.

She'd hated him then. But did she now?

"I'll get off here." Amalie pointed to the side of the lane, and the man pulled the horse to a stop. Amalie dropped to the ground and winced, her backside aching and her legs stiff. She stretched and then forced herself to start running. The sun was dropping low, and she needed to get to Oren's before dark.

Amalie raced through the streets of Mordelles, then retraced the path she'd taken hundreds of times out of town. She took breaks, walked, and ran until she hit the stone wall.

The gate was open when she pushed, and she rushed through the yard, jumping the steps. Amalie burst through the front door, nearly unhinging it in her haste. She didn't bother closing it behind her. "Bethany! Maurielle!" Her pulse thudded in her ears as she waited for a response.

Nothing.

She gasped for breath and took off down the hall. "Bethany! Maurielle!" Her voice was desperate, her hands beginning to go numb.

The only answer was the echo of her voice against the walls.

The house still looked lived in. Exactly as she'd left it. Hope sparked in her chest as she flew down the hall and threw open the door to her uncle's study.

Amalie skidded to a stop, unable to understand the scene in front of her.

Uncle Oren.

Hunched over his desk, inspecting something.

With Theo bent next to him, a hand on his shoulder.

36

1836 COUNTRYSIDE BEYOND MORDELLES,
FRANCE

Amalie stared at the man who'd been like a father to her. She blinked several times, not understanding what she was seeing. Her guardian—the man who'd raised her after her mother had died—was standing *next to Theo.*

A vampire.

Who, up until a week ago, he denied the existence of. "You know each other?" She gritted her teeth, desperately fighting the urge to curse her uncle out in his own home or run to him and make sure that what she was seeing was real.

He looked like himself. He didn't have marks on his neck. "I heard you were attacked," she rasped, her emotions locked in hand-to-hand combat.

Oren's jaw worked. "You said you'd be here in the morning."

Amalie's jaw dropped. "That's what you're saying to me right now?" He was alive. He was human. That mattered more than the fact that he'd lied to her again, didn't it? She nearly choked on the rage punching its way through her chest.

Theo lifted his hands. "Let me explain."

"Explain?" Amalie's eyes burned. "Do you plan to *explain* this like everything else?"

Oren's brow pinched, and he turned to Theo, his face flushing red. "You know my niece?"

Amalie laughed out loud, clawing her hands in her hair. "This is unbelievable!" She spun in a circle, searching for something she could punch or shatter.

Amalie whirled, her eyes filling with tears. She ran to Oren, throwing her arms around him.

"Amalie—"

"How are you here?" She squeezed him tight, and after he'd gotten over his shock, he returned the embrace. "Are the girls safe? Maurielle?"

"Yes, of course." Oren pushed back, cupping her face in his hands. "Amalie—"

"You." Amalie rounded the desk, storming up to Theo. "You knew about this and forced me to stay behind?"

Theo rounded the desk, his eyes dark. "Knew about what?"

Amalie opened her mouth, but the words died on her throat. What had he kept from her? Oren was here. Safe and sound. She frowned, thinking back to Ren sitting outside her bedroom door. He'd told her that Allard was the name of the attacked Guardian. Had it been a mistake? Had he gotten the surname wrong?

Theo took a step closer. "Amalie, it isn't safe for you here. The attacks—"

"If there are attacks, then none of us are safe." She looked between the two of them. "Why are we not taking the girls somewhere? Why is a vampire *in our home?*"

"Amalie, sit down." Oren pointed to the chair in the corner by his bookshelves. The last thing she wanted to do was sit, but the room was beginning to spin. She'd traveled all day. She hadn't taken a single breath that didn't ache.

She did as he asked, her throat beginning to burn. Theo was there. Oren knew him. She'd been with Theo for days and he'd said nothing. She'd lived with Uncle Oren her whole life and *he'd said nothing.*

Oren exhaled. "Your sister is well. Bethany is out back in the garden with Maurielle and my girls."

A pang shot through Amalie's middle. She'd been here. Standing in this very room, a ring dropped on his desk as proof that vampires existed. Now he stood here with one of them while the girls he was supposed to protect were out back picking flowers? Amalie's chest cinched so tight, she could barely breathe.

Oren ran a hand through his thinning hair. "Theo has been working with us for years to protect the guardianship. Your mother made me promise—made me swear I wouldn't tell you about our history until you were eighteen. I'm sorry—" His voice broke, and Amalie felt the urge to go to him.

She didn't. "I didn't realize 'our history' included colluding with the vampires that killed my mother."

Theo's jaw ticked. "We have protected the guardians since the beginning."

"Who's 'we?'" She couldn't take any more of his cryptic talk.

Theo turned to Oren, and something flickered over her Uncle's face. Oren turned to her. "How do you know Theo, Amalie?"

"I tried to kill him."

"More than once," Theo muttered under his breath.

Amalie's eyes flashed. "With your *permission.*"

Oren stared at her a moment too long. Finally, he turned to Theo. "You believe it is her?"

Theo nodded. "I know it."

"Have you tested—"

Theo shook his head. "Her blood won't work on me, and I haven't had access to anyone outside of my coven."

"What the hell are you talking about?" Amalie stood, her hands shaking. "My entire life you told me these creatures didn't exist. Now you want me to believe you're in league with them? Why would Theo care to protect us?"

"Because you asked me to." Theo's voice was raw.

His words didn't make sense. *They never made any sense.* Amalie stood. Her body felt so heavy it could sink through the floor.

Uncle Oren sighed. "Amalie—"

"No. You two can have your secrets. I came to make sure you were safe." Her eyes flashed as she pulled off Olivie's cap and let her hair fall around her shoulders. She turned to Theo. "Ren followed me from the sand flats to Servon. I believe I lost him, but I'm not sure. I assume since he's not here with you, that's significant."

Amalie spun on her heel and stalked from the room. Neither of them followed her up the stairs, and she was glad for it. She needed time to think.

It felt like years since she'd entered her bedroom. Had it only been a week?

She closed the door behind her, and took in the narrow bed pushed against one wall and the armoire standing guard opposite. She gazed over her rumpled covers. Her mother's face swam before her eyes, smiling gently as she brushed Amalie's hair back from her forehead. How many times had she sat on this very bed while her mother told her a story? How many nights had she woken from nightmares only to be comforted by her soothing voice?

Amalie's throat burned. It had been more of Maurielle at the last. Had she ever thanked her aunt for that? When her mother had been gone, she'd been the one to rub her back and sing her to sleep.

Amalie crossed to the window and yanked open the shutters. The window made her think of Theo, and she gritted her teeth as she sucked the cool evening air down like water, trying to calm the racing thoughts tumbling through her mind.

Her mother had known all of this. She'd had the answers, and she'd asked Oren to keep them from her. *Why?*

There had been so many times when she could have asked her questions, but she hadn't known she held secrets. The mother she'd seen was such a small sliver of the woman she might've known and loved.

She would have told her. Amalie had no doubt about that. Had she learned of vampires, her mother never would have lied like Uncle Oren. If she'd been there, Amalie never would've left. She never would've thought she could vanquish vampires.

Amalie collapsed onto her arms and let the emotions of the past two days wash over her. She still wasn't safe. Her family wasn't safe. Even if she found the relic, how could one sword be the answer?

A bird chirped and she lifted her head. The little starling sat on a bougainvillea branch. The flowers were gone this time of year, and yet . . .

Life went on. The vine deepened its roots. Birds called. The sun rose and fell.

Amalie swiped the tears from her cheeks and closed the shutters, then dropped to her knees beside the bed, her fingers scrabbling at the loose floorboard beneath. The wood lifted easily, revealing a hollow space where a small wooden box lay nestled among the dust and cobwebs.

Amalie pulled it out, setting it on the bedspread and tracing the intricate carvings. This had belonged to her grandmother, then her mother, and now it was hers. They'd touched it. Held it in their hands.

She tried for the thousandth time to open it. It wouldn't budge. Her fingers burned as she dug her nails into the seam between the lid and base, prying until her fingers ached, then switched tactics and tried to press along the edges. When that failed, she stood and searched the room for something to use as a lever—a letter opener, a hairpin—but found nothing suitable.

Finally, she returned to the bed and glared at the box, her breath coming fast and shallow. "Open," she hissed through gritted teeth, gripping either side of the lid. It refused to give way.

With a growl, she raised the box above her head and hurled it across the room. There was a crack of wood, and splintered pieces flew in all directions.

What if there had been something delicate inside? Something irreplaceable?

Amalie stared at the shattered remains of the box. Jagged pieces of wood and scattered trinkets lay strewn across the floor. She dropped to her knees, her hands trembling as she reached for the fragments.

She sifted through the debris, moving splinters of wood as her eyes burned. The box had been a precious link to her mother, and now it lay in ruins. *But she could've made it easier to open.*

Amalie yanked her hand back when a sharp sting pulsed through her finger. Panic surged through her, her mind flashing back to her pulling on a piece of skin. To her window surging open. To Theo Vallon standing in front of her.

Amalie pulled the sliver out quickly, bringing her finger to her mouth to suck on the wound and stop the bleeding. *Stupid.*

She held her finger out to dry and watched. It was a small enough prick, the bleeding didn't last long, thankfully. She resumed cleaning, that time more carefully, not allowing her thoughts to drop to Oren's study below.

After forming a small pile of wreckage, Amalie paused at the sight of a delicate paper swan with crumpled wings. The sight of it hit her like a bag of bricks.

Her mother's hands folded in her lap. "Take this piece, and fold it over."

They sat together in the garden after lunch while the sky darkened with rain clouds, making birds from the colored pages in her storybooks.

"You make it look easy." Amalie fought with the edges of her bird.

"It's all about patience and attention to detail. You're almost there."

They'd finished their swans just before the storm broke, running inside and setting them on display next to her bed, where they'd stayed until they moved away a few months later. Amalie clung to the memory, unable to believe how easily she'd forgotten those moments. How focused she'd been on losing her instead of remembering.

She clutched the mangled swan and shifted her focus back to the pile before her.

Next, she found a small notebook bound in leather. Its cover was worn, the pages inside were empty. Another image of her mother sitting up late at night by candlelight, her quill scratching across the yellowed pages of those same notebooks. There were dozens of them shoved behind books on the kitchen shelf and others scattered around the house.

"Why do you write everything down?" she'd asked once, annoyed that her mother couldn't take her outside because she needed to finish whatever she was working on.

"Because someday I'll forget."

Those words hadn't made sense to Amalie then, but now . . .

Amalie tugged the end of a delicate gold chain from under the armoire. Her mother's locket. She remembered it hanging around her neck, which meant her mother had found a way to open the damn box.

She turned over the gold oval charm in her palm, again searching for a clasp that didn't seem to exist. Perhaps it was only decorative. Her mother had never opened it, at least not in her memory. She slipped the chain over her head and pulled her hair free of the it.

Only one more item lay within reach. Amalie picked up a glass vial, turning it over in her palm. It had no cork and wasn't much larger than her finger—empty except for a bit of residue stuck to the bottom of the container. What would her mother have used something like this for? Perfume?

Dust from the floor finally caught her nose, and Amalie sneezed twice, holding her arm over her mouth and blinking into the dim light. Where could the other items have landed? She crawled forward, peering beneath her desk and feeling for anything that might've fallen between the cracks.

A flash of silver caught her eye at the corner of the room, and Amalie's blood rushed. She scrambled toward it on her hands and knees, reaching out and grasping it tight. She turned her hand over, and frowned.

A ring.

Masculine.

Amalie furrowed her brow and shifted closer to the window. She hadn't realized how low the light had gotten.

As soon as the light hit the face of it, her body stilled. An oval. Tilted on its axis. Half light, half dark.

37

1836 COUNTRYSIDE BEYOND MORDELLES, FRANCE

A knock sounded at her bedroom door, and Amalie jolted. She slipped the ring into her pocket and jumped up from the bed.

"Amalie?" Bethany's voice. Amalie rushed forward, pulling the door open and sweeping her little sister into her arms. She ran a hand over her braided hair, crushing her to her chest.

"Amalie, I can't breathe." Bethany's voice was muffled, and Amalie relaxed her grip.

"Sorry. I'm so glad to see you." Amalie pulled her into her room and closed the door.

"It's only been a few days. You owe me an explanation, by the way." Bethany was about to flop onto the bed when Amalie stopped her. She crouched and scooped up the items she'd spread out on the quilt, moving them to the nightstand.

"What are those?" Bethany asked as she sat.

Amalie crossed the room and used a match to light the candle on her writing desk. She pointed at the pile of splintered wood still sitting on the floor. "I opened the box."

Bethany's eyes widened. "It looks like you took a rock to the box."

Amalie stubbed out the match. She sat next to Bethany on the bed and sighed. "I couldn't figure out how to open it."

Bethany's eyes locked onto the collection of items she'd moved off the bed, and Amalie felt a pang in her middle as she fingered her mother's locket. Her sister didn't remember. She'd only been two when their mother passed.

Amalie had vivid memories of their mother. Of the way wisps of her hair escaped and brushed over her face as she worked in the garden. The way she chewed on her lower lip when she was studying one of her books.

"This was hers." Amalie held the necklace out, allowing Bethany to inspect it.

"It was in the box?"

Amalie nodded.

Bethany held it up, turning it this way and that. "Does it open?"

Amalie shrugged. "I don't think so."

"Please don't take to it the way you did with that." Bethany pointed at the remains of the box.

Amalie snorted. She scooped the other items from the nightstand and placed them in her lap.

"Were these hers, too?"

"This was." Amalie handed her the notebook.

"Have you read it?" Bethany asked. Amalie shook her head, and she handed it back to her. "I won't look before you do." She picked up the vial and inspected it.

"I thought it could be for perfume, but there isn't any lingering smell."

Bethany pulled out the stopper and held her nose close to the opening. She nodded in agreement. "Did she wear perfume?"

Amalie considered this. "I think so. But I'm not quite sure. She smelled fresh, like sweet pea blossoms."

Bethany handed back the vial. "I wish I remembered more."

Amalie's throat tightened. "Me too." She had the sudden urge to tell Bethany everything. To assure her their mother wasn't gone, not really. That she would be reborn, and so would they. But the complexity of it overwhelmed her.

Who were they to each other if they were new in every life? How often did they find themselves living again, and where did their spirits go in the interim? She didn't know if they'd ever see their mother again, and that tinged the entire story black at the edges.

"Your clothes are strange," Bethany said, and Amalie laughed. She'd forgotten she was still dressed in Olivie's pants and shirt.

Amalie stood and crossed to the armoire. She unlatched the belt and pulled off the trousers, exhaling at the sudden freedom around her middle.

"Where have you been?" Bethany's voice was timid, and Amalie hated that she'd given her sister a reason to be hesitant around her.

"I was traveling north. In Normandy."

"Were you with them?"

Amalie pulled on a clean pair of slacks. She glanced at Bethany who fiddled with a loose fingernail, not meeting her eyes.

Bethany knew of her work with the Pourfendeurs. No doubt it was a regular topic of dinner conversation. How she was a terrible example and Bethany should never follow in her sister's footsteps.

"No. Not this time." Amalie set Olivie's shirt on the desk

and pulled on a clean tunic. A soft knock came at the door, and Amalie jumped a second time.

"It's Aunt Maurielle. May I come in?"

"Yes." Amalie crossed the room and set the items from the box next to her right hip on the bed, obscuring them from view.

Maurielle opened the door and leaned into the bedroom. She gave Amalie a small smile. "Would you like to come down for supper?" She turned to Bethany. "Since you and the girls have already eaten, I was hoping you might be willing to put your cousins down for bed."

Bethany seemed to read something in Maurielle's expression. "Of course." She squeezed Amalie's hand and walked to the door, then turned back. "I still want that explanation."

Amalie huffed a laugh. "In the morning?"

Bethany shot her a look, then slipped past their aunt and disappeared into the hall.

Amalie stood. She barely made it two steps before Maurielle was folding her into her arms. "I'm so glad you're safe." Her body was warm and soft, and she smelled of herbs and strong soap. "Come," Aunt Maurielle said, stepping back and holding out a hand. "I'm sure you're hungry."

Amalie followed her aunt downstairs. She patted the ring in her pocket, and her pulse quickened. It was from Theo's coven, which meant he knew the vampire who had been meeting with her mother. He knew the vampire who killed her.

The only question was, did he know he knew? Was this another piece of information he'd been keeping from her?

But she'd asked him if he knew who killed her, and Theo hadn't avoided answering. Even though he'd kept things from her, he'd never lied, not directly.

Amalie held her breath as Maurielle rounded the corner to the dining room. Would he be there? She assumed Maurielle sent Bethany away because Theo was in the house, but she hadn't realized how much she'd been hoping to see him until she stepped into the candlelight and found him seated next to Uncle Oren.

The dining room was quaint. Just as she remembered it, with a muslin tablecloth and a small vase of fall blooms in the center. She took her seat across from Theo where a plate already waited.

Theo's eyes flicked to the locket around Amalie's neck, but he didn't say anything. She wondered if he could sense the ring hidden in her pocket.

Amalie picked up her fork and glanced up at Aunt Maurielle. "Thank you. It smells delicious."

Uncle Oren waited for her to take the first bite, then began cutting his meat. Theo swirled a glass in front of him. Absinthe, she assumed by the color. She held back her surprise that Oren and Maurielle would have any in the house.

Theo looked tired. She hadn't noticed how his cheekbones were dusted with shadow in the office. She'd only seen him look like that one other time. In the castle. When he'd been about to leave and she'd stopped him.

The memory of him next to her in his closet. His lips against her skin . . . Her cheeks heated, and she focused on her plate, shoving a piece of potato into her mouth.

When she looked up, Theo's eyes were on her. *Because you asked me to.* His words in the study thrummed through her.

He had been protecting guardians. Working with Uncle Oren all this time. Is that where he'd gone when he left the castle? He would be a perfect ally, powerful, and free to walk during daylight. Had she known that about him in a past life?

Amalie speared a tender piece of chicken and placed it in her mouth. Who was Theo Vallon to her? Who did she want him to be?

"I've brought down books for you." Uncle Oren swiped at his mouth with a napkin. "I know it's long overdue, but I'll answer your questions, Amalie. Whatever you want to know."

Amalie looked up from her plate. Her uncle's eyes were sad, almost glassy in the candlelight. "My mother's books?"

He nodded. "She read them more than I did. They were passed down to us by our—" His voice caught, and he coughed into his napkin. "By her mother," he finished, his voice strained.

The air in the room grew thick. "Her mother?" Amalie's fork sat still in her hand.

Oren drank from his glass. "Rachel and I weren't family by birth. She was in need of a home. We adopted her in." He glanced up at Theo, but Theo's eyes were still trained on her.

Amalie suddenly felt like a rabbit caught in a trap. She set her fork on her plate. "Where are the books?"

Oren nodded to the hall. "In my study. I set them on my desk."

Amalie stood and placed her napkin on the table. "Thank you." She dropped her eyes and strode from the room.

She couldn't make it down the hall fast enough. She entered the study and closed the door behind her, pressing her forehead against the cool wood.

It felt as if she were staring at the sea, watching a tidal wave rushing toward the shore, ready to swallow her, but her feet were buried in sand.

There was something in her past that neither Oren or Theo wanted to tell her. The way they looked at her, sitting in wait.

Was she supposed to remember? Had she remembered before?

Amalie straightened and strode to her uncle's desk, the scent of dust and aged paper settling in her nostrils. Her heart galloped as she saw the stack of books below where her uncle had been standing earlier when she'd caught him with Theo.

She hunched over and pressed her hands against the desk, her dark hair falling into her face. She brushed it behind her ear in an irritated flick and pulled the first book from the pile. The spine was cracked, the book bound with worn leather, and the title was almost unreadable.

Le Livre de la Garde. Amalie sat in her uncle's chair and opened it. The pages were fragile, the words penned in ink. Theo's voice sounded in her head. *Human histories are necessary because your life spans are short. Those stories must be recorded more permanently.*

Amalie shivered and began to read.

Lovely.
Deadly.
Cloaked in shadow,
Bound by light.
Two sides of
The same eternal night.

The Great Eclipse.

In the time of eternal twilight, Solène and Le Sombre existed in perfect harmony as one being, a union of light and dark, maintaining the delicate balance of the world created for humanity. Together, they ruled over all, a peaceful force that mirrored the beauty of the dawn and dusk where their realms of light and shadow met. The gods, pleased with this balance, watched over the world with pride. However, as the ages passed, even the gods grew weary of endless harmony.

They began to tease and prod at the unity of Solène and Le Sombre. The gods planted seeds of discontent until finally, the tension between light and dark became too great. The harmonious being that was Solène and Le Sombre fractured, torn into two opposing forces, each desiring dominion over the world. Solène embodied the purity and brilliance of light, while Le Sombre claimed the depths of shadow.

But both were incomplete without the other. Le Sombre, filled with longing and ache, created dark companions to share in his misery. These beings were birthed from the shadows and cursed with an insatiable thirst, never able to truly possess the life force they craved.

Solène pleaded with Le Sombre, begging for an end to suffering. But without her light, Le Sombre could not see past his own darkness.

Amalie paused, reading a note in the margin in her mother's hand.

You were not made merely to fight the darkness, but to bring forth the light within it. Help them see beyond the shadow.

She read it again, her vision blurring as tears filled her eyes, then flipped the page. She read the last paragraph of the introduction.

What follows is a record containing the fullness of the guardian bond and the light we wield. Until the Day of Light, guardians will wait. They will serve. They will protect. And when she who is sent to bind appears, they will follow.

Amalie had barely begun to absorb the words when she startled at the sound of a boot scuffing on stone.

Her head snapped up, making tears drop onto her cheeks. Amalie stood and wiped her cheeks with the back of her hand.

"I'm sorry. I didn't mean to startle you." Theo's voice was low.

Amalie worked to swallow the lump in her throat. "I don't think there's much you could do to startle me at this point."

Theo's eyes shuttered. "Fair enough." He took a step closer to the front of the desk. "Did you find what you were looking for?"

"About the sword? No." She shook her head. "I—"

"I wasn't talking about the sword." He was in front of her now, only Uncle Oren's desk between them. Amalie breathed him in, giving in for just a few moments to the desire that constantly hummed beneath her skin when he was close.

Or even when he wasn't. She was like a compass, always pointing toward him. Whether she was in the castle or alone in her hotel room in Servon.

"Is there something I did?" Amalie dropped her eyes, her throat working. "I mean in the past. Did I hurt you? Is that why you attacked in my room. Why you were cold—"

"No." Theo's body tensed.

"Then why?" She finally looked up, not trying to hide the new tears pooling in her eyes.

Theo's hands trembled at his sides. "You wouldn't have believed me."

"You could've tried."

"No. I couldn't." He turned, dragging a hand over his face. "I had to take you to the island. I needed you to be safe."

"Because of the wards?"

His eyes snapped to hers. "How do you know about that?"

"Ren. I told you, he—"

"I came to tell you I'm leaving," Theo snapped. "I need to find him. He wasn't supposed to be at the castle."

Amalie's breathing quickened. "He was in Servon. He may have followed me, I don't know."

"I'll find him." Theo turned, but the idea of him walking out of the study and leaving the house made her feel as if a hand was clenched around her windpipe.

"Wait."

Theo glanced back, and Amalie shoved her hand into her pocket and pulled out the ring she'd found in her mother's box. She placed it on the desk.

His eyes locked onto the circle of silver, and he moved like a shadow in front of the desk. Theo picked it up and inspected it. "It's not mine. Where did you get this?"

Amalie opened her uncle's desk drawer and pulled out the ring she'd taken from him the night she'd stabbed him in the heart. "I know it's not yours." She placed his ring on the desk, and Theo snatched it up.

"Where did you get this?" he asked again.

"It was hers. She left me a box, and that ring was in it. I only just discovered it." She scrutinized his face, searching for any flicker of . . . something. Recognition? Guilt? Theo's face was a mask of stone. "She had been meeting a vampire, Theo, and then this ring—"

Theo slid his own ring back on the ring finger of his left

hand. Had she noticed that was where he'd worn it when she'd taken it from him?

As he straightened, Amalie felt the same chill from the hallway. When they'd found Penelope broken, crumpled on the stone. "Theo—"

"This ring belongs to a member of my coven. I will find him." Shadows seemed to press in around him, soaking into him like water on dry soil. The shadows around his eyes grew deeper, his eyes dark pools of midnight.

"Let me help you." Amalie's breath hitched. The idea of Theo leaving the house made the knot in her middle cinch so tight, she thought she might snap in two.

"Amalie, you can't—"

"You need to feed. I know. I can see it." She thought of him with the knife in his hands. Ramon's fingers against the blade. "You can—we can take care of it the way we did last time. Quickly."

Theo seemed to groan under an invisible weight on his shoulders. "I don't think that's a good idea."

"You need to feed."

"I'm well aware," he growled.

"Then let me help." Amalie rounded the desk and reached for him.

Theo caught her wrist, and she gasped as he pulled so fast and hard, her feet flew out from under her. Theo caught her waist, righting her. "It's too dangerous."

She shook her head. "You didn't hurt me last time."

"*That's not what I meant.* You don't understand."

"Then *let me.*" She snatched her hand back, her eyes flashing. "I will not let you leave like this. You'll kill someone."

"If I stay, I'll—" A strangled sound escaped his throat, and something tugged hard in her middle.

Amalie reached out and touched him. She'd never done it before, not like this. Not because she wanted to.

Theo froze, besides the rapid rise and fall of his chest, every part of him so still, it was as if he'd been cast in stone.

"You won't hurt me," she whispered. "I know you won't." Amalie ran her hands over his chest, feeling the beat of his heart through her fingertips. He was darkness. Deadly. And her body ached for him.

"I can't do this again." Theo's voice was so low, she wasn't sure if she'd heard it.

Amalie stretched a hand to his face, and he shivered under her touch. "Please, Theo. Let me help."

38

Amalie pulled the door open, her eyes adjusting to the dim light. The house was silent, the only sound the soft crackle of the fire in the other room and the occasional creak of the old wood.

"I can go up. You could come in the window," she whispered.

Theo didn't answer, but before she could turn, his arms were around her, lifting her as if she weighed nothing. "I can—"

"Yes." Amalie gasped, her hands instinctively gripping his shoulders. They were upstairs in seconds, the only proof of their movement the rush of air against her skin.

Then they were in her bedroom. Her feet were on the floor, and the door clicked closed behind them. Amalie's heart bruised her ribs as she wrapped her arms around herself, the chill of her room hitting her like a wave.

A thin strip of light snuck through the shutters, dusting the floor. It was enough that she could make out Theo's silhouette. "I was so afraid. When I saw you in the window."

"I know," he murmured. "I'm sorry."

Amalie wanted him to stop apologizing. He was right. She wouldn't have believed him. If he would've appeared in her room and told her he'd known her from a past life or that her blood was meant for him, she would have laughed in his face. And then probably stabbed him again. She never would have gone with him. She wouldn't have listened.

Theo's breath was hot against the crown of her head. "I shouldn't be here."

"You keep saying that."

"Because it's true." His hand grazed her hip. "But it seems even when I try to make you hate me, I can't quite commit."

Amalie turned to him, the heat from his body lighting her up like a struck match. "I feel something here." She lifted his hand and placed it at the base of her ribs. "It reaches for you."

"I know." His breath was ragged, his lips brushing the shell of her ear.

"What is it?"

Theo brushed his hand over the inside of her wrist, then trailed his fingers up her arm, pausing and circling—

"What are you doing?" Amalie snatched her hand back, stepping away from him.

"Has it appeared yet?" Theo unclasped the button on the cuff of his shirt. He rolled it up and walked toward the window, exposing the runes on his skin in the pale, silvery light.

She took in the scrolls of ink. The symbol she'd seen everywhere in the castle he lived in. On the rings they wore.

Blood rushed in her ears as he watched her, his eyes flicking to her hand wrapped around her arm. She was back in the forest, pulling her shirt over her head. *What is that?*

Amalie trembled as she unwrapped her fingers and stepped into the light. She held her breath. "How is it possible?" Her head grew thick, her chest tight as she stared at the symbol on her arm. It was no longer smudged.

It was a perfect replica of Theo's signet.

Theo was in front of her, his hand on the hem of her shirt. "I didn't want you to understand. I didn't want you to remember."

"Why, Theo?" Amalie lifted her arms, allowing him to pull the shirt over her head. He caught her arm, the one he'd used last time. The one with the mark. Amalie thought of those moments in his closet, his hand wrapped around her hip, his lips brushing her skin. "We aren't safe. What if—"

"It doesn't matter now." Theo's voice was a low rumble, vibrating through her until her bones quivered. "Nothing matters now."

His lips were on her, kissing her knuckles, her wrist, the inside of her elbow. "You're mine, Amalie. You've always been mine."

Her head tipped back, her hand wrapping around his waist, willing him closer. "I know." The words slipped out of her, light exploding within her.

Theo sucked on her skin, a low growl in his throat. "Tell me to stop. If you want me to—"

"No. Take it. Please—"

Theo's fangs pierced her skin, her feet leaving the floor as the force of him pushed her up against the wall. She wrapped her legs around his waist, clinging to him as warmth spread through her like spiced wine.

She couldn't stop herself from touching him. Her free hand found his neck, her nails biting into his skin one moment, her fingers threading through his hair the next.

The heat within her built, coiling until she could barely stand it. "Theo—" she gasped for breath, liquid fire consuming her from the inside out. And then the mark on her arm, the symbol she now shared with Theo, ignited.

Her mind splintered, sending shards of flickering glass through her consciousness. She was falling. Tumbling. Whirling into darkness.

39

Aurelia stood behind the shroud, extending her wrist. The fabric was rough against her skin, ancient and worn. Her hand shook and she cursed herself. Her parents had prepared her for this, and she hadn't been afraid. Not until she'd heard the stories.

A hand encircled her wrist and she sucked in a breath. His hand was large, his grip firm, but not cruel. He could snap her bones in an instant. Pull her through the shroud and devour her whole.

"You're frightened." His voice was low and soothing. "I won't hurt you."

Aurelia exhaled, heat rising to her cheeks. "That's what they say." *Please, don't choose me. Just take my blood and let me leave.*

His thumb brushed over her skin. "You believe the rumors, then?"

"I've heard enough to make up my own mind." Her words were sharp, but she couldn't erase the tremor from her voice.

The vampire didn't speak. Aurelia's palms started to sweat,

her wrist still at his mercy. When she thought she might burst, he finally lifted her hand, and his breath whispered against her skin.

"My name is Theo. So you'll know who to blame if you have any complaints."

40

Alba ran through the tall grass, her breath misting in the cool night air. *Where were they?* She scanned the trees, willing herself to see shadows moving on the ground and not streaking from the sky.

A hiss broke the stillness, and she stumbled to a stop, a shiver down her spine. She scanned the shadows. *There.* At the edge of the clearing, a figure writhed against the barbed fence.

From the size of it and the dark black wings glinting in the moonlight, it was a stryx. One of the bird-like creatures that had attacked with the vampires. She should leave it. After everything the creatures of shadow had done that night, she should be happy for any one of them to suffer. The creature let out another whimper, and she gritted her teeth.

Her heart pounded as she approached, her eyes fixed on the creature's wings. The delicate membrane was torn, the flesh beneath exposed and bleeding. She winced as the stryx thrashed, his fangs bared.

"Hold still," she reached out a hand.

The stryx's gaze snapped to hers, and he snarled, his eyes

flashing. Alba's breath caught in her throat, but she didn't back away. She knew what he was. Knew the danger he posed, but she couldn't leave him like this.

"I'm trying to help you."

The stryx's nostrils flared, and he stilled, his eyes narrowing. Alba took a step closer, her fingers brushing against the cool metal of the fence. Her fingers trembled as she brushed the edge of the creature's wings.

"This will hurt." She stayed clear of the stryx's talons and yanked, working the wing free from the barb.

When it finally released, she stumbled back as the creature dropped to the ground.

"There." She wiped her hands on her cloak. "You're free."

The stryx's eyes gleamed, and her stomach dropped. Before she could react, the creature lunged, his claws raking across her arm. She cried out, stumbling back as she fumbled for the dagger at her waist.

She didn't have time. The creature was on her, a blur of claws and wings. Her vision blurred as she finally caught hold of the hilt and flung the blade forward, twisting and slashing.

Then, suddenly, the creature flew into the night. Alba sucked in a breath, her lungs burning and frantic. She rolled onto her side and pushed up to her hands and knees.

"Run." A man loomed over her, his dark hair windswept, his eyes nearly black.

She scrambled to her feet, but she didn't run. She couldn't tear her eyes away from him. *Vampire.* He had helped her. They'd come to attack, and yet he—

"Run!" he repeated, and that time, he didn't give her a choice.

41

Alba panted, sweat dripping down her face, her muscles straining as she faced Theo. She blinked from the light pouring through the arched windows behind him.

A smirk played on his lips. "That won't be good enough."

"This isn't a fair fight," she growled. She lunged at him, but he moved like smoke, fluid and impossible to predict.

"It won't be tomorrow either." He gripped her arm and twisted, sending her to the marble floor with a grunt.

She forced herself up as soon as he released her, gritting her teeth and forcing the tears in her eyes to retreat. Her chest felt like it might crack in two as she drove toward him for the hundredth time, and then the pressure suddenly released. It was as if she'd been drilling in the earth and had finally broken through the bedrock.

Energy surged through her, flooding every inch of her with raw strength. Theo moved, and Alba struck with a kick that connected, her foot slamming into his chest. The impact made her teeth rattle, and she dropped to the floor as Theo flew backward, his body slamming into the stone wall.

The force of it sent a shockwave through the room, and the stones behind him crumbled, dust and debris falling to the floor.

Theo lay on the ground a moment before pushing up and finding her eyes, the smirk wiped from his face. "That's more like it."

42

Alba stood before the crumbling stone altar, her heart beating slow and steady. This was it. She was supposed to be there, she could feel it.

The altar was weathered and cracked, vines winding their way through the crevices, as if nature had already laid claim to what lay beneath. She reached out a trembling hand, her fingers brushing against the cool, rough surface.

Theo put a hand on her lower back, centering her. "Let me."

Alba nodded. Her breath hitched as Theo plunged his hand into a thin crevice and pulled at the rock. The side of the altar gave away easily under his strength, and in seconds, she was able to reach into the musty sarcophagus.

Her fingers brushed something cool and metallic. "It's here. I knew it would be here."

As soon as she said it, the stone walls around her began to disintegrate, and she was standing in a richly decorated hall. The distant sound of water flowing broke through her awareness, and she turned, her eyes widening as she saw the Loire river stretching out before her through the window.

"It's here. I knew it would be here."

"Amalie."

She frowned, turning to look down the hall. *Who was Amalie?* The corridor was empty. Alba looked down at the sword in her hand, then back out the window at the river. "It's here. I knew—"

"*Amalie.*"

The walls around her shook, and she dropped the sword to the floor. "It's here. I—"

43

1422 BLOIS, LOIRE VALLEY

She was gasping, lying in a bed of grass, the air heavy with the organic scent of sweat and blood. She turned her head to see Theo kneeling beside her, his face drawn with worry. He reached out and brushed a strand of hair from her forehead, his touch sending a jolt of electricity through her.

"They're alive?" She panted.

Theo nodded. He leaned down, his lips brushing against her temple. She closed her eyes, feeling the warmth of his breath on her skin. He pressed his lips to her cheek, then her jaw, and finally, her mouth. "You are a warrior, Alba Joan."

Her hands fisted in the fabric of his shirt as he kissed her, her body sinking into the earth. "I love you."

"I loved you first . . ."

"Amalie."

"Amalie, I'm here."

44

1836 COUNTRYSIDE BEYOND MORDELLES,
FRANCE

"Amalie, please. Look at me."

Her eyes rolled back in her head as the grass beneath her dried up and crumbled. She drifted through darkness, spinning until she slammed against something solid.

She sucked in a breath, her body arching as her eyes flew open.

"Amalie." Theo's hands were on both sides of her face, his eyes wild.

She gripped onto his wrists. "I know where it is. The sword, Theo. *I know where it is.*"

45

Amalie jumped up from the bed and would have crumpled to the floor had Theo not caught her.

"Shh, wait a second." He smoothed her hair, and she turned to look at him. There was a lit candle now sitting on the desk, and the flickering light made his skin glow.

That face. She'd seen it again and again. She'd been called by different names, lived in different bodies, but *that face.* Amalie searched his eyes, peeling away the layers of what she'd seen. What she knew in this life and what she'd found in others. She'd trusted him. Known him. Loved him.

"How many times did you find me?" she whispered.

Theo's fingers trembled. "Three."

"Only three?" Amalie exhaled. He'd lived for two thousand years, a human lifespan was fleeting, and they'd only met three times? "When?"

Theo's hand dropped to her waist. "You were there at the beginning."

Amalie pressed her hand over his and drew a deep breath. "Which was?"

"The first time, we lived in the south. During the Roman Empire. Guardians and vampires together."

Amalie let out a long exhale. She'd lived during the Roman Empire? "How did I die?"

Theo's eyes darkened. "The first time?"

She nodded, swallowing hard. The idea that she'd died more than once made her insides flip.

"Your blood gave power to those who drank it. We had a friend who wanted it for herself."

The answer was simple, and yet so complicated it made her head throb. Amalie pressed at the edges of her mind, stretching it like taffy. She wanted to ask him everything.

Theo cleared his throat. "After our parting, I waited sixteen hundred years, three months, and—"

Amalie put a finger to his lips. "Sixteen hundred years?"

Theo's eyes were glassy.

"And this is the third time?" she whispered.

He nodded, clenching his jaw. As she gazed at the profile of his face, the layers of her knowing seemed to suddenly snap into one solid picture. She knew Theo Vallon. He'd never changed, after all this time, and she had. Sixteen hundred years.

Amalie reached out a hand. His dark lashes brushed his cheek as her fingers reached his jaw. "Look at me." A soft "hmm" left his lips as he turned, his eyes meeting hers. "How did you find me? You said you weren't sure until you scented my blood, but you were here. How?"

"You bonded me. Under a blood moon. I can always feel when you're reborn, but I never know exactly where. I watch. I wait. It's how I found you the second time. This time," Theo shook his head. "It proved more difficult."

"But you found me."

"I did."

She thought of him appearing in her bedroom and roughly pulling her into his arms. *Don't make this harder than it needs to be.* Of him stoking the fire in the shed that first night. How he barely looked at her and made her feel like a fool. How he'd left her alone in the castle, answered her in clipped sentences. Never once had she thought he'd cared for her in the least.

Then lastly, she thought of the bitter look on his face in Uncle Oren's study. *Even when I try to make you hate me, I can't commit.*

Tears pricked her eyes. "Why did you want me to hate you?"

Something flashed behind Theo's eyes, and his grip on her tightened. He swore under his breath and reached for her arm. "We have to go. Now."

"Theo, what—"

He lifted her arm, turning it so she could look at the mark on her skin. His mark, and—

"What the hell is that?" She stared at the blood red symbol darkening in her skin above Theo's oval signet and clutched her middle as a needling pain threaded through her. "Theo, what is happening?"

"Helena. The friend I told you about. There's no time to explain." He pulled her up off the bed. "Pack now. Enough for at least two nights. I'll get the others."

Before she could stop him, he disappeared from the room. She glanced back at her arm and stared at the mark. Two chains, twisted together. One barbed and jagged, the other smooth and unbroken. What did it mean?

Her hand still clutched her middle, aware of that slicing shard settling next to the warmth that stretched toward Theo.

A friend. Helena.

She'd heard that name. On the rooftop, when Theo had been talking to Ren. What had he said? She couldn't remember, but the thought of it made her shiver. It had been a dig, and Ren hadn't taken it lightly.

She needed to move. If Theo said she was in danger, she believed him. Amalie had left her satchel downstairs in Oren's office, but she could still gather her things. She pulled open the doors of her armoire, and paused. Her mother's dress. The pale blue fabric and white swans. Bethany said she'd put it back.

She fingered the soft fabric, worn with time and use.

"It was yours. Your favorite."

Amalie's breath caught at the sound of Theo's voice.

"I—" His breath caught. "I bought you the fabric. The last time."

The last time. This fabric couldn't have been more than forty or fifty years old. "It was my mother's."

"It was her mother's before that," he whispered, his hand brushing her neck. "It was her favorite."

Tears welled in her eyes, her hand frozen to the door of her armoire. "That strip of fabric. In the castle."

"Yours. I kept it."

Amalie's mind reeled. Her mother. *Her mother's mother.* She had lived, she had died. How was it possible?

Theo's hand landed on the small of her back. "Are you ready? The others are—"

"You can't do that." She spun, her hands clenched at her sides. He was so close, she had to tip her head to meet his eyes.

"Do what?"

"Say something like that and then tell me I need to rush out of this house. That we're in danger, when all I want is—" She sucked in a breath, heat flashing through her center.

Theo stilled, his eyes liquid pools. "What do you want?"

You bonded me. Under a blood moon. She didn't know what a bond meant or how it was accomplished. She'd only seen flashes of what Theo had been to her in her other lives, but she knew what he was to her in this one.

Her heart momentarily forgot it was supposed to keep rhythm as his scent invaded her senses. She didn't fight it. *She didn't ever want to fight it again.* "I want to know what this feels like." Amalie threaded her hand around the back of his neck, urging his head toward hers.

Theo's eyes glinted in the candlelight, his expression tortured with want. His scent swirled through her as his lips brushed hers, soft and tentative. Theo pulled back just enough to say, "I've never forgotten—not for a second—what this feels like," and Amalie tugged harder, angry that he'd wasted a second of this moment on words.

Theo huffed a laugh as their lips crashed against each other, this time desperate and bruising. Amalie fisted her hand in his shirt, willing him closer even though his chest was already flush with hers. She wanted more. She wanted—

Theo parted her lips with his and flicked his tongue over her lower lip.

"Yes." *That.* She wanted more of that. Amalie tasted him. Teased her tongue against his as her hands fought with the fabric of his shirt. She thought of every time Theo had been in his room shirtless. How she'd watched him, traced the swirls of his runes with secret glances, imagined the feel of him. Even when she'd hated him, she'd wanted to run her hands over his skin, and now—

The creak of a board in the hall sent her heart into her throat. Theo jolted, and in a flash, hid behind the open door.

The door was open? Of course it was. Theo had come in, and she hadn't even thought to check before groping him like a feral cat.

When she looked up, Bethany stood in the doorway. Her sister's sleepy eyes narrowed. "Are you alright?"

Amalie nodded, pursing her swollen lips. "Mmhmm." She turned and grabbed a pair of slacks and two tunics from the shelf with trembling hands. "I'm coming."

"Uncle says he needs us in the parlor now."

"Right. I only need to find socks."

Bethany frowned, and her eyes crinkled at the corners. "Was this how it was? The first time?"

Amalie thought back to that night. To her screaming in the woods and Uncle Oren hauling her back to the house as she stretched back toward that clearing in the trees. Toward her mother's lifeless body. How Maurielle had held onto her as Oren had thrown their belongings into a cart.

"No." Amalie shook her head. "It's nothing like the first time." Bethany's teeth worried her lower lip. "Go. I'll follow you down."

Bethany did as she asked, and Amalie swiped socks and undergarments from her drawer. When she turned, Theo was still standing in the shadows, pressed against the wall.

"You're coming with us?" Her voice trembled imagining him disappearing into the night.

Theo nodded, his brow drawn. "I drew up a plan years ago for this eventuality. I have a place."

"You expected this?"

His shoulders tensed, his voice tight. "It's the same every time."

"Helena." Amalie spoke the name faster than necessary. She didn't know what it meant, but she knew it wasn't good.

"She will find you, Amalie. Her bond is slower to form, but when our mark appears, hers is quick to follow."

Amalie twisted her arm, inspecting the two marks. Theo's hadn't appeared until the day before. "Does it always take so long? After rebirth?"

Theo shook his head. "I was careful this time."

With those words, the pieces tumbled into place. His vigilance. The bite in her room. The distance, the cold glances, the refusal to answer her questions.

"You gave me your bedroom." Amalie strode toward the door, stopping in front of him.

"It was always meant for you." His thumb brushed over his signet. "And this mark, it was never mine, Amalie."

Images of that signet flashed through her mind. On the doors at the edge of the sand. The ring they all wore on their fingers, the carved wood in the castle. Her voice caught in her throat. *It was always meant for you.*

"Amalie!" Her uncle called up the stairs.

"Coming!" She called back, her voice strained.

"No, stay in your room. I need Theo. Now," he growled.

Amalie turned, and Theo's expression darkened. He was gone in an instant, followed by Bethany, Matilde, and Ghislaine stumbling back up the stairs.

Amalie flew to the window and opened the shutters. As her eyes adjusted to the darkness, she searched the gardens below until her eyes landed on a shadowed figure outside the gate.

Her breath hitched at the familiar features illuminated in the moonlight.

Ren.

46

ow was Ren outside her uncle's gate?

Beads of sweat formed on her forehead. She'd done everything she could to get here without him following, but she'd failed. *But what had taken him so long?*

Amalie turned to find the girls huddling together on her bed. She closed the shutters. "Wait here."

"Uncle Oren said—" Bethany started, but Amalie held up a hand.

"I'll be right back." She set her clothes on the writing desk and descended the stairs. Maurielle sat in the parlor, but she didn't give her aunt a chance to stop her. She rushed outside, stopping only when her uncle turned and flashed a look of pure murderous intent.

Theo blocked her view of Ren through the open gate, and she shifted to the side to get a clear view. "What are you doing here?"

Ren held out his hands. "There's no time to talk. The Pourfendeurs are coming. We need to get out now."

Amalie's brow pinched. The Pourfendeurs? She'd left

Marcel and Olivie in Servon only a day prior, and they hadn't said a thing about coming to Mordelles.

She took a step closer, emboldened by Theo's presence even though her uncle hissed through his teeth. "The Pourfendeurs are my friends." She wouldn't listen to any more of his lies. He'd insinuated it was her uncle who had been attacked, then insisted Theo had asked him to protect her. Neither of those had proven true.

Ren gave her an apologetic look, then turned his attention back to Theo. "I tried to keep her safe, but she refused to stay put."

"I didn't ask you to keep her safe," Theo snapped.

"Well, it's a good thing I took it upon myself. She could've been killed on her way to Servon. She had no money—I had to pay for her to spend the night at a reputable inn."

"I would've made do." Amalie took another step.

Ren ignored her. "I followed her here and heard the rumors in Mordelles. They know you're here, Theo. They know what you are." He looked innocently between the two of them. "Is this where the attack happened?"

Amalie watched him for any hint of betrayal, but couldn't find it. Ren looked glad to see Theo and honest in his desperation for them to act. Theo's hands fisted at his sides.

Ren's eyes flickered. "I mean what I say. Whatever dealings you have here, they can wait. This family doesn't need their house to be burned to the ground."

"They wouldn't do that without proof," Amalie said. "I know them. They aren't witch hunters, as much as people make them out to be."

None of what Ren was saying made sense. Unless . . . had Marcel and Olivie followed her, too? Had they been watching her home since that night she showed up with a mark on her skin? She thought of Marcel's accusations in the town square.

How he'd changed his tune the next morning after she'd stepped into the sunlight. Had it been a bit too easy to convince him?

"I think this might be yours." Theo pulled his hand from his pocket, and Amalie snapped back to the present. Theo stood in front of Ren, holding out the ring.

Ren's eyes widened. His jaw went slack as he stared at the silver band in Theo's palm.

Theo's eyes darkened, his jaw set. "Answer me."

Amalie's hands began to shake. If Theo thought the ring was his, then Ren must've known about her mother. Could it have been Ren that she loved? The entirety of her childhood replayed in a split second. Her mother leaving late at night to meet Ren in the woods. Ren's hands on her mother's waist. Ren's lips dripping with her mother's blood.

Amalie thought she might be sick.

Ren's eyes narrowed. He took one last look at the ring and tilted his head. "It's not mine."

Theo slammed his hand against the stone wall, directly next to Ren's head. "You're a liar."

Theo said he'd watched over guardians, but from the way he'd acted at the castle, it didn't seem like any of his coven knew about it. But they'd known each other for thousands of years. Was it so hard to believe that they knew each other well enough to parse out each other's secrets?

So why hadn't Theo seen Ren's? How had he not known that Ren was hunting for her mother near the river?

The shard in her middle pulled so intently, she thought she might collapse to her knees. *The river. The sword.*

"I swear to you, I know nothing of which you speak." Ren tugged at the collar of his shirt, fishing for something. Finally he pulled it out. Strung on a gold chain. His signet ring. Safe and sound against his chest.

Theo took a step back. He stared at the ring in Ren's hand, then at the one he held in his palm.

Ren clapped a hand on Theo's shoulder. "Now, I'm assuming you'll tell me the details later, but it's obvious these humans are colluding with our kind. You, specifically, so can we please get them out of here?"

None of this was right.

The sensation of someone watching her prickled her skin. What was she missing? Ren hadn't told her the truth, but then he'd shown up as if it was the most normal thing in the world to be warning a man and his family who was supposed to be cursed.

Was it possible he didn't know of whom he spoke? Had he gotten information from someone else and never connected the two? But what Theo had said in the bedroom . . .

Either Ren's version of events was true or Theo's was. She knew what she wanted to believe, but hadn't her mother fallen prey to such thinking?

"I'll go to the Pourfendeurs. I'll show myself. Distract them while you get them out." Theo nodded, then closed the gate and turned to Amalie and Oren. He'd let Ren go, just like that. But what proof did they have to accuse him further?

"We should go with him. Marcel and Olivie will listen to me." Amalie's fingers felt numb at the ends. They *would* listen to her. She would tell them every last shred of information if she had to.

Oren shook his head. "No. We're leaving this house anyway. Let them burn it if they wish."

Amalie's heart sank as she glanced back at the house. The roses that bloomed along the foundation. The pear tree that always flowered pale pink in the spring.

Maurielle walked outside with Bethany and her two younger girls. All of them looked wide-eyed and flushed. They must have been watching from the window, and now all three of them stared at Theo. If Oren had hoped to wait until they were eighteen, she doubted very much that he'd be able to reach that mark. It was for the better.

"I left my clothes upstairs." She started for the house, and Oren herded Maurielle and the girls to the second gate along the side of the house.

Theo had drawn up a plan. Her curiosity clawed at her as she ran into the study and pulled her satchel from the chair, then took the stairs two at a time to her bedroom. She stuffed her clothes from the bed into the bag, then glanced at the armoire. She could fit the dress, couldn't she?

Amalie crossed the room and pulled the door open, then released the dress from the wooden hanger. She pulled it out and closed the door, then jumped as a figure moved in her peripheral vision.

"You forgot something at the castle." Marx waved his fingers through the flame still burning on her writing desk, then straightened and pulled a strip of pale blue fabric from his pocket. "Sentimental, yes?"

47

Rachel wrapped her arms around herself, her fingers fidgeting with the hem of her sleeve. The forest darkened. Shadows used to make her nervous, but now they felt almost comforting.

Florent stood in front of her, his tall frame relaxed and composed. His hair fell to his shoulders, and the fading light highlighted his chiseled features. He turned to her, a small smile playing on his lips.

She'd waited nearly a week for this moment, and it felt like an eternity. The air grew colder as the sun fell deeper below the horizon. Rachel shivered, her breath nearly visible.

Florent reached out, taking her hand in his. His touch was warm. Steady. "Are you ready?"

Rachel nodded. She'd wanted to ask a thousand questions about the ceremony, but Florent had been so hesitant. He'd barely allowed her into his world, and she didn't want to do anything to spook him.

But tonight was the night. She and Florent would be bound together.

She knew what he was and had no illusions that he would transform into a husband like Romane. He moved in the night. He kept his secrets and lived with a burden she could never fully understand.

But this ceremony would strengthen him, and he would be hers.

Florent placed a chalice on a stump next to them and squeezed her hand. "You must follow my instructions exactly."

Rachel nodded, then tensed as another figure emerged from the trees. His eyes glowed amber in the twilight, and he wore a cloak that flowed around him like mist. A deep calm washed over her, pressing against her shoulders.

"Who is he, Florent?" Rachel swallowed hard, her throat dry. *This vampire was strong.* She wanted to trust him, but this was not a part of the plan. Florent had never mentioned the need for another. Though, in a traditional marriage ceremony, they would have enlisted a bishop or priest. Perhaps this was a tradition he'd forgotten to mention?

Florent pulled her closer as the vampire in the cloak raised his arms, and the air around them suddenly hummed with energy.

Rachel's heart raced as she watched, her breath coming in short gasps. Her mortal mind screamed for her to run even as her body rocked in the waves of his glamour. She knew what he was. She'd been taught to see the signs. Yet her guardian blood seemed to sprout like a seed soaked with water.

She was made for this. Her blood was meant to seek his.

Florent leaned in. "Listen carefully."

Rachel nodded, her legs trembling as she took a step closer.

The man began to speak, his words flowing like the Loire in a language she didn't recognize. After a moment, he turned to her and spoke more slowly.

"Repeat the words," Florent whispered.

"I don't understand them."

"Just do your best."

Rachel's voice shook as she repeated the strange syllables. An odd sensation, like a sustained bolt of lightning, surged through her veins.

Florent had explained the oaths they'd be making. That she would be sacrificing blood to share a bond with him. But repeating foreign words from a creature she had no experience with made her skin crawl.

She gripped Florent's hand tighter and finished the last sentence, gasping as her ribs cinched around her lungs. "Florent—"

"Nearly there, love." His tone was flat as he reached into his pocket and pulled out a small, ornate box. He opened it, revealing a sleek silver dagger with a glistening blade.

Rachel's eyes widened, her pulse quickening. She knew what came next. She had to trust him, to let him complete the ritual.

Florent plucked the dagger from its velvet casing. "Would you like to do it or shall I?"

Rachel's throat tightened. She reached out and took the dagger with trembling fingers. With a deep breath, she brought the dagger to her palm. She hesitated, her mind screaming at her to stop. But she couldn't. She had to finish what they'd started, and this was only a meager offering.

Florent stepped closer, his breath warm against her cheek. "Do it."

Rachel closed her eyes and dragged the blade across her skin. She hissed as it sliced through her flesh, a sharp pain radiating up her arm.

Florent's pupils dilated, his fangs descending at the scent of her blood. He'd explained the pleasure her blood brought to him. How he craved it.

Florent caught her hand as crimson pooled in her palm. He guided her to tip her hand over the silver chalice, her blood dripping into the vessel. Rachel's heart pounded in her chest as the droplets fell.

Florent took the dagger from her and slid the blade over his own palm, then held his hand over the cup. Their blood mixed together in the bowl, and the man in the cloak began chanting again.

"Is it done?" Rachel whispered.

"Nearly." Florent didn't look at her. He stared at the chalice, his blood dripping past his wrist and staining the cuff of his shirt.

He still gripped the dagger with his right hand, his knuckles white.

"Here." Rachel reached out for the box, but Florent stopped her.

"Don't move."

"Florent—"

His eyes flicked to hers, and Rachel's voice died on her tongue.

48

Amalie stumbled back, clutching the dress and her satchel to her chest as his cool, sharp scent washed over her. "How did you find me?" She took short, purposeful breaths, fighting back the sudden urge to smile at him.

Marx dropped the fabric on her writing desk, keeping his other hand behind his back. "I told you, I'm not going to hurt you."

Amalie's heart jumped against her ribs. "And yet you're standing in my childhood bedroom refusing to show both of your hands." She wanted to scream, to call for Theo, but she knew how fast vampires could move when they wanted to. It was true that Marx hadn't hurt her, had barely touched her, during both of their encounters.

But perhaps he hadn't know what she was. Did he know now?

Marx pulled his hand from behind his back, and Amalie sucked in a breath.

"Where did you find that?" She stared at the blade in his

hands. It was exactly as she remembered it. Its blade was long and narrow, shimmering with a silver hue even in the golden glow of the candlelight. The hilt was encrusted with black opals and white diamonds, and the grip wrapped in faded leather. The sword's crossguard curved upward like outstretched wings.

Marx lay the sword on the floor between them. "Consider this a gift."

"Where did you find it?" Amalie repeated, her hands beginning to shake. She'd seen it in her dream, she'd felt a pull to the south. How was it here, and how was Marx the one to bring it to her?

"I know someone who's quite interested to meet you." Marx's eyes flicked to her arm, and Amalie turned it toward her body, hiding her runes.

Amalie's throat worked. "It's her, isn't it? Helena. Have you worked for her all along?"

Marx raised an eyebrow. "Not going to pretend you're studying botany, then?" She paled, and Marx's lips pulled into a wide grin. "What have they told you? All terrible things, I'm sure." He sat, throwing his arm over the back of her chair.

"I don't want anything to do with her."

He chuckled. "First impressions can be misleading. You of all people should know that by now." He glanced lazily at the armoire, then back to the bed.

Amalie's cheeks flushed. "You don't get to talk about Theo."

"Ah, but he's the reason we're here, isn't he? Wasn't this what he was after?" Marx nodded to the sword on the ground. "So desperate to find it, he was willing to risk your life."

Risk her life? That was the last thing Theo had done. She wanted to tell Marx to take the sword and leave her room, but . . . he was right about one thing. Theo had been hunting for the sword. Her heart twinged in her chest. *I want the relic for the same reason you do. You can vanquish me yourself. And then I don't care what you do with it. Kill them all if you want.*

"Ah, Amalie, you look so conflicted. Are you having second thoughts? This was what you wanted, was it not?" Marx dropped his arm and leaned forward on the chair, resting his arms on his knees.

"Yes." Her tone was clipped. *You can vanquish me yourself.* Why had Theo said that? If he'd gone to all this trouble to find her, if he'd waited sixteen hundred years, why would he want a sword? Why would he want Amalie to take his life, to release him permanently from the world?

She glanced at the armoire, imagining his hands on her hips, his lips pressed against hers. Had he been lying about that? Had he only been trying to find common ground?

"Theo and I haven't known each other for long. But Helena . . . well, she's known him since he was bitten, and trust me. She knows him almost as well as he knows himself."

Amalie's grip tightened around her satchel. "Why are you telling me this?" She glanced at the door, wondering when Oren or Theo would get worried and come looking for her.

"Because I think it's only fair you get both sides of the story." Marx's expression was suddenly deadly serious.

"I need to help my family."

Marx shook his head. "You can't help them. Not like this."

"Then what do you suggest?" she hissed.

Marx stood, straightening the fine shirt he wore tucked into his trousers. "Have a conversation with her. She'll make sure nobody touches your family. They can remain here in their home, and you don't have to promise us anything. Just a talk."

Theo. Amalie silently pleaded for him to climb the stairs.

Marx glanced toward the door. "I'll give you time to think it over. Personally, I can't wait to see what Theo thinks of this."

He nudged the handle of the sword with his boot. "Delivered right into his hands." Marx crossed the room, giving her a wide berth, then paused at the open window. "One last thing, did you know it was possible to make replicas of jewelry?" He glanced down at his hand, twisting a ring on his finger. "It's quite simple with a talented silversmith." He grinned. "But under certain circumstances, it's embarrassingly easy to spot the original."

Amalie's pulse pounded in her ears. "How is that?"

Marx's eyes glittered. "When a silversmith dies, his signature dies with him. The small number inscribed in the back of his pieces. It makes his work truly one of a kind."

49

Rachel's body arched, her muscles seizing as pain radiated from the gaping wound in her neck. Her fingers were slick with her own blood, the coppery scent filling her nostrils and sending her stomach roiling. Her vision blurred, but she could still make out the dark figure standing over her, his eyes glinting in the moonlight.

"Shh, shh. I have you." Florent's voice was a low, soothing murmur as he eased her down onto the forest floor. His hands supported her head. "It will be over soon."

Rachel's breath hitched as her back pressed against cool earth, the dampness seeping through the thin fabric of her dress. Florent's face hovered above hers, his hair falling forward as he leaned over her. Why had he done this? She'd given her blood, watched it swirl with his in the chalice. Why—

"You're strong, Rachel. So strong." His voice was a purr, his breath hot against her skin. "You were chosen for this. You will be reborn."

Rachel's mind was a fog, her thoughts sluggish as she tried

to process his words. Reborn? Her heart pounded in her chest, forcing blood out of her body too fast. She couldn't heal—couldn't regenerate.

She tried to speak, to ask him what he meant, but her throat wouldn't work.

Florent's hand cupped her cheek, his thumb brushing over her skin. "Rest now. It will be over soon."

Rachel's eyelids fluttered, her vision narrowing to a pinprick as the darkness closed in. The night air whispered over her skin, the rustling of leaves in the forest around them. It was so quiet.

Her mind drifted, memories of Amalie and Bethany flashing before her eyes. Their laughter, their smiles. The way they would curl up next to her in bed, their warm bodies pressing against hers. She wanted to hold them, to tell them how much she loved them. But her arms were heavy, her body a leaden weight on the forest floor.

Florent's voice was a distant hum, his words slipping through her consciousness like water through her fingers. She tried to focus, but it was like trying to grasp smoke. Her thoughts fragmented, her mind splintering as the darkness closed in. Words like "transfer" and "bond" floated through her mind, but she couldn't grasp their meaning. She was slipping, her body sinking into the earth as the world faded, slow and thick.

Tears mixed with the blood on her cheeks, her chest heaving as she tried to force the words from her throat. "A-Amalie." The name was a breath, a mere exhalation of air. Her mind fractured, her thoughts scattering like leaves in the wind. She couldn't hold on. She was slipping.

"A-Ama—" She tried again, her lips trembling. Her daughters' faces swam before her eyes. Amalie's dark curls, her wide eyes filled with curiosity. Bethany's rosy cheeks, her chubby fingers wrapped around Rachel's thumb.

Florent's eyes softened, his expression one of understanding. "Your girls will be safe, Rachel."

Rachel's heart clenched, her breath stuttering in her chest. The memory of her daughters was all she had left, the only thing anchoring her to this world. She wouldn't let go. *She couldn't.*

She tried to speak again, to tell him to keep his promise. To make him swear on his life. But what good was his word? He'd told her they'd be together . . .

Had he said that? Or had he told her this ceremony was life and death?

Another wave of darkness crashed over her, pulling her under. Amalie's eyes, wide and curious, staring up at her as she read from the old leather-bound book. She'd failed them. She should have seen the signs. She should have—

"Can you feel anything?" A man, not Florent, spoke. His voice was tight.

Florent knelt beside her, his eyes scanning her face. "Not yet. The bond won't transfer until she's gone."

The other man froze mid-pace, his eyes narrowing as he turned his head to the right. He inhaled deeply, his nostrils flaring. Florent stilled next to Rachel. He frowned, his eyes darting around the dark treeline.

"He's here." Florent pushed up, pulling his hand from behind her head.

She didn't see them go, but she felt it. She was alone. She dragged her fingers over the soft clover as her eyelids fluttered.

So quiet.

So cold.

Then there was nothing but black.

50

1836 COUNTRYSIDE TO MORDELLES, FRANCE

Amalie rushed down the dark stairs, her satchel bouncing against her hip. The chilled autumn air bit at her skin as she stepped into the garden, clutching the sword. Theo stood next to the wall and Oren paced, his head bowed. Maurielle whispered to Bethany, Matilde, and Ghislaine who stood with their backs to the stone wall.

Theo came to life when he spotted her, and she ran to him, resting the blade of the sword against her palm to make it easier to carry.

"Is that what I think it is?" His voice was low, the shadows around him already moving toward him like waves in the sea. Amalie nodded. "How?" Theo reached out a hand, and Amalie's heart skipped a beat. She imagined him gripping the hilt, holding it up in the moonlight, then burying it in his own chest. *You can vanquish me yourself.*

Her head began to throb as she pulled it closer to her body. "We need to find Ren. Now."

"How did you get this?"

Amalie set her jaw. "Does it matter?"

"Yes." Theo's voice was sharp.

Amalie opened her mouth, then closed it again. It was a simple answer, but she struggled to give it. "Don't make me say it."

Theo's placid expression cracked, tension coiling beneath his skin. The veins along his throat pulsed, and the darkness of the night seemed to pour into him. The shadows around them flickered.

"She was here?"

Amalie shook her head. "No. She sent a messenger." She wanted to tell him about Marx. About how he'd been at the castle, how he'd found her in the stairwell and on the roof.

Theo held out a hand, and Amalie took a step back. She shook her head. "I have to find him, Theo."

He took a step toward her. "Give me the sword. Please."

Her eyes flashed. "I'm going to find—"

"We should stay together." Theo moved, and she instinctively thrust out her knee, but he pushed back, taking her arm with him and launching her off balance. "Not as simple when my hands aren't bound."

Her blood boiled as she regained her footing, her eyes shooting daggers at him. "Why would you defend him? He killed my mother."

Theo's jaw tensed. "We don't have proof, but he did betray my trust. I promise he'll pay—"

She struggled against him. "Pay how, Theo? He took a life—"

"Amalie, stop." Theo's arm trembled as he held her back. "I'm not defending him. I'm trying to protect you."

She laughed. "You think you're protecting me? You think you know what's best for me?"

Theo's eyes locked onto hers. "I know—"

"You call yourself a protector, but you still think like *them*." The words came unbidden, her hurt coating every thought in her head, making it impossible to think clearly. She wasn't angry at Theo. It wasn't his fault, and yet she couldn't stop the onslaught.

Theo sucked in a breath. "I have no choice but to survive."

"Neither do I." She twisted, throwing out her free arm, and Theo seemed to evaporate and condense as he avoided contact.

"This isn't survival, Amalie. You're hunting. You're becoming the very thing you hate."

Amalie's chest heaved, his words like a slap. "You wouldn't understand."

"I wouldn't understand?" Theo's breath came in quick bursts. "I've watched you die—watched you murdered *twice*. I held you in my arms. I saw the faces of those who sought to control you. Sought to *own* you."

He forced her arm up, the sword glinting in the light of the moon. "This is not a gift, Amalie. This is a flaxen cord."

Amalie's arm dropped a fraction, and then he was there. Pressed up against her. "I know where this leads." His eyes searched hers. "I've seen it. I won't let you do this."

Amalie's chest tightened, her lungs refusing to fill. He was too close. Heat radiated from his body, and she shivered at the brush of his clothing against her skin. "I'm not asking for your permission."

His nose brushed her cheek. "You don't know what you're doing."

His scent enveloped her, sending her head spinning. "I want justice."

"It's a cheap reward," he snapped. "Trust me."

Amalie held his gaze until she saw something retreat, a door closing behind his eyes. Theo cleared his throat and turned back to Oren, Maurielle, and the girls.

Bethany gaped at them, and Amalie dropped her eyes.

"We need to leave." Oren ushered his girls toward the gate.

"Yes, keep them safe." Amalie's voice shook. "Theo can—"

"I'm going with you."

She paused, her eyes lifting. Before she could protest, Theo turned to Oren.

"I'll meet you there. After."

Amalie swallowed hard. "Ren is with the Pourfendeurs. I can speak to them." Her cheeks flushed, hearing how feeble the words sounded in her own ears. She had no desire to speak to the Pourfendeurs. She wanted the truth. *She wanted Ren dead.*

"Show me the rings." Amalie motioned to Theo's right pocket, the deep well of anger and grief beginning to simmer within her. If Ren had been the one to kill her mother, if he'd lied to her and then tried to cover it up?

A cold, dark calm settled over her like a veil as she ran a finger over the crossguard. Theo did as she asked, pulling out the ring she'd found in her mother's box, then showing her the ring he wore on his own finger.

Amalie's blood began to hum. "Check the back. The signature." Theo frowned and twisted the ring, holding them up to the light. "It should be a small number pressed into the back of the metal."

Theo drew a breath. "Thirteen."

"On both of them?"

He nodded.

"You had them made by the same silversmith." She spoke faster, already striding toward the far gate.

"Years ago, yes. The old man's probably gone by now."

Amalie glanced over her shoulder. "Which is exactly my point." Actually, it had been Marx's point. She shivered, thinking of him lounging in her bedroom chair. How did he always know where she was? How did he always know exactly what to say? *She will find you, Amalie. Her bond is slower to form, but when our mark appears, hers is quick to follow.*

She felt as if her head was underwater by the time they reached the gate. Bonded. Theo could feel her. Helena could feel her. Why had one of their friends wanted her blood? Had she chosen this bond, or was the blood-red swirl on her arm proof that she'd rejected it?

Amalie stumbled once, and Theo lifted her into his arms. She dropped her satchel inside the wall, then clung to him as he pushed out onto the street. Theo didn't say a word.

"You know where they are?" She asked before thinking. Of course he did. He'd watched her go to Marcel and Olivie the first time he bit her.

Theo began to move, and the world blurred around her. She held the blade of the sword pressed between her knees, safe from jostling against Theo's body, then buried her face against his shoulder as they moved. With the wind against her cheeks, she could pretend they were flying.

In minutes, they stood at the end of the street. Theo set her feet on the cobblestones, and Amalie stared at the house ahead of them. Light filtered through the glass. It was the only house on the street without darkened windows.

"You believe he killed her." Theo's voice was low, his hand still resting on her elbow.

Amalie nodded. "Don't you?"

Theo's fingers tensed. "Ren is complicated. He was with us then. In the beginning. He was betrayed by Helena just as you were."

Maybe that was why Theo couldn't see it. Amalie didn't remember Ren then. She only saw him for what he was now.

She drew a deep breath. "You know why I hunted you."

"I do." Theo's voice was clipped.

"Then you understand what I have to do." She ignored the

pang in her gut as she walked up the street, struck by how different it was this time. She wasn't hiding marks on her neck or working to cover her sobs as she climbed the front steps.

The house was silent. Calm. If Ren was planning a distraction—

"I told you to get them out." Ren dropped onto the porch from the roof of the house, his boots barely making a sound. He looked between the two of them.

"Show me your ring." Theo's voice was low and calm. Deadly.

Ren scoffed and pulled the chain from his shirt. "I already showed you—"

Theo ripped it from his neck, and Ren growled. Theo ignored him, pulling the ring from his pocket and comparing the two. Amalie knew what he'd seen the second his eyes lifted.

"They don't match." Theo hurled the ring at him, and Ren stumbled back on the porch.

"I don't know what you're talking about."

Theo lunged forward, and lights suddenly exploded in front of him, so bright Amalie stumbled back. The whistles and bells came next, and her heart jammed in her throat. No. This was an attack. The Pourfenders— "Marcel!" she screamed, willing her body up. She blinked, trying to make her eyes focus through the white spots in her vision.

But when the smoke cleared, she saw she was too late. Her hands. They were empty. Ren held the sword to Theo's throat.

"Ren." Theo spat the name, and Ren clenched his jaw.

"Don't pretend to be angry, Theo. I haven't betrayed you."

"Let him go!" Amalie screamed, stumbling back to the porch steps. "Marcel! Olivie!" She was going to kill them— both of them—for going along with this. Her thoughts spun back to Servon. How Marcel had dismissed her, then taken her to breakfast in the morning. Ren. Of course, it had been Ren.

He hadn't followed her. He'd known exactly where she was going. Had it been a coincidence that Marcel had been in the town square?

Ren's face twisted. "Don't take another step, or I'll finish what you started."

Amalie froze on the step, her ears ringing. "I know you're out there," she hissed, scanning for any sign of Marcel, but there was nothing.

Theo's eyes were fixed on the sword hovering beneath his chin. "How long were you with her?"

"It was only the summer." Ren's expression darkened, and Amalie felt like she had suddenly fallen through a ceiling made of glass. Only the summer.

Lapping streams. Plucked bluebells.

It had been the best summer of her life. Until it wasn't.

"How did you find her?"

Ren's throat worked. "It wasn't hard. Once I tracked—"

"Paul. He told you." Theo's hands shook. "You were watching her."

"I thought you knew—that you'd found her again." Ren chuckled. "You're always watching, and you're meticulous. Always spending time in strange places, trying to make sure nobody sees your true focus. You left for years, never visiting the Clermonts. Never visiting anywhere close to the river."

Theo growled low in his throat, but Ren pressed the sword closer to his neck. "I was curious," Ren continued. "That's all. I was curious if she was what I suspected. And when I found out she was a guardian, I knew it must be the same bloodline."

Amalie's breath came in shallow gasps. *I was curious.*

Ren exhaled. "I did care for her, you know. She was lovely. So selfless. But then I tried the ceremony, and it didn't work—"

"What ceremony?" Amalie's throat grew so tight she could barely draw breath.

Ren ignored her. "I didn't know *for sure.*"

"You were wrong." Theo struggled against his grip, but Amalie's heart skipped a beat. No. One flick of Ren's hand and Theo would be taken from her. He'd never wait for her. He'd never watch.

"I was wrong then. But I'm not now." Ren lifted his eyes and looked directly at Amalie.

Theo's face twisted. "Even I don't know that for sure."

Ren's eyes gleamed, and he gave her a wicked smile. "He knows." He dropped his gaze back to Theo. "I've known you for over two thousand years, and I was there the first time you got that look in your eyes. At the castle. The way you looked at her before she sliced through your spine. That's when I knew she was the one."

Amalie's mind spiraled. They'd been hunting her. Theo, Ren, Marx, whoever this Helena was. But why had her mother died? If she was the one they wanted, why had Ren targeted her?

None of it added up. Theo needed her to find the sword which now sat in front of them, its hilt grasped in Ren's right hand.

Helena had the sword. She held the power to vanquish any vampire she wished, so why hadn't she come for them? Why had she offered it as a gift?

"Why kill her? If she was meant to find this for you, why take her life?" Amalie's voice shook. She needed to end this. She needed answers and she needed to get Theo to safety.

Ren's eyes darted between her and Theo. "You haven't told her?"

Amalie stepped forward. "I know who you think I am. I know I was meant to find the relic—"

Ren laughed out loud, his voice caustic in the still night air. "Oh, Amalie. Is that what you believe? Theo, I'm impressed. You've truly outdone yourself this time."

"I told her what was necessary." Theo's jaw worked.

"Necessary to keep her pliant." Ren took a step closer. "I understand why you're upset. I should've told you about Rachel, but you of all people should have compassion for my circumstances." He lowered his head. "*I told her what was necessary.*"

"You broke the bonds of our coven. You killed a guardian." Theo gasped as the blade bit into his skin, beads of blood forming against the side of his neck.

"You wanted this!" Ren hissed.

Amalie clenched her jaw to keep from screaming. Ren's words made a pit open up in her stomach. She'd wanted Theo dead. She'd tried to take his life.

But then she'd seen too much.

Ren dropped his voice, his breathing ragged. "I did this for both of us, Theo. I swear to you. I was only trying to get us what we wanted. There is a way for neither of us to suffer, you only have to allow me to complete this."

I did this for both of us. Amalie couldn't keep silent a moment longer. "Theo, what is he talking about?" She needed to get the sword out of Ren's hands, but how? He was faster than her. Theo was stronger than both of them combined, but with the blade tight at his throat, he could barely draw air into his lungs.

"What am I talking about? Isn't it obvious?"

She glared at him. "That Theo wants to die?"

Ren's eyes glinted. "No, Amalie. That Theo doesn't want to live in a world without you. And he's willing to take both your lives to make it so."

Movement caught her eye, and she held her breath. Marcel

stalked around the corner with Olivie trailing him. He didn't look the least bit surprised to see Ren standing on his porch in the middle of the night holding another vampire against his will.

"Marcel. Olivie—" Amalie started, but neither of them looked at her. A sob choked her as Marcel lifted his hand. A small glass vial glinted in the moonlight. It looked like the one that fell from her mother's box.

Theo's eyes dragged to hers, and he looked more creature than human. "Amalie, I didn't—" he rasped, as Marcel plunged the needle into Theo's flesh.

51

Amalie's vision narrowed to a dark tunnel as Theo's body went limp. The thread of light inside her flared, making her gasp. *I didn't, what?* What words had he been about to speak? Didn't want to tell you the truth? Didn't want to kill us both in the end?

Tears pricked her eyes as Theo's strong body hit the stone with a sickening thump. Marcel didn't even pretend to break his fall. His eyes were still open, the dark liquid of his irises like pools of ink as he stared at her sideways. His chest still rose and fell. He wasn't dead. Not yet.

Amalie forced herself to breath, though it felt as if she were sucking air through a siphon. The urge to throw herself at Marcel, at Ren, to drive her blade through both of their ribs, was unbearable.

But Marcel was trained. Olivie too. And Ren held the sword. One swipe from that blade would end her life. Would she be reborn, or was it capable of vanquishing her blood, too?

"That's better." Ren clicked his tongue, but there was sweat on his brow. He was nervous. Why? It seemed he held all the cards. "I have to thank you, Amalie. None of this would've been possible without your help."

Her limbs trembled. She had to do something. Theo was defenseless, and Ren watched her like a hawk trained on a rabbit.

"I'm sorry about your mother. Truly. But you must understand by now that guardians are never truly gone." He gave her an apologetic smile.

She knew it now, but at ten years old, she hadn't known it. She hadn't known it as she'd grown up and dreamed of dark eyes and blood-soaked grass, or when she'd discovered she hadn't bled like other girls and had no mother to comfort her. Yes, she knew it now. But she'd suffered for twelve years because of him.

"Not talkative?" Ren sighed. "I understand. But I promise this won't take much longer." He turned to Marcel and Olivie. "You can let go. He won't be waking up any time soon."

She wouldn't die like this. Amalie needed to move. She scanned the front of the house, searching for anything she could use as a weapon, sweat soaking her shirt. She could fight Marcel or Olivie one at a time, but together? They would disarm her within minutes. And Ren held the sword.

There was no way out of this. She couldn't protect Theo. She couldn't even protect herself.

"I'm sorry you had to hear it from me." Ren turned toward her, descending the steps. "I'm sure Theo had some romantic gesture planned. Some Shakespearian tragic ending."

"Don't come any closer." Amalie dropped into a defensive crouch, and Ren's eyes widened.

He barked a laugh. "Or you'll what?" He glanced down at the sword, then back at Theo slumped on the ground. "You should thank me, Theo. This way she doesn't have a choice in the matter."

"If you're going to kill me, then do it." Amalie seethed. She would not go out without a fight.

"Do you think I'm going to battle you to the death?" Ren's mouth quirked up at the corner. "No, no, no. You're not understanding. You think I want you to die, but I don't. I simply need something you have, and unfortunately . . . it does require your death for me to take it." He stepped forward, and Amalie lunged at him.

Ren easily caught her by the arm and forced her against the trunk of the oak tree in the yard. She blinked at the pain as the bark bit into her cheek and shoulder.

He dropped his head to her ear. "You won't have to change your shirt this time." Ren pulled back and forced her to look at the marks on the inside of her arm. "This. This is what I want." Amalie stared at the mark of her bond with Theo, then at the blood red chains. "Helena took something from me, and now I'm going to take it back."

He released her, and Amalie dropped to her knees on the sanded path.

Ren snapped his fingers, and she looked up to see Marcel approaching, a book in his hand.

"Your death destroyed him, you know?" Ren murmured. "Both times, actually, though with the last he didn't have to wait long for your return."

Amalie's chest pinched as if she'd been run through with a blade. *Sixteen hundred years.*

Ren's voice was like sandpaper over raw flesh. "He didn't want Helena to know you were reborn. He thought she would come for you if she did."

Marcel took his place at Ren's side, and Ren glanced over at the page he held open in the book. He nodded approvingly.

Ren turned his gaze on her as she lifted to her knees. "But Theo didn't know about our little bargain. Your friend Marx and I came to an agreement. I would let him know whenever Theo took an interest in a woman, and in return, he would ensure the sword came to me when I needed it."

Olivie appeared on Ren's left, offering him a chalice.

"Why are you helping him?" Amalie spat.

Olivie flinched, but Marcel's stare was even.

"We do what we must," he answered, his eyes flicking to the sword in Ren's hand.

Amalie let out a sardonic laugh. "Is that it? He promised you the sword? I told you about the relic. I told you—"

"You didn't know where it was. He did."

Amalie exhaled. It was always that simple with Marcel. You were either useful or you weren't. "Olivie—"

"Don't." Olivie pursed her lips. "I'm sorry Amalie, but you defended them. You—"

"I'm of guardian blood!" Amalie's voice was raw. "There is so much more that the Grimoire doesn't begin to cover—"

"You're a hypocrite!" Olivie screamed, her face darkening in the moonlight.

Amalie's arms trembled with rage. "Do you think he'll hand that over? The power to vanquish, and he's going to let it go?"

"You were my friend, Amalie! You didn't come to me. You trusted that creature instead!" Olivie pointed an accusing finger at Theo. "You claim to be a vanquisher and yet you showed up here tonight with the sword in your hand and Theo Vallon standing next to you, his heart still beating."

Amalie's words died on her tongue. They wouldn't understand. *She* didn't understand.

She'd walked out of Uncle Oren's house with the sword, and not once did she consider using it on Theo. *Not once.*

Olivie was right. She was a hypocrite. When she left the

castle, she'd intended to give the Pourfendeurs information to vanquish others, but not him. *Never him.*

Tears welled in her eyes as she stared at Theo's shadowed form behind the three of them. *I loved you.* She wanted to shout the words at him. To hurl them at him like daggers. *I loved you, and you kept this from me!*

Ren approached, flicking a dagger between his fingers. "Your arm, Amalie. Don't make this harder than it has to be."

A whimper worked its way up her throat. Had her mother felt like this? Like her heart was being ripped from her chest? Had she fallen to the forest floor knowing the man she loved had kept his true intentions from her, or had she gone willingly?

Ren knelt next to her. "Shh, little bird."

This was it. He was going to slit her throat just like he had her mother. Amalie's heart pounded, her mind working furiously. She could hit him in the soft space below his ribs. She could—

Ren growled as a shadow darted between them. He flew back, the chalice flying from his hand.

52

Amalie scrambled to her feet, scanning the yard and the street for any explanation of what just happened. Marcel and Olivie ran back to the house, yelling for reinforcements. Were they under attack? By whom?

Amalie ran toward Theo, then skittered back as three more members of the Pourfendeurs bled from the house. She didn't have time to figure out who they were before striking out. "I'm sorry." She grunted as her fist struck home. They were blocking her way. She needed to get to him and somehow retrieve the sword and get away from Ren, and the Pourfendeurs.

She shouldn't have come. Theo had told her they should stay together, and she hadn't listened. But Marx had been right. Ren had killed her mother, he had made a replacement ring to hide the fact that his had gone missing.

Rage welled up inside her, whistling like a tea kettle and begging for release. There was a sharp crack as her elbow connected with bone, and the woman she'd been fighting dropped. Amalie didn't hesitate. She flew toward the steps, but before she could reach them, the light shifted, and she caught Ren hovering in the shadows behind Marcel and another Slayer.

He was letting them fight his battle? Her pulse quickened as she took in the weapons they wielded. Whips with barbed tips, batons that burned with white hot flames to blind and singe. These were new weapons, ones she'd never used. The smell of burnt skin and clothing filled the air, and Amalie nearly gagged.

A whip cracked, and a frustrated scream tore through the air. Amalie was nearly to the steps when she saw blood red lips. Clémentine. Amalie's jaw dropped as the vampire threw herself toward Ren, only to be hit again by the wicked barbs.

Clémentine was here. Was Etienne as well? Other members of Theo's coven? Hope bloomed in her chest. She was close. *So close.*

She reached Theo, and just as she threw out a hand, a blade flew toward her, nearly taking off her fingers. She whirled back, her eyes locking on Olivie who stood over Theo like a guard dog.

"Olivie, you have the sword. You don't need us."

Her friend flinched. "He won't leave this if he doesn't get what he wants."

Amalie scoffed. "He won't leave it regardless. You've hitched your cart to the wrong horse."

Olivie frowned, then tightened her grip on the blade. Amalie was ready when she lunged. She'd trained with Olivie for years, and knew her fighting style, though Olivie had the same benefit. Amalie spun, but Olivie was faster than she remembered. She twisted, her arm snaking out, allowing her to snatch Amalie's wrist.

Amalie grunted as Olivie wrenched her arm at the same

angle Ren had moments before, and pain shot through her shoulder. She kicked out, her foot connecting with Olivie's shin. She stumbled, and Amalie took the opportunity to twist free.

They circled each other, their eyes locked. Amalie's heart bruised her ribs as she panted. When Olivie lunged again, Amalie met her head on.

"I don't want to fight you."

Olivie let out a huff of air. "Then you shouldn't have whored yourself to a vampire."

Amalie's eyes flashed. She gritted her teeth and pushed, using her weight to force Olivie back. Olivie snarled and twisted, the blade of the relic slicing through the air. Amalie ducked, but not fast enough. The blade caught her arm, and she hissed as pain seared through her flesh. She stumbled back, her vision blurring.

Olivie pressed her advantage, her strikes coming faster and harder. Amalie's muscles screamed in protest, but she pushed through the pain. She couldn't let Olivie win. *She would not die like this.*

Amalie's foot slipped on the slick cobblestones, and she fell to one knee. Olivie was on her in an instant, her blade arcing toward her throat.

Amalie's instincts took over. She rolled to the side, her shoulder slamming into Olivie's legs. Her friend yelped and tumbled to the ground, and Amalie was on her in a split second.

She straddled Olivie's chest, her hands wrapping around her throat. Olivie's eyes widened, and she clawed at Amalie's hands, but she held firm. Her muscles burned with the effort, but she didn't let go.

Olivie's face turned red, and her eyes bulged. Amalie

squeezed tighter, her vision narrowing. "I'm sorry. I'm so sorry, Olivie," she murmured, looking anywhere but at her friend's face. Olivie's struggles grew weaker, and blood rushed in Amalie's ears.

Tears stung her eyes as Olivie's body went limp. She dropped her hands, shaking as she fell onto the stone. She wasn't dead. She hadn't held on long enough for her to die.

The sword lay on the stone next to her, and she lunged for the handle. Her hand caught only air as the blade skittered across the stone. Amalie growled, throwing herself after it and catching a boot to the ribs.

Her palms burned as she slid across the rough sand. She caught a flash of dark hair and leather before the heel of Marcel's hand caught her underneath her jaw. How was he coming after her? If Clémentine and Etienne were there, they should have taken out the Pourfendeurs easily.

Blood filled her mouth as she rolled, catching him in the stomach before scrambling again for the hilt of the sword.

"This is mine," he growled, but Amalie's hand closed around the worn leather.

This had to stop. She flew to her feet, swinging the sword from the ground. "Enough!" she cried, whirling the blade over her head.

She had sought this blade to protect. To avenge her mother's death and vanquish the darkness that plagued their villages, townships, and cities. She would not use it to kill her friends.

Marcel dropped into a ready stance, and Amalie fixed her eyes on his. "I don't care what he promised you, Marcel. This ends now." Marcel's eyes flicked to hers, then back to the sword. He took another step forward, and Amalie tensed. "Marcel—"

"All of them will die," he hissed. Amalie spun as he lunged, bringing the blunt edge of the sword up to deflect his blow. She would not kill her friends. The force of the impact reverberated through her bones, and before she could recover, Marcel's knee cracked against her ribs. He was stronger, more experienced. This wasn't a fair fight.

The vision of her training in the room with windows flashed through her head. She'd found strength then. A force strong enough that she'd caught Theo and thrown him against the stone.

Marcel smashed his fist against her temple, knocking her to the sand, then ground his boot into her wrist. Amalie cried out in pain, forcing her fingers to stay clamped around the hilt of the sword.

Pain flashed in her head, sparking like kindling, making it impossible to think. Her thoughts fractured, stabbing like shards of glass. Her family. The guardians. They had hunted her. Theo watched for her. Her blood—someone had wanted her blood. The relic would vanquish. Theo had a plan. Her family needed him. They were defenseless. Theo was defenseless.

Those last thoughts ignited like absinthe, surging through her veins and scorching her insides. The thread of light became a beacon, and the shard that pinched her gut became a blade through her center.

Amalie reached for them both, wrenching against them until they snapped forward. Amalie gasped as energy crashed over her like a tidal wave, drawing her under, threatening to snuff her out.

And then the world went still. Marcel's boot against her wrist froze. Amalie blinked, the sounds of clashing bodies and feral growls heightening into a roar. Her vision sharpened, and she could suddenly smell the granite from the sandstone beneath her cheek. The leather of Marcel's belt, the salty sweat soaking his shirt.

Amalie flicked her hand, and Marcel stumbled back in slow motion. She gripped the sword and before she'd thought it, she was on her feet. Then her boot was in the center of his chest.

Marcel flew backward, crashing against the steps, his head snapping. She was there. Standing above him, the sword raised over her head.

"Amalie," a voice rasped, and she faltered. *She knew that voice.* Her head lifted to find dark eyes boring into hers. "*Amalie.*"

She blinked, and the world snapped back into frame and her body no longer felt weightless. Theo's finger twitched against the stone, and she spun, taking in her surroundings. Marcel cowered beneath her, gasping for breath, blood pouring down his face. Olivie pushed up from the ground, her skin bruised, her eyes bloodshot. Clémentine and Etienne stared at her as the Pourfendeurs fled, disappearing behind the house.

And then her eyes landed on him. Ren. His gray eyes wide with shock. She'd barely thought his name before the flood-gates opened again and she was flying through the air. Ren's figure shimmered, and he began to fade into a swirl of smoke and shadow, but Amalie's strike was like lightning.

He was slow. So slow. And weak.

"You killed my mother. You took her from me, tricked her into loving you, then killed her." Amalie's vision blurred as she threw him against the tree he'd pressed her against moments before. She was Amalie d'Acier. *Amalie of Steel.*

"How?" Ren gaped at her, terror warping his features. "You're a human. You're—"

Amalie slammed the blade through his chest, driving it home into the bark behind him. Ren's body jolted from the impact, and his arms flew wide. Amalie waited, watching like she had on the roof for his wound to start healing, for his chest to rise and fall as his heart reformed and began to beat.

But Ren's eyes were dark. Lifeless. When she pulled the sword from his body, he dropped to the ground, his legs splaying at unnatural angles. His skin faded, growing pale and ashen.

Amalie dropped to her knees and stared into his stony features. "I am a *guardian*."

As Ren's body began to crack and crumble, Amalie pressed up from the earth. The sword felt like an iron weight in her hands as her whole body trembled. Power seeped from her like water, and she drew in a shaky breath.

She turned to find the yard empty besides Etienne sitting on the steps next to Theo, and Clémentine standing a few feet away, watching her.

"Damn, Amalie. Where was that on the rooftop?" Clémentine raised an eyebrow.

Amalie exhaled, nearly losing her balance. "How did you know?"

Etienne frowned. "Theo hadn't returned after we scouted the attack. Ren was supposed to meet us, and he didn't show, either. Then I found a note on the gates to the castle. It listed this location."

Amalie's brow pinched. "A note?" Who would leave a note? Who else had known where she and Theo were heading besides her own family?

"My family." She exhaled in a rush. "I need to find them."

Clémentine eyed the sword in her hand warily as Etienne lifted Theo from the ground.

Amalie turned, feeling Theo's eyes on her. She didn't want to look at him. Not yet. "I can do this myself," she said, her voice unsteady as pressure built behind her eyes.

"We're coming with you," Etienne said simply, walking up to stand next to her.

Amalie nodded once, scanning the dark, empty street. What had she done? She'd fought against her friends, she'd left Olivie bruised and unconscious on the ground and Marcel cowering in front of her.

She'd vanquished.

Her hand flew to her shoulder, running over the lifted mark on her skin. He was going to kill her. Ren was going to—

"Amalie?" Clémentine nudged her shoulder, and she sniffed.

"This way." Amalie led them down the street, crossing through the center of Mordelles and back onto the lane that led to Uncle Oren's house. They didn't complain about her pace. Theo limped along next to Etienne, his arm slung over his friend's shoulder.

Had Theo planned for them to die tonight? Would they have taken her family to safety, and then . . . what? Would he have taken her aside? Would he have told her anything or would he have held her close and slammed the sword through their bodies at the same time?

The moon seemed to shrink as it rose, and by the time they reached the gate, it was dangling over their heads. Amalie pressed her hand against the door. She'd told Oren to leave, to take the others to safety.

"They may not be here."

Etienne nodded. "We'll check."

"I know where they are if they didn't stay." Theo's voice was raw, slurred, but she could understand him. The sound of him clawed at her insides, leaving open wounds.

She gritted her teeth and pushed into the garden. Etienne, Theo, and Clémentine followed.

It was exactly as they'd left it. Calm. Peaceful. She scanned for Bethany or the girls, for Uncle Oren or Aunt Maurielle, but nobody waited in the shadows near the back gate.

Amalie was about to open her mouth when something flickered in her peripheral vision. Her eyes narrowed, staring at something fluttering on the front door.

"That's what it looked like," Etienne whispered. "The note on the gate."

53

1836 COUNTRYSIDE BEYOND MORDELLES,
FRANCE

Amalie slung her satchel over her shoulder and tore the note from the dagger that held it in place, then yanked the blade from the wood. Words were scrawled on the paper, but she needed more light. She pushed into the house and strode down the hall to her uncle's study. He'd put out the candle, but she remembered where he kept his matches. Setting the note, her satchel, and the sword on the desk, she found them and struck a flame, then protected it with her hand while she crossed the room and lit the wick in the oil lamp.

She tamped out the match, leaving it to smolder, and strode back to the desk. Etienne helped Theo to a chair while Clémentine trailed her hand over the spines of books on her uncle's shelves.

Wish I could have seen you in action. Helena

says it's a sight to behold. I do hope you enjoyed yourself. -M

*   P.S. Your family is being cared for. Do join us when you have a moment.*

Amalie read the words again, then retraced the letters a third time as if that would fill the pit opening up in her stomach. Theo was right. Marx had played her like a fiddle. She couldn't tell if it stung more or less knowing she'd wanted to be played.

She wanted vengeance. He gave it to her. But she hadn't recognized the cost.

"Well?" Etienne's voice was soft.

"She has them," Amalie snapped.

"Of course she does," Theo grunted.

Amalie whirled. "Don't, Theo. I don't need—" She crumpled the note in her hand. *This is not a gift, Amalie. This is a flaxen cord.* Amalie fell back against the desk, allowing it to hold her weight. Bethany, Matilde, and Ghislain. They were guardians, and they were now in the hands of vampires. Vampires that Theo hated, or worse, that he feared.

Theo hunched over his knees. "I didn't mean—"

"I know what you meant." She struggled against the lump swelling in her throat. "I have to go," she whispered. She didn't give any of them a chance to speak before snatching her satchel and the sword from the desk and bolting into the hall.

She stormed into the kitchen, throwing whatever supplies she could find in with her extra clothes. A tin of sardines, the last bit of sausage and aged Comté, and a handful of dried figs.

She'd seen the sword at the river, and could still feel the pull south. That journey would take at least three days on foot.

She'd have to find water on the way. Amalie strode to the front door, her arm still aching where the sword had cut.

"Wait." Theo's voice sounded behind her, but she didn't turn.

She strode through the still-open door into the garden.

"Amalie, stop." Theo gripped her elbow, and she yanked her arm away from him. This time he didn't back down. He pressed forward until he was there in front of her, his hands pinning her arms to her side.

"I don't want to hear what you have to say." She struggled against him, turning her head and refusing to look at him.

Theo didn't speak, his chest rising and falling against hers as she fought against his warmth, his scent.

Amalie began to shake, her grip on the sword faltering. "Theo—"

"I'm not asking for your forgiveness."

Her stomach dropped to her knees. "It's true, then? What Ren said?" Her neck began to ache. She didn't need to ask the question. She'd known it was true the second she'd looked in his eyes.

He did want to die, to be released from his curse. He'd just left out the part about taking her with him.

"If you're not asking for forgiveness, what are you asking for?" Her voice trembled, and she flinched as Theo pressed a finger to her chin, tugging her face back to his.

"Will you look at me, please?" Theo's voice rumbled through her, warmth flooding her veins.

No, rang out in her head, but her body refused to listen. Her chin tipped up, her eyes finding his.

Theo's expression was soft. Pained. "I only want you to understand."

"I understand plenty."

His eyes shuttered, his thumb tracing along the edge of her

jaw. "Indulge me, then." Amalie's breath caught as his fingers trailed beneath her ear lobe, feathering down the side of her neck. "I've watched this play out twice before. I've watched you fight. I've watched you be brave. You were born with strength Amalie, and you won't be dissuaded. I've always admired that about you." He exhaled, his tongue flicking over his lips. "The problem is, she won't stop either."

She. Helena. Amalie's pulse quickened.

Theo paused, his jaw working. "I've tried to be honorable. I've tried to be brave. You asked me to protect your family, and I did—I have. But I don't believe in the prophecy, Amalie. Not anymore. The relationship between vampires and guardians will never be healed, the light will never bond with shadow. It's you and me. That's all. And I don't want to see you suffer— I can't—" his voice caught, and he gritted his teeth.

His words floated around her, barely sinking in. *The prophecy*. Theo had never mentioned a prophecy, but as the word left his lips, her memory flared.

Theo's downcast eyes. *Your blood gave power to those who drank it. We had a friend who wanted it for herself.*

Oren looking between her and Theo in the dining room. *You believe it is her?*

I know it.

The smirk on Ren's lips. *I was wrong. Then. But I'm not now . . .That's how I knew she was the one.*

. . .

The scrawled text in her mother's book. *Until the Day of Light, guardians will wait. They will serve. They will protect. And when she who is sent to bind appears, they will follow.*

Power.

She was the one.

I know it.

"When was I born, Theo?" Amalie worked to clear the lump in her throat.

Theo stilled. "Which time?"

Her lip trembled. "You know what I'm asking."

Theo cupped his hand over her cheek. "Amalie—"

"Answer me. Please." Tears spilled over onto her cheeks, and he searched her eyes.

He opened his mouth, then closed it, his fingers trembling against her skin. "Don't make me say it."

"Please, Theo."

"I love you," he whispered, kissing her temple. "I have to save you."

She exhaled in a rush. "I don't think you can save me from this." The truth of it settled over her in layers. *She who was sent to bind.* What did any of it mean?

"I want to. I can." Theo pulled back and dropped to the ground, picking up the sword. "All of this can be over."

She shook her head. "Theo—"

"This isn't a game, Amalie!" His face twisted in anguish. Amalie's ribs seemed to pierce her lungs. Theo gritted his teeth. "You were born on the Day of Light. You hold power never before seen, and still, she took you from me. It's been over two thousand years, and the rift has never been repaired. We have fought together, and we have failed."

Theo stepped closer, his eyes insistent. "Helena is a snake. She has one goal, Amalie. Kill anyone who could challenge her. You're a guardian with power she's desperate for, it's why she bonded you in the first place. As soon as she has what she wants—"

"What does she want?"

He dragged a hand through his hair and gave an exasperated sigh. "I don't know. Ever since—" He hissed air through his teeth. "I don't know what she's after this time, but I do know this. As soon as you're not useful, she will make you suffer. You'd be a fool to go to her."

"Then I guess I'm a fool," Amalie snapped. Her head throbbed as her mind scurried to gather the thousand threads whirling inside her and somehow weave them into a picture she could understand.

She glanced down at the sword in Theo's hand.

The muscles in his arm flexed. "The prophecy was written thousands of years ago. It isn't true—it *can't* be true."

Her chest felt as if it were cleaving in two. She could give him what he wanted. She could go to him, wrap her arms around his waist, and kiss him. Then close her eyes and ask him to take her with him.

She could pretend it didn't matter. That her family would be reborn, that their lives would continue whether she chased after them or not. Theo had lived for thousands of years, and he didn't believe she could make a difference. Who was she to say differently?

You were not made merely to fight the darkness, but to bring forth the light within it. Help them see beyond the shadow.

. . .

Amalie met his eyes. "Give me the sword."

Theo's shoulders tensed, his hands beginning to shake. "Amalie, please."

She blinked back tears and held out a hand. *She loved him.* Not only in past lives, but in this one, as well. She knew it, could feel the truth of it pulsing in every cell of her body.

But there was another truth beginning to swell within her. One she couldn't ignore, even if Theo had decided he would.

"I won't watch this happen. Not again." He threw the sword to the ground, his eyes burning as she stooped to pick it up.

She stood, and Theo moved toward her, a feral growl in his throat. Amalie raised the sword on instinct and Theo froze, his eyes locked onto hers.

"Do it then," he said. Amalie's skin flushed as she sucked in a breath. Theo didn't blink as he dropped to his knees in front of her. "I made you a promise. I swore you could vanquish me if we found the sword, and now you have it."

Amalie stared into his eyes, reading his pain and fear, letting it wash over her like rain. She reached out a hand, threading her fingers in his hair, then dropped to her knees in front of him. She reached for his hand and placed the hilt of the sword back into his palm, then held her arm next to his, pulling up her sleeve and forcing him to stare at the mark they shared. A piece of him etched into her skin.

"Who did you make a promise to, Theo?"

He gritted his teeth. "I told you—"

"Not that one." She shook her head. Theo's breath came in ragged gasps. "I love you. Whatever you decide, I *understand.*" She brushed her lips over his cheek as her heart shredded to pieces. She pushed up from the ground, allowing her sleeve to fall back to her trembling wrist. "This promise is yours, Theo. Only you can decide to break it."

Amalie gave him one last look, then turned and strode to the gate, leaving the sword at his feet.

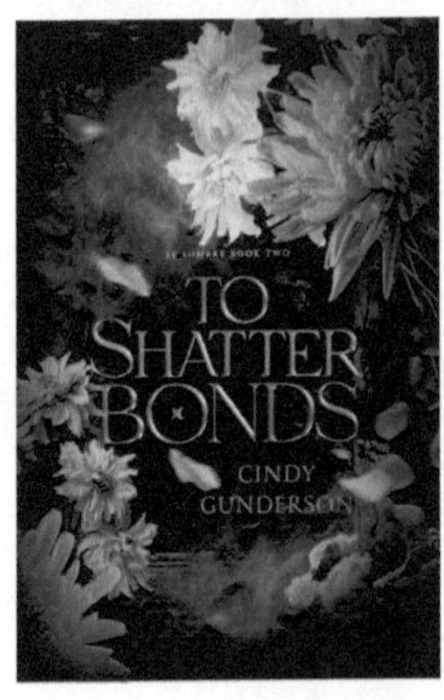

Preorder Book 2 or Subscribe to the Reader's Club for notifications on the next special edition!

www.CindyGunderson.com

NEXT IN THE SERIES

Preorder Book 2 or Subscribe to the Reader's Club for
notifications on the next special edition!

www.CindyGunderson.com

ALSO BY CINDY GUNDERSON

Tier Trilogy

Unreal Series

The Blessing Giver Series

www.CindyGunderson.com

Instagram: @CindyGWrites

Facebook: @CindyGWrites

www.ingramcontent.com/pod-product-compliance
Lightning Source LLC
Chambersburg PA
CBHW021239190726

48289CB00005B/1396